Erica JONG

OF BLESSED MEMORY

BLOOMSBURY

First published in the United States of America
by HarperCollins Publishers, New York, 1997 as

Inventing Memory: A Novel of Mothers and Daughters

First published in Great Britain 1997
This paperback edition published 1998

Copyright © 1997 by Erica Mann Jong

The moral right of the author has been asserted

Bloomsbury Publishing Plc, 38 Soho Square, London W1V 5DF

A CIP catalogue record for this book is available from the British Library

ISBN 0 7475 3918 9

10 9 8 7 6 5 4 3 2 1

Printed in England by Clays Ltd, St Ives plc

Best Friends:
Kenneth David Burrows
Gerri Kahn Karetsky

The only truly dead are those who have been forgotten.

—Jewish Saying

Gladys Spatt Burrows
1917–1996

Selig S. Burrows
1913–1997

Of Blessed Memory

Acknowledgments

*Special thanks to Gladys Justin Carr, editor extraordinaire;
Annette Kulick, tireless amanuensis; and my devoted first
reader and* landsman, *Ed Victor. I thank him and all those who
shared their family stories with me.*

Special thanks also to the YIVO Institute for Jewish Research.

E. J.

DESCENDANTS OF SARAH (SOPHIA) SOLOMON LEVITSKY

(Sukovoly, Russia)

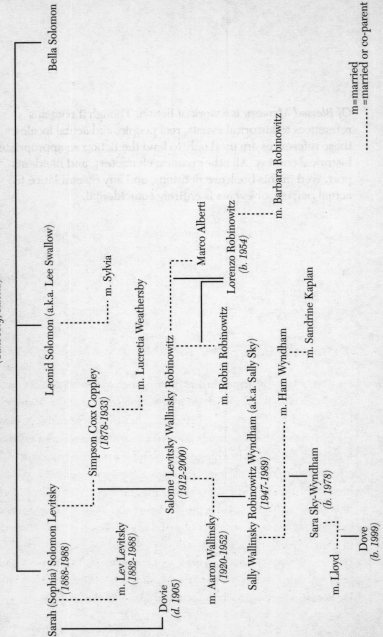

Bella Solomon

Leonid Solomon (a.k.a. Lee Swallow) ---- m. Sylvia

Simpson Coxx Coppley
(1878-1933) ---- m. Lucretia Weathersby

Marco Alberti

Lorenzo Robinowitz
(b. 1954) ---- m. Barbara Robinowitz

Salome Levitsky Wallinsky Robinowitz
(1912-2000)

m. Robin Robinowitz

m. Sandrine Kaplan

Sarah (Sophia) Solomon Levitsky
(1888-1988) ---- m. Lev Levitsky
(1882-1988)

m. Aaron Wallinsky
(1920-1952)

Sally Wallinsky Robinowitz Wyndham (a.k.a. Sally Sky)
(1947-1989)

m. Ham Wyndham

Sara Sky-Wyndham
(b. 1978)

Dovie
(d. 1905)

m. Lloyd

Dove
(b. 1999)

m=married
----- =married or co-parent

SARAH'S STORY ✦ PEOPLE WHO CAN'T SLEEP
1905

Death does not knock at the door.

—YIDDISH PROVERB

Sometimes, in dreams, my firstborn son comes back to me. I think he is my guardian angel. "Mama, Mamichka, Mamanyu, Mamele," he says, "let me warn you . . ." And then he tells me something about some man in my life, or some business deal—and always it turns out that he is right, though I never quite remember his words when I awake. He speaks in that dream language of the dead. His presence itself is a warning. I can't remember his voice either, but I do know what he looks like: he wears a tall black silk hat, a fur-lined silk pelisse. His cloak is trimmed with sable. He has a long beard—he who never learned to walk, let alone to grow a beard. He is a man—who was always only a baby—but that baby smell clings to his sweet neck, and in the dream I know he is both baby and man for all eternity. I have lost him and yet I have not lost him. He lives in a country to which only death provides the key.

I had come home to Sukovoly from Odessa, where I was apprenticed to a photographer, retouching sepia portraits of the gentry. Only seventeen and as foolish about boys as I was smart about pictures, how could I know I was pregnant? How could I know how I got that way? Another long story for another rainy night.

When my mama realized what was happening to me, she raved and screamed and tore her hair. Then she calmed down. "With babies come blessings," she said, murdering some proverb. And she got excited about her first grandchild.

He was such a sweet baby, my David, my Dovie, my little man. He latched onto my breast and sucked as if all the world were in my nipple and he meant to devour it. But that night the Cossacks came and we hid in Malka's barn, I knew that my life and Mama's and my sister Tanya's and my cousin Bella's and my little brother Leonid's all depended on silence. So when my darling Dovie started to whimper, I took out my breast and crammed it in his mouth, hearing him suck, suck, suck, and be silent.

My heart was beating like a drum, my breath was almost held with fear, the metallic taste of terror was in my mouth as if I were drinking from a rusty cup put down into a cold clear well. I was praying with my whole soul for all those lives (including mine and his), and for a while God must have heard, for the baby sucked and sucked and all I could hear was the pounding of my own heart. But then the little wiggling one squirmed and began to whimper. He needed to be held upright. He needed to be burped. I was not sure I could do this without betraying us all. Biting my tongue, I carefully raised him to my shoulder, patted his little back, and held him until he gurgled up from his depths a noisy air bubble and then he spit sour milk over my breast and my shoulder.

The Cossacks had been stomping around below us, sticking their bayonets or swords or whatever they had into bales of hay, but when the baby started to whimper, they stopped and listened. Then there was no sound but their boots dragging the hay with a sort of swishing.

I clapped the baby on my breast so fast I might have been a gunfighter drawing for a shootout in one of those silent movies they had when I first came to America. The baby sucked and sucked again, and I very quietly let the air return to my lungs and felt them expand beneath the baby's moving mouth. When he became quiet and seemed to sleep, I did not notice, because of the ruckus and screaming down below. The Cossacks had caught a calf and were running him through with their horrible instruments and he was making wild animal noises, almost the noises of a child—a child who would never nurse again. It was only when the Cossacks had gone galloping off to the next slaughter, the next *shtetl*, that I realized my boy did not draw breath.

Later I sat dumb for two weeks, neither eating nor sleeping, staring into the middle distance but seeing nothing. I could not cry or scream or even speak. And Mama brought me soup and said that many mothers who had the strength to kill their babies lived to give birth and love again, and that her mother had known no less than three women who had put their hands over their babies' mouths in just such circumstances. One died. One was made strange for life. And one limped like an idiot. This made me feel worse, not better. I had not the will to say, "Mama, I did not choke him. I only nursed him." But really I cannot remember every motion I made in that dark barn, with the rats scuttling and the Cossacks stomping and my terror that once again my little Dovie would whimper and doom us all.

"What does not kill you makes you stronger," goes the proverb. And surely losing my firstborn angel made me know how hard the world is and that life is no picnic.

But Dovie comes back to me again, a grown man with angelic inky baby eyes and a full beard, whenever I need him most. Why he had to go ahead of me to the other world I will never understand, but in some way he is a herald. He watches over my life.

"He is an angel," Mama said, "and we are alive."

I hated her for thinking I had killed him, but perhaps that is what I thought myself. I will never really know until I meet my son again in the other world.

It was not only his death that caused me to go to America. It takes the sacrifice of at least three men for a woman to set out on her road.

A week later the Cossacks came back and burned down the *shul* and everyone in it, including my twin brother, Yussel—may he rest in peace—and my father, of blessed memory. Yussel already had the precious ticket to go to America. Despite her grief, my mama dressed me in my brother's clothes—though it was forbidden—gave me his ticket, and ordered me to go to America. That was the sort of woman my mama was. Of course, I was to bring them all to the Golden Land as soon as I could.

"You are the man of the family now," she said, giving me permission for the rest of my life.

Death can be a blast of courage, fuel for a journey you are afraid to take. Death can make you seize whatever courage you have. And it was the force of these three deaths that propelled me across the perilous border, across the dark continent on foot, through haystacks alive with biting insects, through breakfasts and dinners of sour black bread, through humiliating searches and seasick nights that seemed to go on forever. It was Dovie's death—and my brother's and my father's—that took me across the sea and deposited me in a basement flat in skyless New York, right next to a coal vault, where the dumping and shifting of the coal substituted for the sounds of the crickets on a starry night.

All the stories that have ever been told are the stories of families—from Adam and Eve onward. When I think of my child and her children (including my darling great granddaughter Sara) and how they live, I realize that no leap of empathy can make them understand how close to the bone we were on that journey, on that crossing, in that coal-black flat belowground. My *kinder* live in London, Lugano, Venice, Hollywood, Montana, Manhattan—nothing's too good for them. Interest rates they worry about—and development deals and final cut. They collect first editions, Georgian silver, polo ponies, contemporary art. They accumulate heavy things that cannot be moved in a pogrom. This is a measure of how secure they feel. They do not expect that the Jews will be trapped in Benedict Canyon as in the Warsaw ghetto. They do not expect to be chased over the Rockies as over the Pyrenees. They are complacent, their troubles are psychological. I made them that way. I made them secure—I with all my insecurity. Or perhaps it was Dovie; perhaps he is the guardian angel of the whole family.

1

Sara's Story

2005

Parents can give a child a dowry but not good luck.

—YIDDISH PROVERB

The Council on Jewish History in New York City (called the CJH for short) is located in a limestone mansion built by a turn-of-the-last-century robber baron in imitation of some great European pile. Rows of scallop and nautilus shells circle the ground-floor frieze. Bronze dolphins dance the quadrille in the cascading fountain of the inner court (used for spring fund-raisers, cocktail parties, and the occasional doomed tryst between resident scholars). The rose window from a deconsecrated Gothic cathedral forms the centerpiece of the library skylight, although stained-glass figures of Adam, Noah, Moses, Maimonides, Spinoza, Einstein, and Freud—no women are in evidence—flanking the great dome give the ceiling the requisite patina of Jewishness. Around the library wainscoting, carved in Hebrew letters, the motto KNOWLEDGE IS

POWER appears, and potential donors being given the grand tour of this sanctum sanctorum are often moved to remark on the almost sacerdotal feeling of the place. What they mean is that it is a portentous and gloomy space—the gloom broken only by shafts of colored light, indicating the divine presence of the eternal unnameable one.

An *aron,* or ark, from a small synagogue in Ferrara, later destroyed by Mussolini's Blackshirts, was propitiously transported to the Council on Jewish History in 1928 by a grateful Ferrarese Jew who had made his fortune in New York real estate during the Roaring Twenties. It still stands at the back wall of the reading room, where it is used to display the CJH's priceless collection of Renaissance silver Torah crowns, *kiddush* goblets, and chased silver *menorahs* given through the years by other donors (who doubtless believed that a gift to the CJH would guarantee admission to that obscure heaven of the Jews). The CJH is that sort of place—the oldest Jewish research institute in New York and the most prestigious.

Sara was taken on her first tour of this impressive edifice on a brilliant day in April, when the inner courtyard was ablaze with cherry blossoms, brought back from Japan by a horticulturally inclined Warburg—or was it a Rothschild? (Even afterward, when she had been toiling in the library there for several months, Sara could never remember.) The sky was that sublime Côte d'Azur blue of isolated spring days in New York, and birds were singing in the blossoming trees. The medieval herb garden, laid out in a pattern of eighteen aromatic herbs to symbolize *life—chai,* in Hebrew—was just starting to return from its winter hibernation.

Sara followed CJH's director of development, Lisette de Hirsch, a stalwart but fashionably anorectic woman in her late fifties, white-haired, blue-eyed, who was partial to black vintage Chanel suits with gold buttons, brilliant scarves with rampant suns and moons, and low-heeled shoes handmade in Venice by a cobbler who also supplied the dancers of the Fenice and La Scala theaters. She was an old family friend of Sara's not-quite-stepmother, Sandrine, who had always encouraged Sara to call her for a job.

Lisette de Hirsch did not need the salary her position provided. Her husband was from an ancient Jewish family that had quadrupled its money in every boom since the Civil War and preserved its capital in every bust—including the Great Depression. But Sara was not so fortunate. Not yet thirty, she had masses of wavy auburn hair, a voluptuous but somehow also slim-waisted figure, green eyes with yellow flecks that made you think of topazes one moment and emeralds the next, and an aristocratic aquiline nose like an Italian Renaissance beauty painted by Bronzino; she tended to chew the lipstick off her full crimson lips when nervous, as she was now. She desperately needed the grant she was interviewing for. She had booted her husband out on New Year's Day, after discovering that he was bewitched by his twenty-two-year-old graduate assistant, Stoddard (nicknamed "Stoddi") von Meissen—the Nazi *shiksa* from hell. This left Sara with their six-year-old daughter, Dove, to support, the rent on a rambling West Side apartment, and not a penny in child support. Lloyd now had his Ph.D. in history, and Sara, despite having supported all three of them, had most of hers—all but the dissertation. They had both received fellowships to grad school, but there had been the costs of baby-sitters, preschool, and the other unexpected expenses of parenting, so that by the time Lloyd fell under the spell of Stoddi, Sara's small savings were long gone. Lloyd had promised to support the family while Sara finished her dissertation. But before that could happen, Prinzessin von Meissen waltzed into Lloyd's seminar on modern Jewish history at Columbia and sang the siren song of youth and shiksatude that lures Jewish men from the partners who have increasingly begun to remind them of their mothers and grandmothers. Lloyd was now beginning to make noises about wanting to come back, but Sara was suddenly not so sure she wanted him. She had come to like her independent life, rigorous as it was.

"It's an amazing building," said Sara, hoping to ingratiate herself with Lisette de Hirsch, who absolutely glowed with pride during the tour.

Privately Sara thought the place over the top, a mishmash of architectural styles—none of them in the best taste. The library, with its gaudy ark and priceless silver (all accompanied by donor plaques almost as big as the objects), was crammed with leather-bound volumes housed in dark mahogany bookcases, one of which revolved to expose a spiral staircase leading down to several levels of library stacks and a secret conference room with a green baize door and a round conference table that has been built into the bedrock of Manhattan. Nobody knew whether the chamber had originated as a wine cellar or if the Vanderbilt who created the house circa 1905 had added it as a hideaway during World War I. The subsequent owners refashioned it into an underground dining hall or conference room, with a dumbwaiter to the kitchen on the ground floor.

Lisette opened a paneled door and pressed a button; elevator cables whirred as the dumbwaiter descended. It was fitted out with circular depressions for decanters of wine, dish racks for china, and a flat shelf for conveying large servings of food.

Lisette proudly displayed this gadget to Sara. "They didn't *have* a servant problem in those days," she said, not knowing how much she sounded like a caricature of a rich woman. "One butler was waiting here to plate and serve the food and two kitchen maids to send it down after the chef had done his final seasoning. Some menus from those days survive. They were inordinately fond of seven-course meals, from soups to savories."

Sara laughed rather too appreciatively. After all, this woman was one of the three who would decide whether or not to anoint her. She didn't want to sabotage her chances of getting the grant.

For the moment, she would have to forget that her husband possibly believed himself in love with the Nazi bitch from hell, that since Daddy moved out her daughter had been wetting her bed and had begun therapy with a child psychiatrist who charged an outrageous three hundred dollars per forty-five-minute "hour." She had no wealthy relatives to bail her out and she was already behind with her rent and Dove's school bills.

Sara knew she was short-listed for the plum of resident scholar at CJH, and she'd be damned if her habitual ironic defiance would lose it for her. She couldn't afford irony and defiance now. She had a kid to support.

"What days those must have been!" Sara exclaimed in her best ingratiating manner. "Those days before income tax, those Edith Wharton, Emma Goldman, days . . ."

"Edith Wharton—though not Emma Goldman—was said to have dined in this very room." said Lisette, the buttons on her suit gleaming. "Apparently there was a literary dinner, and Henry James was also here. This was before they both abandoned New York for Europe."

"I would be honored to work in such a house," gushed Sara, wondering if she wasn't laying it on a bit thick.

Lisette's eyes lit up behind her expensive gold-rimmed granny glasses.

"Oh, I do so wish more young people felt like you," Lisette said. "After the Holocaust, Jewish history *must* be preserved. It has never been more important. How did *you* get interested in Jewish history?"

"When my mother died last year, I decided I had to know everything about our family—and naturally I was drawn here. . . . There's some rumor that my great-grandmother—whom I'm named after—was part of an oral history project before I was born or just after, but nobody seems to know where the tapes are."

Lisette looked blank. Fund-raising, not what the money was *for*, was her domain.

Sara hurried on: "I've become passionate about the history of the Jews . . . particularly the stories of the women in these families. . . . I would like nothing better than to rescue these women from oblivion. . . ."

Now Lisette looked like she would burst with pleasure. Sara knew in her gut she had the position—and with it the grant that would save her life.

She trailed Lisette back to the gloomy library stacks (which were groaning with the sort of research materials Sara needed for her dissertation) and watched her pull out a large leather box and open its clamshell top. It was filled with turn-of-the-century photographs of serious-looking women, many in wire-rimmed glasses, who wore "waists," hobble skirts, feathered hats.

"We are determined to computerize our photo archive," said Lisette, "and that would be one of your first challenges." (Lisette was the sort of person who habitually employed words like "challenge." It made Sara think she was not being given some essential piece of information about the sort of expectations that went with the grant.)

Lisette closed the box of antique photos and carried it to a carrel in the stacks, where she placed it with a thump, flipped it open, and began holding up the photographs one by one. Some were dated in an old-fashioned hand and some were undated. Many were stamped with the names of photographers in Odessa, Novgorod, Kishinev, Warsaw, Vilna, Hamburg, London, New York.

Suddenly Lisette held up a photograph of a dark-hatted woman with huge, light, luminous eyes.

"She *looks* like you!" Lisette exclaimed. "If you imagine the clothes updated, the hat removed, and the hair unloosed."

Sara took the faded sepia photograph and examined it carefully. There was no question of the resemblance—or perhaps her desperation was just making her supersuggestible.

She turned the photograph over. On the back was stamped the name *American Studio, Odessa and Novgorod,* and in light pencil, something in Hebrew script, then in English and almost rubbed out by time: "Sarah S., 1905."

◆

Sara felt like something of a fraud as she walked across blossoming Central Park to her own apartment. Her sense of her own Jewishness was not as unambivalent as she had let on. She had not really known she was Jewish till she started living with her mother, the mythic folksinger Sally Sky, at the age of fourteen. And sometimes she felt that the sufferings of the Jews were all their own fault for being so damned insistent on their chosenness, specialness, superiority. She had been raised largely in Montana by a poet-father who believed that fly-fishing and religion were the same thing, and later in Europe by a divorced mother who worshiped only at the shrines of AA and room service—and who died long before Sara was ready to lose her, leaving plenty of unfinished mother-daughter business. Even when her mother or father *was* around, Sara had often felt like an orphan. Both parents were so self-centered. Typical products of the sixties, they believed that their self-expression was all that mattered. They *loved* Sara. Of course they loved her. But they were always so busy with their own dramas that their love for her hardly seemed like a priority in their lives. To Sara anyway.

Sara's father, Ham Wyndham, was forever busy reinventing himself as the Thoreau of Bear Creek, Montana. And Sara's mother—before she died, at any rate—was busy atoning for having become one of the most famous singers of her generation. Sally Sky alternated between running from her notoriety and secretly courting it—just as she alternated between sobriety and drunkenness, celibacy and promiscuity, accumulating money and compulsively squandering it. She *loved* Sara, wrote songs for Sara, drowned Sara with gifts, goodies, all that money could buy—but she was too much of a child herself to give Sara stability. Searching for that elusive commodity, Sara had married young. Now that her search had proved delusional, she felt adrift—fiercely independent one minute, terrified the next. If only she could find some anchor, some identity that would sustain her through the crisis of divorce that seemed imminent. If only someone had left a note in a bottle, some sacred text that would give her the strength she needed to go on.

She had studied with a professor at Columbia who insisted that "ancestor worship is the only true religion." He used to say that line of descent was the earliest way of organizing historical information and that the Book of Genesis was so full of genealogy because it was the way the earliest humans fixed and celebrated identity.

Sara had always instinctively felt he was right—even though her own ancestors were wrapped in fog like gods who dwelt on misty mountaintops. Nor was she so sure she liked a world where ethnic identity was more important than anything. She was not certain it would not lead to anything but more of the tribal warfare that had so far marked the millennium.

Sara arrived at her door just in time to hear her phone ringing.

"Congratulations to our new resident scholar!" Lisette de Hirsch crowed.

"How on earth? I thought you had to consult with the board and your other development directors."

"I *am* the board," said Lisette, "and the only development director who matters."

"I can see that," said Sara.

"We'd like you to start as soon as possible," said Lisette, restoring the fiction of a "we" behind her autocratic decision.

Sara felt a cold knife of fear in her heart. If she took this position, would she be free to finish her dissertation, or would they find a million other tasks for her? It was true that the Council library—brimming with exactly the research information she needed—would be at her disposal, but would she find the time to use it for her *own* research? She was never very good at saying no to authority figures, and that could greatly impede her progress, but she tried to convince herself otherwise—and with a divided heart, she accepted.

That night, after she put Dove to bed, Sara couldn't get the image of that early-twentieth-century woman out of her head. Normally she was contemptuous of people who undertook a search for their roots, feeling that they were cloaking their sentimentality in history—or at least sociology. Whenever friends of hers made pilgrimages to Vilna or Prague or the East End of London, she would accuse them of tracing their "joots"—her shorthand for Jewish roots.

But a picture is capable of hypnotizing as few other artifacts can. There was something in that face—defiance mixed with an undeniable prettiness—that made Sara feel she was encountering a reflection of herself. Back in that vanished world of bowler hats, hobble skirts, sawdust saloons, tenderloin parlor houses, rattling trolley cars, horse-drawn wagons, and brand-new subways, there was a woman who might have been her twin.

What brought this Sarah to America? Did she come alone? Did she succeed or perish? Create a dynasty or become dust in a potter's field? Where was the rest of her story? Would it somehow predict Sara's own?

2

Sarah in the Golden Land

1906

> *It's not as good with money as it is bad without it.*
>
> —YIDDISH PROVERB

It started on the boat—my American life, I mean. The boat was called *Der Goldener Stern*, its home port was Hamburg, and from the outside it looked like a floating palace, strung with lights. But within, you descended a ladderlike stair to the very bowels, past half-naked coal-dusted demons with contorted faces who shoveled black nuggets into a fiery furnace, and you discovered a stinking steerage, full of tightly packed bunk beds, the roar of ventilating fans, and the stench of seasick humanity.

I can still close my eyes and see the darkness of that hold, hear the creak of the ship's sides, and smell the monkey-house smell of poor people packed together. It has been the curse and blessing of my life to have a better smeller than other people.

"I smell, therefore I am," I used to tell my daughter, Salome, Miss

Smarty-Pants, the avant-garde writer. And she would say: "Mama—you *inhale,* therefore you are . . . otherwise it seems like *you* stink."

"Forgive mine greenhorn accent, dollink," I'd reply. "To me it sounds fine to say: 'I smell, therefore I am.' It's a *double entendre,* nu?" And Salome would throw up her hands with exasperation and shout: *"Mama!"*

"So your mother is a greenhorn—get used to it," I'd say, but really it made me mad. What else are daughters for but to make you mad?

Back to the ship: There I am in steerage with the smelly people. I escaped as often as I could, wandering the decks, gazing at the sea, sketching in my notebook everything I saw. At first my fiery auburn hair remained tucked up in my twin brother's cap, but eventually I let it down and allowed myself to be a girl again. Eventually I found my way through a passage where steerage intersected with second class, and then I stumbled upon the secret place where second class led to what they called "saloon" class. Fearlessly I opened the unlocked gates, ignoring the warning signs. After what I'd been through, no warning signs could keep me out. And on one of these walkabouts, I met a pale young man with startled blue eyes, faded brown hair parted in the middle, a stiff collar, and a flowing silk tie. I thought his face was kindly. (Later I learned it was weak.) He introduced himself as Sim Coppley.

I said, "How do," which was probably the only English phrase I dared say at the time. And then I gestured for him to sit down, and I did a pencil sketch of him right there and then. In five minutes, I had a telling likeness—I could always get a likeness—and he was amazed. I tore out the sheet of paper, curtsied, and gave him the portrait. Then I ran away.

Back in steerage, I wondered what on earth was *wrong* with me? Was I so afraid to make an American friend? Mr. Coppley seemed nice enough. Why was I so terrified? "The entire world lies on the tip of the tongue," Mama would have said. (She would, of course, have said it in Yiddish: *Af der shpits tsung ligt di ganse velt.*) For the lack of speech was the whole world lost. Was I so ashamed of my igno-rance of English that all I could do was run away? Yes!

For the next two days, I searched everywhere for the blue-eyed Mr. Coppley but could not find him. Despair! Self-loathing! I reproached myself for my cowardice.

And then I saw him strolling the steerage deck, making notes in a little book, stopping to ask questions of a young woman with a child. Jealousy stung me! Mr. Coppley was speaking Yiddish with this cow! And she was preening and flirting and exposing bad teeth. Just then her baby—my rescuer!—started to howl. *Ven dos mazel kumt, shtelt im a stuhl,* Mama whispered in my ear. (When luck walks in, pull up a chair for him.) The cow was putting the baby at her breast—but not without coyly displaying it in all its fullness to the well-dressed American man.

"Beg pardon," I said, rushing over to him. "*Kum mit mir!*" And I dragged him by the arm to the edge of the deck railing, where my rival could not follow.

"*Kunst du lernen mir Englisch?*" I blurted out. *Why* I thought this man would want to teach me English I do not know, but there was something schoolmasterish about him. And in truth, I had him dead to rights. His azure eyes lit up with delight at the very suggestion.

"*Mit geschmecht!*" said Mr. Coppley. I thanked God for my good fortune and Mama for her good advice.

I realize now that Sim Coppley must have fallen in love with me on the spot. Or else it was the effect of my drawing, which had always opened doors that otherwise would have remained shut to me. Besides, Sim was attracted to the exotic and to compulsive do-gooding. He was writing a book, he said, on the "Hebrew immigration"—as he called it. I was his research text and he became my teacher. None of these encounters is by chance. *Beshert*, we say in Yiddish.

Soon I found out that Sim was the scion of a famous New York family—an "Astorbilt," as I later learned his type was styled in New York—who had found the rounds of debutante balls, dinner parties, and weekends at country cottages in the Berkshires not to his liking and had sought to use his wealth for more serious pursuits. He took me on like a cause. Later I would come to resent this, but at the time he was my benefactor, and I had nothing but pure gratitude.

He was never quite clear about what he had been doing in Europe. Trying to escape from something or someone, I thought. Why else would anyone leave the Golden Land?

Whoever gives you a language also gives you a window on the world. Sim Coppley had been taught to hide his emotions, to dissemble, to cloak his yearnings in intellectual garb. (That was no doubt why he was so attracted to me.) Much of what he taught me on the rest of that voyage had to do with filling the air with pleasantries that substituted for true communication.

"Nice weather, isn't it?" he would say in his role as pedagogue. The wind was howling and rain was spilling out of the lowering gray clouds. The anthracite North Atlantic was troubled by foaming white caps.

"*Meshuggeneh!*" I finally found the courage to call him. And then I found the words: "If rain is *nice weather,* I'm the czarina of Russia."

"Sophia," he said—for he had proposed that I change my name from Sarah to Sophia—"we are not talking about what we *seem* to be talking about. We are merely filling the air with words that link us in sociability."

"Feh!" I spat. "Who wants words if not to communicate?"

"Very good," Sim said of the sentence I had made. (I thought it was pretty good myself.) "But you cannot call people names in polite society even when you think they deserve them."

"You are *meshuggeh*—and this is hardly what I would call polite society!"

Sim laughed and laughed. I think he fell in love with me because I could always make him laugh. From then on, *meshuggeh* was his favorite Yiddish word. And he always wanted to hear me pronounce it.

Of course, he pronounced it like a *goy: mee-sugar.* That made *me* laugh.

"*Meshuggeh* is . . ." I made a sign for scrambled brains. "Brains like eggs," I said.

"Like eggs?" Sim asked.

"Eggs *after* you break them," I said.

"Oh, Sophia," Sim said in his best schoolmasterly manner: "Civilized conversation means *never* commenting upon the mental state of your interlocutor." And we *both* laughed and laughed. Still, I understood that this was his *real* lesson, and that there was something in it that was *not* a joke.

My walks and lessons on the deck with Sim, our splendid teas in his saloon class suite . . . and then the return to the bowels of the ship—it was a long way to traverse, the jump of several generations attempted in one crossing. I knew this, and from time to time I felt a stab of guilt for my good fortune. Why was *I* alive when Yussel was dead? (A twin walks with you always like a shadow.) Why was *I* alive when Papa and Dovie were dead? (A dead father and a dead son weigh down the heart as if with stones.) And then I remembered what Mama had said as I was leaving: "*A mensch trakht un Got lakht.*" (People struggle, God laughs.) And I resolved to banish guilt. All of life is a dance on a grave. The only way for a woman to get ahead, I realized even then, is to flaunt her talents and not to care about being too good. Being good is the curse of the female of the species. Even men get tired of good girls. And good girls get oh so tired of themselves. I would have to measure myself by a different standard than goodness. But what would it be? It was already clear that America and Russia were two different planets, not two different countries. And I wasn't even *in* America yet! Still, I could tell it was a place where clinging to the past meant being left behind.

As long as I had a charcoal in my hand and I was drawing, I did not suffer moral dilemmas. I felt that all those deaths were *beshert,* as was my own departure. The idea of destiny is always strangely comforting. "You need some luck even for *bad* luck," Mama used to say. (*Tsum shimazel darf men oych haben mazel.*)

The arrival at Ellis Island—the island of tears—was as awful as everyone has said. The nakedness, the clothes carried in a bag, the smell of disinfectant, the eye examination, the waiting, the waiting. Some people were marked with chalk on the shoulder and set aside like baggage. *H* meant heart trouble, *F* was for a suspicious rash, *E* signified eye trouble—and with a chalk letter on your shoulder, you had to go in a wire pen, like an animal. But I was spared. Some children became ill on the ship and came to Ellis Island only to die. Their mothers saw their little bodies wrapped in sheets and buried in the so-called Golden Land. I was glad I had buried my baby in the old country and had come unencumbered except by memories. They weighed enough.

People had died on the ship, too, and were buried at sea. One young woman tried to jump in after her dead mother. The splash of a corpse hitting the water is a splash you never forget.

The truth is, I never saw anyone kiss the ground at Ellis Island. Mostly they looked lost, confused, uncertain: maybe they should return to the troubles they knew. Some of the people who were sent back for trachoma of the eyes actually looked *relieved*. (Nobody ever talks about the people who went back.) At least they avoided the crowds of sharks and *starkes* who waited at Castle Garden for the immigrants to come ashore. Pimps, sweatshop owners, policemen, madams, all set upon the innocents.

I still laugh when I remember the salesmen with their cartons of alarm clocks! An alarm clock was the *symbol* of America—a place where the ticking of the clock was drowned out by the sound of the cash register. Or were they both the very same sound? *I* thought so. "Time is money" was the motto of the Golden Land. I thought this was stupid even then. Time is not money; time is priceless. I had never seen people *move* so fast in my life. You may think those old silent movies were speeded-up for fun? Not at all. People *walked* that way! America in Charlie Chaplin's time was the country of "Time is money." "The Land of Hurry-Up," we called it. The land of dollars.

Where was I? Ellis Island. So much mythology has grown up around those immigrants, because America *needed* a myth of huddled masses yearning to breathe free. . . . In fact, the boats were filled with all manner of humanity—swindlers and innocents, rebels and sheep, whores and virgins—and the same sort awaited them. Afterward, you could lie to your American-born children and make it appear that all the immigrants were saints. Far from it.

Sim had already been dispatched in a little boat with the other saloon class passengers. Our parting had been melancholy. Would I ever see him again? Oh, he had given me an address on Madison Avenue—as long as I lived on the Lower East Side, I thought it was pronounced *Medicine* Avenue—and urged me to contact him as soon as I was settled. (I had made it seem that the America to which I sailed was full of rich relations who would look after me—nobody likes a *schnorrer*.) But I knew I would be too shy to contact him. I had used up all my *chutzpah* on the boat. So I was not certain I would ever lay eyes on him again. Perhaps all his benevolence was just shipboard loneliness, I thought, feeling myself totally abandoned when he waved goodbye with a handkerchief from the little boat, saying, almost singing, *Sophia, Sophia,* and blowing a phantom kiss.

Who was Sophia? I wondered, not responding to the name. And then I realized it was me—the new person I would become in America.

I was sent, of course, to a relative, a huge woman with a crooked wig and many chins with as many wens, who called herself my aunt Chaya and would only ever call me greenhornish *Soora*. She was the one who rented me a slab of a bed in the cellar by the coal vault, which I shared with three other boarders. Chaya was a "sweater"—she ran a sweat-shop in which newly arrived girls from Russia sewed knee pants for a few pennies a pair.

"Sleep faster, we need the pillows," goes one of Mama's favorite sayings (*Shlof gicher, me darf di kishen!*), and "Aunt" Chaya took it literally, rotating the girls who worked on different shifts in that very coal cellar and letting three beds serve for six boarders. The bed-clothes always reeked of someone else's underarms or monthly blood. Bedbugs—bursting with the blood of immigrant girls—were constant companions. There were also fleas and roaches. And rats as big as lapdogs. Remembering, I shudder. I was resolved to get out of there as soon as possible.

Whose relative *was* Chaya anyway? I had only a scrap of paper with her name, but even then I wondered whether Mama could have been mistaken, for Chaya didn't treat me like a relative at all.

Do you want to hear about the other jobs she found for us? Turning worn collars over and resewing them: poor clothes for poor people. Sewing buttons, sewing buttonholes, washing, pressing, the steam flying up in our burning faces. And always hanging over me the thought of the money my journey had cost—the equivalent of twenty-five dollars for the steamship ticket (the precious *shifskarte*) and kopecks for the bribes of the border guards—and more kopecks for the packed train to Hamburg.

How would I repay my family by bringing them one by one across the sea? Turning collars would not do it, nor would making caps in a locked factory with twenty other girls, nor even draping pretty spring-colored evening dresses on a mannequin, whom I talked to as if she were Mama, wetting the chiffon with my tears. My perfect little stitches would not bring them all across the water. I had to find another way.

◆

And then it was a Sunday in spring and my day off, and I was walking down Rivington Street in a swelling tide of people. They pushed and shoved, argued in a mélange of languages. Boys stole apples and pears from pushcarts. Girls danced frantically around the hurdy-gurdy man. Drunks guzzled beer. Babies howled from tenement windows. Corpulent, red-faced mothers leaned out to watch the pageant of the streets—their only entertainment, distraction, pleasure. The fire escapes were hung with worn featherbeds, torn sheets, tattered blankets. The roofs were alive with flapping laundry, pigeons, adolescent boys at their dangerous play. And suddenly my eyes were drawn to an open window on the street level, and I wandered over as if in a trance.

A naked girl—pink, plump, large-breasted—was arranged among folds of fabric on a low wooden platform at the room's center, and a variety of men were sketching her. One man had a gold stopwatch, protuberant eyes, and a bushy black beard. His eyebrows were like black caterpillars. They jumped up and down on his forehead as if possessed by their own will. Instead of the usual skullcap, he wore a sort of embroidered beret. Every five minutes or so, he clapped his hands, and the girl changed her pose.

The other men, those who were sketching, were young, old, thin, fat. Some could draw like demons, some were awkward and slow. One of the laggards complained, "Levitsky—not so fast!"

"Out!" shouted the man with the stopwatch and the funny eyebrows, and he sent the *nebbish* of an artist packing. The girl changed poses again, and seeing the door was open, I walked in.

"May I watch?" I asked politely with my heavy accent.

Levitsky immediately replied in Yiddish: "A pretty face is half a dowry." It was a proverb my mama always used. Then he added in English: "How can I say no to such a beauty?" His accent, strong too, was redolent of Russia: *beautzy*.

I stood and watched through various cycles of poses. The odalisque was now on her back, now on her stomach, now standing, now sitting cross-legged among the drapes of fabric. I was fascinated with the folds of her fat and couldn't stop staring.

Levitsky came over to me and put his arm around my shoulder—I almost jumped.

"Are you an artist too?" he asked.

"A retoucher," I said. "But I can draw as well as this lot."

He looked cynical—as if he didn't believe a girl could draw. Then he handed me a board with paper pinned to it and a piece of charcoal.

"Draw!" he commanded. And draw I did. I had never sketched a nude before, but I was *born* knowing how to draw. How could a nude be different from the other things I'd drawn—houses, animals, portraits? Levitsky sucked in his breath as he watched me draw the sprawling nude. Then she changed poses, and he gave me another sheet of paper. I drew the next pose as well.

"I'll be damned," said Levitsky, in English. "You're better than my other slaves."

"Slaves?" I asked.

"Slaves who can draw fast!" Levitsky barked. "Heads, hands, legs, feet, shoes, hats. To mine opinion, if you work quick enough and specialized enough, you can make quite a lot from the catalogs, but you have to hustle. These *schmegegges*"—he gestured at the drawing fools—"would love to be my slaves, but they ain't good enough. I got the commissions—more than I can handle—but I need the hands to draw 'em. If it were only me drawing, I couldn't make enough to buy a pot to piss in, let alone what I have in mind. . . ."

"And what do you have in mind?" I asked.

"I ain't telling a girl I just met," he said rather roughly.

"Begging your pardon," I said, "but with a hardworking woman with a business head on her shoulders to help you, you could be, *eppis*, a millionaire."

What gave me such *chutzpah* I do not know, but Levitsky was piqued by my brazenness—as brazen people often are.

"So *nu*?" I said.

And that was how I came to leave the coal cellar and work for Lev Levitsky.

The first night I spent in his studio, we drank tea with damson jam, ate walnuts (which we cracked with our teeth), and talked in Yiddish like two prisoners who had been in solitary confinement. Such talk, talk, talk! It warmed my heart. Levitsky was the greatest talker I had ever met—and I had met some great ones.

Then he showed me his drawings. He was a cornucopia of ideas, and his drawings brought back the old country to me and made me homesick for Mama. (In those days, *everything* made me homesick for Mama. I used to read the Yiddish poets in the *Forverts* and weep.) Not only Levitsky's work but his way of speaking made me homesick. And his *smell*. He smelled like my dead papa. His drawings depicted towering tenements, trains that ran on single rails through the air, strange flying machines that could be harnessed to the backs of humans. At the root of it all was a sad wooden village, with skinny goats and hollow-eyed children and tumbled houses arranged around mud ponds. It could have been Sukovoly.

His masterpiece was the huge oil painting he was doing of heaven and hell. All of heaven was made of rosy, creamy clouds encircled by the arms of a rosy-cheeked, white-bearded God, whose body also seemed to be composed of fluffy clouds. His eyes followed you wherever you moved in the room. And below his realm, hell began: demons climbing tenement buildings, hanging from the teeming summer roofs, from fire escapes, from careening streetcars, leaping on people who walked in the streets, dragging them down through manholes into a darker realm—a realm of sewage pools and flesh-denuded humans who crawled on what was left of their knees and howled for mercy. It was the Lower East Side, transformed into a vision of hell!

"A Michelangelo I could be," he said, not without bitterness. "But that's no way to get rich in America. To get rich you have to skim the fat of other people's bones, multiply your hands, and lose your heart. To mine opinion, you have to be a *boss*. And a boss can't be an artist. When the Messiah comes to America, he should come in a private railroad car like Mr. Frick or Mr. Rockefeller! Who would listen to what he would say otherwise? No one! America only listens to what the rich have to say. And to get rich in America, you have to use other people as if they were animals, beasts from burden. One man's hands and heart will not make you rich in America—that's the truth of it, the *emis.*"

I sensed that his bitterness had something of rationalization in it, as if there were a fear inside him that he was not good enough, or that by painting and drawing he would raise *dybbuks* and affront the Almighty. For a Jew to paint in those days was to rise in rebellion. Books we were allowed—books we worshiped—but images always smacked of the devil for us. The Jew who painted was always torn, whether Chagall or Pascin . . . or others I came to know later. But I held my tongue. I needed the job I had so audaciously demanded, and I was not about to block my own way.

Better to be Levitsky's slave than Chaya's. Better to be Levitsky's slave than a Sidewalk Susie or a white slave in a brothel. The streets of the Lower East Side were full of Jewish girls who made their living on their back. They strolled the streets wearing nothing but their vivid kimonos, flashing a bit of breast or lewdly propositioning potential customers. They lived—if you could call it that—in storefronts, in tenements, in shacks behind tenements, and they charged fifty cents a night at a time when you could buy something for a penny—a lemonade, say, or a hot dog, or halvah covered in powdered sugar. Their pimps were as brazen as the girls. Some of these men became song pluggers or Second Avenue producers or later even Hollywood agents. A man who can figure out a way to get paid for what a girl does in bed with another man can figure a way to get paid for *anything*. In Yiddish, we call such a person a *dreyer*—a smooth operator.

As Shakespeare said, *chutzpah* is all. On the Lower East Side, *chutz-pah* was meat and drink and a roof against the rain.

Once I began working for Levitsky, I had no time to mope about the family I left behind—neither the living nor the dead. Now I was run-ning at double speed, like some heroine in a picture show. Levitsky was a ferocious taskmaster, driving his ghost painters on to greater and greater feats of productivity. First he had to conquer the catalogs, then he became fascinated with the possibility of making animated cartoons, and he would sit day and night drawing twenty or thirty pictures of the same horse, but slightly different in the legs, sewing them into a book-let and flipping the pages until the horse seemed to move. At such times he was so engrossed that I feared bringing him anything, even a cookie or a glass of tea. Sometimes he would show me what he was doing. And sometimes, when I expressed greater interest, he would draw sugges-tive female figures, again with slightly different motions of legs and arms, and flip them for me until I blushed. And he would laugh rau-cously, delighting in shocking what he presumed was my innocence.

As for that commodity, I both was and wasn't innocent. *Wasn't* because I had borne a child. *Was* because I had never known the love of a man. Perhaps that was why it was so simple for me to decide that if I was going to work for Levitsky, I would sleep with him too. There was no sense in being coy, I told myself. Men were men, and if you couldn't celebrate the Sabbath in America—Saturday was a work day in America then—you might as well give up all your other illusions about virtue. But Levitsky was a funny man. He would not *let* me into his bed, saying (in Yiddish) that when the cock stood up, the brains lay in the ground, and that he would rather have my help than my distraction. Sometimes he would stroke my hair or put his arm around my shoulder, but that was all. Nor did he visit the whores. He spat at them when they importuned him in the street, saying, "Go to the *mikveh*" or *"Shande! Shande!"*

"You're a nice piece of goods," he used to say to me, "but go to your own bed."

And I would obey, thinking him the most peculiar man I had ever met.

"Better an honest smack in the face than a false kiss," Mama would have said.

Oh, *Mamenyu!* Where are you? It seemed to me I needed my mama now more than I ever had. I carried my little mama with me in my head and heart every minute of every day. Sometimes I even spoke to her as if she were in the same room.

"What's wrong with Levitsky, Mama?" I asked. And: "Will I ever see the *shaygetz* from the ship again?" And: "Will *he* reject me also?" For I hardly knew then how attractive men found me. I was like catnip to them, but I did not know yet what sort of power that was.

The *shaygetz* from the ship was in my mind as much as Mama, if the truth be told. I kept hearing her say in Yiddish: *"Dray zakhn ken men nisht bahaltn: libe, hustn un dales."* (Three things can never be hidden: love, a cough, and poverty.) Those pale-blue eyes had betrayed love as insistently as a consumptive's cough foreshadows his death.

I am speaking of my first year in America, when everything was fresh and new and had a halo around it like the ring around the moon on a frosty winter night. For a stranger who walks alone in a foreign land, every ordinary thing pierces the heart. Every policeman is fearsome. Every encounter may change your life for better or for worse. Every man you meet is a door into comfort or disaster.

As a little girl, I used to fear the outhouse in our back courtyard. When I had to make caca in the middle of the night, I imagined invisible demons who would rise up from the stinking pit beneath the hole and drag me down into their hellish realm. Sometimes I would use the chamber pot or else hold everything in all night, tossing and turning, unable to sleep till the dawn came. But if I was sick in my *kishkes,* I had no choice but tiptoe out to the hell gate of the privy. What terror there was in creeping outside in the cold, hanging my little *tush* over the entrance to the underworld while the demons prepared God only knew what tortures for its sweet pink flesh.

Being in America alone was a lot like going to the outhouse at night in Sukovoly. No wonder Levitsky became mother, father, brother, comforter, to me. I clung to him as I would have clung to my mother had she braved the perils of the outhouse with me (which she only did when I was feverish and sick). If you wonder, as this story proceeds, how I stayed with a man whose very claim to manhood was so uncertain, remember the story of the outhouse. I stayed with him because he stayed with me in the dark night, when the *dybbuks* howled under the privy's hole.

Meanwhile, what was Sim doing? I found out only much later. Sim returned from Europe to his digs on what I thought of as Medicine Avenue (did only doctors and apothecaries live there? I wondered), to find himself obsessed and distracted by dreams of the goddess he had met on the ship. The goddess! That was me! How different I seemed from the women he knew in New York, he said. I was alive, and they seemed like walking corpses. Even before I could express much in English, I had said more to him than any other woman he had ever met. Or so he claimed.

How would *he* do if deprived of the life he knew and thrown into a whole new world in a teeming metropolis? Not well, he suspected. There was in Sim a black melancholy that was activated by disorder, uncertainty, the upsetting of routine. Even his plunges into the abyss followed a pattern. And now a descending goddess had threatened to throw him into chaos!

"If a man is destined to drown, he will drown even in a spoonful of water," Mama used to say. Was I destined to be Sim's spoonful of water?

Levitsky had no carnal passions, it seemed, but Sim was accustomed to ruling *his* with an iron hand. Only he knew at what great cost he accomplished this. His mother believed he would eventually marry his cousin Lucretia Weathersby. But what the intimidating Mrs. Coppley could not know was that after every extended audience with bluestocking Lucretia, whether in her family's town house on Fifth Avenue or in their bogus Tuscan *castello* in the Berkshires (Fontana di Luna was its ostentatious name), he went immediately to a notorious brothel in the tenderloin and lost a day and a night in the arms of the latest child bride the madam, a certain Mrs. Rottenberg, had found for him. After the debauch, he would carefully lock the memories of those guilty hours in a secret chamber of his brain and throw away the key.

Lucretia was clever, was, God knows, rich. But a stroll with her up Fifth Avenue or through the greensward of her country place left Sim gasping for breath as if he were dying. He suspected that Lucretia felt the same about him, but being a woman and *required* to marry in order to escape her mother and join the world, Lucretia had seized upon him as the least of all possible evils. He was, after all, bookish like her, loved dogs, loved cats, loved horses. But apart from her animal passions, Lucretia was seemingly a disembodied spirit. Sim, however, *had* a body—though he always managed to forget it between trips to Mrs. Rottenberg's. Now, his body was alive all the time.

I am speaking, of course, of things Sim told me when I had been in America so long I was beyond being shocked. He told me later that when he visited Lucretia and watched her pour tea from a Georgian silver pot, he fancied he was sitting opposite "the goddess from the boat." He imagined me pouring my breasts out of the top of my corset and playing with my brown nipples until they were erect. He imagined me throwing my petticoat over my head and inviting him into my moist, warm center.

"How strange you suddenly look," Lucretia had said once to Sim. "What is it?"

And Sim longed with all his heart to tell Lucretia what he was thinking, but he would have as soon put a bullet in his brain.

"How is your research on the Hebrews?" Lucretia asked.

"Far more absorbing and penetrating than I supposed it would be," said Sim.

Lucretia was sitting at the tea table, staring into Sim's blue eyes with her eyes of identical hue. Her bosom was almost nonexistent, even when pushed up by the corset beneath it. She tapped her foot in her delicate black kid boot with its licorice buttons.

"Sim—I want you to take me to the ghetto next time you go. I have to see your beloved Kike Town!" (Though Lucretia's ruling passion would indeed turn out to be her anti-Semitism, in those days terms like "Kike Town" were freely used by all, as if they had no negative connotation whatever. We Jews were too newly arrived to be touchy about names. The same went for the other immigrants who burst the asphalt seams of downtown New York: Wops, Chinks, Guineas . . . how could they complain? Complaining is the privilege of the secure.)

Lucretia's request to see the ghetto seemed entirely mad to Sim, who could never imagine his cousin Lucretia outside of an environment in which the upholstery and the draperies matched.

"If I were a man," Lucretia said, "I would go on my own."

"Happily, my dear Lucretia, it is impossible to imagine you as a man."

She stamped her licorice foot again. "I *hate* being a girl," she said.

"Surely you can't mean that," said Sim.

"Surely I can," said Lucretia. "And so would you. The clothes alone are enough to drive one mad! If I were a man I would go *everywhere*—Kike Town, Nigger Town, Wop Town, Pigtail Town— and you would go with me!"

"Lucretia—such lingo is wholly unbecoming for a lady."

"I don't want to be a lady!" said Lucretia. "I've been a lady long enough!"

Sim was thinking of that odd conversation as he walked the teeming streets of the Lower East Side in search of the woman he had met on the ship. (I had never contacted him.) "*Kreplach* that you see in a dream are no *kreplach*," my mother used to say, and to me Sim was a *kreplach* seen in a dream. It was not for eating. The truth was, I did not *expect* Sim to turn out to be real. I must have suspected even then that he needed his life of luxury: the shafts of light that fell on the silk cushions in the drawing room at Fontana di Luna, the Gothic windows and Renaissance fountains plundered from a different Europe than mine, the gardens made in imitation of eighteenth-century France or sixteenth-century England. But I could not possibly know then that he was even more stimulated by the strong smells of my downtown streets—the sweat of the peddler women with their heaving bosoms, the aroma of pickles and smoked fish, of knishes and blintzes, of beer and ale and strong cigars. Pushcarts overflowing with tumbling toma-toes and staring fish, large barrels filled with pickles, foamy brewed drink tapped from kegs, the wildly bearded men in their bowler hats, haggling and arguing, the women in their kerchiefs, the half-naked children playing in the Rutgers Square Park and scrambling for their piled-up clothes when the lookout boy whispered, "Cheese it—duh cops!"—these were sights and sounds that filled Sim with an excite-ment he could not find in the purer precincts of his uptown world.

Sometimes he would become so bewitched by the ghetto that he was in danger of being knocked down by a careening horsecar. He went into a trance on Hester or Ludlow or Orchard Street or East Broadway, and he would say to himself that he could never properly write a book about the "Hebrews" (as he called us) unless he rented a flat down here and lived among the tenements and pushcarts day and night. Sim was particularly fascinated by the way whole families came to sleep under the stars on sweltering summer nights, leaving the air-less caves of the railroad flats to the roaches, rats, and bedbugs. The roofs came alive with humanity on such a night. And sometimes Sim would wander from roof to roof, gazing down at the sleeping immi-grant women, looking everywhere for his "Sophia."

But the goddess from the boat was nowhere to be found.

Oh, he saw women who were as juicily attractive, as full-breasted and full of life, yet their eyes (he later said) lacked the same mischief.

"Mister!" came a call of a peddler with a tower of derbies on his head. He advanced to grab Sim by the lapels and drag him into the darkness of his little hole-in-the-wall: "You need a zoot? A coit? A new pair of shoes?" The man rummaged furiously among an amazing array of goods, then leaped forward, tore Sim's topcoat off his back, and substituted a heavy tweed much too dense for this hot weather.

"*Nu?*" said the man. "*Nu, nu, nu?*" He raised a cracked fragment of mirror. Apparently Sim was so overwhelmed to be interrupted in the midst of his reverie that without even bargaining, he bought the lumpy thing the man had pressed on him.

The peddler was astonished, perhaps even disappointed. He kept throwing in extra goods "at no extra charge" for the sake of sweetening the deal.

"I'm looking for a woman," Sim Coppley said, and the snaggle-toothed peddler, as if to show that nothing was beyond his capacities as a procurer of human needs, excused himself, ran up a flight of narrow stairs at the back of his dusty lair, and brought down a dirty young girl with feverish black eyes, a smudged apron, and a nimbus of frizzy hair. She began to whimper pathetically, revealing yellow teeth.

Horrified that even this disgusting peddler knew his predilections (or so he imagined in his guilt), Sim turned and, leaving both his dollars and the heap of clothes, ran down the street, darting and weaving amid the pushcarts. Secure in his escape, he suddenly realized he was wearing the peddler's heavy tweed and had left his own bespoke London topcoat behind.

A few days later, Sim wrote a letter to the column called "A Bintel Brief" in the Yiddish newspaper:

Esteemed Editor:

I hope you will give me advice even though I am a "goy" who has learned Yiddish from books and dictionaries rather than at the knee of my mother.

Returning to America from Europe on a ship called Der Goldener Stern *some months ago, I met a Hebrew woman from steerage whose beauty, liveliness, and intelligence captivated me. I helped her with English and she drew my portrait, which I treasure. But now she has disappeared from my life forever.*

Tell me, dear Editor, how shall I find her—or am I insane to think of making her my wife? I cannot forget her.

I know she is poor, but as the poet says: A pretty face is half a dowry. I can supply the other half. Please advise your desperate reader.

An uptown man whose heart is downtown

ANSWER:

We cannot advise this writer concerning this matter. Some mixed marriages are happy, some are not. Also, the writer seems not to have considered the woman's feelings. The advice to the writer is: honor the young woman's opinion.

We print this letter in the hopes that the woman will contact him if she has the desire. If she does not contact him, we advise the writer to let the matter drop.

3

Sarah ✦ YENTL MEETS *THE AGE OF INNOCENCE*
1906

> *Darkness, the old mother, has not forgotten my East Side.*
>
> — MICHAEL GOLD

When I saw the letter printed in the *Forverts,* I immediately tore it out and hid it in my corset so that Levitsky would not see it. Somehow I knew that despite his reticence about sex, he would not be happy about the existence of a rival for my attentions. He might be afraid to make love to me himself, but that didn't mean he was not possessive. The territorial drives of men are not only about sex. Possession is a fiercer joy. Levitsky had made my life better, and I had no intention of giving him up.

It was not only the work but the newfound sources of entertainment. He would take me to the Yiddish theater, happy to have a pretty woman on his arm and to have people think we were lovers. At first I was glad to conspire. With the money I was making from my catalog work, I could afford new clothes, and the theater was the

place to show them off. Afterward we would tour the Yiddish Rialto
on Second Avenue (this was even *before* the Café Royale), and
Levitsky would beam with *naches* when all the theatrical riffraff—or
slumming Avenoodles—looked hungrily at me.

What myths have grown up about the Yiddish theater! You'd think
it was the old Globe itself and that every playwright was Shakespeare.
Not that they didn't plunder him—and everyone else they could steal
from. Like Hollywood, which it in fact gave birth to, the Yiddish theater stooped to conquer. Respect for the intelligence of the audience
was hardly rampant. Everyone went for the cheap laugh, the croco-
dile tears—and the audience loved it. The audience made more noise
than the actors. Still, the Yiddish dramatists stole from the best—
Shakespeare, Ibsen, Chekhov. In one offering, Hamlet (played by the
great matinee idol Tomashevsky) was a rabbinical student who came
home to find that his uncle, the old rabbi, had married his mother
and knocked off his father—with a poisoned matzo, no doubt. What
shreiing there was! Who would have guessed that all of Denmark was
inhabited by Litvaks! (Tomashevsky was a rather *plump* Hamlet—not
exactly Valentino—but the Litvak ladies swooned nevertheless!)

There was also the Jewish *Doll's House*. (Ibsen, of course, was
claimed by all progressive Jews as a landsman.) In the Yiddish version, Nora was called Minna and took in a handsome young anarchist
boarder with bedroom eyes who immediately enlightened her and
her daughter about female emancipation and woman's suffrage, not
to mention the eight-hour day. Having renovated their brains, the
boarder now commenced to renovate those parts that were sacred to
Venus—excuse my French—while the old papa *dovened*, turned a
blind eye, and went on paying the bills. Ibsen, meanwhile, rolled over
in his grave.

Not so different from show business today, when you come to
think about it. My grandson, Lorenzo—God help him—has just produced a gay musical *Hamlet* in which Hamlet and Horatio are lovers,
Rosenkrantz and Guildenstern run a bathhouse in Wittenberg, and

Ophelia and Gertrude are making it in the throne room behind the arras—where they run into Claudius and Polonius doing the same. At first he was afraid to invite me for fear I would be shocked. Shocked! I should only be shocked. In my younger days I saw and did plenty of things that would curl his hair—if he had any.

Lorenzo . . . I hardly have to tell *you* about your uncle Lorenzo. He was spoiled rotten by my dear daughter, Salome, and fancies himself a producer—a name anyone can assume, talent or not. My deepest wish is for Lorenzo to get his act together, stop plundering Shakespeare and get a job. I should live so long.

Just like Lorenzo, the anarchists of the Lower East Side thought they invented sex. But New York was already Sodom and Gomorrah *before* they got off the boat. Besides the tenderloin and the Dutch village, the Bowery with its bedbug houses and Irish saloons, there were streetwalkers and hoboes, singing waiters who doubled as pimps, second-story men, and girls—plenty of them nice Jewish girls, you should excuse the expression—who started out in the tenderloin and drifted down to Fourteenth Street and eventually to the Bowery, until they wound up in potter's field, the last stop. The whole Lower East Side was a red-light district when I got there, and a house was not necessarily a home.

I may be a Yiddishe mama, but I'm a *red-hot* Yiddishe mama! I knew couples who lived happily with the husband's mistress and couples who invited the male boarder into the conjugal bed. Back then it was done in the name of anarchism and free love. Later it was done in the name of Communism. The intelligentsia always likes to find an intellectual reason for *schtupp*ing—of that you may be sure. Whatever the excuse, *schtupp*ing is still *schtupp*ing. And it is the rhythm that cranks the world on its rusty old axis. Moralists may march, pass laws, blame the Jews for it, but it will never be eradicated. Which reminds me, for some reason—who can chart the vagaries of the ancient female brain?—of white slavery.

The subject of white slavery was all the rage when I came to

America. (Black slavery they took for granted.) Havelock Ellis and Emma Goldman got all worked up about what they called the scandal of white slavery. Politicians would denounce it to get elected. Girls at Ellis Island would whisper about it—half in fear, half in titillation. It was said that some girls we actually *knew* were contracted to bawdy houses and compelled to stay there until they paid back their passage or—more likely—came down with disease and died. They never lasted more than two or three years, it was said. Syphilis was the scourge of the ghetto.

But I knew even then that if I had been contracted to a white slaver, I would have got the better of him. Somehow. I had seen too much to be afraid of a penny pimp—you should also excuse the expression. I knew I was alive only because of the hard bargain God had driven. I was borne up by the bodies of babies—Dovie first among them. And I walked with a phantom twin, having to be both girl and boy.

We are all borne up by the bodies of babies, though we prefer not to think about it. I remembered a crying child who tumbled through the ice as we *fussgeyers* crossed the frozen border into Germany. Over the lamentations of the mother, the ice child was left behind in its cold blue cocoon. When you have seen and heard things like that, you either give up and die or become a fighter.

I took the clipping from the *Forverts* from my bodice and made up my mind not to let Levitsky and Coppley meet. Levitsky was my impresario, and he was jealous. Coppley would only make him more so. That much I had learned about men. There would be a time to use this jealousy to my advantage. But the time had not yet come.

Meanwhile, I drew. I drew hats and shoes, petticoats and corsets, money belts and suspenders. I drew overalls and work boots, shirts and waistcoats, coats and trousers and hobble skirts. The more valuable I was, the quicker and better I drew, the more possessive Levitsky became.

And I learned to manage him: to mix sugar and tongue-lashing, to wheedle and seduce, to tease and taunt until I got what I wanted. All my aim in those days was to earn enough to bring my family over from the land of *pogroms*. To this end I saved my money at a Jewish bank. (It went bust in the depression of 1907—another story for another rainy night.)

We made a funny family—Levitsky and I and the few other catalog artists who worked with us in Levitsky's tenement on Rivington.

We had drawing tables and high stools, and sometimes the corsets and shirts and blouses and jackets would be stuffed or hung on tailors' dummies.

Since our place was on the ground floor and since we always had food and drink aplenty, homeless urchins who lived everywhere and nowhere—street Arabs, they were called—used to flock into the studio to beg for scraps. I took to one of these urchins and fed him behind Levitsky's back. The child's name was, he said, Tyke, and he sold newspapers and swept streets; he may also have been a pickpocket. Who knows where he slept? Those homeless boys slept in alleys behind Irish bars or on the steps of wine cellars or anywhere they could till the snow came and froze them out. What they did then, God only knows. But even though Tyke was half black, he looked to me like my lost boy, so I was always glad to see him.

One day, I gave him a little sketch I had made of myself and asked him to bring it to Sim Coppley's house and slide it into the mailbox. I had not put my address or name on it. I meant only to whet Sim's appetite. But apparently Sim caught the boy and bribed him with chocolates until he confessed to my whereabouts.

The very next day, who should come strolling through the doors of our street-level studio but Sim Coppley himself!

He fell to his knees before the stool where I was drawing. "'Thine eyes are as doves,'" he said, quoting the Song of Songs.

"Thy *kopf* is *dumm!*" I said, quoting myself, though my heart thudded in my chest.

It was my good fortune that Levitsky was out delivering drawings when Coppley arrived. "You must never come here again!" I said. "My boss will fire me."

"You don't need a boss, you need a husband," Coppley said.

"A husband *is* a boss!" I said, flaunting my—or Levitsky's—anarchist ideas. "A husband is a form of white slavery!" (I had begun attending radical lectures at the Educational Alliance, and this is the sort of thing I'd picked up. Only six months in America, and I was already a low-rent Emma Goldman!)

"If you were *my* wife, Sophia, I would give you everything you needed and freedom too."

"Freedom cannot be *given!*" I said. "If you think you can give it to me, it shows you don't know what freedom *is*. Besides, I am almost a stranger to you!"

"We have crossed an ocean together," said Sim, dazed with desire. And then, seeing a bowl of fruit on the table, he sighed: "'Comfort me with apples! I am faint with love.'" (Later he would woo me by translating Elizabeth Barrett Browning's "How do I love thee? Let me count the ways" into Yiddish: *"Vifiel hob ich dir leib? Loz mir tzelen: / Ich leib dir azoi tief und breit und hoich / Vie mein neshomeh ken dirgreichen, ven / Zie sucht dem lebens tachlis und die shchineh."* Oh, he believed that poetry and psalm would cover a multitude of sins!)

Just then Levitsky strolled in, smoking his stinkiest cigar.

"Pfui," I said. Coppley, for all his delirium, had the presence of mind to say: "I greatly admire this lady's work, and I would like to propose a business deal to you."

The word "business" always riveted Levitsky. Business was his religion. I went on coolly drawing a corset as if it would contain Sim's rash tongue. Levitsky and Coppley retreated to a corner to bargain. I heard them haggling in raised voices. Finally they shook hands.

Coppley then came up to my drawing stool and said, "I shall look forward to welcoming you in the country, madame."

And he took his leave.

When Sim departed, Levitsky was excited.

"He will pay us fifty dollars for you to draw pictures of a party in the country. And we are to go this very weekend in a private railway car!"

"A full pocket will heal the sick," Mama would have said.

Fifty dollars was a fortune in those days. It had cost me twenty-five to come across the sea. Now I would cross an even wider ocean, into the world of the rich *goyim*. And *they* would pay *me!* Incredible.

Clever Sim, I thought. He had immediately realized that Levitsky's heart was imprisoned in his wallet.

It was on a Friday evening in May that Levitsky and I departed the infernal city in the private railway car, a paradise of *marron-glacé*–colored velvet sofas, polished brass, etched mirrors, and velvet easy chairs more embracing than the womb. An ebony butler attended to our every whim. First he brought us cordials and water, then he set a table for dinner with beautiful linens and fresh flowers. Presently he served us foods such as I had only read about in books: terrapin soup, scallops in cream, *coq au vin*, lemon tarts, French cheeses, coffee, oranges in liqueur, and bittersweet chocolate—all with the appropriate wines.

In an hour or so, I was so tipsy that I fell back in my chair and slept. I did not awaken until we had arrived at a sweet-smelling station in the country, where the summer night was alive with crickets and stars.

We were met by a coachman driving a one-horse shay. The conveyance swayed and bumped over the rutted roads and brought us in some minutes to a grand edifice that the coachman called "the cottage," with a curving tree-lined driveway. There we were put in the care of a housekeeper, who brought us to adjoining rooms with huge four-poster beds, polished pier glasses, velvet chaises, and tufted settees. Flowering branches bloomed in Chinese vases. An applewood fire burned in each hearth, scenting the rooms.

I fell asleep that night watching the flickering fire and knowing that I could never explain to Mama about this or about the other things I had already seen and tasted in America.

"Forgive me, *Mamele*," I whispered, falling asleep. "I did not mean to run ahead of you, but fate presented me with this rolling road."

And I thought I heard Mama say: *"Kayne hore."* (May no evil eye fix you in its gaze.)

Some mornings, Sim Coppley awoke unable to breathe. He would gasp for breath, making wheezing noises in his lungs. The feeling of choking was so real that sometimes in a panic he would wet himself like a hanged man on the edge of death. He would leap out of bed and jump about the room as if that way, somehow, he could pull more air into his lungs. A gurgle in his throat and a shortness of air told him that he was in danger of drowning in his own secretions. He would cough to try to dislodge them, increasing his own panic. There was always a moment when he was sure he would not survive the attack. Then, miraculously, air would return to his passageways and he would know he had been reprieved. When he had these attacks, Sim felt that somehow he was being punished for his lechery and deserved to die. He was always surprised when he was spared.

The morning he was to greet me at Fontana di Luna—which was Lucretia's family's palazzo—he apparently had one of the worst of these spells. He soaked his nightshirt back and front, wet the rug, and found himself unaccountably on his knees like a dog, coughing and sputtering and gasping. He thought that if I could see him this way I would loathe him.

"Weak, weak, weak!" he railed at himself when he found his voice. His father had been contemptuous of his asthmatic wheezing, and Sim's nursemaid had tried to hide these fits from Father when the boy was small. The fact that he was still visited by them seemed to Sim proof of his undeservingness. He had the feeling that I could fill his lungs with breath.

✦

When I awoke in the cottage, sunlight was streaming in my window and I was troubled by the shreds of a dream. In the dream, Sim Coppley and I had to meet the President of America, but when I looked down at my shoes I saw that both they and my stockings were unmatched. One shoe had a strap across the instep and one did not. One stocking was brown and one was green. How can I meet the President like this? I asked Sim in a panic. And then I thought of what Mama would say: "Even a prophet's dreams are not always prophetic."

There came a knock at my door, and a serving maid in a ruffled cap arrived to bring me my breakfast in bed.

The dream of unmatched shoes disappeared with the first sight of the breakfast tray. The white linens, the silver cutlery, the basket of hot cross buns, the tea in porcelain cups as thin as eggshells, the little pot of amber honey, the fresh country butter, the brown-speckled eggs in their cup and cozy, the sausages under their silver *chuppah*. So transfixed was I that I never wondered if the sausages were *trayfe*! And there, neatly folded, was the *Berkshire County Eagle*.

I am still amazed to inhabit a world where some people pick food out of the garbage and some eat on silver trays. The first time I had white bread at Ellis Island, it seemed like cake to me. Do all Americans eat like this every day? I wondered. But my first breakfast tray at Fontana di Luna was an absolute marvel: a whole little universe of silver and porcelain and creamy linen. What effort had gone into this breakfast alone! How many cooks and craftsmen had labored to make the breaking of bread into a work of art! Even though I believed in the brotherhood of all men (no one mentioned women then), I knew I could get used to breakfast in bed in the wink of an eye!

This is what memories are made of: the first breakfast tray, chalk letters on the rejected at Ellis Island, a private railroad car clacking along the Housatonic Railroad line, a dream of unmatched shoes.

To travel backward in time a century or so—you're not going to trap me into saying how old I am!—and re-create these early days is not easy, but it is always the smells and the objects that take me back.

What I remember from that weekend: the ladies in their pastel frocks and parasols playing croquet on the lawns of Fontana di Luna, the paneled library with thousands of leather-bound books, the trellis of white roses trained into a living, fluttering canopy, humming with bees.

At that time, the worst thing on earth was to be a greenhorn—*a greener,* as we used to say on the Lower East Side. Embarrassed about my accent, my uncertainty about which fork to use, I hid behind my sketchbook and spoke as little as possible. What if I should mispronounce something!

When Sim came to fetch me that morning, having first sent maids to fit me with new clothes—a mutton-sleeved, high-necked linen waist, a blue-and-green tartan skirt with matching fitted jacket, a wonderful green hat with parrot feathers and swaths of green veiling—he found me admiring my green suede high button boots with scalloped edges.

"Oh, what I dreamed!" I said.

"I dreamed of you," said he, "all night long."

"And what was I wearing in your dream?" I asked.

"Nothing at all," said Sim, blushing pink as a marzipan pig and starting to cough in nervousness.

He brought me pastels and paper and an ingenious French folding easel which could be unfolded and placed on the grass. It even had its own parasol to shield me from the sun. He carried this folded contraption as he took me on a tour of the grounds and showed me the beauties of the Berkshire countryside.

The "cottage" was immense—fifty rooms or more—and was perched whitely on the hilltop. With its gabled windows and many chimneys, and its terraces of Italian gardens, sundials, fountains with rearing horses, it seemed a place of enchantment, such as I imagined Versailles—which I had seen in pictures. My job was to memorialize the weekend with my pen. The house, the gardens, but most particularly the guests . . . all these I was expected to sketch.

I will never forget the way Levitsky trailed us, watching from afar as if he expected Sim to steal me away.

Sim was very solicitous of my needs, wanting me to participate in the croquet, the archery, the lunches, teas, and suppers. But feeling sure I would make an utter fool of myself among these swells, nobs, and brownstoners—what did I know of archery from Sukovoly or even Odessa?—I pretended such sport would interfere with my work and that I preferred only to sketch. I meticulously laid out my pencils, inks, and pastels, and I disappeared into the creamy drawing paper.

Impressed as I was by the purple hilltops, the deep-blue lakes, the sloping lawns like the dark-green velvety suede of my boots, I was even more impressed by the women, who seemed a breed apart from any I had ever known. Their slimness could hardly be due only to corseting! One among these took a particular interest in me.

"Meet Miss Lucretia Weathersby," said Sim, leading over to my easel a thin, almost pinched lady with what appeared to be a pair of pigeons taking flight from her huge white straw hat, whose gossamer streamers lifted in the wind and fluttered. Miss Lucretia had eyes hard as crows' beaks and little crinkles at the cruel corners of her mouth.

"Show us your temptress of the tenements, Sim!" she said with a bitter laugh. Then she minced over to be presented to me where I stood next to my easel under its spot of silken-parasoled shade.

She put out her bony hand. I clasped it and found it cold. She appraised me like a pawnbroker appraising a stolen watch.

"Ah, Sim," she said, not even deigning to address me, "you did not say your little Hebrew protégée was also a juicy morsel!"

Beads of sweat broke out on my forehead, and my cheeks prickled with heat. I hated her on sight and might have shown it had not Levitsky stridden forward to be introduced.

"Madame," he said, "let the lady sketch your likeness in that becoming hat!" And fetching a wicker chair from a nearby gazebo, he placed it on the emerald grass for Lucretia.

She arranged her shroud-white skirts and crossed her bony ankles, then pierced me with her birdlike gaze.

I thought for a moment of drawing her as the bird of prey she seemed. Then I remembered myself and made a likeness, but a flattering likeness in which all the sharpness I saw in her was softened. Sim stood behind me, watching, while Levitsky clowned for Lucretia. He was obnoxiously playing the stage Jew—with gestures stolen from Tomashevsky—and she ate it up!

"You people are sooo talented," I heard her say. And Levitsky played on her *goyishe* sensibilities like a ham Shylock. She would give him *her* pound of flesh—if only she had any! Sim, meanwhile, hovered over me. *That* was the day he pressed his Yiddish translation of Mrs. Browning's "How do I love thee? Let me count the ways" into my hand. I hid it promptly in a pocket of my borrowed finery.

By the end of the afternoon, I had sketched several of the ladies, and they were all oohing and aahing over their little pastel sketches. Some began to bargain with Levitsky for me to paint proper full-length portraits of them. Yet for all that I had flattered Lucretia, she still eyed me warily. She knew me for her rival, and I surely knew her for my enemy.

I think of Lucretia as I saw her then (now that she is long dead) and she seems like such a black-and-white villainess. But remember, I viewed her not only through my own eyes but through the eyes of Sim, who had confused her somewhat with his own imperious mother. Sim was bound to Lucretia by manacles forged in childhood, and the crueler she was to him, the more bound to her he felt. Pain binds more securely than pleasure.

◆

I have been asked to tell you everything I remember—perhaps because it is presumed that my great age gives me wisdom of some sort, or perhaps because I am now so old that my recollections are museum pieces. The young need to believe that the old know something. Otherwise life seems too random, too full of chaos. So I am dictating my story to your mother, because I want to give you something of value, and life is always of more value than *things*. Perhaps when you are old enough to read this I won't be here anymore. This is my testament for you, Sarichka, my spiritual will. "Writing an autobiography and making a spiritual will are practically the same," says the great Shalom Aleichem. So what if I am not writing but talking? I imagine you listening, *mayne leben, mayne neshoma, mayne libe.*

You were born in that generation whose parents were all divorced when you were young, so perhaps continuity means even more to you than to other generations. The class of 2000! Whoever thought we'd come to such a year! And who'd have thought we'd have a generation like yours, so deeply cynical about love, about sex, about politics. Perhaps you were reacting to your parents' belief that a drop of LSD in the water supply would bring world peace. With parents like that, no wonder you're confused.

Sitting here, talking into this machine, my mind wanders. Painting is really much more comfortable for me than writing—or even dictating. Speaking, I see everything in pictures. I wish I could tell this story that way. But time is my subject, and time requires narrative. That's me: the ancient narrator.

I never look at myself in the mirror anymore, because I am no longer the self that I remember. It dislocates me to see that old crone in the mirror. I'd rather remember myself as I was then—auburn-haired, beautiful—as you are today. I'd rather look at you and see myself.

Since you have followed me this far, you are probably wondering how much of all this is true. I can only say it is as true as memory, and memory is a notorious deceiver. Mama used to say: *"Oyf a mayse fregt men nisht keyn kashe."* (With stories, you don't ask questions.) Like all records of a life, it is a sort of note in a bottle cast upon the waters, to be found perhaps by a future survivor of life's shipwreck. I hope that future survivor is you.

Time is an undertow. Most of us live in the past our whole lives, and when death confronts us, we surrender and are not surprised to rejoin our lost loved ones. I find that the older I grow, the more real Russia is to me, though I lived there only seventeen years. But I know it is an imaginary Russia, which no longer exists; perhaps it never did. Nevertheless, it is where I live in these last years of my life. Often I find myself surrounded by relatives who died long ago. The worst thing about being this old is that the telephone seems useless because you cannot call up the people you are mostly thinking of. No telephones in heaven! (Though probably the other place is wired for sound!)

I try to remember all the things my mother told me, so that I can pass them on to you. "You may have doubts about love, but you can't doubt hatred," I repeat.

"Another pessimistic proverb!" I imagine you saying. "Didn't your mother ever say anything cheerful?"

"By her, that *was* cheerful," I say.

Yiddish wasn't just words, you see, it was an *attitude*. It was sweet and sour. It was a shrug and a kiss. It was humility and defiance all in one. "A worm in horseradish thinks his life is sweet," Mama used to say. "If God wills it, even a broom can shoot" was another favorite.

What I wish for you, my darling, is that all the brooms in your life should turn into magic wands and that you travel always from horseradish to honey, knowing the sweetness for what it is and having keen taste buds to appreciate its savor.

◆

It was a world of outdoor privies, Irish cops, whalebone corsets, dumbbell tenements, and Beaux Arts (or brownstone) mansions— but the griefs and heartbreaks were the same. The panic about being broke, the thud in the heart when love came to call, the hopelessness of the old and the arrogance of the young—all these were the same.

Human beings do not, after all, have such a varied repertoire. For more than a hundred years, people have been saying that new machines will remake the creature, but I have seen people remain the same from horsecar to automobile, from clanking railroads to supersonic jets, from outhouse to rushing indoor cataracts.

After the weekend at Fontana di Luna, Levitsky decided there was more to be made on portraits of the rich than on catalog art, so he began to look for a proper studio for me.

He found one near Union Square, in a gloomy brownstone with a wide stoop and a parlor floor backed with glass that gave onto a northern sky.

We furnished the place in what seemed to us splendor: a fainting couch covered with Oriental rugs, a model's platform raised up on ball-footed legs, Turkish lanterns and a Turkish corner, embroidered shawls over the round table, plaster casts of Michelangelo's slaves, Donatello's David, Bernini's Daphne turning into a laurel tree.

And then the clients came, the women tittering and titillated by taking off their clothes and going into costume—for some wanted to be painted not as they were but as they wished to be: Juliet, Portia, Ophelia. (Men preferred to be painted as their heroic selves.) Many women changed into their own brilliant ball gowns and hovered over me to see that I highlighted every pearl.

Painting portraits is a good way to listen to the soul of a person hanging in the air. For the more silent I was, the more my sitters spoke.

They began by establishing their wealth and station, as most people do, and ended by revealing the depths of their desires. And I would paint—the greenish shadows that define a nose, the yellow shine across a forehead, the wedge-shaped chocolate shadow below a lip. The portrait painter knows that all God's children are multicolored.

All day, I would listen to my sitters preen and talk of balls and entertainments, engagements broken or dreamed of, grand tours to Europe planned or canceled.

They spoke to me as if I understood, and soon I did. I came to know that money prevents no griefs, cures no illnesses, and that a person can be as happy standing at an easel painting as having dresses fitted in Paris and arranging balls for four hundred. Happier, in fact. As my mama used to say: "The reddest apple may also have a worm."

At night the uptown sitters vanished and the hairy downtown anarchists arrived to argue and eat, and eat and argue.

We would drink tea with jam in the Russian fashion and slivovitz and vodka, smoked fish with black bread, and when there was money enough, black caviar.

The downtown world was intent on one thing: improving the human race. They really believed that if only their ideas were adopted, mankind could be saved. This was the principal difference between then and now: intellectuals really did believe that a better world was at hand. Utopias sprouted on the old Lower East Side like tubercular children. Capital was bad, it was argued, but people were essentially good. Thus many reasoned that the abolition of capital would change the world and bring back Eden. Anarchists in their cups spoke of which capitalists they would like to shoot. They discussed weapons. They ridiculed my portraits of rich ladies (which paid for the slivovitz and smoked fish). I ridiculed them too. I referred to my fine ladies as stuck-up *shiksas* and my fine gentlemen as *shaygetzes* with watch chains. I spat on the source of my good fortune to prove it hadn't changed me. I was still Sarah from Sukovoly—no matter how much English I learned, how many rich clients I had, how much money I saved or sent home to Mama.

My uptown sitters *liked* the world the way it was—except for one thing: it was changing too fast. Too many "new people" with money, too many "foreigners," too many anarchists, unionists, troublemakers. Balanced between two worlds, I listened to the innermost secrets of each. Often I wished I could tell the poor anarchists how unhappy the rich were—or tell the rich how angry the anarchists were.

But it was my role to hear everything and hold my tongue. Everyone was poised for flight. The uptown people sought to flee the strictures of their proper families, while the downtown people thought only of saving their pennies to reunite with their relatives. Everyone was discontented, but in opposite ways.

The anarchists in our circle presumed Levitsky and I were lovers, and I think this suited him just fine. He wanted me safe on a shelf—but he did not want to climb up there with me.

One night when we were alone, I asked him about this.

"Why do you let our world think we are lovers?"

Levitsky stroked his bushy beard. "Do I?"

"You know you do," I said. "It's enough to keep any man from courting me."

"You need to paint, not court," Levitsky said solemnly. "Any little hen can make chicks. Not everyone can paint as you do."

"But what about being a woman!" I raised my voice.

"Being a woman gets you married and buried," said Levitsky. "Why do you think men bless themselves for not being women? Painting will make your fortune."

"You're afraid of me," I said.

Levitsky gave me a hateful look. I knew then that I was right.

Not that we did not try. One day, he embraced me in the studio and I felt the unmistakable hardness in his trousers that told me he was not as indifferent to me as he claimed. Possessed by the *dybbuk* of dominance, I was mad to have him and dragged him to the model's dais. There I undid his buttons, flung my breasts into his mouth, and searched in his shirttails for his bauble—it was no bigger than a field mouse. It put its head up tentatively, seemed to pulse in search of pleasure, and then retreated. Neither tongue nor moist lips could give it courage, and had it buried itself in me for shelter, I would have felt less than nothing.

I wept bitter tears of frustration—for what can be worse than a woman eye-to-eye with that conqueror who should subdue her but instead is subdued? I was sick with disappointment. Here was a man close to my heart in every way but that which makes man and wife. I hid my head in his breeches buttons and wept.

That night Dovie came back. "A dream not interpreted is like a letter unread," Mama used to say. In my dream, Dovie was grown, and he approached me like a lover.

"You are my son," I warned, holding him off, but he seemed ready to transgress the moral code. Then suddenly he was an infant again—but with a man's penis. It was bigger than Lev Levitsky's and more insistent. I awoke with a sense of dread and foreboding. Something horrible was sure to happen.

It was a time of heroics. We had an anarchist friend whose dream was to assassinate John D. Rockefeller in the name of the workers of America. She was a small, pretty woman, and she bought a pearl-handled pistol that looked like a toy.

When she entered Rockefeller's office and informed his well-dressed male secretary that she was there in the name of labor, unionism, and the eight-hour day, the secretary gave Rockefeller a prearranged sign to leave by another door. Then he flung off his father-killer celluloid collar, his braces, spats, and shoes, and had his way with her right there on his massive rolltop desk. Thinking herself a heroine of the revolution, our disheveled friend rose from the rape, brandished her preposterous pistol, and declared: "Tell Mr.

Rockefeller that if he doesn't stop starving the miners, I will empty the contents of this pistol into him."

"I'll give Mr. Rockefeller the message, miss," said the smug secretary, and he showed my friend to the ornate carved door.

She boasted of her exploits at my next anarchist evening and proudly showed us the bruises the fabled furniture had left on her back. Of the rape she was even proud since she fancied the secretary's lust would gain her admission to Mr. Rockefeller's sanctum sanctorum again. Next time she would kill him and save the world! Those were the days, my child!

The question under discussion that evening became whether sex could be useful to the revolution.

"I bet your sitters could be useful to the cause," said one of Levitsky's cronies, a dapper little droopy-mustached man in a Russian peasant blouse whose name was Aaron Plotnik. (I have learned, in my much too long life, never to trust people named Plotnik.)

"Bite your tongue!" Levitsky admonished Plotnik.

It was all an act. He was as obsessed as any of them with the idea of changing history with a gun. More, perhaps—because his own gun was so useless. He read books on daring assassinations and hungrily followed all the news of anarchists at home and abroad.

I tried never to think of the slaughters that had brought me to America, the little bodies laid out in the *shul* after the *pogrom*, the dead fathers, the weeping mothers. Usually I was so busy with my work that I had no time. But when I dreamed of Dovie, all the past would come tumbling back—the sour smell of Russia, the fear, the time in Odessa when the photographer came to my narrow cot in the dark.

If you are innocent and expect no harm, it is not easy to be protected against evil. I used to fall into my bed exhausted from retouching pictures all day. My hands and feet were always numb with cold and my *tush* was numb with sitting. So when the big, smelly, vodka-breath bear came to my cot, all I felt at first was heaviness and warmth and fear of reprimand. He was my master after all.

A rough hand groped between my rags. Sandpaper skin, and a sour mouth muttering, "No harm will come to you." I pretended to be asleep because I was so afraid of resisting, and I prayed for Mama— who was hundreds of miles away—to save me. Here is the strange thing: I was ashamed of what was happening as if *I* were at fault, not he! Even after it was over, I was not sure what had occurred. Separated from myself, I believed my virginity had not been breached. So when Dovie came, I thought of him as the Messiah and rejoiced in him as if he were sent by God.

Attended by ghosts, I came to America. They were always there with me, whether I painted or prayed. Dovie, my father, my brother—they choired around me like cherubim as my brush made its dry sounds on the canvas.

I had discovered that most of my fellow immigrants in *der fremd*, the foreign world, dreamed always of the wretched homes they'd left. And the Yankees dreamed always of Europe, as if it would civilize them and make them whole. Those who could afford it sent half of Europe's bric-a-brac home by ship. I had seen this plunder at Fontana di Luna: stained-glass windows from France, altarpieces from Italy, statues from Greece—the furnishings of Europe transported across the seas to civilize the Americans. It didn't work. The Americans murdered each other even more often than the Europeans—especially on the rough-and-tumble Lower East Side.

"I dream of seeing my darling daughter again once more before I die," my mother writes to me, along with gossip about people I have almost forgotten. Everybody is dreaming. When will we all wake up?

When I didn't have a sitter, I would take my sketchbook and char-coal and roam the poorest sections of the city, with Sim as my guide—Jewtown, Chinatown, the foundling hospitals, the tenements, the tumbledown houses on back lots and the desperately poor children sleeping in back alleys, the Polish-Jewish families who subsisted on pickles and black bread, the Irish cops who cudgeled the barefoot boys on the street for stealing apples, the Italians who grew tomatoes in soup cans, and the Chinese who deadened their pain in opium dens. I would sketch the "sweaters" (whom I had so lately escaped) as Sim interviewed the pale girls coughing their lungs out with consumption, the skinny boys of eight or nine pretending to be older when the inspectors came.

The poverty of New York gave the lie to those who thought of it as the Golden Land. (My mama had a friend at home in Sukovoly who always said: "People tell me that in America the sugar is not sweet," and on dark days I was tempted to agree with her. But madness lay that way. The only thing that has preserved our people for six thousand years is hope. When we lose hope, we doom ourselves as Jews. Hope is our bread, hope is our honey, hope is our means of survival.)

There were flophouses with hammocks where the refuse of the city could sleep for a few cents a day—but even worse were the streets, where many lived, if you could call it living, including children whose lives were mercifully short. They either perished of exposure as infants, died due to the neglect of orphanages, or expired in the streets at eight or ten, having helped to enrich some boss.

I sent my sketches to the *Forverts* under the name "Sol," and I signed them with a sun. It was presumed the artist was a man—for what woman would dare impersonate the sun? Besides, they were paired with writings by "Sim."

After a while, my sketches were much talked about, and so were his writings. Some people complained that Sim and Sol were slandering New York, and others said that we were honestly depicting the need for reform.

But "Sol," the sketcher of the ghetto, lived a separate life from Sarah Solomon, the fashionable portrait painter.

Levitsky hated these excursions to the ghetto, but he felt powerless to forbid them because Sim had launched my other career.

Sketching as "Sol," I felt utterly liberated. It was the freedom of the mask, the fact that I need not sign my own name to these drawings and so could depict the cruelty of the city as I saw it—the orphans, the shopgirls, the street Arabs, the newsies, the consumptive waifs, the rum-soaked beggars, the porkpie-hatted gang leaders, the urchins who slept on the sawdust floors of bars.

Tell me the story of a foundling dropped on the doorstep of a wealthy house and saved. I will tell you of another foundling, dead and buried in a pine box. The rich are not so tender of the children of the poor. They may lecture them, preach to them of the joys of labor while they give them their dust to sweep, but do they ever bestow charity without a plaque to commemorate their goodness? What became of anonymous charity? Is charity true charity when it embellishes a rich name? I bless the man who gives without a plaque to commemorate his giving. In those days, all charity was private, and bodies of babies found floating in the river testify to its efficacy.

America was supposed to be the place where challah was served on weekdays, where the workers walked from factory to bank laden with bags of gold, where greenhorn girls wore feathered hats like duchesses. When I began doing these sketches and sent some of them home with the money I was making, my mama was outraged. She did not want to hear that America was not a perfect country, and she reproached me with my ingratitude to the new land. I unburdened my heart to Sim about this.

"You are taking away her dreams," he said. "People can forgive anything but that. I know, because you are taking away my dreams."

"Sim!" I exploded. "Do you want to be an outcast for all your days? Marry me and lose the world."

"Gladly I would," he said. "Otherwise I creep into my coffin early, with only Lucretia to row across the river Styx."

Even if Levitsky did not like my rovings with Sim, he tolerated them. No doubt he thought Sim would open more doors for him. I wanted to keep Levitsky happy. He was essential to my business. Also, he was *landsleit*. We shared a way of speaking, a way of thinking, a way of looking at the world.

Levitsky (as I always called him), a big man with a grizzled black beard, big dark eyes, those distinctive larval brows, and a paunch, looked older than his years—he was only a few years my senior. His greatest assets were his ready, easy way with strangers, his joke-telling, his fluent talk. He was a born salesman who could ensnare the unsuspecting with clever words and separate them from their thrifty intentions before they knew what was happening.

"Any fool can paint a picture," he used to say. "But it takes a genius to *sell* a picture."

I took him at his word—not recognizing for a very long time that it was *my* contribution to our partnership that was being maligned.

One day, I was due to meet Sim down on Orchard Street for one of our sketching and note-taking jaunts, and he did not arrive. I waited for him, got a penny coffee from a vendor, and looked anxiously along the street. But still Sim did not come.

"I know where he is," said a small voice.

I wheeled around. It was Tyke, the street Arab, who had trailed me, looking for a tip, some food, errands to run, a mother, a friend.

"Follow me," he said.

He led me along Orchard Street, which in those days was a riotous old-country market, almost impassable, with pushcarts, horse-drawn carts, boys carrying towers of tagged garments, dancing street *speilers* with flying pigtails, frenziedly following the hurdy-gurdy man, market women trundling baskets and barrels. Orchard intersected such streets as Hester and Delancey—all of them lined with tenements, whose roofs and fire escapes held as much teeming humanity in these hot summer days as their crowded railroad flats.

Tyke led me into a groaning tenement on Delancey. The stairs were dark and garbage-littered. Hungry cats roamed the halls, turning up their clean cat noses at the rotting refuse. The smell made you reel. On the top floor, several curtains had been improvised as doors.

We entered a darkened room furnished with pillows and opium pipes and crumpled bodies seeking such oblivion as could be found there. Deeper into the den we went, and when our eyes adjusted to the gloom, we saw a warren of little cubbyholes and in each one a waiting girl (or boy—who could tell?), painted like a woman and trussed in corsets, lace, and high button boots.

Sim was caressing one of these creatures.

I stood and watched, my eyes burning a hole in his back, as Sim parted the child's legs.

Suddenly he turned. His face went pale. He started to cough convulsively.

I pulled money out of my pocket and gave it to the little girl (I had decided it was a girl). Taking Sim's arm, I led him back to my studio.

Levitsky was not there. To Tyke (who had trailed us home) I gave some pennies and had him guard the front door. Then I locked the door to my studio and led Sim to the Turkish corner.

It was then that I entered Sim's fantasy and did all the things he dreamed of when he sat with Lucretia, sipping tea, at Fontana di Luna.

How I *knew* his fantasies I cannot say, but they rushed into my head as if I knew. I loosened my corset, played with my own breasts, tweaked my nipples, then presented them to his mouth like ripe berries. In a tangle of clothes, we fell back on the scratchy wool of my carpeted couch. His breeches open, my petticoat over my head, he slowly fed on me as if I were all the nourishment he needed. When the throbbing was so intense I thought I'd scream, he entered me and pressed his hardness into the Garden of Eden I had never known existed inside me. I was in blossom. I knew now why I had come to America.

◆

From then on, Sim became our boarder. Strangely, Levitsky never questioned it. Outwardly, the two men became the greatest of friends. Whenever we could, Sim and I would stoke the fires of our obsessive passion—though never flaunting it before Levitsky. And yet he *knew*. I told myself it comforted him—as if he were my lover himself—but I was wrong. Surely sex is the province of imps and *dybbuks,* but the need for possession cannot be eradicated from the human heart.

Levitsky appeared to cede the field to Sim and seemed content to do so as long as people thought the three of us were lovers. I told myself it was as if Sim relieved him of a burden, as if this strange *ménage à trois* fulfilled his own sexuality, as if Sim were somehow his lover too. The truth was, I needed to believe in the two men sharing me and becoming great friends. Since my idol was Emma Goldman—"If I can't dance to it, it's not my revolution," was her credo—and she certainly had far more lovers than I, I felt I was merely following her example.

"A sin repeated seems to be permitted," Mama would have said. But I wrote none of this to Mama, though I sent her money every week.

"You can't ride two horses with one behind," she would also have cautioned, or perhaps, "You can't dance at two weddings with one behind." (Her proverbs were forever changing to suit whatever point she wanted to prove, or else memory—that great editor—has rewritten them.)

Levitsky, Sim, and I appeared to live like three comrades, sharing everything but bed. If ever conflict arose, we would discuss our revolutionary principles and recommit ourselves to the task of overcoming jealousy.

It was true that Levitsky seemed to be more and more often absent, but Sim and I were so drunk with our passion that we hardly noticed. From the moment we awoke, we were looking for a space of time to connect flesh to flesh—as if only this linkage proved we were alive. When we joined our bodies we were lost to the world and might as well have been in the land of faerie, tasting forbidden fruit. For that was part of the attraction. I can still close my eyes and see his parchment-pale skin with blue veins next to my honey-colored nakedness.

Sim wanted us to escape with our love, go to Europe. He knew his family would be fierce in reclaiming him once they knew of his defection. How could I travel to Europe and disappear into love when I had pledged to bring my family to the Golden Land (they were due to be arriving in the next few months)? Besides, how could I marry a *goy*—however much I loved him? I had *slaved* to bring my family over: how could I betray them and myself? This was the dilemma that entrapped us. We hesitated—and we were lost. To Sim, Europe was escape, but to me it was *pogroms* and heartbreak.

We drifted along in this state—neither ready to give each other up nor ready to part. The ecstasy of a forbidden love fills the whole mind, crowds out all practical considerations. Our love was a place where the barriers fell and everything was open, flowing with milk and honey. No wonder people are so afraid of love and ecstasy—you can lose the world for them. But love makes you feel so alive that you never stop to question your foolishness. You run over the tops of clouds. Your life seems to have meaning for the first time. Love may be commonplace, but the lover is no snob. However many times love has existed before, it is new to the lover.

But this was a troubled love, a love my mama never would approve. Not only was Sim a *goy* but he was promised to another. My mama took such things seriously. Breach of promise was still a crime in those days—both in Europe and in America. How low I had sunk since I came here! I worked on the Sabbath. I was sleeping with a *goy*. I was living with two men like a bigamist. My ancestors had said *kaddish* for me from their graves. Easy enough to rationalize all this

in the name of Emma Goldman—but in the dark of night I was
wretched. I believed I had condemned myself to hell.

And since it is we human beings who create hell for ourselves, hell
arrived in the person of Lucretia.

Lucretia had begun to wonder at Sim's absence. She had a detec-
tive trace him—women like Lucretia *always* know where to find
detectives. One day, wearing garish face paint and a cheap red dress,
she burst into my studio, crying. I was priming a canvas for my next
portrait. Fortunately Levitsky and Sim were both out.

"I *tried* to become what he wanted—but I can't even do that!" she
bawled. "Nobody wanted me! Finally an old man took me home,
gave me some money, and said, 'Give it up, girl—you're not cut out
for the streets.' Even he didn't want me! And neither does Sim!"

I knew this was true, and I also realized she was insulting me by
implying that Sim Coppley only sought sex from me, but I tried to
comfort her.

"Lucretia," I said, "you will always be unhappy if you live for men.
You need a cause, something to contribute to the world. Look at the
poverty of New York! Look at the hungry children! You can do something worthwhile here without walking the streets!"

"Would it make Sim love me?"

"It would make you love *yourself*."

I gave her tea and cookies, told her she looked beautiful in her
bedraggled red dress, and soon her sharp look returned. Lucretia had
the soul of a headwaiter—at your feet or at your throat—and when
she came back to herself, she came back to her meanness. I gave her
some clothes of my own to wear, and she took off for the streets
again, making me promise not to tell Sim she had come. Why I kept
that promise I will never know.

"Only an honest man worries about keeping his bargain with a
gonif," Mama used to say.

You probably wonder at my gullibility. I wonder about it myself. But even when people were cruel to me, I always tried to be kind to them in return, and I have never regretted my refusal not to be corrupted by my enemies.

I actually felt *sorry* for Lucretia, out there on the downtown streets. For a moment, I felt honor bound to protect her. In those days there was a song that went, "Heaven help the woikin' goil!" Remember that we are back in an era when cigar stores doubled as penny brothels, when downtown New York was famed for its parlor houses and its panel houses (where thieves lurked behind movable walls until gentlemen were engaged in taking their pleasure), when "magnetic water massage," freak shows, and vaudeville still entertained the populace, and when the vote for women was still a distant dream. In those days, part of a woman's power was knowing how to cosset men, and cosseting their kin was an essential part of that. It still is. Or has it all changed so drastically in less than a hundred years that you hardly know what I mean?

About a month later, Sim and I were strolling across Union Square when our way was blocked by a demonstration. Jewish and Italian garment workers were marching for a *unione* and an eight-hour day, and who should be marching with them, wearing a sandwich board in Yiddish and Italian, but Lucretia! She was dressed like a factory girl and chanting at the top of her lungs.

My first thought was to get Sim out of there as soon as possible. But I was not quick enough. He saw her and began to wheeze and sputter until he had a full-blown asthmatic attack. Lucretia pretended not to notice him. Nevertheless I saw that she saw him and was biding her time. I knew then that she would have him if she had to wait forever.

Levitsky had got me a prize commission. I was to paint one of the richest of the robber barons—a man named Theophilus Johnson—

and his good lady wife Eliza. It was to be a double portrait, full length. Even their prize Thoroughbred horses and their colts were to be painted gamboling in the background. Of course, a man as important as Mr. Johnson did not have much time for such trivia as posing for portraits, so he sent his wife with swatches of his suiting material, his gold watch fob, a lock of his hair, and a full-length photograph of himself and his horses. He even sent studies of the horses' heads. When the portrait was almost done, he would deign to come for one hour so that I could put the finishing touches on his face.

The whole radical Lower East Side was abuzz about this commission. There were even those who whispered of kidnapping Mrs. Johnson so as to make Johnson—who was a mineral and mining magnate—yield to the strikers' current demands.

From what his wife said of him while posing, it wouldn't have been such a good idea. To hear her tell it, Johnson might not even have ransomed her. His horses were a different story.

Oh, she poured out her heart as she posed, and her heart was not a pretty place. It was rank with neglect. Whatever she had dreamed as a girl has been dashed in womanhood.

So I painted the highlights on her pearls and the shimmer of her gown and roughed in her consort from a photograph. I left his face ghostly if not entirely blank.

And then came the red-letter day when Johnson himself was to come to the studio. I was extremely agitated—as if somehow I knew my life was about to change.

Johnson arrived in state, with a liveried chauffeur driving a gorgeous automobile whose brass lamps alone could have lit a palace. His bodyguards were former cops—Irish, of course, as all cops were then. The street outside my brownstone vibrated with people—some gawking, others begging—but all were pushed aside roughly by Johnson's goons. I saw Levitsky and his cronies milling about just beyond the police barricades.

Sim Coppley stood at attention, making appropriate obeisance at the curbside. He even thanked Mr. Johnson for taking the time to pose.

Johnson was a vast man with a belly, waxed handlebar mustaches, and a red face. He was puffed up with his own importance.

When he posed, he did so in a fidgety way that seemed to imply he was far too busy for such female foolishness. He coughed, suppressed belches, and squeezed out deadly, smelly silent farts. He dictated to me as if I were his secretary. I hated the man thoroughly. Every five minutes, he broke his pose and got up to look at what I was painting.

"It's too soon to look," I told him. "Wait, and you will have a nice surprise."

But it was impossible for him to sit still. His knee jerked, his chin bristled, his jaws chewed imaginary delicacies. He wiped his bulbous nose with a handkerchief, picking out boogers and examining them before my eyes. The rich think they can do anything at all in front of their servants—and to a man like Johnson, an artist was merely hired help. He repeatedly consulted his pocket watch and spoke of an appointment far more important than this.

When, at last, he was ready to go, I couldn't wait to be rid of him.

One of his Irish bodyguards helped him with his beaver coat; another held his black derby and silk scarf. His wife nattered and apologized, though she had nothing to apologize for.

I accompanied him to the door of the studio, as far as the Turkish vestibule. Then time slowed to a crawl. He turned and tipped his hat to the crowd in slow motion, as if he were a king acknowledging his subjects. And then shots rang out, and the crowd began to roar. When I came to the edge of my stairs—oh, higher than an Aztec temple they seemed on that day—I saw a huge fat man crumpled facedown on my stoop and dark blood dribbling down the steps as if in geological slowness. Sim was feeling the dead man's pulse. The bodyguards had seized two Italian workers and were letting them know they were the wrong kind of Americans. Levitsky had absolutely vanished.

✦

"There's always money for matzos and shrouds," Mama would have said. Or: "For death you always have time." How would Mr. Johnson have behaved if he'd known that posing for his portrait was the last act of his life?

After long interrogations, threats of deportation, and humiliating searches of my property, I was cleared of guilt—but not before my reputation had been ruined by the newspapers.

Sim had the worst of it. Because he had published scathing attacks on New York's poverty and inequity in the Yiddish press, he was pilloried as "a traitor to his class." The evidence against him was purely circumstantial, but Lucretia came forward to swear under oath that she had heard him plotting the murder in an anarchist café. Sim had once made the mistake of telling her that he would rather die than live the life of a member of New York Society. It was this statement— quoted everywhere—that sealed his fate. Sim was indicted as an accessory to the crime.

Levitsky could not be found. Those two Italian union men received the tender mercies of the police until they confessed to Johnson's murder. Anarchist protests, poems, broadsides, were not enough to keep them from being sentenced to execution for the crime of being foreigners.

"America is rich and fat because it has eaten the tragedy of millions of immigrants. . . ." Who said that? It was Michael Gold (who was later erased from the golden book of poets for turning into such an enthusiastic Communist). Mike Gold was born Irwin Granich in an East Side tenement—people changed their names in those days— and he fell in love with the dream of the workers' revolution and gave up literature for what he considered a higher calling. But what he said in *Jews Without Money* was true then and it's true now: The immigrants have changed, but the *tragedy* of the immigrants is the same. America's melting pot is a cauldron of boiling tears. And even the real Yankees sometimes drown in those immigrant tears.

◆

Portrait commissions, needless to say, dried up. By the time my mother and Tanya and Bella and Leonid arrived at Ellis Island (looking like greenhorns), I had been forced to indenture myself to the picture fakers and become a ghost painter. My bosses were those art con men who set up swell studios in Palm Beach and Beverly Hills and on Fifth Avenue and posed as artists, while they farmed out the work to hungry immigrants like me.

Of course, I resented the picture fakers for the huge percentages they took, but I have to admit they saved my life. I worked mostly for a certain Mr. Filet (the name was pronounced in a Frenchified manner as "Fee-lay"—though its owner was born Feeley in County Cork). Filet had as his partner a fellow named Cooney, who hailed from Killarney. He called himself "Coo-nay." Filet and Cooney certainly had a good racket going. Filet was the one who posed as the artist—flowing smock, beret, the absentminded air of a *luftmensch*— and Cooney was his manager, agent, all-purpose factotum—and artist's wife. For these two gentlemen were pederasts, to use the quaint terminology of the time. On the East Side, we were blunter: *feygele*—bird—was our term of art. I knew, knew by Filet's bouncing blond mustaches and the feathery way he talked and walked, knew by his uxoriousness and Cooney's mincing, that they ate together, slept together, and banked together, and that the fine ladies of Palm Beach were thrusting out their bosoms for naught. "Such charming manners," they said of Monsieur Filet. "Such delicacy and tact," they said of his partner. "Such talent," they said, as I painted the portraits Filet pretended to paint and Cooney charged a fee that was ten times my take. Still, I was glad for the work.

Filet and Cooney were favorites in all the best society. Matrons introduced them to eligible daughters, whom they never, of course, married. At Palm Beach, they had a rented Mediterranean mansion on the sea, complete with potted palms and a liveried staff of lackeys, maids, and laundresses as well as handsome young equerries and grooms. I would arrive by train in the dark of night—Jews were not welcome in Palm Beach in those days—be concealed behind the arras like a *gonif,* and proceed to paint the actual portrait while Filet posed as the artist. He played the role so well he had begun to believe it himself. He talked about the paintings as if they were actually his.

"I learned everything I know about painting lace, my dear, from Van Dyck, and my flair for drapery was the gift of Veronese," Filet would tell his sitters. "Rembrandt van Rijn taught me about light. And the divine Tintoretto tutored me in *chiaroscuro.* Yes, Cooney *ed io* toured Italy together—just *noi due*—so I could apprentice myself to the dear dead masters. Carpaccio, Raffaello, Botticelli, Bronzino . . ." He would roll the *r*'s in the Italian fashion. "I would forever be copying, copying, copying, until I learned all their beautiful tricks. . . . I learned to grind my own pigments—cobalt, ocher, titanium—to prime canvas so it will last for at least a thousand years, to underpaint and overpaint and overpaint and underpaint, until the paint itself metamorphoses into flesh! Ah, 'tis but the magic of art!" He'd rattle on, miming the painting of the portrait—dabbing his brush on the canvas, wiping it theatrically—then flinging a damask drape over the easel before the sitter got up to stretch. Meanwhile, ensconced behind the tapestry, or behind a screen decorated with birds to do Mr. Audubon proud, I would be peering from a pierced pair of eagle's eyes. While the painted eagle ambushed the painted mouse, Monsieur Filet would ambush his sitter.

Did the deception delight me? It did. And so did the money. My daughter, Salome, later attacked me for "hiding my light under a bushel." But I hardly wanted more notoriety after the madness of the trial. I wanted merely to disappear as Levitsky had done. Since *he* seemed never to be coming back, I took his name and gave it to my daughter, to spare my mother's fragile heart. I was an abandoned woman, as far as my mother knew. As for the friend I visited in prison

every week, how could Mama know that he was more than a col-
league and friend fallen on hard times?

It was sometimes my misfortune to visit at the same time as
Lucretia. I remember one occasion when both of us were waiting
outside the jail for visiting hours to begin and Lucretia brazenly came
up to me and said: "I will win this round."

"I didn't know you were a prizefighter, Lucretia," I said.

"A winner," shrilled Lucretia, through pointed teeth.

If Sim goes to his enemy, I thought, he is weaker than I suspected.
I hadn't counted on Lucretia's tenacity and Sim's lack of it. Weak men
always find tough women, and vice versa. But how could Sim do anything but spit on his betrayer? Was he so deeply guilty for his affair
with me? It never occurred to me that Lucretia would convince him
that I was his betrayer and she was his savior. But I am rushing ahead.

Have I forgotten to say that by the time Mama, Leonid, Tanya, and
cousin Bella arrived at Ellis Island, I knew I was pregnant? This time
it was a comfort to me, because I felt so alone in the world. I will
never forget seeing my mama come off the boat looking like an old
woman. On her coat was chalked the remains of the letter *H*. We
were lucky they let her into the Golden Land despite her bad heart.
In her European shoes, handmade shawl, and crude false teeth, she
resembled someone I could not know. And then I took her in my
arms and smelled the smell that told me I was home.

I turned myself into a drudge. Painting under a false name is liber-
ating because the element of self-judgment is gone, the sentinel at
the gates that inhibits all wildness, all brilliance. At times I turned out
two or three portraits a week. Often I traveled with the picture fakers, posing as their secretary or assistant by day, painting all night by
electric light while they went to the swell parties and gathered the
commissions. Extra men—"Champagne Charlies" or "men about
town" they called them—are always welcome at swell dinners. Not so

"women about town"—which then as now meant prostitutes. Oh, the double standard is still alive and well!

When Salome was seven, Levitsky returned like a bad penny. He quickly took advantage of the situation, announced to Mama that we would marry again in the synagogue because we had only married in City Hall. He legitimized my Salome.

I disappeared into marriage, motherhood, and work. Work was my drug, my anodyne, my aphrodisiac. Meanwhile, Levitsky squandered my money, opening a variety of downtown galleries, which failed. I anchored myself in the comforting certainties of stretching canvases, mixing paint, and watching the everyday miracle of the flat plane of the canvas turning into three-dimensional life. Salome became my compensation for all that I had lost. I cared about her too much. Our relationship was so intense that she had to run away. There is an old proverb that equates an only daughter with a needle in the heart. I am here to vouch for the truth of that.

4

Salome's Story ✦ FROM THE GOLDEN LAND TO THE CITY OF
LIGHT AND BACK AGAIN
1929 and after

> *We are not born all at once but bit by bit, the body first*
> *and the spirit later.*
>
> —MARY ANTIN

NOTEBOOK

The Dôme, Paris

21 May 1929

My mother named me Salome after a novel written by one of her
Lower East Side cronies, though by the time I remember anything,
we had long since moved uptown to Riverside Drive—Allrightniks
Row—with my old Nana, who never quite learned to speak English,
and my weird old squirrelly cousin Bella from the old country.

They were shocked when I became a flapper at fifteen, hung out
with girls who were called "speeds," haunted the speakeasies in
Greenwich Village, the chop-suey dance joints in Chinatown, and did
all the various black-and-tan joints in Harlem during its heyday as a
so-called sepia sin spot. But my uncle understood—and whenever I

fought with Mama, I had a place with him and Aunt Sylvia. They had no children and were happy to claim me as a surrogate daughter. They were already rich in the linen supply business, driving a mile-long Packard with a liveried chauffeur and having penthouse parties that lasted till dawn—parties where you saw starlets and jazz babies, whoopee mamas and John Held, Jr., girls (with their sheiks, jazzbos, and *soi-disant* jelly beans), as well as the usual political bosses, gangsters, publishers, and starving poets. Uncle Lee said that parties were good for business. But Mama and Papa never came to any of them.

Uncle Lee spent his days in the laundry plant on Tenth Avenue. He would walk the plant, staring at the floor like a Zen monk, picking up the little bits of string that otherwise would get balled up in the wheels of the laundry carts and stall them. He was forever muttering curses in Russian about the stupidity of "the help."

Mama painted every day in her studio at Seventy-second Street and Riverside Drive, with its perfect north light. She wore little half-moon-shaped glasses and rested her hand on the maulstick, and Papa came and went, bringing her more commissions, more pictures of these dull-looking capitalists with center-parted hair, high collars, and diamond stickpins, more swatches of tweed or silk, more bank checks. Mama did well, but it galled me that when the time came to sign the pictures in beautiful vermilion script, she never signed her own name. Sometimes she signed one name, sometimes another. She never signed our name—Levitsky—either. And Papa had long since stopped painting. He spent all his time stirring up work for Mama and scheming about galleries he wanted to open. His biggest dream was to establish a downtown gallery and sell the latest avant-garde painting, but Mama thought it was a waste of money—and Mama ruled the roost. I felt sorry for Papa and vowed that when I became famous myself I would give him everything Mama had denied him.

I told Mama this.

"You're a little *pisher* who understands nothing," she said.

"And *you've* given up your dreams," I would shout. "I never want to be like you!"

"And I never wanted to be like my mama either," she said, "but look at me now!"

And it was true that she and Nana looked more and more alike, spent more and more time together, spoke Russian so that I could not understand, and seemed in league against me.

But Uncle Lee gave me the money to go to Paris when I was eighteen. And sent me a generous allowance too. Mama was furious, but I sailed for the City of Light without so much as asking her permission!

In May of '29, I sailed on the *Bremen,* a German ship known for its flowing (real, not bathtub) gin, good-looking pursers—we called them *pursuers*—and endless nights. With my shorter than short beaded flapper dresses and coy strapped shoes, I always had plenty of admirers.

On the very first night, I was tight (as usual) and dancing a mad Charleston in the cabin-class cabaret with a German student who wore a monocle, white tie, and tails. His name was Emil von something. (In the novel I should call him Erich—with an *h.*) He had dueling scars from Heidelberg.

We were red hot, and the whole shipboard *boîte* was watching us.

Suddenly Emil stopped, scanned the onlookers, and said to me: "I smell *Jew.*"

I was stunned. I felt as if my face had been slapped. For a moment, I didn't know what to say.

"But, Emil," I said, "didn't you *know* I was Jewish?"

Now it was his turn to look shocked.

"You can't possibly be a Jewish cockroach," he said with a mixture of lust and loathing. Nevertheless he turned on his heel and walked away. He avoided me for the rest of the crossing. Oh, Thomas Wolfe is right that Atlantic crossings are filled with "the life, the hate, the love, the bitterness of six-day worlds!"

That was my first taste of the nastiness that was beginning to megaphone in Germany—not to mention my first inkling of what it meant to be a Jew away from Gotham. In New York, being Jewish is entirely unremarkable. Everywhere else, it is a source of shame. Or mad pride.

[This appears to be Salome's initial journal entry from her fabled first trip to Europe in 1929. She was not quite seventeen and a half—though she claims to be eighteen! Her story is told in letters and journals, which, like her mother's taped oral history, I have arranged chronologically so the reader can follow. Ed.]

2 June 1929

Dear Theda,

    I'm finally in Paris! I have taken a flat—a room with a bidet really. (Do you know what a bidet is? Hint: it's not for washing socks!) It's on the top floor—seven flights up—of a dive on the Rue de la Harpe. Paris is everything it's cracked up to be and more. And how. You should definitely come over.

    This city never sleeps. The cafés are swept at four in the morning and they reopen at six. I sit in the Dôme—where the artists are—every night and scribble all my ideas for the great American novel. In the book, I'm going to disguise you, don't worry. To protect the guilty. (Do you think, by the way, that you and I are best friends because of our names? I do.)

    I absolutely haunt the cafés—the Rotonde, the Select—meeting everyone: artists, of course, and queens dressed in women's clothes, and artists' models like Kiki de Montparnasse, who drink real absinthe (the kind with the worms in it).

    The first ones to discover you are the Sapphists, of course, just like in the Village. They all write cryptic poems and sign them with initials. They are often very beautiful, but a lot of them are wasting away from too much absinthe, *not to mention* opium. *The Sapphists wear the most elegant clothes and some of them dress like dandies. Some of them prefer men's tailoring and some are so exquisitely feminine you can hardly tell* what *they are. Pale faces, arched eyebrows, marcelled bobs, filmy dresses, gallons of Arpège. I have written some cryptic poems too.*

I am much more cryptic in Paris than I ever was in New York. Will you come over? You will never regret it if you do!

Love, Love, Love,
Salome

NOTEBOOK

13 June 1929

With Uncle Lee's money, I have decided to start a magazine—everyone starts a magazine here—called *Innuendo*. Access to the printing press gives power. And sex. (At least, that's what I'm hoping.)

Poets of all races and genders will flock to me because of my magazine. Already I am not unknown on the Left Bank and in Montparnasse. (That's too modest—I am seen as a *figure* if not quite yet a *legend*.) Mostly the medium of exchange is sex—chocolate boys who play the trumpet, piano, and clitoris; vanilla boys who claim to have been wounded in the war. I will sample them all! Quantity if not quality! I am also picking up paintings for a *song:* Pascin, both Delaunays, Picasso, Man Ray, Tanguy, Braque. (For my old age, if I ever *have* one—ha!)

Dear Theda,

    What do you mean, your parents won't let you come?
    *Don't ask them. You can't cling to your parents forever. If
they have their way, you'll wind up married to Artie
Lefkowitz and making chopped chicken liver and brisket
every Friday night. You'll wind up in Brooklyn, for God's
sake. And then what will be the use of all we've taught each
other? Be firm. All great women flaunt convention. Think of
Edna St. Vincent Millay! Would she listen to her parents?
Courage!*

    Love, Salome

Dear Theda,

    *Of course I wish you well. Of course you can still be a free
woman and a flapper though married. Of course I will never
stop being your best friend. Of course I know you are not doing
it for your parents. The only reason I am not coming to the
wedding is Innuendo. Love is love but I have a responsibility to
my deadlines. This is what it means to be a publisher—even an
avant-garde publisher.*

    Love, Salome

5 Sept 1929

Dear Theda,

   Life gets crazier and crazier here. Last night I went to a
ball where most of the women exposed at least one breast and
were painted gold or silver. Before that there was an art show
with no lights at all—very Dada—we were given flashlights
and lanterns to see the pictures. I am learning more here
than I ever learned in school. And I have met everyone. The
talk of literary Paris is a book published privately in Florence
by a chap named Lawrence which details a love affair
between a lady and her gamekeeper. He twines violets in her
pubic hair! And other things too unprintable to mention. I
will try to find a copy for you as a wedding present. Hot
stuff!

   Love, Salome

12 Sept 1929

Dear Theda,

   It didn't require a cable. Stop. I will keep the book for myself.
Stop. Don't want to shock your old man. Stop. Keep the aspi-
distra flying! Stop.

   Salome

3 April 1931

I am overcome with guilt for not writing in this notebook for so long, but everything changed after the Crash! A lot of the Americans packed and went home, and the ones who stayed were a different breed. The remittance kids went home, I mean—except for me (since linen supply is a depression-proof business)—and the ragamuffins arrived. One ragamuffin in particular, a certain H. Valentine Miller of Brooklyn and Yorkville and Greenwich Village, arrived. I decided to stay.

12 June 1931

Sex in the thirties—just like in the twenties—is plentiful if not always dependable: a tremendous amount of passing out goes on because of the *absinthe*. I'm told that when Pernod (an artificial absinthe that the old-timers always complain about) came in, it was an excuse to drink even *more*. And then there are the *fins à l'eau* everyone drinks and drinks and *drinks*. Sex and drink do not great sex make—as Zelda Fitzgerald was forever telling everyone. The Fitzgeralds *too* have gone home after following the Murphys to the South of France. I met all these birds since *Innuendo* gave me entrée everywhere.

But the most exciting person I've met is this bald writer on a bike—he calls it his *racing wheel*—who always needs a meal or a place to stay. He's from Brooklyn, is in love with astrology, philosophy, and sex—in reverse order—and he is definitely the sort of vagabond who comes into a woman's life and turns it upside down.

Dear Theda,

So I was sitting in the Dôme and writing one day—because even though I have been away from New York almost two years, I still have only bits and pieces of my novel. Too busy leading the literary life to actually write, I guess. (No wonder Flaubert said, "live like the bourgeois." Or words to that effect.)

Anyway who should be writing at this other table but a sinewy guy with Asiatic-looking eyes, a slouch cap on his head, and a wide mocking mouth. As I walk to the back of the café to find the W.C., I peek over his shoulder. The Land of Fuck, I read, in his sloping rhythmic hand. Suddenly he turns around, looks in my eyes, and asks:

"Do you wanna go there?"

This with a heavy Brooklyn accent.

"Every cunt needs to go there regularly, don'tcha know?"

I laugh and continue to the W.C. But the phrase strikes me. In fact, like Lady Chatterley, I start to throb you know where! "The Land of Fuck" is what I have been looking for in Paris— as you know better than anyone—and have not yet found. It's not as available as avant-garde literature might indicate! Not really.

As I squat over the stinking bowl, flanked by two giant ridged footprints (you should see these toilets!), I conjure "The Land of Fuck"—a wild place, a steaming jungle of smells and tastes, everything forbidden even for flaming youth forbidden nothing.

I return to my table. The asiatic Brooklyn eyes leer at me.

"And just where is The Land of Fuck?" I ask.

"Where the Seine mingles with Alph the sacred river of Kubla Khan, wafting you to the stately Pleasure Dome beyond

*the sunless sea. It is bisected by the River of Dreams, guarded
by Morpheus and Kali. It runs with menstrual blood and
sperm, the primal ooze of creation. I am drunk on its fumes as
on poppy fumes."*

I move over to his table.

"Tell me more," I say.

*"Literature," he says, "is over. What is wanted now is a pro-
longed insult, a gob of spit in the Face of Art, a kick in the pants
to God, Man, Destiny, Time, Love, Beauty. . . ."*

I am riveted. That's what I want too.

*"There is no more hope for civilization," says the bald man
with the slitty eyes, "nor for literature. What we need is what is
in the open street, not derived—life, not literature."*

*He also needs a place to stay, he says, so I take him in. He
tells me he has survived up to now by making lists of his
acquaintances and rotating among them for dinner, singing for
his supper—a thing he does well.*

*He also does another thing well, with a kind of abandon
and—shall we say—moxie that makes you think your womb
has been visited by a shower of golden rain—but it is also the
most purely innocent act you have ever known. And that is
another thing about The Land of Fuck—its innocence. Who
would have thunk it? Oh you kid. (More later.)*

*It is now later. I am back at my place with Val, who is sleep-
ing like a dead man. Don't get me wrong. He is no rapist—
everything is courteous, by invitation only. Nor is he tight all
the time like Scott and Zelda always were (dipsomania seems a
prerequisite for the literary life). But suddenly he tells me that
his wife has arrived. She's called June and she's quite mad—but
then mad girls always bewitch writers. (I learned this from
Scott if nothing else.) Then it turns out he is also involved with
someone called Anaïs, who is married to a banker! They must
be discreet. The long and the short of it is they want to use my*

*place! They even want me to stand guard on the floor below
and rap on the pipes as a kind of human alarm when her husband or his wife comes to surprise them.*

*And why do this? Henry says it will help my novel. For
art . . . the last refuge of a scoundrel. I already have the title
of my novel:* A Bad Girl in Paris. *I know it will be too shocking
to ever be published in America. So much the better! I will
have it printed in Paris and smuggle it into New York! That
way, everyone will want it more!*

Love, Love, Love,
Salome

Dear Theda,

*What do you mean, Artie—or, as he pronounces it, Ahtie—
found the letter and has forbidden you to write me? What do
you mean, he burned my letter? Good thing I keep carbons!*

*What use is the vote for women if Artie can burn your/my
letters? Please send back all my earlier screeds. It is one thing
to give a man your body—but your mind? S.*

---

*[To place the undated entries, I have had to use my own knowledge of
Salome's life from other sources. Ed.]*

<u>NOTEBOOK—UNDATED</u>

The most incredible thing has happened. I have met Mrs. Edith
Wharton at her elegant manor house, Pavillon Colombe, at St.-Brice-
sous-Fôret north of Paris. I wanted to bring Val, my guttersnipe and

vagabond, but Scott Fitzgerald—who gave me the letter of introduction before he left Paris—warned me that Mrs. Wharton was a bit stiff, so I did not.

A few years ago, Scott was invited for tea, since he and Mrs. Wharton shared an American publisher. Apparently Scott disgraced himself with the reigning dowager of American Literature by telling her a long, unfunny story about an American couple who stayed in a brothel in Paris, thinking it a hotel. "I did not object to the coarseness, but only to the lack of humor," said Mrs. Wharton. "Coarseness unleavened by wit can never be forgiven." Not the sort of comment you'd expect from her, but then she is not the sort of *woman* you'd expect.

I came expecting to find nineteenth-century reserve and icy propriety—but what I found instead behind the pearls, the silver tea set, the leather-bound books, the old-fashioned French, the beeswaxed furniture, was a shy but clever and most amusing elderly lady. She told me that she wanted to meet me because she wanted to meet "a real flapper." If only I were! I felt she was studying me, sucking me up with her eyes as a stone-still lizard sucks up flies with her tongue.

Here's the amazing part: wandering around Pavillon Colombe, I found a portrait of a young man with sandy hair and blue-gray eyes, against a background of purple hills, copper beeches, and red maples, that had my mother's signature—her real signature before she mysteriously abandoned it: "S. S. Solomon."

Somehow, I dared not ask the venerable Mrs. Wharton about the portrait. She was pouring tea and telling me quite amusingly how Scott made a fool of himself—but she did not hold it against me.

"Authors," she said sagely, "do not exhibit the best part of themselves except in their books." I certainly had learned *that* in Paris—if nothing else!

Later, Teddy Chanler, who was showing the house and grounds to me, burst out:

"That man in the portrait *looks* like you!"

"Not only that, but it has my mother's signature," I said.

"Who in blazes is it?" Chanler asked.

"I've no idea," I said.

"I'll find out," said Teddy.

And he trots off to Mrs. Wharton, a great friend of his mother's, and whispers in her ear.

Now, *this* is a moment. Like the moment that an automobile flips down into a ravine after you have miraculously escaped. My whole being hangs on this moment, and I know it.

Teddy Chanler strolls across the polished parquet floors.

"A cousin," he said. "Mrs. Wharton will explain." Mrs. Wharton—whose books I unfortunately read only *after* meeting her—now settled herself in memoir mode and mused:

"Sim Coppley is a cousin by blood and by marriage. He lives near my former home, The Mount, in the Berkshires—in the town of Lenox. His life has been tragic. Went to jail for love of a foreign woman, mixed up with anarchists and Bolsheviks, lost everything, married now to my cousin Lucretia, that gorgon. Why do you ask?"

"How did the picture come to you?"

"Arrived in a shipment of furniture sent by my family in Lenox, and I thought it a handsome portrait—decorative. I have *always* been interested in the decoration of houses. It was rolled up, lacked a frame, needed varnish. Nor was it the *only* one."

Mrs. Wharton went to a cupboard, opened it, and produced a rolled-up canvas, unvarnished, somewhat scratched. Slowly she unrolled it.

It was a self-portrait of my mother as a young woman, her hair loose to her waist, a palette smeared with colors in her left hand, a brush in her right. And in a mirror behind her, a reflection of that same young man, his eyes full of adoration. It was not signed, but my mother's style is unmistakable.

I felt as if I had been struck by lightning. Later I drove back to the City of Light with Chanler, who pointed out the beauties of the countryside and gossiped about Scott.

"Who can blame poor Scott?" he asked. "Mrs. Wharton can be hard to amuse, and one sometimes gets so nervous one says *anything!*"

"I liked her," I said. "Under the stuffy-old-lady act is a flapper longing to get out. Probably Scott got drunk and insulted her considerable intelligence. He gets drunk with the hope of drowning his shyness," I said, "but his judgment drowns *with* it."

"A rummy," said Teddy.

"I wish there were another word," I said.

"Lush, dipsomaniac, drunk," said Chanler.

Me: "Scott is obsessed with Zelda and his cock, though not always in that order. He makes a play for me and everyone else, but then he's always too drunk to follow through."

"I thought so," said his supposed friend.

[Salome was always alert to betrayal and hypocrisy. She was far more vulnerable than she seemed underneath her brisk flapper act. Seeing the self-portrait of her mother as a young woman must have triggered her homesickness and yearning, for folded into the notebook, one finds the following letter. Ed.]

LETTER FROM SALOME LEVITSKY
TO SOPHIA SOLOMON LEVITSKY

Dear Mama,

I always felt somehow inadequate because I was not a boy and I could never replace the baby you lost in Russia. He will always seem more important than me—as if his death annihilated my life, as if Russia annihilated America.

Your productivity dazzled me—your skill, your discipline,

your capacity for work. What was there left for me but to be a wastrel and make a mockery of all your hard work?

Anything I did seemed small compared to your immense skill. So for a long time I did nothing. When, as a little girl, I wanted to paint, you made me draw in charcoal first, saying that painting was a privilege that had to be earned, not a right that was automatically granted. This ruined painting for me. I wanted it to be play, not work.

Once you introduced yourself as critic between myself and myself, I could not enjoy art—or anything my clumsy baby hand could draw. It had become a test, a competition with you, a tournament to win. So I turned to writing—because there I could play. And I wrote the most shocking things I could think of—like this book, A Bad Girl in Paris, *which you have never seen before. It was written expressly to outrage you, and I fear I have done my job so well that I will never be able to send it to you. . . .*

[Here the letter breaks off, unfinished. It was written in 1932, it seems, on stationery from the Closerie des Lilas—and apparently was never sent. Bundled up inside is an extremely rare copy of A Bad Girl in Paris, *inscribed "To Mama from her good-bad girl . . ." Ed.]*

Dearest Salome,

When you were born, I felt that all the holes in my life were healed. Not like patchwork quilt, but like miraculous new skin. I never compared you to Dovie, my dead angel. You were whole, complete in yourself, and I spent hours leaning over you, cooing, singing, sketching. I loved you so much that for the first time in my life, something was more important than my work. I felt I would give my arms, my legs, my eyes, my liver, to protect you.

But daughters grow up and beat their fists against the breast
that suckled them. The more they cling, the more they beat. I
understand this. I left my mama when I was seventeen and
broke with tradition, Sabbath, synagogue, to make a living in
America. America liberated me but also exhausted me.
Exhaustion breeds defeat. It is a country that distrusts and in
fact hates the artist, the questioner, the woman, the mother, so I
found that to survive, I had to hide behind men.

You are angry that I sign my paintings with men's names. I
will tell you that this gives me the peace to do my work. Who
cares about the name signed to a work? All paintings are God's
paintings, all poems are God's poems. Praxiteles, Michelangelo,
Leonardo, El Greco, Rembrandt, are only fleeting names for the
Spirit that is great within.

When a daughter grows breasts herself and begins to beat
against her mother's breasts, it is easy for the mother to feel
demolished. This is an enemy against whom one has no defenses!

It is a part of you that turns on you—a tumult in your cells,
like cancer. For years, as a mother, you lead your own life quietly but your little girl's life out loud. You push your own needs
into the background. Your little girl's life is more important. All
your hopes take root in her. You want her to become everything
the world squeezed out of you. But your little girl cannot fight
your wars. She first must fight her own. The first of her own
wars to fight is her dependency on you. She is cruel to you to be
kind to herself. She hates you in order to love herself. She ideal-
izes everyone unlike you—Aunt Sylvia, who plays mah-jongg
and charges dresses at Bergdorf's and Bendel's; Uncle Lee, who
pays off gangsters to beat up rivals in the linen supply racket
who won't price-fix with his cartel; Papa, who disappeared for
seven years of your life and left everything to me. . . .

Of course, Papa was the one who brought me your book—
because he knew it would hurt me. The harsh portrait of the

*mother who drives everyone, including herself, but is a hyp-
ocrite for "giving up her dreams." Do you think you are the
first daughter in history to feel this way? Every daughter is
taught to blame the mama and exonerate the papa! That is how
the papas stay in power. If mamas and daughters ever formed a
union—that would change everything! But instead we fight
each other, and the papas go free like the capitalist bosses.*

*Perhaps you will understand when you have a daughter of
your own. Darling, what I understand now is that we are all
part of a chain. We are ripples in a river.*

*As on a rosebush, the single rose does not matter, but the
stumpy root with its stubborn life. Like a vine, not the grape
itself, but the gnarled, pruned stalk.*

*What we pass along is life. The leaves drop, the grapes rot,
the rose withers—but the sap has been transferred. It is life—
by any name. Grasp it. Seize it. Write what you like about me,
about anyone. Find your own truth—and follow it to the ends
of the earth. . . . I love you, my heart, my own, mayne libe. . . .*

Mama

[This letter, dated 13 April 1932, was also apparently never sent. Ed.]

EXCERPT FROM *A BAD GIRL IN PARIS*

Vassily says that anonymity is the secret of art. Vassily sits
at the mirror, squeezing his pimples. When one goes *ping*
against the glass, he is jubilant and brings it to me to share
the white worm in the bloody chancre. It is the only orgasm
he can have. Vassily was wounded in the war. Which war? I
ask, I always ask, as if that would answer anything.

—All wars, no wars, he says.

And then I am in the Hôtel des Etats-Unis with Val. He claims to have an unbreakable bone in his prick, but *I* will break it. I will swallow it whole again and again till it stays wilted.

But no! Up it pops again, harder than before. What am I—an houri, one of the Bacchae, that I can harden pricks so reliably? All over Paris—in the Dôme, the Select, the Dingo, the Ritz, the *Closerie des Lilas*—pricks are hardening and preparing to spit their white worms like Vassily's pimples. . . . And I came here to write a book. Left America so I could chronicle America. But the last thing we need at the end of the world is another book! The last book for the end of the world! All over Paris, books are dying for lack of faith, lack of pus, lack of maggots.

Now we are on Val's bicycle, rolling along the Seine. The sun sparkles from the river to my nipples, Val's indefatigable prick is in my reamed-out cunt, and all is right with the world. O delirium of foiling death! Prick of Ages! Thank you God for making me a woman.

I collaborate with the Cosmos! I fuck saints and savants, syphilitics and Seventh-Day Adventists, cannibals and choirboys.

My cunt encompasses the universe. It is vast as the upper and lower kingdoms and mythological as The Land of Fuck. Yes, I say to Val, as he watches me swallow all the pricks of history—yes, my cunt contains multitudes. . . . It ruminates on the ravages of history, meditates on Maya, contemplates Karma, antagonizes Isis and Osiris, hugs Horus, undoes Diana and her dogs (or are they stags?). It reaches from St. Sulpice to Broadway, from Sunset Boulevard to the primal volcano—yes, it is the cunt of creation. . . .

One of the best things about Paris is the constant stream of visitors to whom one can show off one's superior knowledge of the City of Light.

Uncle Lee and Aunt Sylvia are here, staying at the Ritz. They took me to Lapérouse, and I reciprocated by letting *Innuendo* make them a party—which everyone but Mrs. Wharton attended.

They were all there—from Kiki to Kuniyoshi, Miss Stein to Sam Beckett, Val Miller to James Joyce.

How the great ones *avoid* each other! Still, there was a moment when Beckett, Joyce, and Miller all pulled up chairs near each other, but they were accosted by their sycophants and admirers before they could speak a word.

To Miss Stein, however, the very fact of the chairs being pulled up connotes conspiracy.

"A chair is a chair is a chair is a chair is a chair is a chair," she says. "And where three chairs converge, it is a men's club, and *chair* means flesh in French."

"What do you think of his work?" I hear Jolas—or perhaps it was McAlmon—ask Joyce.

"Whose work?"

"Oh, him . . . ," said McAlmon nonchalantly (or was it Jolas?).

Joyce looks dimly through unseeing eyes and does not recognize Miller. "Poached eyes on ghost," as Bloom says in *Ulysses*.

"Trash," he says. "In Ireland we set the dogs on men like that."

Another writer is berating Sam Beckett for imitating Joyce: "His mannerisms are not what make him the genius he is. Rather his *brain*."

"The brain is an overrated organ," says Val.

My uncle Lee loves that—and how! He thinks Val is *corking*! (Ever since he made a pile in linen supply and changed his name from Leonid Solomon to Lee Swallow, he's gone soft on artistic types. His dream is to elevate himself from linen supply to show business. "Restaurants are entertainment, aren't they?" he says.) Just as Mama's ambition is to make painting *pay*, Lee's ambition is to turn business into art. This is the grand canyon that divides first-generation Jewish-American families: The artists want to be businessmen, and the businessmen want to be artists!

Val meanwhile is taking the measure of Aunt Sylvia's silk-stocking-clad knee, admiring her white instep under a diamanté buckled strap.

"More bubbly for Mr. Valentine!" she orders.

"You look as young as your niece," says Val cannily.

This has the desired effect on Aunt Sylvia, who dimples like a bride. (She met my uncle in London, where her family tarried for several months on the way to America. From a well-to-do timber-merchant family in Odessa, she was staying with her married sister in the East End of London. Even though Leonid was a greenhorn, she saw in him the brute ambition that would make him rich, so she hitched her wagon to his rising—sanitary—star. Which indeed became the name of the business: Sanitary Star Linen Supply.)

Sylvia has come to Paris to shop, and her husband has come to Paris to get fucked. I figure it is my job to facilitate both simultaneously, if possible.

This is where Val comes in.

"Take my uncle to the Rue des Lombards or Rue Quimcampoix and get him fucked," I tell him, "and we'll meet you at Les Halles for breakfast." And while Val goes cunt crawling with Uncle Lee, Sylvia and I go back to the Ritz and flirt with gigolos in the bar. Then we order gin fizzes and plan our shopping trip for the next day.

Sylvia and I are only twelve years apart, and we had our hair bobbed on the same day back in New York. She is as dark as I am auburn, and has a heart-shaped face, Cupid's-bow lips, one adorable dimple, and a wardrobe full of Paris frocks. She believes in style above all things. I think my uncle married her because he *knew* he was a greenhorn who needed reforming. She never interferes with his pleasures but extracts ransom in the form of jewelry for each lapse. She is one of those women who know how to turn male guilt into diamonds. *I* have never possessed that skill.

Her fingers glitter with rocks of various sizes. Even her cigarette holder has real rubies in the band where you unscrew the two halves. She has a platinum swizzle stick and matching cigarette case, and she collects jewelry the way other women collect shoes.

"If God had meant us to sleep with men for nothing, He wouldn't have made diamonds," she says. She is a regular Russian-Jewish Lorelei Lee.

When we get to Les Halles at seven, the boys (as she calls them) are not there. In fact, they don't turn up for forty-eight hours. Sylvia is supremely unruffled.

She looks at her tiny platinum Cartier watch.

"The longer he plays, the more he pays," she says.

The shopping that goes on in the next two days is inspiring. An art form in itself. If Cocteau could make a film of it, we would really know the toy shop of a woman's heart.

"You and your mother," Sylvia says, being fitted for a whole evening and daytime wardrobe at Chanel, "*give* it away. That's the biggest mistake a girl can make."

"Do you think Mama ever had an affair?" I ask—like a little girl inquiring about Santa Claus.

Sylvia rolls her eyes. "Don't press me," she says.

"What do you mean?" Now I am alarmed.

"Your mama is a peach. Ask me no questions and I'll tell you no lies."

I stare at Sylvia and see that she is torn between the urge to gossip and the urge not to.

"Your mama was a follower of Emma Goldman," she says.

"So . . . ?"

"Someday ask her about your uncle Sim," she says, and then I cannot get another word out of her.

When Val and Uncle Lee come back, red-eyed, staggering, they both look very pleased with themselves. Until I say:

"And who is Uncle Sim?"

"*Oy vey,*" says Uncle Lee. "Let's just call him your mama's *shabbas goy.*"

Books that influenced me growing up: *This Side of Paradise, Winesburg, Ohio, The Green Hat, Flaming Youth, The Sheik, Renascence and Other Poems.* Didn't know *Ulysses*—except by rumor—until I came *here.* But the feeling of the books, the jazz, the poems, the artists' costume balls, the Village speaks (like Three Steps Down, et cetera), led my generation to believe that sex was invented between 1920 and 1922. We were *certain* that our own parents had never known or sought such raptures.

[The durability of this delusion is amazing. Is it perhaps a necessary delusion, enabling youth to break out of the Oedipal shadow long enough to mate and pass along the flame? Ed.]

Papa arrives in Paris soon after Sylvia and Lee go home (burdened by boxes and—it turns out—the clap).

Papa is no Ritznik. He stays on the Left Bank in a ratty hotel he remembers from his days as a poor artist who had walked from Russia.

He is *amazed* at the paintings I have hanging around my bohemian flat—by now I am living on the Rue des Saints Pères—and he begs me to bring home as many as I can.

"But, Papa, I am never coming home," I say.

"We all promise this," says Papa. "We all come home in the end."

He looks old. His shaggy beard is streaked with gray. His broad-brimmed black hat and flowing cape make him look like a ghost of the Belle Epoque. He still says "To mine opinion" when he wants to issue a philosophical dictum.

"Mama has never written me a letter," I say. "She's angry."

"Maybe you are *broykis* with her. By her, you never pick up a pen. You should see how she looks when she asks that *yenta* Sylvia for news of you. Her heart could break."

"So could mine."

"How could you—a baby—have a broken heart? Mama, she kills herself to earn a piece of bread."

"She lied to me."

"Never! Bite your tongue!"

"Remember Nana's favorite saying: 'A tongue is the most danger-ous weapon'?"

"So *nu*?"

"So who is Sim Coppley, and why did Mama paint his portrait?"

There is a long pause.

"This is something your *mamele* should be the one to tell you."

"But Mama is not here and you are, and I need to know!"

"Let me tell you something else first, and then we'll see . . . ."

I can see that Papa is settling in for some serious storytelling, so I put on the kettle for tea.

"Everybody talks about *pogroms* in Russia, but nobody born in America knows what means *pogrom*. Imagine nine little boys, too young to be *bar mitzvah*, laid out in the *shul*. Imagine their sweet faces—*cheder* boys dead for nothing. Maybe they were the *lucky* ones. Luckier than boys who went to the army for twenty-five years—or tried to shoot off a toe and shot off something else instead."

"Papa!"

"You don't know. We were so poor some people made a living picking rags or flicking chickens. That was already a *good* job. . . . My mother, of blessed memory, may she rest in peace, *oleha ha-sholom,* was a ragpicker, and when she died, Papa could not keep the family together. My sisters went to work as maids or factory girls. I began to walk to America. But I was caught. And sent back to the town where I was born, the town on my papers, where nobody I knew was left alive. I was only fifteen. I thought myself a man, but I was a boy. And the big fear was being caught by the *khapers*—the kidnappers for the Czar's army. You can't imagine. . . ."

"I can't."

"You felt like a trapped rat. You cursed God, the Czar, the capitalists. You would do any crazy thing not to go to the army, to get away from Russia, and if you met with a group of good talkers who gave you bread, you would believe whatever they told you. In jail, I fell in with such people. They filled my head with anarchist *narishkeit,* the dignity of the common man, the uselessness of wealth, the writings of Bakunin, the Internationalist Socialist Congress held in Paris in 1889, at which May Day was proclaimed the holiday of the laboring classes. . . .

"Angry and rebellious, I sought theories to clothe my rage, and theories were always more plentiful than food in Russian jails.

"A plot was hatched to escape when the next transport came. We were taken by filthy cattle car from town jail to town jail until, by slow degrees, we were brought home—or to our place of birth.

"My anarchist friends flew free, but I received the gunshot wound in the groin that has marked the rest of my life—to which my comrades responded with anarchist slogans instead of sympathy.

"'At least you are unfit for the czar's army now,' they said, 'and can devote yourself to the revolution.'

"When, months later, I had lost touch with the anarchists and I finally came to Paris with the *fussgeyers,* I was gravely ill with a systemic infection and lingered between life and death. *Tsum shtarbn darf men keyn luach nit hobn.* You *fersteh?* For dying, you don't need a calendar.

"In Paris I would have starved and died, but for a girl called Marina on the Rue Monsieur-le-Prince, whom I reminded of her Russian father. Or so she said. She made me the mascot of her *bordel* and cured me during the several months I stayed there, sketching the girls. It was a good *bordel* and the rooms had themes and the customers had a choice. In the cheapest houses they had none, and the girls were scarred or ill. These *bordels* or *maisons* or *bobinards* of Paris were full of traditions at that time. They were synagogues of sin. When, after a time, I was healed, I made my way to New York, arriving in the very year the century turned. By the time I met your mother, I was well established as a catalog artist and boss."

"What then? What then?"

"From the moment I met her, I knew she was the woman of my life, but since, because of my wounds, I could not possess her as a lover, I possessed her as a business partner. What I wanted was to control her life, and I achieved it.

"But I knew she was a flesh-and-blood woman and that our truce with the body was uneasy. . . . And then the anarchists came back to find me in America, and I drifted secretly into their orbit. Mama prospered as a society-portrait painter, thanks to her love-struck *goy.*"

"What love-struck *goy?*"

"The one she met on the boat coming over—you must ask your mama. This is not my truth to tell." Here he broke down and began to sob. "If you are a man and not a man—how do you keep a wife who is a woman?"

I wanted to hear no more. My head ached. My eyes were starry as if I had been hit in the face.

"But I could have kept the crazy balance of our lives if only I had stayed clear of politics. Yes, I was jealous—though I had no right to be—and at the meetings I let it be known how important Mama's sitters were. After that they were all over me, prying secrets out of

me, trying to use me for their ends. I meant not to, but I gave away
too much—or maybe I wanted to hurt them both, Mama and her
lover—"

"Her *what*?"

"Salome, you are not the first to have a lover."

"Papa!"

"I am not your papa—but I am your friend."

There is no doubt I am going to leave Paris and make my way to
Massachusetts. But when, I do not know. To tell the truth, I am
scared of what I might discover. So I linger. "Only get desperate
enough and everything will turn out all right," is Henry Miller's
motto. I am becoming more desperate by the day.

---

*[In 1932 the Depression hit bottom, hard times were at their hardest.
Hoover was President. He cut his own salary to give hope to the people—but it was a matter of too little, too late. He appointed a woman,
Mary Emma Woolley, the president of Mount Holyoke College, to the
Geneva disarmament conference of the League of Nations. She was
quoted in* Time *magazine as saying that women wanted peace most fer-
vently because "only a woman knows what a man costs." Ed.]*

Val Miller has disappeared into his mad dash to write *Tropic of
Cancer.* He writes as if his life depends on it, as if only pounding the
keys of the typewriter (as if it were a mortal weapon) could save his
life.

Paris grows dingier as the Depression deepens. Without the rich Americans to buoy things up, the desperation of bohemia shows its true face. Kiki de Montparnasse is swelling up like a Christmas pig— a pig with green eyeshadow and black mascara. And the girls of the Rue de Lappe look more diseased and sordid than ever. Brassaï wanders about with his camera, taking night pictures of all that is seediest about human nature. I feel like someone who has stayed too long at a beach resort when the cold weather comes, like someone who has overstayed her welcome at an orgy. It's time to go home.

But where *is* home? Home used to be Riverside Drive and Seventy-second Street, where my mother lives with my grandmother and my "friend"—formerly my papa—Levitsky. Like so many others of my generation, I feel I *can't* go home again. I don't even know where home *is*. So I close down my magazine and make my way to the country of my birth. Deliberately, I sail for Boston, not New York. (I am *that* afraid of seeing my mother again.) I have been in Paris almost three years.

5

Salome ✦ Tree of Life in the Berkshires

1932–1941

> *A mother is always attached to her daughter but not so*
> *a daughter to her mother.*
>
> —Talmud

<u>NOTEBOOK</u>

November 1932

It is a bleary, chilly November when I arrive in Boston and head by train for Lenox, Massachusetts.

A gray sky and mist rising everywhere. Pockets of fog fill the valleys. Outside the ornate railroad station, built at the century's turn for the private railroad cars of robber barons, I find a taxi and ask the driver if he knows where Mr. Sim Coppley lives.

"Jump in, miss," he says. Then he loads my trunk, turns on his engine, and takes off over the rolling Berkshire hills. Where am I going? And why? I have three years' worth of Paris clothes and Paris memorabilia: manuscripts, rolled-up canvases, photographs. I have no idea where I belong.

On the train from Boston, I saw the face of the Depression in the shantytowns along the railroad tracks: hungry-eyed children wrapped in tattered blankets, women cooking on outdoor fires, men collecting sticks, rags, anything to warm body and keep soul from fleeing to a better place.

On the train, I also read—at last!—*Brave New World*. Oh, to be an Alpha and go to "feelies," wearing a "malthusian belt," to be generally "pneumatic" and dance to the music of the "sexophone." What a contrast between Huxley's deathless, childless, motherless utopia and the world outside the windows of the train! How strange to be in bleak America again after syncopated, sleepless Paris!

A long, curving driveway. Yew trees bending somberly at either side, their tops whipping in the wind. The house, once grand, has broken, boarded windows and a bedraggled air.

The driver helps unload my trunk and waits while I ring the bell. No answer. I ring again. Finally, dim footfalls. A dog barks. The door is opened by a sharp-faced middle-aged woman in a tattered red velvet dressing gown.

"I would like to see Mr. Coppley," I say.

"Why?" asks the woman rudely. "Mr. Coppley can't be seen." She starts to slam the door.

"Because I have come all the way from Paris and I believe he is my father," I say.

The door slams. Now what? I am trembling like those yew tops in the wind. How to get back to New York and my family?

I hear shuffling and faint noises inside. The sounds of argument. Eventually a tall, thin elderly-looking man with disappearing hair the color of weak tea opens the door. He looks at me quizzically, then intently. He grabs his heart.

"Salome! My little one!" he exclaims. And then he swoons and falls facedown, cutting his nose on the doorjamb.

"You see!" the woman says accusingly.

The driver, the woman, and I carry him up to his bedroom—a

grand affair like the rest of this house meant to be staffed by hundreds and falling into disrepair for lack of maintenance. We lay out Mr. Coppley on the oaken bed. His eyelids flutter.

"What happened?" the apparition asks.

"You fell," I say.

"Suddenly I was queasy in my stomach, and after that I remember nothing. Is Sophia here?"

A thin red rivulet descends from his nose.

He reaches a bony finger up, feeling the warmth of the blood.

"What's this?" he asks.

"Apparently you still have blood if not your Sophia," says the woman tartly, applying a white linen handkerchief to stanch the flow.

"Can this be Salome?" he asks.

"It can be and is," I say.

"Oh, my dear," says Coppley. "You were a little, little girl with titian curls. I saw you between bars. In your mother's arms." And then he passes out again.

Mrs. Coppley, as I assume her to be, leaves my trunk on the verandah, dismisses the cabdriver, then addresses me. "Don't get the idea there's money in any mattresses, but let me offer you tea—even if you *are* an impostor! Titian curls, my ass. I guess you see what I'm up against, taking care of him!"

I follow this madwoman downstairs to the cavernous turn-of-the-century kitchen, meant for flocks of servants but containing none, and we huddle at a small table near the fireplace, drinking tea out of earthenware cups and eating cake from a common plate. In the glass-fronted cabinets are porcelain and crystal services for fifty, which tinkled softly as we passed them.

"How did you find us?" asks Mrs. Coppley.

"Luck," I say.

And then I tell her about Paris and the visit to Mrs. Wharton and the portrait.

"Edith was always a strange bird," says Mrs. Coppley. "A woman who stays in bed all morning, scribbling and having her maid collect the pages and bring them to her secretary. It's queer. And her books are queer. She's a bolshevik, I'll wager."

"It's queer enough just to write books—to separate yourself from the whole world so as to re-create the world in paper and ink," I declare.

"I don't know why anyone would do it," says Mrs. Coppley. "Do you?"

"Because it gives you back your life, calms your soul, bestows the ecstasy of understanding. And you hope it does the same for your readers."

"A strange obsession," said Mrs. Coppley. "But then so many of the things humans do are strange obsessions. My husband, for example, worries constantly about a book he never finished that he began in youth."

"What book?" I asked.

"Oh, some silly book about the silly Jews," said Mrs. Coppley. "*You* know, your chosen people—those troublemakers who think they're so damned smart. Without them, we'd have no income tax, no financial collapse, no Depression. They run *everything* for their own benefit—except that it never benefits *us.*"

"Excuse me," I say and dash to the nearest bathroom, where I throw up my tea, the cake, and the remains of my lunch.

My so-called father is as welcoming as his wife is hostile. But he is frail. His legs are as thin as chopsticks. Sometimes I think I've come only to bury him.

Jail almost destroyed him. He was raised too delicately to survive its horrors.

"Thank God Lucretia waited for me," he says, referring to Mrs. Coppley. "What I would have done without her, I do not know."

He is grateful for her most grudging ministrations. Like a beaten dog, he is grateful to be stumbled over rather than intentionally kicked.

What are so dead as the passions of the previous generation? My father—or so he declares himself to be—wants me to know all about his illicit obsession with my mother, but this is one of the things a daughter cannot hear. I listen but register little. Maybe I'm too young to want to see my parents that way. But he also tells me of a safe behind the Bordeaux in the wine cellar. Whatever is left of the Coppley legacy is there, he says. He wants me to memorize the combination. And never share it with a living soul. That will be simple as long as I stay in this house of the dead. I think constantly of Mama and Papa, and I long to contact them, but I feel so disloyal for having sought out my mother's secret life that I'm afraid to. I consider myself a traitor, and staying here is my punishment.

The Coppleys have been buried in a pie-shaped plot for the last two hundred years. They had names like Ebenezer, Ezekiel, Anna, Edwina, and Hermione. They look down on the Housatonic River from their granite graves. Snow falls early here and the ground freezes, and anyone who has the ill luck to die in midwinter waits for the ground to thaw in order to be buried.

I spend a lot of time in the cemetery, staring at the Coppley graves, trying to understand what strange destiny brought me here.

You'd think a cemetery would be an unlikely place to find a lover, but that is where I first met Ethan.

"Looking for anyone?" he asked.

His eyes are gold, his body slight and slim and muscular. The snow seems to melt around him because of his warmth.

"Want to meet my mother?" (This from him.)

He leads me to a grave marked with a stone that says SARAH FOR-RESTER LYLE, 1881–1932, identifying her only as "beloved mother." She was interred last summer, he tells me.

"My mother is called Sarah too," I say.

"Fancy that," says Ethan. "I knew we had something in common."

He looks at me pruriently, as if he had just given me a good fuck—as Henry would say. He is the sort of man who takes possession with his eyes.

Ethan is supposedly the groom, but because most of the horses have been sold off, he does everything from chopping wood to odd jobs around the house. In better weather, he landscapes. He's the life of the old place, makes it run. From the moment I bump into him, I abandon indefinitely the idea of going back to Paris—or New York.

His mother was Sim Coppley's mother's housekeeper. My grandmother's housekeeper—though I can't think of a woman I have never known as *grandmother*. My real grandmother speaks mostly Yiddish and Russian and is inclined to spout paradoxes and proverbs in Yiddish.

"My mother told me it was once *splendid* here," said Ethan. "But then Mr. Sim went to jail and times changed and the Crash came and their banker jumped out the window and the banks all closed. But I know there must be something of the old fortune left, or *she* wouldn't bother. She's not the type to bother." Ethan had a swamp Yankee accent, and he looked good in overalls. He seemed like the sort of man who wouldn't take no for an answer. His eyes were wild.

"Who?"

"You know—Mrs. Coppley. That harpy. My mother was sure she was poisoning him. Slowly, I mean. I shouldn't tell you all this."

"Tell me," I say. "It's waking me up, and so are you. You're very good news."

"And you," he says. "You're a fire on a rainy night, hot biscuits on a winter morning, brandy to an avalanche victim. . . . Watch out for *her*. There's nothing she won't do."

From the moment I met Ethan, I found I couldn't think about him without a tumult in my belly. I would lie in bed at night, dreaming of going down to his apartment over the stables, appearing, as if in his dream, and making love to him: his wiry little body, his muscular rump, his arms with the hard, lean muscles. I fought the attraction, but I knew it was just a matter of time. One always knows it. There's that mist in the air when one meets someone who gives off matching molecules. Besides, Ethan has that wildness I like in men, that smoldering devil-take-the-hindmost air. He is unafraid. I like men who are unafraid.

But Lucretia is watching us. Each of us is a threat to her power. And together we are a bigger threat. A man and woman together can do anything. God knew that when he dictated the Bible.

(What shall I call Ethan in the new novel? He reminds me of Mellors the gamekeeper!) In the apartment over the stables, we melt the snow and ice. Ethan sucks the honey out of my hive and I drain him to the dregs. He kneels on the bed above me, his cock ready to plunge and his eyes soft. Hell may gape, heaven may be proved mere myth, but I have to have him.

Ethan is teaching me self-sufficiency—how to chop wood, fix the roof, do simple carpentry. He is teaching me how to ride, how to hunt deer with bow and arrow. He is making an independent woman of me.

Meanwhile, Sim gets weaker. He sits in his bed, trying to finish his old book about the Jews, but he is mostly too frail to write. And the book is out of date. He knows it. He has lived his book, not written it. He is not happy about the way his life has turned out, and his life force seems to be ebbing away. He looks as if someone has emptied him with a straw and the skin and muscle have collapsed around the bone.

Being around old people makes the time go slowly. Ethan is my antidote. But when I am in the big, dilapidated house, with most of the rooms boarded up, I think I'll die of boredom. I spend as much time as I can quizzing my supposed father about his past. But his memories break down into set pieces, and he seems to tell the same story again and again. How he met my mother on the boat, the obstacles to their affair, his family's disapproval. It is as if he made it all up long ago, locked it in his brain, and never revised it. He needs to repeat it again and again simply to prove he is still alive.

"Promise you will write my story," he says.

And I promise. But how can we *ever* write another's story? What we write is always some version of our *own* story, using other characters to illustrate the parables of our lives. I make furious notes, to please him and because I hope I may someday know what to do with them.

"We might as well be allies," Lucretia says to me. "We will be saddled with the responsibility of cleaning house together, so we might as well agree now," she says.

"Agree on what?" I ask.

"Don't pretend you don't know what I'm talking about," Lucretia says.

How do people die?

First the organs go, then the blood, the bone, the will, and finally the breath. The heart is the last to stop. The heart beats like a crazed clock when everything else is gone. Yet the will is the most important part—excuse the pun. Sim has apparently always been asthmatic, but before he also *wanted* to breathe. However low he sank, he intended to return. Now he fades in and out of consciousness and finds it sweet. He is more than half in love with easeful death.

"I don't know why I'm here," he says. "I let go a long time ago. There must be a reason I remained."

"To meet me," I say.

"Of course." And then the wheezing begins, the sound of death in the lungs, rattling the cage of life. He calls out for someone I've never heard of. Neither has Lucretia.

"Margery! Margery—help me! Make them stop! Make it stop! Help!"

"Who is Margery?" I ask Lucretia.

"How should I know?" Lucretia says. "His nurse, maybe. He's back in the nursery."

Lucretia sits doing her family's coat of arms in needlepoint, pushing the sharp silver needle in and out. I feel utterly helpless.

"*Please* don't die," I say to Sim, "until I have learned how to live. I'm not ready to be an orphan yet."

"I am wondering," Sim asks in a moment of clarity, "if when animals die they worry about being remembered, of having their stories told. They are so like us in so many ways—the quest for dominance, the urge toward reproducing their own kind—but do they have *memory*? Is it memory that makes us human? Is memory the crux of all that we invent . . . poetry, sculpture, painting? I loved your mother for many things but above all because she belonged to the people of memory, the people of the book. What is so great as memory?" The question was clearly rhetorical.

"The body breaks down, but memory remains," I say.

"Only if transfused into another body, another brain. And only love transfuses the life force." And he begins to wheeze again.

Lucretia runs out to phone the doctor. Sim takes note of this and quickly says to me:

"Whatever she or her family may imply, we aren't really married."

"Am I the only one who knows this?"

"Ethan's mother knew, before she died."

"And have you left proof that I am your child?"

"The safe. Everything is there. Take care of your mother."

And then he begins to drown.

"Please stay," I say, clutching his hand.

"Please don't ask me to do the one thing I cannot do. *You* are *my* memory now," he says.

My heart feels as if it is cracking as I hear him struggle with his breath, draw in air, choke on it, and turn it into strange music. A hurricane is brewing in his lungs. It blows away my selfish resolve to keep him here.

Let him go, I say to myself. Release him. That is the kindest thing you can do. But it takes an active effort of will to accomplish this. His dying requires both his and my letting go. It is not a simple matter. People may be summoned into the world thoughtlessly, but they do not leave it that way. Too much thought, memory, regret, holds them back. Every death displaces a great weight from the shoulders of God.

What does his life mean? I feel I need to know that in order to know what mine means. By the time the doctor comes, Sim has ceased to breathe.

We can't bury him, because the ground is frozen. His body is to remain all winter in the icehouse, as if he were still with us. Lucretia plays the part of the grieving widow so well that she must believe it. Her family lost everything in the Crash, so her only claim to comfort is Sim's legacy—this house (nowhere as grand as her family's lost mansion, Fontana di Luna) and whatever the Coppleys have preserved.

Ethan and I speculate on the contents of the safe. We are afraid to open it for fear of Lucretia's treachery. Ethan is now convinced that Lucretia killed his mother and is not beyond killing us. And the winter is so cold and snowy that we are all confined here with Sim's corpse till the spring thaw.

NOTEBOOK

December 1

Lucretia is becoming more and more irrational. She is given to outbursts:

"Don't think you can just waltz in here and take everything," she said today. "I gave up my life for him, nursed him, waited for him! I could have had a family but for him! I could have had a brilliant career!"

She visits him in the icehouse and has long dialogues with him as if he's alive. She supplies both sides of the conversation. Her theme is always the Jews: how it is our corruption, pollution, and money grubbing that has destroyed the world. She reads aloud from her well-thumbed copy of *Protocols of the Elders of Zion*; she quotes Henry Ford's *Dearborn Independent* (to which she subscribes); she denounces "the International Jew."

I suppose that's me.

"At home nowhere and everywhere," she says, "hucksters who make nothing but only resell what others make—these are the people with whom you have mingled your pure Christian blood."

(That his pure Christian blood is frozen does not seem to occur to her.)

"Don't just lie there!" she screams. "*Say* something!"

And then she reads to him from the Bible and glosses the texts to make them seem to refer directly to her own situation. She lies down beside Sim's corpse and says: "I'm your Margery now."

NOTEBOOK

December 7

Why do I believe I have no other options but to stay here? Often I feel as orphaned as Jane Eyre. The house encourages it. It seems to have a madwoman in the attic. I am paralyzed with fear. Even Ethan cannot melt me. I feel I have burned my bridges—Mama, Paris, Papa—and I have nowhere to go. Here I am with a corpse and a crazy woman, confined to a frozen, crumbling, boarded-up mansion in the Berkshires.

NOTEBOOK

December 18

Some mornings, I find that Lucretia has left messages for me. Crucifixes and biblical quotations and scribbled exhortations about the necessity of loving Jesus. DENY NOT YOUR SAVIOR! I read. Or: CHRIST-KILLER! Or: DARE TO BE A COMPLETED JEW! (Lucretia has some batty theory that Jews are cursed because we are "incomplete"; we spawned the savior but did not recognize him, and that is why we are doomed to wander the earth.) RECOGNIZE HIM! HE IS HERE! I am an odd choice of target for her—my mother was too busy painting to give me a religious education. But to Lucretia I am heretic incarnate, the source of all her troubles, the reason she has been replaced. I might as well *be* my mother.

My life in Paris now seems like a lark to me. How spoiled and unserious I was! How little I understood the darkness in the human heart.

NOTEBOOK

December 22

Today I joked to Ethan that it is too bad we can't lock Lucretia up in the attic like Mrs. Rochester. But from his look of fascination, I am sorry I said anything.

"Who's Mrs. Rochester?" he asks.

I am suddenly terrified that Ethan, in possessive passion for me, might attempt foul play. He is a man who recognizes no limits.

Some nights, Lucretia lies down beside Sim's body and I have to rouse her and bring her indoors before she gets too cold.

"Why don't we let nature take its course?" Ethan asks.

NOTEBOOK

Christmas Day

Last night Ethan got me drunk on eggnog, his mother's secret recipe. I slept like the dead. In the morning, I found Lucretia lying

beside Sim, her lips quite blue and a fine frosting of ice in her delicate nostrils.

Ethan claims that someday freezing will be seen as immortality. I
think he may be going mad too. Did Lucretia freeze to death out of
sheer hatred? Stranger things have happened.

NOTEBOOK

December 26

Ethan has packed both bodies in ice chests and covered them with
snow. When I say I am afraid they will rise up and haunt us like *dybbuks,* he piles more logs and kindling on top of the chests. And laughs.

"What if somebody finds the corpses?" I ask in a panic.

"If I had a penny for every house in New England with a corpse in
it, I'd be a rich man," says Ethan. "They died of natural causes. God
grant we go as easy."

"Is freezing painful?"

"It's better than boiling oil," he says. He is starting to frighten me. I
hide my notebook so he won't find it.

"Did you get her drunk too?" I ask.

"A lovely death—tipsy and losing body heat. You melt away into
the snow with no regrets. Painless," says Ethan. "Christian martyrs
were not given this choice. . . ."

NOTEBOOK

December 28

What did we find in the safe?

No rubber mouse. No gold bullion. But a will leaving the Coppley

house to me and my mother and a quantity of stocks and bonds
whose value could not be immediately determined. Sim's partial
manuscript was there, of course. A romanticized view of the Jews,
attributing to us superhuman warmth, charity, intelligence. "The only
people who worship a scroll with words written on it; this is why the
Jews have made their mark in every age. They worship learning. We
worship death. They pray to a holy book blazing with light."

And then there was an amazing letter to Sim from Levitsky, con-
gratulating him on his courage and regretting his own cowardice:

My brother:

*When you first came into my life, I regarded you as a rival for my
love's attention and I resented you bitterly—though I never said so,
pretending instead to be above jealousy. My lies festered inside me,
leading me to let slip information which I knew would hurt the one I
claimed to love. You were innocent of this and risked your life to save
hers. Nor did you ever seek to implicate me. Instead, you took the
punishment which should have been mine. If there is a heaven for
those who love without stint, you will be there. Since there is no
chance we will meet in that place, farewell and bless you.*

Levitsky

LETTER FROM SALOME LEVITSKY TO LEV LEVITSKY

21 April 1933

*Dearest Papa (I know you are not, but despite everything, I still
feel that you are)—*

*We buried Sim and Lucretia this morning. During the five
months we waited for the ground to thaw, I had plenty of time
to think about you and Mama and Sim and Lucretia and what
it all meant. I am not willing to give you up as my papa. You*

are the only papa I have ever known, and I feel closer to you
than I ever felt to Sim Coppley—whatever you may say. I know
we both owe him a debt for saving Mama, but I'm sure there
must be some mistake about the rest of it.

I seem to have got myself into a bad situation with Ethan.
When we first got together he seemed wonderful—but more
and more I am afraid of him. He is given to rages. He threatens
to accuse me of terrible things. He is physically violent, and at
times I think he may kill me. It was passion that drew me to
him, and passion has a fierce brightness, but it also has a dark
side. His kisses are sweet, but must I die for them? I am afraid I
am in deeper than I dare admit. I feel like a prisoner in my own
house, and Ethan keeps pressuring me to marry him. I think he
reads my mail and also my notebook. What should I do?

Your loving Salome

Dear Salome,

This is not a dress rehearsal. This is it. Your life. Save it. You
are always welcome here. Your grandmother always said:
"Kindness is the highest wisdom." This goes double when it is
toward yourself. Mama and I love you with all our hearts.

Papa

Dearest Papa,

Your letter itself was balm to my soul. It gave me the
strength to stand up to Ethan. The money I got for the stocks
in the safe also changed his mind rather quickly. He has gone to
California, where he dreams of being discovered as an actor.

*Good luck to him. It is not easy to remain here alone, but I feel
I must do it. Tell Mama I also love her with all my heart.
Perhaps I will make you proud of me yet.*

Salome

[A number of years go by without any letters or journal. When these
writings resume, their tone is different. Ed.]

December 1942

Dear Papa,

*I have opened my house as a school for refugees from
Europe. The first few were sent to me by some of my artist
friends in Paris. They tell incredible stories about what is going
on in Europe: children being sent away by their parents
because of fear that the National Socialists will kill them all.
There is a program called the Kinder Transport. In England,
children are being boarded with various families, and most will
never be reunited with their parents. The word is that the Nazis
plan to kill all the Jews. Some refugees even whisper about
killing factories that are being built. They have already killed
many more than are generally known about. The more I hear,
the more I believe that anything can happen and will.*

*Aaron Wallinsky is one of the refugees. He survived the
Aktionen (as the Germans called their first murders) in which
his parents and brothers were all killed. The SS and their
enthusiastic native helpers took all the Jews to a forest in
Poland—hundreds of people—made them dig their own graves,
and began mowing people down with bullets.*

Because he was young and strong, Aaron was put in charge

of piling up the discarded clothes. He says he went into a trance doing this to the sound of bullets, blocking out what the bullets were doing, blocking out the screams of the dying. He was sure that he was next to be killed, but as he piled the clothes, he created a tower behind which he could hide. Then, propitiously for him, one of the naked prisoners attempted to escape, and the SS men went off after him. For all their methodical madness, the Nazis sometimes abandon the goods they so carefully collect for the Reich. In this case, they were completely distracted by the runaway, and they broke off the killing to pursue him.

At first Aaron couldn't believe his luck, but then, as night fell, he layered himself in the clothes of the dead and began to wander away from the bloody pits filled with the dead, the half dead, the buried alive. He wandered until morning, when he came to a lean-to on the banks of a river, which was being used by rebels against the regime. A series of impossible coincidences saved his life and brought him to this promised land. But America is ignorant of what is going on in Europe. America wishes to be ignorant, Aaron says. He has become my soul mate, my teacher, my friend.

Lovingly, S.

P.S. I find myself more and more meditating on the fate of the Jews in Europe, which could be our fate. Aaron has told me of horrors which no one here wants to know about. I have written the following poem, which I want to dedicate to you, Papa of my heart.

THE GOD OF THE CHIMNEYS

For what angry God
arching backward over the world,

his anus spitting
fire, the fetid breath of his mouth
propelling blood-colored clouds,
his navel full of burnt pitch and singed feathers
have we given
our eyes, our teeth
our eyeglasses, bales of our hair,
and the magic of our worthless gold?

For what angry God,
who tested Job,
and Abraham,
Moses, Esther, Judith
and the severed head of Holofernes—
for what atonement do we walk
again and again
into the fire?

Invited
with our industry, our instruments—
bookbinding, goldhammering, silversmithing—
given a ghetto, gold stars, curfews,
after some centuries,
we burst its seams
with our children and riches. . . .
Then we are invited
into the ovens to die,
leaving our gold molars behind.

Who are the Jews after all—
but a people without whom
we would have to confront
the void in our own echoing hearts?

The symbol
of our phoenix yearning

to rise on the ashes of death?

People of the dream,
moving through history's
insomnia,
people who can't sleep.

6

Salome ✦ EMBLEMS OF ETERNITY

The Jew is an emblem of eternity.

—TOLSTOY

LETTER FROM SALOME LEVITSKY TO SARAH LEVITSKY

Lenox

28 March 1948

Dearest Mama,

What to tell you after all these years of silence? That I admire you? That I love you more than words can express? That I know now all the things you did for me? That I am a mother now and understand everything? That I am ashamed of how long it took me to understand?

My little one was born two days ago in Pittsfield. Aaron and I do nothing but stare at her in utter amazement. Where did she come from? Surely she cannot have come out of my body. She looks like you. . . .

The school we started is going well. We have staffed it mainly with "displaced persons," refugees from Hitler, survivors of the horrors of Europe. The stories they tell!

Most are the sole survivors of all their kin—siblings, cousins, not to mention parents and grandparents.

How can you and I be separated when such horrors go on in the world?

Tell me, how is your work going in California? Papa says you are the toast of Hollywood and that every movie star has to have a portrait by you. Nobody deserves this success more.

Why didn't you tell me how remarkable babies are and how they change your views of everything? Sally is sunshine itself . . . for the first time, I feel my life is whole.

But I am so afraid I might do something wrong. When she coughs, I am afraid she is choking. When she sleeps soundly, I am afraid she will never wake up.

I have only one wish: that you should know her and know her father—a remarkable man, made more remarkable by the things he has endured.

All my love,
Salome

1 April 1948

Dearest Salome,

Of course when I didn't hear from you directly for what seemed like an eternity, I knew you were in a rage at me for my lie, and there was a part of me that sympathized. I worried about you and wondered.

But as my mama used to say: "The whole world is one town"—so news of you drifted back. A Bad Girl in Paris was *rubbed under my nose not only by Levitsky but also by my brother Lee and various smart-aleck "friends" who carried it home from Paris or even found it under the counter at the Gotham Book Mart in New York. Another of my mama's pessimistic proverbs goes: "A mother is always attached to a daughter, but not necessarily vice versa." I never stopped writing to you, but I could not always bring myself to send the letters. By the time I gathered courage enough to mail them to Paris, you were no longer there.*

I was never really angry at you. You were warming up for the great things you would eventually write—like that poem you sent Papa, which I have been carrying back and forth to California all these years. It is almost in tatters. I will not recount how fearful we were for your welfare at times, how we worried. All that is over now.

As you know, my fortunes improved and so did Levitsky's. A Hollywood actress—Loretta Young—whose portrait I'd painted (under one of my aliases) sought me out and made me her pet artist. At the height of the Depression, here I was doing movie posters and portraits and making a fortune—or it seemed like a fortune to me.

Of course you know that Levitsky's new gallery finally hit. The paintings by the Jewish artists in Paris found a ready market with the Broadway and Hollywood alter cockers who, like Levitsky himself, want to own art especially if they can't create it! It gives them the feeling of being artists even though they are parasites.

God is the true artist—and what glory he created with California! California is full of orange groves, smudge pots, dusty canyons. Whales frolic in the waters near Catalina. It is really the West—the land of impossible dreams. Levitsky and I go out on the train with our pockets full of nothing but talent and ambition and come home heavy with Hollywood gold!

Dotty Parker says that Hollywood money melts in the hand like snow. Only if you dissolve it in booze, I think. The danger is staying out here and starting to live like the moguls. Then nothing is ever enough. But our needs are not so great. We still remember how to save string.

Levitsky is a pessimist, and he is always afraid that a new Ivan the Terrible will take over America, so he saves like a Russian peasant. Or do I mean a French peasant? I think the Russian peasants mostly drank vodka! Now he worries about some committee in Washington. Always something.

"Shrouds have no pockets," Mama would say. How I miss her! I seem to quote her more now that she's gone.

I cannot wait to see my granddaughter! Blessings on you all!

Your Mama, who loves you more than her life,
Sarah

[Salome's mother, the first Sarah, always signed her name with a bold flourish, in an old-fashioned European hand. She made her S with an almost eighteenth-century largesse. As the years passed, her letters became bigger. At the end, they trembled like her hands. But they were always as bold as she was. Ed.]

NOTEBOOK

1 September 1948

Aaron is working on his memoir. He is in despair most of the time. He says that no words can possibly convey what he witnessed and that in attempting to write of the horror, he experiences it all over again. He seems to feel guilty rather than happy about the baby. Just at the time he should be celebrating life, he is still in the grip of death.

I tell him: "Just tell the story straight. It does not have to be the most literary—it only has to be true to the feelings of human beings." I try to encourage him with what I learned in Paris from Henry: *Life, not literature, matters most.* He gets angry at me and says: "How can you possibly understand?" But I feel I *do* understand. Often I think he is trying to destroy our happiness because he is so guilty about all the people who died when he did not.

"Don't you understand?" he shouts. "We who survived were the worst and those who died were usually the *best* among us! It was a death factory. Only the broken, imperfect, insensitive ones were cast aside and did not make it to the ovens!"

The first chapter he wrote was called "The Boy with Too Many Coats." An astonishing description of a boy piling coats in the forest. Only at the very end do you understand that the wearers of the coats have all been methodically murdered, that the drumming in the boy's ears is the sound of machine guns.

But Aaron was not happy with it, and he burned the chapter.

"How can I make embroidery with words when they are *dead*?" he shouted.

I tried to comfort him, saying that being a witness was the worthiest goal, that to a Jew especially, words were life-giving things, living things, that we all die eventually and that if no one tells our tale we are doubly dead. I urged him to consider his memoir a *Kaddish,* a hymn to life sung over all those graves. "Stories endure but flesh does not," I said.

Funny I should say this when I have largely given up my own writing to nurture him and the baby—but I deeply believe it. And I feel betrayed by his burning the chapter, because it seems a slap in my face. I also loved it, and I rocked the baby so he could write.

How did the story begin? "The boy was piling coats in the forest. Every time he saw one he fancied, he pulled it on over his own— until he was wearing a half-dozen coats and with them, it seemed, the souls of the people to whom they had belonged. . . . After a time, the weight of these souls was so heavy that he could barely move. . . ."

Everything written is only a pale approximation of the vivid specters in the mind. If we stopped communicating because of such disappointment with our own poor productions, we would have long since fallen silent. . . .

"Are the dead more honored by silence?" I ask Aaron. He puts his head down on the desk and covers it with his hands.

When at last he looks up, he says: "Do you know that whenever I get dressed in the morning, I panic, looking for my patch with the Star of David on it? Then I remember I'm in America—the land of the free, the home of the brave." He laughs bitterly.

"So I suppose I should throw Sally in a pit because of all the Jewish mothers who lost their babies!" I scream. "But I *won't* let death win, and neither should you! Everything that has been done in this world has been done because of *hope*! How dare you give up hope? How dare you do that to our daughter?"

So it goes. But you cannot argue someone out of despair. Aaron goes so deeply into despair that some mornings I see him sit at the edge of the bed staring at his shoes, wondering whether it is worthwhile to put them on. He is dragging me down into despair with him. Once, I screamed at him: "You might as well have been shot!" Then I groveled on my knees and apologized. But in my secret heart I am starting to believe that the Nazis killed his soul. It just took the birth of Sally for the murder to emerge.

NOTEBOOK

In New York

18 October 1948

Have taken the baby and gone home to see Mama, who is briefly back from California. Mama and Papa have bought a rather grand

town house on Fifty-sixth between Fifth and Sixth, where they have
the Levitsky Gallery and a pied-à-terre for themselves. "All de-
ductible" as Papa says. "Uncle pays."

"I see you're saving string," I said. Nobody laughed.

The whole place is white, with shoji screens and pickled floors and
all those wonderful paintings everywhere. Mama and I fell into each
other's arms and wept. She insisted on kissing the baby nine times for
luck, until Sally began to fuss.

I wanted to talk to Mama—there were so many things I wanted to
ask her—but the first night there was a huge cocktail party in my honor,
with everyone famous there—from Gypsy Rose Lee to Tennessee
Williams to Leonard Lyons—and the second night I'd planned a secret
dinner with Uncle Lee and Aunt Sylvia (Mama doesn't speak to them,
blames them for my Paris period and a lot else). And then Mama had a
portrait to do, of course, and she had a sitter in her white studio—some
socialite named (can you believe it?) Babe. And before long our time
together was almost up and we had hardly talked.

How I've dreamed of really *talking* to Mama—and how impossible
it is when we're together. Why is communication so difficult between
the generations? Will Sally and I be the same? Perhaps it is easier
when several generations are skipped. Maybe if my grandmother had
spoken English and had not been a greenhorn, I might have really
known her. As it is, all I remember is the smell of old Persian lamb—
which I thought of as the smell of Russia—and some cologne that
smelled old-fashionedly of lavender. Whenever I smell Yardley's
English Lavender, my old Nana appears.

Went to see Theda, who lives in Great Neck and has three maids, a
chauffeur, and a butler—not to mention three children and a husband who has made a fortune in Brooklyn real estate . . . in the very
neighborhoods she would never again live in.

"What happened to that copy of *Lady Chatterley's Lover*," she
asked. "I understand now it's a collector's item, *takeh*."

"Your husband forbade it," I said.

"You're kidding!"

She had forgotten the whole story, and now she blamed me. It was clear she was jealous of my life—Paris, underground success, my small fame as a denizen of the Left Bank in *les années folles*.

Oh, how the rich want fame and the famous want riches! Is that a rule of life?

Theda does not seem happy at all. She is fat, claims her husband has a mistress, and takes all kinds of pills for her "nerves." She is seeing a fat psychiatrist who practices in Greenwich Village. She even wanted me to meet her, for advice about my dismal marriage.

"She saved my life," Theda says.

"How?"

"Well, when I was feeling sick at heart about Artie's affairs, his never coming home, she showed me her *pushke*—"

"Her what?"

"You know—a box for donations."

"So?"

"So every time I had an orgasm with another man, I was to put a dollar in the *pushke*. This was to show me that I could still be attractive to men. And it worked! Dr. Magid and I have quite a stash—and it's our little secret. She is so pleased for me every time I put another dollar in the box. It's really helped me get over my sexual inhibitions."

I tried to digest this. (When I first knew her, Theda never had sexual inhibitions.)

"Well, once a flapper, always a flapper," I said diplomatically.

Would I have been happier had I made a conventional marriage? I would be just as miserable as Theda, no doubt. (Theda wears makeup to bed, by the way, because Dr. Magid suggested it, and she gets up at four to reapply it before her husband wakes up.)

Oh, yes—I nearly forgot to report that when she and the good doctor have enough money in their *pushke,* they are going to buy Theda some really fabulous sexy present—a silk peignoir, perhaps. Am *I* crazy, or is it the world?

Mama tells me that a *schnorrer*—one of her favorite words—
named Ethan Lyle approached her in California, claiming to be a
"close personal friend" of mine. He had become a "business manager" to celebrities, and he wanted to make a deal with her: he would
bring his clients to have their portraits done, if she would cut him in
for half the fee. Mama was outraged.

"In the first place, young man, I have *more* clients than I can paint,
and in the second place, I don't pay *schnorrers* to bring me sitters. As
George Bernard Shaw said, *you* may be interested in art, but I'm only
interested in money."

"How did he look?" I asked, feeling the old throb in the belly his
name always evoked.

"Like a snake," said Mama, "in moccasins." She paused for humor-
ous emphasis. "With a suntan."

We laughed and laughed. And hugged.

There was no way to talk about Aaron's depression. Somehow I felt
it was disloyal to share all that with Mama.

Papa said: "If you're not happy, you can always come home. To
mine opinion, unhappiness is the only sin." He knew.

"I have a school to run, you know." Too proud to accept help.

But standing there in the familiar smell of Mama's turpentine forest—so different from Aaron's forest of many-colored coats—I suddenly said to Mama: "What was it like when you were young?"

"They had spittoons everywhere and telephones that cranked—but
the griefs and heartbreaks were the same. Always the same: when
things go wrong, they blame the Jews," Mama said.

"You should tell your story, Mama," I said. "If not for me, then for
your granddaughter."

"I'm too busy making a living," Mama said, "but when I have a
great-granddaughter . . . maybe by then I'll have the time."

"I'll hold you to that promise, Mama," I said.

"Promise, schmomise . . . *You're* the writer in the family,
Salome—you should be writing, not waiting for a man to do it. Men

are weak. Wait for men to get strong, and you wait forever: that's the truth of it."

So I had my message from Mama at the end. I am finishing this journal entry four days later on the train back to Lenox. Her words are ringing in my ears.

Mama may be more intimate in letters than in life, but if you wait long enough she always delivers.

"Ach," said Papa, "still a follower of Emma Goldman."

NOTEBOOK

Lenox

November 1948

Often I think I fell in love not with Aaron but with his heroic history. After Val Miller, all those lost boys in Paris, after lost Ethan, Aaron's martyrdom seemed *important*. I wanted to love something important. I wanted to love something Jewish. Now I do: Sally.

Aaron seems like a big, cranky baby—writing and burning, writing and burning. I'm supposed to fetch his manuscripts out of the fire—aren't I? But I don't care anymore. He seems so self-indulgent. There is something about the immediacy of a child that makes everything else seem like vanity.

The difference between writing a notebook and a novel: With a novel, you describe people; with a notebook, you assume that the reader—yourself?—already *knows*. Aaron has reddish hair and a reddish beard. His skin is pale and freckled. His front teeth are large, and one is misshapen. When I loved him—or loved his history—I found this irregularity beautiful. Now I'm not so sure. He can be terribly droll, but in his depression, he falls silent a lot. His cock—which I have not seen for ages—used to be large. Who knows if it even exists anymore?

November 1948

My guilt at walking on this earth as a Jew (when Jewish children had so lately been marched into ovens) made me cling to Aaron past the point where there was anyone to cling to.

I see that I talk about our love in the past tense. This terrifies me. No. It doesn't terrify me enough.

1 December 1948

I have hired a baby-sitter—a lovely woman from Stockbridge named Hannah Weeks—and I have started writing again. This book is very different from *Bad Girl*: I am writing from the point of view of a survivor of the Nazi slaughters—rescuing Aaron's stories from oblivion. But my protagonist is a woman—the woman I would have been if my history were Aaron's. The book is spilling out almost as if by dictation from a secret source. I have no idea if it's any good or not. I only know that I can't stop.

When it comes this way, it's like straddling the globe and galloping through space. Nothing else matters.

Sally is far less trouble at this point—nine months old already!— than Aaron. He sulks. She smiles. Mama used to quote *her* mother as saying: "A hair shirt is bad enough, but worse if you weave it yourself." I told that to Aaron, who was not amused.

"I come last in this house," he said. "First the baby, then your writing, then your students . . ." I feel he is choking me with his grief. I refuse to let myself be choked.

But depression is contagious. Sometimes I think I can't go on. He drains all my energy.

21 December 1948

Dearest Mama,

Happy Hanukkah and Merry Yule Log and all that. It must be odd to be in California at this season. Here it is snowing as usual—though not as madly as last year, when I was heavily pregnant during the great blizzard of '47. I will never forget the cars buried in snow, appearing as blue-white humps whose identity was uncertain. I still remember your telling me on the phone that all of New York was under a drift of white and you couldn't get a train back to L.A.

My snow baby gets more and more wonderful every day, Mama, so many things in life turn out to be disappointing—but babies are even better than advertised. This still amazes me.

The bad news is that Aaron has not been well. He is in a place called Chestnut Lodge (in Stockbridge), and he is in treatment with a doctor who seems to know how to help him. Needless to say, it costs a fortune, but there was really no choice. He seems to have had a "nervous breakdown"—whatever that is. I only know it was terrifying for me and the baby. He claimed to be Jesus Christ and preached from the Sermon on the Mount. He walked along the highway, exposing himself and stopping cars, saying, "Didn't you know that your Lord was circumcised?" In the bitter cold, he was found strolling across the ice on Stockbridge Bowl, wearing only a loincloth. He accused me of being the "woman dressed in purple" from the Book of Revelation, and he called me the "mother of harlots and of abominations." It is impossible to tell you how terrified I was when he also became violent. He dragged me into the cemetery where the Coppleys are buried and threatened to dig up Sim Coppley's grave to "prove" my "abominations." Finally the school's philosophy professor, Laurence Wilder, and

*I took him to the Lodge to see Dr. Bartlow, who has been very
kind. Aaron is under sedation, but what the next step is, I
don't know.*

  Love to you and Papa,
  Salome

---

*[The next item in the file is an illustrated letter done on a sheet of water-
color block and creased to indicate quarter folds, quarters perhaps to fit
it in an envelope. The words are made as pictographs, so that "dear" in
the salutation is a picture of a deer and the references to birds and nests
are illustrated, not written. A baby is illustrated as a cherubic red-
headed toddler in watercolor. Of all the pictographs, the most confusing
is "memory," depicted as a woman's face with eyes upward as if in a
trance; a cloud over her head shows a distant landscape with birch
trees and little wooden houses. Translated, this letter seems to read:
"Dear Salome, my mother, of blessed memory, used to say: 'You can't
stop the birds of tragedy from flying overhead and doing their business
wherever they please, but you can refuse to let them nest in your hair.'
Papa and I have enclosed a check to help you with these unexpected
expenses, but you are not your husband's keeper. You and the baby
come first. Mama." The bank check is seen as a little blue rectangle with
wings flying over a snowy landscape. Ed.]*

NOTEBOOK

26 December 1948

Dr. Bartlow says that Aaron has constructed an imaginary world to
shield himself from all the things he cannot face. The Jesus Christ
thing is probably only the latest identity. In Poland, as a child, he
made up other imaginary kingdoms and lived in them—but in the

stress of wartime and the Hitlerite abominations his family faced every day, his "delusional system" was overlooked. How can you call your son mad when the whole world has clearly gone mad? Aaron's family may have seen that something was amiss, but how could they focus on it? Bartlow says that when a disturbed adolescent experiences the fulfillment of his violent wishes (parents and siblings killed), he begins to believe the gods of his inner world really are in charge and omnipotent. He asks me if I ever saw signs before of Aaron's delusional system. Did I?

"He only seemed wildly imaginative to me and on the best of terms with certain inanimate objects. . . ."

"Which, for instance?"

"He used to do this routine where he called down into the toilet to summon certain beings—toilet trolls, he called them—whose bodies he claimed were made of excrement and who could impersonate human beings, sort of like a golem . . . but I always thought it was meant as a joke."

"He seems to have internalized certain Nazi stereotypes of Jews into his mythical system—as if by accepting them, he could save himself."

"Does this mean the Nazis made him mad?"

"He probably would have had delusions even in normal times, but this we cannot know. In any case, we have to keep him from hurting himself and others and hope that he has the will to get well. He may not, you know."

"Then what?" I asked.

"It is too soon to contemplate that now," said the doctor evasively. (They must teach a course in evasion in medical school.)

But they have him in a unit called "Disturbed," so they must be concerned that he plans to harm himself. He asked for his pens and portable typewriter but was told that he could not have them yet on "Disturbed."

"Oh, very good," he thundered to me. "That way you and the

toilet trolls get to steal my book! Very clever, Miss Levitsky!"

Dr. B. talked to him in a way that was probably meant to be sooth-ing, but Aaron found it condescending—as I knew he would.

"I'm not an idiot!" he yelled in a voice that made my blood run cold.

[Handwritten excerpt from what appears to be fiction. Rough draft with many strikeouts and much crosshatching. Ed.]

So she kept silent. And sometimes she could almost deceive herself that it had not happened. But from time to time in her dreams, machine-gun fire exploded through her willed deafness, and the moans and screams of the dying were heard again, and she remem-bered the bad smell when her little brother had lost hold of his bow-els, and the blood that had blinded another boy when he was wan-tonly struck on the head for not keeping still . . . ruhe, ruhe (oh, the memory of being screamed at in a language you scarcely understood, paying with your life for not comprehending—like in some nightmare school . . .).

No. The answer was to not speak of it, to not even remember it, to blot out of her eye's remembrance and her ears' echo and the linger-ing lizard cunning of her animal sense of smell (so linked to mem-ory) any traces of that day, that night, that pit, that cloth tower, that forest. Sometimes she could do this for days and nights on end. And then she would be not happy but not quite sad either. She would just be numb. And for a little while, she could mistake numb-ness for life.

Then, quite without warning, some smell—the smells were the worst—some sound, some harsh word, would flash her back into the midst of it, and she would wish they had shot her too. Oh, sometimes it seemed they had and only her ghost walked around this bland country, far across the sea.

But the suppression of memory carries a terrible price. For it is in

*the territory of memory that we are born and practice to become our-
selves—so if we suppress that invisible, odorless part, we have, in
fact, lost ourselves.*

~~*Territory of memory, territory of the dead . . . Who is so dead as
those who have been forgotten?*~~

*When it was all over and she was safe in another country—though
"safe" was not a concept that had any meaning now—she discovered
that it was a mistake to tell anyone what had happened. Just as she
had not believed it when the shooting of naked people began, just as
she had managed to deafen her ears and blind her eyes while she was
building that biblical tower of coats, she now realized that to tell people in this bland country, which had never known war, what had happened in the east, across the sea, was to rupture their covenant with
their parents and with God. It was as if she were robbing them of
their belief in goodness, their belief in answered prayers, and instead
of pitying her, they hated her for it.*

*Perhaps, she thought, this was why the Jews were so troublesome
to everyone throughout history—they were a reminder of how dark
darkness could be, of how death could triumph over life. So easily, so
quickly! All you had to do was turn some secret key in the brain, and
ordinary people changed into murderers. No. The murderer was
there waiting all the time in each of us. Something or someone simply
had to give it permission to show itself. And then the secret was out—
we were all murderers at heart. We had, in fact, become our enemy.*

—*Halina remembering, long after, in America.*

[Halina was the protagonist of Salome Levitsky's second novel, The
Territory of Memory, *published by Duell, Sloan and Pearce in
November of 1951. Ed.]*

[The review that appeared in Time, *December 1951, turns up somewhat later in the file. I have placed it here. Ed.]*

Existential Angst

Salome Levitsky, that distaff Henry Miller, who like the latter shocked decent folk with her well-nigh-unprintable but extremely collectible—no trip to Paris was complete without it before the war—*A Bad Girl in Paris* some years back, has now attempted seriousness with a capital S. . . . We preferred her as an insouciant flapper—full of *fins à l'eau,* Pernod, and gin fizzes, making whoopee in Gay Paree. In this latest offering, Levitsky has attempted a bleak, existential look through the eyes of Holocaust survivor Halina W., a Polish-Jewish girl so doleful we might wonder why the Nazis spared her. Surely not so that she could narrate this depressing tale.

Once again, however, collectors may want this novel, because it threatens to become another *cause célèbre.* A stunning plagiarism lawsuit has been filed by Levitsky's Polish refugee-possibly-soon-to-be-ex-husband, Aaron Wallinsky, who claims, among other things, that Salome stole not only his life story but his notes, drafts, and research while he was hospitalized for a chronic illness.

Surely the flapper we knew was not capable of a novel some avant-garde critics have called "the blackest chronicle to come out of postwar Europe." Written in stark, almost surreal prose that reminds some of existential poetry, *Territory* has become the most debated book of this literary season. In a pivotal scene, Miss Levitsky describes her heroine putting on coat after coat belonging to Jews who are being liquidated by firing squad. We say: The emperor has no clothes. Enough with these gloomy tendentious chronicles of Nazi atrocities! It's time for Americans to look to the future, not the past, and celebrate victory, not defeatism. Human nature is not as irredeemable as Miss Levitsky would have it. Maybe she is just missing her salad days—with plenty of champagne vinaigrette—at the Dôme! Come off it, Miss L. We liked you better as a member in good standing of flaming youth!

[The inveterate tendency of Time's *lickspittle communal scribblers to diminish anyone who, unlike them, dared to publish under her own name is obvious, but there may also have been a political motivation behind this silly savagery: Lev Levitsky had been called up before the*

House Un-American Activities Committee and was debating whether to
go to jail for principle or hire either California attorney Martin Gang or
former Nuremberg attorney O. John Rogge and save his art collection
and gallery. In Time's *time-honored tradition of brown-nosing dicta-*
tors—the magazine had, after all, put Man of the Year Hitler on its
cover in 1938 and Stalin in 1939—its cultural toadies quickly attacked
anyone in any way connected to anything displeasing to J. Edgar
Hoover.

The HUAC witch hunt may, in fact, be the reason that Salome's
diaries continue from now on in mirror script of the sort used most
famously by Leonardo da Vinci. Fortunately they are not in fifteenth-
century Tuscan, and Salome's fairly regular modern hand makes them
legible with a pocket mirror. Mirror writing became her habit from
1952 on. Ed.]

NOTEBOOK

4 January 1952

I thought I had reached the point where I was beyond caring about
reviews, but the response to *Territory* has been shattering because it
is so overtly anti-Semitic, misogynistic, and politically motivated. Of
course, Howard Fast gave me a rave blurb and Edmund Wilson,
Louis Untermeyer, and Lillian Hellman all went out of their way to
praise the book. But even though I knew that those who attacked me
(Ayn Rand, for example) were motivated by the most cynical of
motives—the effort to distance themselves from me and my family
and prove they were "loyal Americans," as Mr. Hoover would understand the term—it hurt like hell. To see my papa and all the intellectuals of this country groveling before John Wood, J. Parnell Thomas,
and the other creeps on the committee, is nauseating. Those called
up are a Who's Who of the arts: everyone who ever raised money for
the Anti-Fascist Refugee Committee or the Committee for the First

Amendment, everyone who ever belonged to the Screen Writers Guild, every acting great from José Ferrer to John Garfield to Stella Adler—not to mention Sterling Hayden, Morris Carnovsky, and Edward G. Robinson. Artists: the Soyer brothers. Professors: Mark Van Doren. Writers: Budd Schulberg, Yip Harburg, Abe Burrows, Arthur Miller, Lillian Hellman, Dash Hammett, Howard Fast, Clifford Odets. Singers: Paul Robeson, Lena Horne, Pete Seeger . . . I am even nervous writing this backward!

Papa says that by now the only way to beat the committee and not go to jail is to mention a few names. He has convinced himself that if he mentions names *others* have already mentioned, he is not really being a stool pigeon.

He says that in his youth he believed in principle, but he now knows that fifty years from now no one will even *remember* the difference between Albert Maltz, Ring Lardner, Jr., and the rest of the Hollywood Ten—who actually *went* to prison for principle (as Howard Fast and Dash Hammett also have done)—or Elia Kazan and Sterling Hayden, who sang for their supper and got off with kudos from the committee. (Not to mention that scumbag Ronald Reagan, who, along with such right-wing worthies as Hedda Hopper and John Wayne, is busy saving the Screen Actors Guild from Communist infiltration! As if those sons—and daughters—of bitches gave a damn about anything but their billing and their bills!) Apparently all the committee wants is groveling. Groveling gets you cleared. That and payoff. There are "clearance experts" who will certify you anti-Commie for a fee. Papa has bartered a Braque I had my eye on for clearance.

Papa says that Americans have no interest in History but only in God and Free Enterprise—which they believe are the same deity.

"Having become an American myself by now," Papa says, "I see no reason to martyr myself, Mama, you, and Sally. Why? For the *illusion* of principle? Committees will come and go," he says, "but Picassos will continue to go up in value. I nearly lost your mother for politics once, and I'm not going to make the same damn mistake again."

And what about Mama? She also gave money to the Spanish Civil War relief, but apparently she used her *nom d'artiste,* and nobody has tracked her. Yet. She says: "I will support whatever he decides."

Sometimes I wonder why I don't have a marriage like theirs. They are joined at the hip, support what the other supports, never air their dirty laundry in public.

Papa says that the FBI has spent a fortune tailing him and that it's not safe to talk on the phone or send letters or telegrams. He says he never would have believed that America could be as idiotic as Czarist Russia, and he now includes Communist Russia in his denunciation.

"In Russia, Ivan the Terrible used to rule, and to mine opinion, Ivan the Terrible *still* rules. In America, it's Edgar the Terrible— oops, I didn't say that. I may have given money for Spanish Civil War relief, but once Franco won, I repented," he says, doing an imitation of all the guys who caved in to the committee. "I was never a Communist in my *heart,*" he says, laughing.

"Sha, Levitsky," says Mama. "Not in front of Sally."

And what does Sally think of growing up in this terrible time? She is almost four and heavenly. So smart you could cry—because what kind of world is this for smart women? Yesterday she retold "Cinderella" for me, and in her version, Cinderella tells the prince she will marry him only if he will marry her mommy too.

"So that's what Cindar [that's how she pronounces it] says to the prince: You can't marry me unless you also marry my mommy and build her a big *liberry.*"

"Thank you, darling, but when your prince comes, you don't have to take me along."

"Why not?" says Sally, boring holes in my heart with those big blue eyes. "Who will make the peanut-butter sandwiches?"

(Later) Aaron, with his phony lawsuits, doesn't scare me—but Ethan still does. I'm always afraid he'll come back, and then what will

I do? I continue to dream about him. In my dreams, he is always about to make love to me and we are desperately searching for a place where we can be alone together. There are people everywhere! From room to room to room we go, through the Museum of Natural History (with its dioramas of elephants, gazelles, and jackals), through Madame Tussaud's (with its famous waxen murderers), through the Victoria and Albert (with its rooms of costumes), but nowhere can we find a place to lie down.

The dream continues, rambling through all these exhibition halls. I am hot and wet and longing to take him in my arms, starving for his hot stiffness. People are everywhere, waiting to trap us. Then we have found a private place and are ready to shelter each other, and suddenly I awake full of a painful yearning. Damn. *Damn.* DAMN. Then I always want to call him in real life, but I don't know his telephone number. I don't *want* to know it either—too tempting. How is it I can still have fantasies about a man I despise? Would I sleep with Hitler? With Ronald Reagan?

[Pasted into the mirror notebook is a yellowed clipping from the gossip column in Hollywood Life, *probably dating from 1951 or 1952—the date has been cut off—and demonstrating the temper of the times. Ed.]*

Commie Crummies Foiled in Attempt
to Put Red Noose Around Film Industry

The shameful and sickening story of how **Moscow** extended its tentacles into Hollywood's film industry in order to sell America down the river is finally being exposed. Dead set on cleaning out Communism in our country, the fearless Washington House Committee on Un-American Activities is bracing for its biggest sweep ever. Forget **José Ferrer, Judy Holliday, Johnny Garfield,** and the **"Hollywood Unfriendly Ten"** (now cooling their heels in federal prison for contempt of

Congress). **I have the proof** that others who fell victim to **com-mie hokum** include: **Dashiell Hammett,** noted author and creator of the "Thin Man" stories and "Sam Spade"; **Howard Duff,** alias Sam Spade; production boss at MGM **Dore Schary,** a serious schemer, and **Sam Wanamaker,** who supported well-known fronts like the Abraham Lincoln Brigade, **Charlie Chaplin,** a card-carrying member of the CP, **Orson Welles, Howard Da Silva,** and of course the mythical art dealer who sells all these traitors the work of commie artists, **Lev Levitsky,** married to Hollywood portrait artist **Sophia Solomon**, whose famous semi-clad portrait of **Paulette Goddard** has been so often reproduced, scribbler **Dorothy Parker** and her husband, actor and commie symp **Alan Campbell** . . .

[And so it goes. However absurd the tone of these columns may appear to us, ca. 2005, they were, alas, no novelty in 1951. Ed.]

NOTEBOOK

25 March 1952

Odd how things often conspire to happen on the same date. Tomorrow is Sally's fourth birthday and I am selling the house I inherited from Sim. What a relief! Aaron gets the school in the divorce settlement. He wants it more than I do at this point. The heart went out of it with his breakdown and our divorce. At least for me it did. Aaron seems more stable now—though I am still not willing to leave Sally alone with him. Mama and Papa insist that I take the top two floors of their house on Fifty-sixth Street, since they are so often in California. With the money from the old house—the pathetic remains of the Coppley fortune—and the royalties from *Territory,* I can live for a while.

Papa spread his legs for the committee, neither took the Fifth (which they hate) nor denounced them (which they hate even more). He waved the American flag, recanted his belief in anti-Franco activities, said that he was never anti-American but some of his evil companions were. In his *heart,* he always loved Free Enterprise. (It's true, of course.) It sickened me to see him put through that and sickened me even more to see him denounce affiliations that were not considered anything but noble when he espoused them. He was saving his skin and swimming pool, so sick to death was he of having the FBI going through his garbage. But will they stop now? Who knows? It depends on China, the war in Korea—which I hardly understand—and the political opportunism of the committee.

Papa says, "Given the choice between Europe with its ovens and America with its committee, what choice is there? To mine opinion, they're all scoundrels."

Will I be that cynical at his age? I hope not.

Papa says, "Tell no one, but I have secured this family's future, whatever happens."

"Gold in the mattress? Buried treasure?" Remember I had seen what happened to the Coppley fortune. A white elephant of a house practically nobody wanted. Stocks sold at the worst moment of the Crash—and only a few shares, held almost by accident, that appreciated after the war. U.S. Steel wasn't such a bad deal unless it was sold late in 1929. (It eventually slid from 381 to 41, as Papa will never let any of us forget. It was the last time he invested in anything but art.)

"I stake my life on art," Papa says. "Art will keep us warm. It always has. It always will." And then he whispered in my ear about two safe-deposit boxes—one in New York, one in Lugano—containing small but choice Picassos of the Blue and Rose periods, old master drawings, and a few other surprises.

After Sim's promises, I scarcely believed him. But I took down the information anyway.

1 April 1952

Amazing how hard it is to sleep in New York after Lenox. I lie awake all night hearing garbage trucks and wondering if I was mad to sell the house. I get up and look out, trying to see if the garbage men are really segregating our garbage for the FBI, as Papa believes, but I can't see well enough to satisfy myself one way or the other. When the phone rings and nobody seems to be on the other end, I am not thinking so much of Ethan as of the FBI. I suppose I could also come under suspicion for aiding refugees, for being my mother's daughter, for associating with people who associated with people who were said to be anti-American.

Uncle Lee and Aunt Sylvia think the United States may be preparing detention camps for "disloyal" people. I tell them they're paranoid. They tell me I'm a babe in the woods.

"It could happen here," says Uncle Lee. "You bet your boots."

"And they won't execute the Rosenbergs either," I say. "You'll see."

"*You'll* see," says Uncle Lee. "All we need is hyperinflation like in Germany in the twenties, and there'll be Nazis under every bed."

"Under every bed?" asks Sally with a child's earnest literalness.

"What a *punim!*" says Uncle Lee, pinching her cheeks in a way she hates. She cries.

Here we all are, threading our way through history as over a bloody canyon filled with bones. Funny I never felt this way before I had a child.

10 April 1952

Papa and Mama are temporarily back after another groveling visit
to Washington. They tell me stories I can hardly credit. Supposedly,
there is a psychiatrist in Hollywood—with the archetypal priestly
name of Levi—who is rumored to sell his patients' dreams to the
FBI. A former Communist now turned anti-Communist, he's known
for being good with writer's block, divorces, and the like—and writers
flock to him. Also actors. Sooner or later, his patients all testify as
friendly witnesses so as not to have what he calls "career death wish."

Papa says, "Trust no one." He is determined to change the name of
the gallery to the White Gallery.

"To mine opinion, anti-Semitism is here again in the guise of anti-
Communism," he says. "In Washington the political insiders all say:
'Scratch a Jew and find a Communist.' The reason the Jews in the
picture business are falling all over each other to be stool pigeons is
that they remember what Hitler did to the Berlin picture business—
threw out the Jews and took the studios over for propaganda. These
ganaiven want to be more anti-Communist than thou to save their
necks. If I hear of you going to another one of those damned 'Save
the Rosenbergs' rallies, I'll insist you're not my daughter!"

He says that with a straight face, having forgotten that Sim
Coppley ever existed! What's Sim Coppley? Merely a dead *goy*. Papa
has won!

What a world!

7

Salome ✦ Days of Hope, Sex, and the Literary Life
1952 and After

An hour in the garden of Eden is good too.

—Yiddish Proverb

NOTEBOOK

1952

Met a man. The most interesting man since Val or Aaron. He's a composer, worships Mozart and Whitman and Blake, practices Zen Buddhism, has taught me to meditate, taken me to something called a "zendo," and has a view of the world that at last makes sense. We are here, he says, only to train our souls for the next journey—a kind of spiritual practice. We cannot judge this world or its experiences because we are in training for a spiritual marathon.

We met at a party in Greenwich Village full of writers—Anaïs Nin with her face powdered white (lusting after beautiful Gore Vidal), puffy Tennessee Williams (lusting after beautiful Gore Vidal), drunk and puffy Dylan Thomas groping girls and reciting his amazing poetry, publishers wishing they were poets, poets wishing they were publishers—the usual New York madness of drunkenness passing for the literary life.

He is blond, cool, tall, a Greek god. When he plays the piano, I get so excited I'm afraid I'll wet the sofa. He caresses the keys, sings to himself as he plays—and to me. His name is Marco Alberti. His mother's family were Venetian Jews who moved to Trieste in the period when Joyce lived there—between the wars. They knew Joyce, Svevo, that literary lot. They came to Canada next, then to America. Like me, he is a rootless polyglot—Jewish mother, Catholic father whose family may have been Jewish way back. He feels like the other half of my soul.

He had read *Territory* and was moved by it.

"The crux of the human problem is consciousness," he said. "Shall we go to escape these drunks?"

I vigorously nodded my head yes. We went to the White Horse and talked all night—one of those talks that go on and on because you know it's too soon to go to bed but you can't part. At four in the morning, he took me home. The birds were making a racket in the garden behind the house, and Sally was sleeping in Mama and Papa's room. We ached for each other, but could not, would not, succumb so soon. I fell asleep and dreamed that I was in a house that was being built and there were workmen all around. Marco and I found an alcove and dragged a battered old door across it for privacy. Dream details! Then we threw a sleeping bag on the floor and began to make love. His face was tender, and his cock was so long and hard it had no trouble reaching the inside of my imagination. I realized how many moons it's been since I was touched that way. And then I awoke, missing him.

I will see him again tomorrow—and I am terrified and elated. Not hungry, sleepless, agitated—all the symptoms of that sometimes fatal disease called love.

The last thing I want is to make some man the center of my life again. What's the point of it? It has to lead to trouble. And yet without that spark, everything is flat, stale, unprofitable.

Why is there no one I can talk to about all this? I look at the marriages of my intimates—of Theda, say, Sylvia, even Mama—and they all seem to have made such dull compromises. I want my life *not* to be dull, to continually expand into new territory. Is that compatible with marriage? With love? So much of my education seems to have come from the men in my life. I have used them to learn: from Val about how to bring writing to life, life to writing; from Ethan about being independent, a deer slayer and amazon; from Aaron about the heroism of survival, of witnessing. What am I meant to learn from Marco?

NOTEBOOK

Lenox

12 April 1952

Never got to see Marco that day because Aaron—as if he knew I was falling in love—made a suicide attempt, opened his veins in the tub like an ancient Greek philosopher. When I came to see him in the hospital, he was pleased with himself.

"Those of us who survived were exceptions," he said. "We were not meant to. The point of the Nazi machinery was death. Those of us who lasted were the ones most capable of numbness, not heroism."

He had dropped the lawsuit, he said, and wanted me back—as if it were that simple! I was to forget it ever happened and to bring back his daughter. He needed her, he said. He seemed diminished, dried out, as if the blood he lost had desiccated him. He had absolutely no idea of the consequences of his actions. The whole world is supposed to make up to him for the Nazis' destruction of his soul. But how can we? Don't we have our own souls to consider?

"I was wrong," he said, "to deny you the right to your vision of the destruction of the Jews. I was jealous." Now he says it! Now that his lawsuit has done its damage!

I look into his eyes and see that he is still not well. I feel black-mailed by his madness.

"Let's see how you feel after a while," I say. "Let's not rush things."

Back in Lenox, I'm reminded of how strange *goyim* are! All the years I lived here—Ethan's eccentricity, the townspeople with their *goykopf* ways. Such a relief, after all, to be back in New York, with the dirt, the garbage, the artists, the Jews.

"Under the rug" is the philosophy of New England. Have a beef? Bury it like a bone! Frozen ground, frozen hearts.

Went to visit Sim in the Coppley pie. Sat staring at his stone: SIMP-SON COXX COPPLEY, 1878–1933.

Thought about his years, his passion for the Jews—what did we represent to him?—his intuitive understanding that hybrids were the heartiest stock, yet his need to go back to a woman who had betrayed him. Poor weak wandering Sim—meeting Mama on the boat, having tried to flee his roots, and yet being called inexorably back. Is that *all* of us?

And was his philo-Semitism just the obverse of Lucretia's anti-Semitism? And the years he lived through: the gaslight era to the Great Depression, the end of his world of table manners, archery, gentlemanly shooting, and the ladylike suppression of sexual desire—except among the "foreigners."

And here he is, flowering into a weeping cherry—the one I planted at his grave nearly twenty years ago. Can it be twenty? No—nineteen years. In nineteen years, even a weeping cherry grows tall. If I dug here, would I find his skull, like Yorick's? And what would I find in it? Worms?

The riotous blooming cemetery moves me: the blasts of spring rising out of the thawing dead.

What is death like? I wonder, looking at the dappled clouds, the rosy setting sun. Everyone—Hindu, Buddhist, Christian (who knows what the *Jews* believe?)—agrees it is the loss of selfhood. Only, without selfhood, what can one observe, or feel? Is individuality necessary to perception? One with the universal consciousness, can you still observe the beauties of clouds and gardens? Of nature? Or is there no *you* to observe? How perplexing it all is.

Where is Sim? I never knew him at all till he was dying, and then he dropped out of my life like a stone into a deep well.

If only I could write about my family and Sim's family and how these two branches came together: old Wasp, new Jew—or is it vice versa? But as long as Mama is alive, how can I? And do I really know her story anyway? And would she ever tell me? She still believes her mother's credo: "If speech is worth one kopeck, silence is worth two." Nana must be doing well up there in the universal consciousness. With Sim.

Bless them both. Or at least, since neither blessings nor curses can touch them now, bless their memories. May they intercede for me with whoever it is that guides my life. I hope somebody's watching!

NOTEBOOK

17 April 1952

Visiting Aaron in the hospital yesterday, I met another visitor of his—a fellow named Robin Robinowitz, who waggishly introduced himself to me as "a forger."

I was not sure I was hearing him correctly, so I inquired again.

He said: "Some painters paint people, some landscapes; I paint works of art."

Robin is in his thirties, studied art in Italy, speaks fluent Italian, and is very mysterious about what works of art he paints.

"Oh, sometimes I am given assignments. I copy a work and then the owner keeps the original under lock and key." He is sharp-featured, dark, small, very flirtatious.

What the hell—I went back to his studio at Windy Perch, another grand dilapidated "cottage" like the one I sold, and (witnessed by a gallery of jewel-like "Vermeers") slept with him. It was rapturous. Can't decide whether I really like him or whether I'm avoiding what I feel for Marco. Now I am thoroughly confused. Was that the *point*?

NOTEBOOK

9 *May 1952*

A woman with a four-year-old daughter who is having affairs with two men simultaneously does not have an easy life.

But exciting. If the FBI is following me, they're getting their money's worth!

Luckily, Mama and Papa are in California, I have persuaded Hannah from Stockbridge to live here and help me with Sally—and Robin only arrives once a week by train. He stays with an artist friend in the Village, but we go to the Hotel Chelsea for the whole afternoon, then have dinner there at the Spanish restaurant. He is a much better lover than Marco—who, it turns out, is cool and Zen and forever going to some zendo in California to "sit," but Marco has my heart. Together, they add up to quite some man!

My fantasy life has *never* been this rich. Perhaps it was the sense of the fragility of life I got when I saw Aaron with his poor bandaged wrists (going on about the Nazis, the camps, the death machine), but I have never felt so sexy. It is the two men, of course—and my utter lack of guilt about it. Even in Paris, when everyone crowed about free love, I would occasionally be clutched with guilt. But now I feel *everything* is my due. Is it because I am "of a certain age," as the French say, and I realize I don't have forever?

[Salome would have been forty in 1952. From what follows, it appears to be a very erotic age for women. Ed.]

**LETTER FROM SALOME LEVITSKY TO
AARON WALLINSKY, CHESTNUT LODGE,
STOCKBRIDGE, MASSACHUSETTS, MAY 1952**

Dear Aaron,

I hope you are feeling more yourself. I was so happy to see you in Stockbridge and I hope that next time I can bring Sally with me.

I beg you to trust Dr. B. and the other people at the Lodge to shepherd you back to good health. I know it does not always seem so to you, but they have your best interests at heart. Dr. B. is really concerned with you—and not just as a professional. I thinks he believes you have a contribution to make to this world—and so do I.

Darling, do you have a Beethoven or Mozart somewhere back in your family tree? A klezmer at least? Sally's whole face lights up when she hears music, and she runs to the Victrola (or hi-fi, as they call it now) and starts conducting imaginary musicians. Lately I have been listening to this radio "disc jockey" called Alan Freed, who plays a kind of Negro rhythm and blues that he calls "rock 'n' roll"—with the pun intended. Sally claps along with the music and dances and twirls. Nobody in my family ever had this talent—how about yours? Sally did splendidly at her Ethical Culture interview. They

love her. *How could they not? I know you would rather have
her in Lenox, but at least for now, I think she will be happy at
Ethical, which is progressive and artistic and everything you
would want for her. Papa has already promised to pay the
tuition, which is horrendous—almost $750 a year when you
include everything!*

  *Be well, my darling,
  Salome*

Darling Vermeer,

  *You left me glowing from within like your Flemish ladies,
glints of light in my eyes like your laughing girl. I love our
meetings at the Chelsea, using up the "day rate," and our early
suppers at El Quijote, getting sick on* paella.

  *You asked me to save all my fantasies for you, and here is
one—though I refuse to tell you whether it is fantasy or real.
You will have to guess, my little forger with the oh-so-clever
devil's paintbrush.*

  *I am entering another brownstone on Fifty-sixth Street. In
the small paneled foyer between the inner and outer doors, a
Moroccan or Moorish pierced-brass lantern dangles from a
tarnished brass chain. Inside it is a bluish bulb that casts little
blue moons and suns on the tall ceiling and narrow walls of
this hallway. I open the inner door—which is lacquered blue—
and walk up the narrow main stair of the brownstone.*

Suddenly I find that I am walking behind a half-naked woman in high heels. Her high heels are carved of gilded wood, and when I look closely I see that they are carved in the shape of upside-down erect penises. This is strange, I think, but I follow her, fascinated.

The balls form the base of the heel—where it nestles into the black silk of the pumps, so that the weight of the woman's body rests en pointe, as it were, on the stiff glans. I follow these cock-heels, these shoes, this voluptuous naked ass (clothed only in a black velvet garter belt and black-and-gold stockings), up up up the stairs.

I smell burning sugar, vanilla, tuberose, and jasmine. It seems to come from between her legs. There is a thrumming of bass strings and the sound of steel brushes over a drum skin. At the top of the stairs, a Negro drummer is hitting his snare drum with the wrong side of his sticks. He is naked except for an African shaman's mask, which chills my blood—as it is meant to do. As I walk by, he pushes the mask back on his woolly head, and I suddenly see he has your face.

"Love root, silk thread, crotch and vine," someone whispers in my ear. A tongue licks at my earlobe, but I can't see whose it is. I smell burning sugar wafting up from my panties.

I follow to the top of the house under the dusty skylight, and there is a loft filled with half-naked women, beautiful women (though they are masked in black silk dominoes—some beaded, some painted and trimmed with lace—as if for a Venetian masque), but they wear little else. Only those golden-heeled phallic shoes—literally fuck-me pumps—and garter belts with black and gold mesh stockings. Some have pierced navel jewels or navel rings.

As my eyes gradually adjust to the dim light, I see that standing against the wall, there are burly men wearing tights cut out at the crotch to show their erections—for which they have obvi-

ously been chosen. The white men wear black tights and the Negroes white tights, and each of them carries aloft a sort of spear, topped with a golden prick—erect, larger than life, and pointing heavenward as the shoes of the women point earthward.

The thrumming of the bass becomes louder. The tuberose smell intensifies. There is a pungent, heated smell of slippery sex—or is it mangoes and patchouli? Clementines and musk? Vanilla and burnt sugar brought to a boil in my cunt?

And now I am gently restrained by two of the prick-heeled women and eased out of my cornflower-blue cashmere twinset, my white pointy bra, until I stand there wearing only my black toreador pants and my black Capezio ballerina flats.

Zip zip zipppppp—they unzip the toreador pants, under which I am wearing white cotton panties whose damp crotch smells of musk and mangoes and burnt sugar and is caked and clotted with a mangoey goo. One girl insinuates a finger there, touches my clit and crotch, then licks it greedily, while another lingers at my waist to lick the reddish place where the zipper has pinched my flesh; another girl is flicking my right nipple with her tongue.

My twinset is suddenly flung in the air so that the pullover catches on the spear point and the cardigan falls to the floor. My ballet flats and white anklets are removed, as are my white cotton panties, embellished at the crotch with a telltale snail trail of sweet slime, still wet, glistening for all to see my shame.

Then I am laid at length on a silken quilt and my legs are bound in white satin ribbon and held apart by two beautiful cock-heeled girls.

They suck my toes excruciatingly, while other girls bind my wrists with white satin ribbons, attaching these to golden finial-pricks, which suddenly grow up from the floor in four preordained places.

*Now I am masked. My mask, unlike theirs, has no eyeholes. I
am blind. Only touch and smell and hearing enter the mysterious orifices in my body. I feel gentle, teasing fingers holding my
labia apart and a tongue thrumming on my clit and a wet finger exploring my depths. I am full of honey and aching with
desire.*

*I hear the faint clatter of dice on the floor and men urging
each other on with bets. They are betting for me. The girls gig-
gle and tickle me with tongues and fingers. I try to wait but am
afraid I am going to come. And then suddenly my cunt is filled
with a cock so big it takes my breath away.*

*I cannot see to whom it belongs, but I can feel his wet
breath and smell his sweat and feel his knotted muscles and his
weight on me. He holds still inside me, making me want to
move with fury, but watchers at my ribboned hands and feet
will not let me.*

"Still, still," they murmur, "hold still."

*The cock slides in and out until I am almost beside myself
with desire—then it disappears.*

*"Ohh," I moan in disappointment, writhing on the quilt.
Then suddenly another smell, another weight, another cock,
and girls touching my labia and one inserting her greased
pinkie into my ass, moving cunningly around. When at last I
come, I am not sure with whom or whether the prick is spear or
flesh—and I do not care.*

*Later I find myself in a round pink marble bathtub with one
of the prick-heeled girls, now barefoot.*

*"We've been watching you," she says. "You'll do. You'll more
than do, in fact."*

"Where do I get those shoes?" I ask.

"They must be earned," *she says, "like Girl Scout badges.
Just remember: Your fantasies are the most precious thing you
have."*

There you have it, Vermeer. I expect no less from you when next we meet in New York.

In heat,
Salome

Caro Marco,

The night we met, I knew we were destined to change each other's lives, but I didn't know how. Now I know. You are my soul mate, the other half of me, the half that makes music, the music of the spheres.

Do you remember when we sat in the White Horse all night, wanting to make love but holding back? I was filled with delicious longing but too afraid to express it. You were also. Then I was called to Stockbridge to see my poor sick husband. While I was there, I visited the grave of my other father—I will tell you all about him one day—and I had a dream that revealed my past to me. In the dream, I knew Sim Coppley was my real father.

Let me tell you about it: I am holding him in bed. He is too weak even to sit, and he looks half mummified. I am feeding him ice water through a bent glass straw immersed in a tall glass tumbler of frigid water. Suddenly I realize that the glass is broken at its rim, and I turn the tumbler around, looking for a place that is not broken. I keep turning the tumbler around and around, desperate for Sim not to know I have brought him a broken glass, but I cannot find an unbroken part to face toward his wizened mouth.

"Salome," he mutters in his cracked voice. "Salome."

"What, Father?" I ask. (In the dream, I am aware that I am unable to call him "Papa." That name belongs to Levitsky.)

"Call me 'Papa' once before I die," he pleads.

And I look at his withered face, brown and wrinkled like a shrunken head.

"Papa," I say, as I never did in life. "Papa."

He dies in my arms with such a peaceful expression that I wake up feeling whole and healed.

You make me feel that way too, as if my entire life is settled because you have come into it. I long to really learn how to "sit." I feel we have only just begun.

I love you, my soul, my own.

Salome

16 May 1952

Never have I dreamed so richly. I wake up at night in my pristine white bed, my floor lined with tatami mats, the dawn coming up behind the shoji screens, and I hug myself for the pure pleasure of being alive. Then I scribble down my dreams in the notebook I keep for the purpose.

This strange combination of Marco and Robin thrills (and fulfills) me more than I can easily express. My analyst, the inscrutable Dr. Zuboff, says it's because I had two fathers, and I need two men to feel whole. But who is *who*? Is Marco Sim or Levitsky? Is Robin Levitsky or Sim?

I have to confess that Robin's forgeries excite me. Forgers are even more romantic than jewel thieves. They demonstrate the foolishness of attributions. They mock the money paid for provenance and famous names. Robin is a gifted rogue, and gifted rogues have always had my heart—or other parts.

Yesterday he said: "In the sixteenth century in Italy, forging antiquities was considered an art form in itself, at least by Vasari. Forgeries tell you what a society desires. In Rome they wanted Grecian antiquities. In the Renaissance, they wanted Roman antiquities. Today collectors want Vermeer and Rembrandt. Modern *schmearers* they can get *anywhere*. Who is to say my works are not variations on themes rather than forgeries? Haven't artists always imitated each other? Imitation is the sincerest form of flattery. Who's to say what differentiates a forgery from an *hommage*?"

"But you sign *their* names to them, not your own. That's an attempt to deceive!"

"Not at all," says Robin. "Suppose I painted in the style of my time—Jackson Pollock, Robert Motherwell. *That* would be an attempt to deceive. But painting in the style of ages past? Not a deception. I fully recognize that in 1952 anyone who painted like Vermeer would be mocked, so as self-protection—and to get my work to the collectors who crave it—I have to *call* myself Vermeer. The times are out of joint, not I. The times call for those in love with figurative painting to lie, deceive, dissemble. So I sign 'Vermeer' or even 'Rembrandt' and use old canvases and antique stretchers and bake the paint in an oven for good measure. But I only do it for my *paintings*—so they may survive. They are my children after all."

And with that he grabbed me, began to caress my breasts through my clothing, insinuated a swift hand under my Claire McCardell dress, and began to stroke me through my damp underwear.

"When you write about me," he said, "and you *will* write about me, don't say I was an art forger; say I was an artist. Because I *am* an artist, your artist, an artist of essences, musk, mounts of Venus and all the treasures to be found within."

He pulls off my panties, smells the wet crotch with an ecstatic inhalation, and throws me back on the bed, my skirt above my head. I struggle to kick off my Capezio ballerina flats. He looks long and lovingly at my wet vagina, saying, "a flower, a jungle flower," as he caresses one lip and then the other, tweaks my clitoris with his tongue, and lifts his head to declaim rapturously: "Someday I will paint this jungle flower, this Venus mantrap, but first I will subdue it." And he plunges into me with his iron stalk, touching my womb again and again until I weep tears of joy. He cannot stop until he has made me come three times and I am quivering from my thighs to my toes and I plead for a rest, a breather, saying, "Come, come, my love." At last he ejaculates, shuddering and growling, making the noises of a seal baying at the Arctic moon.

"My slippery seal," I say, "my salty sweetheart, my kingdom of the three slipperies."

"What is the Kingdom of the Three Slipperies?" he asks.

"*This,*" I say, as his soft cock curls out of me and I harvest his copious come from my vagina and smear it on my cheeks, my lips, my tongue. "This is the kingdom of which you are king."

"The Three Slipperies . . . hmmm," he says. "Let's make it four."

After our debauch at the Chelsea, we skip our usual meal and take a taxi up to the Metropolitan Museum, "to admire the forgeries," says Robin.

First he shows me the huge terra-cotta warrior sculptures that are labeled "Etruscan" but which he claims were made by an Italian family who flourished near Todi in Umbria at the turn of the century.

"If you wanted 'Etruscan' you came to them—clever little *vantzes*. And *everyone* wanted 'Etruscan' in those days. The British Museum has an 'Etruscan' chariot that I would bet comes from the same family. A dealer in Orvieto by the name of Fuschini was notorious for producing 'Etruscan' antiquities at the drop of a lira note. Terracotta's not my expertise, but I admire a fellow artist when I see one. Such skill! Look at the fierce features, the bellicose stance—you want 'Etruscan,' you got 'Etruscan.'"

Then he took me to see Egyptian fakes, Flemish fakes, Greek fakes—particularly among the Athenian black-figured vases.

"See this supposed sixth-century B.C. lekythos? Not at all hard to make in a modern kiln. The tricky part is oxidizing the ground to red, first covering the figures with a thick mixture of special clay so *they* don't oxidize in the kiln. I had a sculpture teacher in Italy who supported his family with 'ancient' black-figured vases. Forgeries are *always* the key to what we crave, what we lust for. They say more about the *collectors* than the forgers."

As we walked through the museum, I had that deliciously loose-limbed feeling of a woman who has been loved to distraction, then set out in the world again, thighs aching and crotch dripping. I felt that everyone could smell sex on me—the white-haired Helen Hokinson matrons in their sensible laced-up ghillies, the museum guards, the sketching art students. . . . It made me defiant, bold, raucous. Robin and I laughed together over our assorted intimacies. We had just come from bed. We were wise to the world's hypocrisies.

It had already been late when we arrived at the museum—three or so—and when the closing bell rang at five, we were simply ravenous. We went to Schrafft's on Madison Avenue, delighting in the prissy lace-collared Irish waitresses, who—we sincerely hoped—smelled sex, rule-breaking, and defiance on our skins as we ate our crustless sandwiches and drank our prim cups of English tea. We finished with those terribly *restrained* ice cream sundaes they have at Schrafft's.

"Isn't it amazing how the *goyim* make everything taste like cardboard?" Robin asked.

"You could never taste like cardboard," I said, "even if you were a *goy*."

"Impossible, isn't it, to imagine me as a *goy*?"

He fed me vanilla ice cream and gooey hot fudge on his sticky spoon.

"When are you going to introduce me to your dad?" he suddenly asked.

"*Which* dad?" I asked absentmindedly. I had forgotten that I'd written to Marco, not Robin, about my two papas. Sometimes I muddle up what I tell Dr. Zuboff with what I tell Marco with what I tell Robin! Watch out! This could be dangerous!

NOTEBOOK

19 May 1952

Hannah was home with Sally yesterday afternoon when workmen came to repair the roof of Papa's Japanese teahouse. It had been damaged by the spring storms.

The long rectangular backyards of New York brownstones (ours is a limestone—but no matter) can be terribly claustrophobic, and Papa had the brainstorm of doing it Japanese style to match the interior of the house. He also had the brilliant idea of putting a Noguchi off center at the lower end of the rectangle, letting waves of raked sand seem to flow from it as if it were a rock in the ocean. The teahouse is authentic, shipped from Kyoto at great expense.

Well, the roofers worked away on the roof, and assuming that the Noguchi was just a bunch of stones, they disassembled them and threw them in the trash. I came home from lunch with Marco, saw what had happened, and screamed:

"*Hannah—what happened to the Noguchi?*"

"The *what*, Mrs. Wallinsky?"

"The sculpture in Papa's garden!"

"That was a *what*?"

"A Noguchi, Hannah. A very important artist. A very important *Japanese* artist."

"I thought it was just *rocks* too, so help me God."

I ran to the garbage pail to salvage Noguchi's beautiful stones from the debris of fallen tree limbs, bottles, and the other flotsam that falls into New York back gardens.

Thank God the evidence was still there. I had to ask Marco to come and help me haul Noguchi's sensual boulders out of the trash! Looking at photos of the sculpture, we rearranged the stones as best we could. Papa will be furious if he misses anything. And Robin would laugh so hard if he knew. He is so down on nonobjective art!

Reading over this notebook (into which I have pasted carbons of my letters to Marco and Robin), I see I have made Marco seem bland, ethereal, bodiless. I don't mean to *make* him seem that way. Like most spiritual people, his qualities are hard to put on paper.

His beauty melts me, of course. He has those little Greek muscles like Discobolus—you know, the rippled belly and pelvic indentations you see in beautiful marble Grecian boys. His cock is big, but he doesn't quite know how to use it. He either comes too fast or is too distracted with spiritual pursuits to want to focus on sex at all. He always rhapsodizes about retracting his sperm into his brain to conserve spiritual force. I am trying to seduce him with fantasy, but he says he cannot connect with his fantasies. He blocks them out, I think, through fear.

Sometimes I come to his studio and he is playing his strange twelve-tone music and I wonder what I am meant to understand. Am I a moron about music? I don't really *like* the discordant kind. Then he relents and plays Schubert or Chopin or Beethoven or Mozart, and I love him again.

He, too, has ties to the Berkshires and wants to invite me up when he plays at the musical festival there—Tanglewood, it's called. But when I think of having him so near Robin, I panic. Surely I will want to run to Windy Perch as often as possible to renew that life-giving contact with Robin—and surely Marco will know. But maybe not. Marco is a creature who knows nothing about sexual obsession. He is too pure. Hannah has this expression: "You can't warm up cold potatoes!" which she uses on every possible occasion. It makes me think of Marco, and *that* makes me feel just awful.

I just got a letter from—of all people—Henry Valentine Miller! He's wound up in California, in a place called Big Sur, after many travels—Greece, Los Angeles, his much-dreamed-of "Air Conditioned Nightmare Trip" around the U.S. with his painter friend Abe Rattner. Everything has happened to him—as usual! *Tropic of Cancer* made him famous as an underground hero. *Black Spring* and *Capricorn* made him even more famous—though they had to be smuggled past the customs agents. He found Enlightenment, with a capital *E,* in Greece, natch. (He enclosed a signed book, published by a tiny press in San Francisco, which I find glorious—*The Colossus of Maroussi,* it's called.) He has lived in Hollywood, failed utterly as a screenwriter (he cannot write for money, it seems), supported himself by doing these surreal watercolors—which sell when nothing else does! He has tried his hand at paid pornography—thanks to his old houri Anaïs Nin— and found that even for a dollar a page, he just can't write it! The porno collector keeps saying, "Too much poetry!" and sending it back. The real porno aficionado doesn't want his porn spiced with poetry. He wants it straight! Henry has married and divorced a very scholarly and pretty Polish woman called Lepska (this is a change for Val, who usually likes nymphomaniacs or madwomen—or still better, literary nymphomaniacs or theatrical madwomen!), had two children, whom he adores, and is now living in a place called Partington Ridge with a primal woman named Eve, who is, of course, half his age.

Conveniently enough, she is an earth mother with the children.

Nevertheless he wants me to visit, encloses stacks of signed books, watercolors, pamphlets—abundance as usual: Val's cornucopia runneth over. I will send him my last novel and (maybe) the erotic fantasy I wrote for Robin, saying it's for *him*. What mischief I could get myself into. I can't wait!

Oh, yes—Val says he is living in a place "remote as the Andes, wrapped in mist," but "the only place in America I can tolerate." He writes of taking a leak into the Pacific from the height of his cliffs, of joining his "strong stream" with the vast Pacific below—oh, Henry is the poet laureate of pissing! But he misses Paris—so do I!—and he misses the light of Greece (which he has described like no one else). Henry is in love with light, in love with Big Sur, but already, he says, his fans have found him out and come to climb his cliffs, and the press writes of his "Big Sur Sex Cult." In fact, what he seems to be looking for is someone to help him raise the *children*! Life is hard at Big Sur, and the women tend to leave. Henry says that he adores the children but they leave no time for writing. As if he were the first man in history to find that out!

He seems to be getting restless even with his "angelic Eve" and his world of empyrean light!

NOTEBOOK

27 May 1952

I sent Val my novel and the fantasy of cock-heeled shoes—as I think of it—and he had plenty to say about both.

[Letter dated 24 May 1952, from Henry Valentine Miller in Big Sur, California, to Salome Levitsky Wallinsky in New York, pasted in here. Ed.]

Salome of the seven veils,

I worry about your adopting the viewpoint of a survivor of Nazi horrors in Territory of Memory *and I worry about the bound masochist of your New York fantasy.*

New York may be like that, but the rest of the world is not! To me New York seems dark, swarming with men who are cockroaches and cockroaches who impersonate men. *No wonder everyone needs an analyst in New York!* There is no light. *In Greece you voyage into the light. That is analysis enough. In Big Sur you become one with the cliffs and the sky, the poppies, wild lilac, and lupine, rattlesnakes, gophers, the mist unending, the primeval paradise of sea, of living rock, and of the purity of your own nature.*

If you come here, I know you will write a book that explodes out of your heart of light. You have not *done that yet—excuse me for saying so. No one has the sheer force of language you have. Even I am dazzled by your immense talent. But you must mine your talent. You must* make peace *with yourself. No one can write otherwise.*

As the soothsayer told me in Athens, you are wandering in circles, looking for the clear open path. You are born to bring that joy and enlightenment to the world, but you must first accept yourself and stop hiding behind masks invented by others. You have signs of divinity about you, but your feet are chained to the earth.

In your Bad Girl in Paris *you let the guts and the bones and the boners show! You were on your way to freedom then. Now you are* off the track, *trying to please—or mislead—your critics.*

I say fuck 'em! *How can you let critics invade your imagination? I am resigned to the fact that if I am ever really known, it will only be long after my death. When people ask me why I*

don't go to work as a screenwriter for a couple of years and put
away some money to really write (instead of eking out just
about enough to feed a goat from my watercolors), I reply:
"Why don't you send your daughter out on the streets to pick
up a little money and later you can marry her off? Who will
know the difference?"

Just because the world worships whores is no reason we have
to become whores. We are not required to forget our divinity
just because others have forgotten theirs. People often tell me
they envy my free way of life.

"Don't envy it," I say. "Emulate it!"

"But I can't," they say. "My job, my parents, my children, my
wife, blah, blah, blah."

Mankind is afraid of nothing more than freedom. But I
expect more from womankind—especially you!

If you come to Big Sur, bring your little girl. She and Tony
and Valentine will get along just fine! I expect another letter
when next I trudge down my cliff for the mail. Don't make me
wait!

Here the earth will open for you like the Book of Revelation!
It has for me.

Your boon companion and sometime satyr,
Henry

I know exactly what Henry means. If only I had the freedom to go
to Greece or Big Sur! But Henry never takes into account that a
man's life and a woman's life are different! Motherhood changes
everything! Trapped in New York, with Sally at Ethical Culture, my

parents returning from time to time to see their little immortality, my analysis with Dr. Zuboff, my crazy husband in the Stockbridge funny farm, my two lovers dividing me, how *could* I go to Big Sur or Greece and open up my heart to light—however much I *knew* I must?

Why had nobody told me that children become a creative mission in themselves for women, a work of art, a cosmic enterprise. I dreamed of taking Sally to Big Sur when school was out, but in truth how *could* I when Aaron demanded her near him in Stockbridge and all my loves were there, not to mention Sim's bones?

Val (he more often referred to himself as Henry now that he had his own little Valentine, his chip of self set out in the world, his female incarnation) was a passionate father in his fifties and sixties. When he had his first child, Barbara, he had hardly noticed her existence. Now, with Tony and Val, he was besotted with fatherhood. But for all the passionate fathering, he had quickly given up on daily child care. It was impossible, he said, to wipe asses, make meals, bathe children, listen to them, talk to them—and also write! If he was Adam at Big Sur, he quickly found an Eve to be his helpmate.

But there *was* no Eve for me. It all fell on my shoulders. And Marco and Robin—not to mention Papa Levitsky when he came home—wanted to be babied too. *Everyone* wanted to be the baby—so I had no choice but to grow up.

But Val was right. My writing persona was somehow buried by my *life*. Somewhere between my *Bad Girl in Paris* and Halina in *Territory of Memory*, my real writing voice lay waiting to be born. It surfaced in my poems, my fantasies, then went underground again. I needed to hear it, practice it, learn to modulate it. But how could I own it? How could I take the immediacy of my letters and journals and poems and turn them into *books*? They were too honest, too sexual, too unfetteredly *female*. Books were *male*—James Gould Cozzens, Norman Mailer, Irwin Shaw. *This* was my dilemma. And my worry was whether anybody would *want* a book that showed the raw feeling of the female heart? All the big best-sellers were about men. Even women writers impersonated men!

Emily Dickinson was virtually unpublished in her time, Sappho's poems were lost, etc. Nor do I find *myself* in the women writers of my own time and place: neither in Mary McCarthy's brittle, cold satire, nor in the draperies, houses, and asterisked love scenes of our popular novelists—Margaret Mitchell being the best but dead.

The book I want to write would be open and immediate as this journal, would show the difference between man's abstraction, his dreadful ability to generalize pain and suffering, and woman's oneness with the womb of creation, her feeling every grief as if she were God.

It would be sharp, sweet, sour, satirical, strange, loving, and hating all at once. It would have the clarity of life, the mystery of dreams, the wild, unexpected dividend of spring after a long winter. It would be Persephone's book, not Apollo's—but *when* shall I write it, if men and children keep chaining my feet to earth?

I have this fantasy that I am trying to write but some man is pinning me to the bed, fucking my brains out. "Let me up!" I scream. "Let me up!" But I am stuck here under a man! *When* will my hormones let me go?

And Sally—Sally has changed my life. I *want* to leave my work and go to her. I do not *want* to give up that pleasure, that annoyance. She is part of me. She is life. She is the future. But sometimes I also resent her and wish she'd disappear.

We women who write are monsters, dipping our scaly fins and mermaids' tails into the dream life, then coming up for air to feed mashed potatoes and carrots to our offspring from hands that have been fins paddling in moonbeams. Half human, half glowering sea monster or twinkling naiad, how can we make peace with our curious lot in life? We are required to be more schizophrenic than madwomen, only to survive and raise our troubled daughters!

Would Val understand if I wrote him this? No, not for all his writer's heart of light. The one being they cannot empathize with is woman. When he says "heart," he means "male heart." When he says "soul," he means "male soul." When he says "light," he means "male abstraction of light." When I say light, I mean Sally's eyes.

8

Salome Surrenders
1952

> *Say it, say it, the universe is made of stories, not of atoms.*
>
> —MURIEL RUKEYSER

NOTEBOOK

1 June 1952

Mama and Papa came back today, cramping my style and spoiling Sally with marvelous smocked dresses which probably she will never wear. She's a tomboy. Loves work clothes, pants, sweatshirts, and those little blue smocks they use at "progressive" nursery schools.

Robin insisted on meeting Papa next time he's in town, and I'm worried about this. What trouble they could cook up together!

Meanwhile, I have been making notes for a new book, saving string, so to speak. I want to write as madly and freely as I do in my notebooks and journals. Even if the book never sees the light of day, I have to know that I possess the courage to write it! I have to claim my voice or die! The subject of the novel will be the contrast between a woman's inner life and outer life—how the two interweave and contradict each other. The book in your head versus the book of your life! How you can be at the dry cleaner or the playground or the butcher and still be having sex in your head with every man you meet. How you can be chained to the earth by domestic duties yet still be climbing your own spiritual mountain path through the mist.

Lately I am giving off such hot vibes that every man I meet seems to notice it. At a dinner party the other night with Papa and Mama and a bunch of art dealers and crazy artists, a very bald, cantankerous artist said to me, *sotto voce,* after talking to me all through dinner, "I could lay you right here on the dinner table."

I smiled like Mona Lisa, giving off that special sex smell.

"And what makes you think I *want* it?"

"You want it. I know you want it. You know you want it. You're wild."

"I have absolutely no idea what you're talking about."

"Like fucking hell you don't," he said, and copped a feel of my right breast.

"I should slap your face," I said, impersonating some spinster from an old play. But I smiled like the Cheshire cat. So he fondled my ass for good measure.

"Nice," I said.

"You're the one that's nice."

"You too," I said, grabbing his ass.

He looked dumbfounded, maybe even scared. Probably no woman had ever done that to him before.

"What's sauce for the gander goes also for the goose," I said. "Or don't you think so?" I sashayed out of the dining room.

What is this perfume I'm giving off? My Sin? It's nice to know I still have the catnip!

3 June 1952

Everything has stopped in my life while Mama and Papa reassert control in the household, entertain their clients and friends, and take over Sally's life. Mama takes Sally to the park—the zoo, the merry-go-round—but fusses over her as if she were made of glass. It is as if she thinks *every* baby will be snatched away by Cossacks. How different her life was from mine. She used to drive me insane, but I have patience with her now, as I didn't when I was younger.

Robin was here to meet Papa. They laughed and talked, hit it off immediately. When Mama was in the kitchen, instructing Hannah about the making of a fruit compote—God forbid she should leave the help alone to *help*!—Papa looked at me, looked at Robin, and waved his right hand from Robin to me, from me to Robin, as if to ask, "You two together?" I blushed. Robin nodded.

"To mine opinion, not a bad match," Papa said.

Later Mama came to my room when Sally was asleep.

"I don't trust him," she said, unasked.

"Neither do I," I said quickly, surprising myself.

"It's as easy to love a nice man as a *vantz*," Mama said. "Since they're all *tsuris*, you might as well have one who won't keep you up at night in worriment."

My mama used to say "worriment" when she was trying to put on her best English.

"When a rogue kisses you, count your teeth," Mama said, quoting, of course, my grandmother.

Then she tucked me in as if I were five, went in to look at Sally and say some special *brucha* over her, and took herself to bed.

Someday I am going to have the guts to ask Mama about her love life. It should be part of the novel I'm writing. And how! What do I remember? I remember that white-haired, blue-eyed Mr. Lobel, who ran a brokerage house, how he used to look at Mama, and that English actor who played Hamlet and was reputed to be a woman-izer. He was cute! Mama painted him costumed as Hamlet, dandling a skull on his knee. He looked fabulous in tights. Hung like a horse. Unless he was stuffed! And then there was Mr. Slansky the producer, who played host at her parties when Papa was away in Europe on buying trips. And of course Sim. She had never even *told* me about Sim. But now she *knows* I know, and we never talk about it. That's my mama. She knows how to keep her mouth shut as my generation *never* did. Is that the secret of her survival?

I fell asleep thinking of all these things. In my dream, Sally was counting my teeth with her little hands. Then I was following her up a mountain on foot while she rode a bicycle. A dog was clambering up behind us—Jacques, our black standard poodle. Every time there was a tunnel cut through the mountain, I'd worry we'd lose the dog because dogs were not allowed in the tunnels. But the dog always scampered up after us somehow, following our scent. I saw that Sally was going to be okay and so was Jacques. At the summit, I put out a bowl of water for Jacques and took Sally in my arms. Way below us, at the foot of the mountain, were Aaron, Robin, Marco. They were wav-ing white handkerchiefs.

"Should I save them?" I asked myself. I woke up pondering this question, and I worried about it all day.

NOTEBOOK

5 June 1952

The Rosenbergs have been in custody for almost two years. Their death sentence was affirmed and committees are being organized to protest it, but things look bleaker and bleaker. Papa warns me against getting involved in the protest, *any* protest, but my heart *breaks* for them—separated from their two little boys, immersed in a political maelstrom, unable to escape the judgment of the mob, of the greedy politicians. I sit here, knowing I am no better than Germans who watched Jews being slaughtered and did nothing.

This is our very own Dreyfus case, and I am turning inward rather than outward, and I am hating myself for it. I feel like such a coward! If they are killed, I shall be one of their murderers. Every night I go to sleep feeling as if I should be in jail with them.

Marco believes the answer is meditation, to reform the human race from the inside out. But it is hard to imagine Senator Joe McCarthy meditating. Sometimes I think Marco has his head in the sand. He stays in his cocoon of twelve-tone music, tea ceremonies, and Zen proverbs, while the world goes down its slimy spiral into hell.

NOTEBOOK

12 June 1952

It seems Aaron has attempted suicide again. We are all in the car on the way to Stockbridge. Papa is driving in his usual maddening way, straddling the center lane, *causing* accidents if not actually *having* them! I can barely read my reversed handwriting. More later.

NOTEBOOK

Stockbridge

14 June 1952

Aaron is dead. He was dead when they found him—dead and bright pink. I kissed him goodbye. His cheek was shockingly cold.

Papa said: "To mine opinion, they had him in the meat locker overnight. What do *goyim* know about the *malech ha-movis*? They would have *embalmed* him at the *goyishe* funeral chapel if we hadn't got here!"

"Sha, Levitsky!" Mama said, Mama always says.

Apparently Aaron locked himself in a running car after having attached a hose from the exhaust pipe into a back window. He was found dead in the garage that the kitchen staff and doctors sometimes use. Supposedly getting *better,* he was no longer on "Disturbed." Nobody knew where he'd got the bicycle chain and the padlock with which he had shackled himself to the steering wheel. The clinic was concerned they'd be blamed or sued: you could see from the way they were busy distancing themselves from the "case," as they called it.

Dr. B. had us all in his office: Mama, Papa, me. Hannah had taken Sally to the Weekses' place, where she was given native strawberries and cream, as if to compensate for having a dead father.

Dr. Bartlow said: "There is a certain point where you have to trust in a person's will to get better, and Aaron's need to die was, sad to say, stronger. We believe here that depression is an *illness,* not a shame or a weakness, but the tools we have to treat it are not yet perfect. Perhaps someday we will understand it better."

But I knew why Aaron kept attempting suicide till he succeeded. The dead had more power over him than the living.

That was the Nazis' primary murder, I thought, the murder of the will to live. Our lives are made of certain things: the presence of predictable schedules, going to school, warm houses, shoes with laces, working toilets, elementary grooming, waiting parents. Take away those lodestars of habit and, predictably, most people will crack open into madness. I certainly would have. I would never have wanted to survive the *Aktionen,* never mind Auschwitz!

"Do you think shock treatments might have helped?" I asked the doctor, who had once proposed them as a last resort.

"We don't know. We never know," the doctor said.

"He always told me he wished he had succeeded in committing suicide," I said.

"But maybe later he would have been glad to be alive," the doctor said.

I didn't answer. I held my tongue, like Mama. I knew the doctor was wrong. Aaron would *never* have been glad to be alive. Aaron could never rest till he joined his dead family. Aaron was too *guilty* to live. What did I feel? Relief. Gladness. Freedom. And then horrible, horrible guilt. The father of my only child was *dead*! His death would simplify my life. And then I doubled over from the weight of my bad conscience.

After I had identified the body, Mama said, apropos of nothing: "Years ago I knew a beautiful woman from Russia called Luba. She worked with me for the sweater—excuse me—in the sweatshop. She used to say to me, 'Sarah, I *danced* all the way to America.'

"'Danced? Who—excuse me—whom did you dance with?'

"'With a very handsome man—who can remember his name? In those days a pretty girl wasn't expected to *sleep* with everyone.'

"'*Nu*, so why didn't you marry him?'

"'He wasn't Jewish,' Luba said, just like that."

"What's the point of this?" I asked impatiently. I knew Mama had a moral here. She never told stories otherwise. "Are you trying to tell me I'm better off with my crazy Jewish husband *dead*?"

"No, but that's what *you* think, Salome."

How could Mama *read my mind*? Can all mothers do this? Will I be able to do this with Sally?

"How *little* you know me," Mama said. "The point is, Salome, even in the sweatshop, we *knew* who we were, what we were, what we were not. Dying you could *always* do. You didn't have to run to it with open arms. 'For death you always have time,' my mama used to say. Your grandmother also said: 'No one can do to you the harm you can do yourself.' Life is a gift, but you have to know how to *receive* the gift."

I knew now exactly what she meant, but I wouldn't give her the satisfaction of saying so. So much that happens between parents and children is unexpressed yet communicated. Somehow, despite all her *mishegas,* all her curious restraint toward me, she had always let me know that life was a gift.

There was no way I could have communicated that gift to Aaron. I *had* tried. But I would communicate it to Sally—or *die* trying! And Mama, in her own way, was trying to give me permission to free myself. She was trying to give me permission to unfetter myself from *guilt.*

Later, as we were walking alone—Mama was with Sally—Papa said to me: "The worst thing about getting old, to mine opinion, is that your *minyan* dies."

"*Minyan?*"

"The ones who have witnessed your life—your friends, your enemies. At forty, it begins. At fifty, it becomes an epidemic. At sixty, they're dropping like flies. 'For dying you always have time,' as your grandmother used to say."

"That's what Mama just said."

"Great minds think alike," Levitsky said.

How do I feel about Aaron's death? Numb at first, then furious. It seems that whenever I start to get my life and Sally's life together, he throws another monkey wrench in. Now we have to plan his funeral, settle his estate, sell the school. It's too late for me to go back to the Berkshires. I'm settled in New York now.

Did Aaron die just to interrupt my novel? I think so. A year will go by before I'm free of this *chazerei.* Ah, well, better to have the storm break, the rotten tree fall. At last it's over. I'm free. Or maybe I *will* be. Someday.

15 August 1952

Deluged by the mess Aaron left by dying. Caring for him had swallowed up my life again, but now I am enraged at him for engulfing me by dying, for being indifferent to the possibility of leaving Sally fatherless. He wants to take away my precious time. He wants to eat up my life, even from the grave! But in the wee hours of the morning, I am writing, writing with the wind at my back, as if the angel of death—*the malech ha-movis*—were pursuing me. And he *is*! Mama and Papa have taken Sally to Beverly Hills with them for the summer. We have not yet told her her daddy is dead. Hannah has gone with them. And I am here in the unearthly peace of the white shoji screens and raked sand garden, trying to make sense of the life I have lived so far, a woman in the dead middle of the century, traveling, as if on a train, back to Paris in the thirties and forward toward the future, the millennium, the end of the century, when I shall be old.

In the year 2000, I will be eighty-eight. Probably I won't remember what wonders I have seen—so I'd better write them down now. Possible titles for this novel: *The Last Century, The Last Jewess, Dancing to America, Inventing Memory, People Who Can't Sleep, Of Love and Memory, Sleepless People, Women of Valor, Of Blessed Memory.*

I am writing the book with Aaron's suicide as the starting point of the story. What happens to a woman who is suddenly launched into her own life by a husband's suicide? How does it change her? How does it make her claim her own will to live? Above all, how does it *free* her? I think I am onto something important. Why do women always have to be abandoned in some way in order to seize their own lives?

LETTER FROM SALOME LEVITSKY WALLINSKY
IN BIG SUR, CALIFORNIA, TO MARCO ALBERTI
IN LENOX, MASSACHUSETTS, SUMMER 1952

Caro Marco,

*On my way to pick up Sally in the City of the Angels and
bring her back to start school in New York, I visited my old
friend from Paris, Henry Miller, who lives here in bohemian
glory, surrounded by merry and hard-drinking hangers-on in a
spot that looks like paradise before the fall.*

*I can see why anyone would stop here—clouds stepping off
into the Orient, rugged country, the free air of the West, an
invigorating life that keeps you mentally and physically
strong—and the light! The light in Big Sur is almost as wonderful as the light in Provence, in Venice, in Tuscany.*

*If only because I am here among the mad bohemians, I long
for peace, order, harmony, and I am tempted to say, yes, let's
join our lives, but I know I cannot do that. In a funny way, I
have never tested my own wings. I have always gone from man
to man. And much as I love you, I have to make it on my own
as a writer before I seek refuge with you.*

Salome

NOTEBOOK

August 1952

Aaron's suicide shifted everything in my head. Suddenly, instead of
my obsession with Robin, I am obsessed with the book I am writing.

Maybe it is seeing Henry and sleeping with him behind Eve's back, behind Robin's and Marco's, the old disorder and chaos from Paris, which is surely a part of my inspiration, versus the other part of me, the part that wants calm and space and peace.

I am enraged with Aaron. In my dreams, I am screaming at him, telling him he had no right to go away and leave me. All this is odd because, in truth, he left me long ago. More and more, I understand that *time does not exist*. Dead people inhabit my dreams, and the living sometimes seem to belong to the past. I drive down to Los Angeles along the old highway that parallels the ocean, and I think about my life, feeling poised between two distinct parts of it, poised between past and future. I am too young for some things and too old for others. What shall I do? Keep driving. Finish the book I've begun. God grant me the time to mine my teeming brain!

There is a French movie by Carné (is it?), in which a woman who is suddenly widowed visits all the men who have been important in her life and *through* them revisits her earlier selves. I tried to do that with Henry. But you simply *can't* return to the past, or reexperience the glamour a man had when he was a hook into your future. Driving along the ocean, I thought of Henry, Ethan, Robin, Marco, and I wondered: *Should* I marry Marco? Should I marry him because he adores me and he will never hurt me? I believe that is why Mama married Papa. Otherwise it is unfathomable. Imagine—he *never* fucked her! Why did she stay? For security. Because they had made a life and a business together. Because she knew how to keep her mouth shut, as I don't! But from Mama's old friend Fritzi Goldheart, who also came to America from Russia in 1905, I learned that Mama had many lovers. I'm really glad for her. My path is different. I will have the heroine of my novel marry and have another child, but *I* myself will not.

August 1952

Here with Mama and Papa at Summit Ridge Road, whence
Pickford and Fairbanks once ruled the tinsel kingdom. The house is
beautiful, white, perched over the city and the sea. Sally has a swimming pool here. Mama wants her never to return to New York.

"Tell me more about the woman who danced all the way to
America, Mama. It was you, wasn't it, Mama?"

Mama wheels around from the easel, her palette in her hand, her
golden half-moon glasses sliding down her nose. She pushes them
back with her right index finger.

"*I wish!*" she says.

"Mama—I know you well enough. You only deny when I'm on the
right track."

"No. It wasn't me, but I always wanted to be like that. Anyway,
what's the difference whether it was me or Luba?"

"Luba who?"

"Before your time—you never knew her."

"Mama—this is what I have to ask. Why did you dance to America
when you were young and then stumble when you got older? Why
did you stop thinking you could beat the system? Why did you surrender."

Mama's eyes flared as if with flame: "Because of you and the
family."

"You mean I clipped your wings?"

"Of course not—I grew them stronger for you. But my focus
shifted. *You* became the focus. Everything else became less important. *Life* became more important than anarchist ideas, than art, than
theories. If this is stumbling, then let me *go on* stumbling. I regret
nothing. I consider this stumbling the real dancing! *Life* is the dance

that never ends! Even if you *can't* dance at two weddings with one behind!"

Did she really say that—or did I dream it? I took Sally back to New York, and the first person I called was Marco. Then I went back to my book.

NOTEBOOK

July 1953

On the day the Rosenbergs were assassinated by the United States government, I finished my novel, which I have decided to call *Dancing to America*. I could have been surging in the crowd in Union Square. I could have been carrying a placard. But I was protesting death in the way I knew best: by giving birth to the book.

Little did I know that I was also protesting death in another way: It may turn out I am pregnant!

NOTEBOOK

August 11, 1953

I am definitely pregnant. Though it is the last thing I wanted, I find myself rather pleased. What if this is my *son*? I think about abortions and quickly rule them out. Who cares who the father is? The baby feels all mine! Marco is thrilled. So is Robin. I dare not tell Henry, for fear he will kidnap me to Big Sur. The baby is due in March. I'm sure I'll be able to sort it all out by then!

[*Dancing to America*, which Salome considered her most important work, was never published. "Too ethnic," said one publisher. "Too

female," said another. "We'll be sued," said a third. "It's obscene," said a
fourth. "We'll all go to jail," said the last of them.

Salome then went into the art business, in which she prospered. She
did have a son, Lorenzo, whose father was anyone's guess. She married
Robin Robinowitz, but Marco remained her best friend, lover, inspira-
tion. She went on keeping notebooks for a while, then gradually
stopped. The manuscript of Dancing to America *unfortunately has dis-*
appeared. Perhaps it will surface someday. Ed.]

NOTEBOOK

12 April 1954

Sally seems utterly distraught by Lorenzo's birth. This is more than
sibling rivalry. She whirls in place until she makes herself dizzy. She
asks me, "What will happen if we close the Bathinette on the baby?"
In my panic to protect my little man, I am afraid I have been too
tough on her. Everyone fusses over Lorenzo the way people used to
fuss over her. I fear for her and for him. I am so preoccupied with
mothering and the gallery that I have almost no time to write—even
in my notebook. Life has devoured me. Somehow I always knew it
would. From time to time, I make little notes, but hardly with my
usual passion. Lorenzo and Sally use me up. What is left of me, the
gallery gets. More and more, my life is like Mama's. Sometimes I look
in the mirror and see her face. Sometimes I hear myself quoting her
quoting *her* mother. "If you're rich, you're wise and good-looking and
can sing well too," I heard myself say to Sally the other day.

"What?" she asked.

"One of the proverbs of my grandmother," I mumbled. And then I
was amazed at myself and laughed our loud. The genes get you in the
end. It's inevitable. *That's* the novel I would like to write.

[Letter from Salome Levitsky Wallinsky to her daughter, Sally Wallinsky Robinowitz, sometimes known as Sally Levitsky Wallinsky Robinowitz, but as Sally Sky to her fans. Ed.]

3 May 1988

Dear Sally,

When you were little and I thought I had committed myself seriously to the writing of novels, I remember how distraught you used to be when I worked at home. I was there, but not there. "Look at me! Look at me!" you used to yell in a panic. The panic only increased when your brother was born. And I remember being suffused with guilt as if I had replaced you— first with writing, then with Lorenzo.

After a while I came to feel that life was more important than writing. How can any mother not? I knew that once I opened the door to that possibility, I would cross some threshold and there would be no going back. I was right.

But there has to be the possibility for women to create life and to create art, otherwise what have we been fighting for all these years? After I had a son, the struggle to write seemed suddenly not worth the candle. I feel I let us both down that way— you and me. You, because I set a bad example. Me, because now I suffer from dreams gone dry.

I have just been remembering how I used to make fun of my mother for "giving up her dreams." But now that she is gone, I understand that she had never really given up. She had simply shifted her priorities. She had become a mother, but she never stopped being an artist, a lover of life. She had a whole secret life, which someday I will share with you.

The demands of life and the demands of art are difficult to reconcile. *There is no way to* pretend *they are not. When I was with you, I wanted to be with my book. When I was with my book, I wanted to be with you. I know now that* many *of us feel this way. We bear the contradiction inside us, and I believe we are heroines for it.*

Why am I telling you this? Because I want you not *to emulate me, not to put away your dreams. Tolerate the contradiction within you. It will make your work richer even while it takes away your time to do it! But whatever you do, don't give up your work. Regret solves nothing.*

If you are ever in a bad moment in your life and you feel that you cannot go on, remember that you are the daughter of a woman who was the daughter of a woman who believed that strength came from accepting the contradictions of life rather than pretending life had no *contradictions.*

This is profoundly Jewish. It is also profoundly womanly. As a people, Jews have had to accept the vinegar with the honey, and we got good at it. All our humor is about that, all our art, our music, our literature. And women also know that life is not perfectible. Only art is. And life is always *more important than art. But art is what remains.*

Eventually, because of what I did and didn't do, what my mother did and didn't do, and what you have *done and will do, women will have more possibilities, less restricted lives. Despair is a waste. We live on in each other's possibilities. We extend our freedoms into the future.*

I never thought my mama would die. She seemed immortal to me. Since she was the ground of my being, her death seemed unthinkable—however much she annoyed me at times. Now I am standing at the edge of the cliff with no one to catch me. I'm sure all daughters feel this way when their mothers die.

The memorial service for Mama was very moving. She touched so many lives. All her old cronies were there, looking

*frail. And her portraits all around. I never knew she did so
many. She painted everyone—Calvin Coolidge to Loretta
Young; Humphrey Bogart to Edward G. Robinson; Betty
Grable to Marilyn Monroe; Babe Paley to Nancy Kissinger—
though (in the early years) not always under her own name.*

*Many famous people spoke—artists, politicians, writers—but
it was her housekeeper, Daisy, who brought the house down.*

*"Miz Levitsky always acted like family, not a boss. She was
so tender of my feelings. She used to say: 'The Jews in Russia
were like the Blacks in America,' and she wasn't just talkin'. She
knew.*

*"One day, she come home when it was pouring rain outside
and she was all wet. I helped her get dry. Then, while we was
sittin' in the kitchen, drinkin' our tea, Miz Levitsky said, nice as
pie: 'Daisy, there was bubbles coming out of my stockings—in
the future, please rinse my stockings.'"*

And the crowd roared.

*But of all the memorials to her, the oral history you did with
her when Sara was a baby, that rambling interview—or whatever you want to call it—is by far the* best *. As I remember, she
addressed her remarks to Sara, whose legacy it will be. Don't
bury it, darling—do something with it. Her story* matters.
*Everyone has an ancestor like Mama, and people will identify.
Give them the* joy *of knowing her. She was one of a kind. Sui
generis. She was a woman of valor.*

*We were never what you would call religious, but we do
believe that each generation carries the previous one forward
by means of memory. Memory is a sacred thing for Jews. That
is why we worship words, books, art, music, all the things that
keep the past alive, all the things that deny death, that rage
against the dying of the light.*

*If we have survived despite all odds, it is because of our rev-
erence for* memory. *We believe the past is with us and* in *us. We*

*do not believe we can eradicate the past, nor that our enemies
can. We document our past as a way of revering it. We are all
historians, in a way. We believe we must lift up the past,
remake it, transform it into the* future. *The secret of our
strength is merely that: we know that memory is the crux of our
humanity. We know that words are sacred. We also know that
though art defines our humanity, life matters too. Life matters
most. Pass it on.*

   I love you.

   Salome (Your Mother!!!!)

9

Sally's Story ✦ In the Sky with Diamonds
1953–1969

> *Jews are the intensive form of any nationality whose*
> *language and customs they adopt.*
>
> —Emma Lazarus

From the time Sally was a little girl, she believed fate had picked her out for a special destiny. This was because her grandfather Levitsky, a bearded man with bushy eyebrows and glittery gold glasses, who used to put her to bed whistling Russian songs and rubbing her back, made it clear to her she *was* special. Every morning, he fixed her boiled eggs and toast soldiers. He walked her all the way from the town house on Fifty-sixth Street to her school opposite Central Park. And he picked her up in the afternoon, dropping everything to play with her.

She also knew she was special because there were portraits of her (painted by her grandmother) at every stage of her life—baby portraits, portraits in Elizabethan costume, portraits in angel gowns and Japanese kimonos, portraits in pastels, oils, watercolors. But most of all she knew she was special because her mother wanted her and her grandmother and grandfather wanted her and when she lay in bed in the morning before getting up she could make rainbows between her eyelashes. There was a black cloud on this rainbow, and that was her father, who lived far away in a sort of hospital place and was whispered about. But if she didn't think of that shadowy being—glimpsed a few times across a green lawn—and thought instead of her grandparents and her mother, everything seemed secure.

At her grandparents' house in California, she had a white tutu and white satin ballet slippers, and at her mother's house in New York she had pink ones. Sometimes she would lie in bed for hours, wrapping pink satin ribbons around her legs and pretending she was dancing on the ceiling *en pointe.* She had all the time in the world to grow up and be the most famous girl in the world, and that was what she planned to be.

"Sally!" her nanny Hannah used to call. "Get out of bed this minute!" But she didn't want to get out of bed. In bed she could imagine she was anything in the world. Bed was her favorite place to be. It allowed enough space for her imagination.

Her mother was beautiful—large tawny eyes and red hair. She was the most beautiful mother in the whole school. She seemed younger than the other mothers, and she liked to skip in the streets and ice-skate at Rockefeller Center and take ballet classes and do things other mothers didn't do. Other mothers were dull and wore beaver or Persian lamb coats. Sally's mother dressed like an actress or a dancer, in Indian silks and silver jewelry that tinkled like bells. Sally's mother had style.

When Sally was five or six, she wandered into her mother's room in the middle of the night, pushed open the door, and saw something she knew she was not supposed to see: her mother's head flung back over the edge of the bed and her stepfather, Robin—was he her stepfather yet?—suspended over her mother, looking angry and rocking back and forth. The door had squealed softly on its hinges. Had they heard? Sally's heart pounded and hammered on her temples. But they did not hear, did not see. They were off in another place. She stood rooted to the floor, watching. She heard her mother moan as if she were being hurt. She wanted to help, yet knew she should not budge. She felt sick, yet fascinated. She literally could not move her feet. Suddenly Robin turned his head and saw her, his eyes wild. She ran away as if she had been hit.

For years she remembered it that way—as if she *had* been hit. And when her brother, Lorenzo, was born and turned her life upside down, she believed he was her punishment for watching. She was bedeviled by the thought that someday her mother would also know her secret and something even more unimaginably horrible would happen. But her mother never spoke of it, and the suspense of this terrible punishment hanging over her head was worse than anything. Sometimes she begged God to strike her dead so that she would not have to wait any longer for the punishment that might come at any time. Anything was better than this waiting. She used to lie in bed thinking that the nail scissors would fly out of its kit and stab her baby brother through the heart. She would get up every few minutes to look in his crib to make sure this *hadn't* happened. And her mother would sometimes rush in and say, accusingly: "*What* are you doing with the baby?" It terrified Sally that her mother could read her thoughts. Now, surely, an even bigger punishment was in store.

Even though she was not such a great ballet dancer, when the TV people came to her school, they picked her to be on TV and talk about ballet because she was different from the other little girls. She was small, but she spoke like an adult. "Ballet is about precision," she said precisely. She carried herself with confidence, with defiance. In a way, this was a cover-up, because she knew she had done things she was not supposed to do—had stolen a toy baby bottle from a play-mate's house because she just *had to have it,* had seen her mother that way, had imagined her baby brother dead, had shamelessly gone on TV when she was not the best dancer, only the best talker. So when people told her how wonderful she was, she didn't entirely believe it. Her sense of a special destiny and her sense of being wicked and guilty were all somehow mixed up together.

When she wanted to feel exquisitely terrible and remember all the things she had done wrong, she thought of herself at five, playing on the floor of a friend's house, debating whether or not to take that bottle with the little red nipple. It was the perfect thing for her doll. But stealing was wrong. If she asked to take it, they might say no. So with a throb of terror in her chest, she put it in her pocket without telling anybody. It burned a hole in her conscience for years after.

She remembered that little bottle so well—even decades later. It had a long, pointed red nipple—not like a real baby bottle at all but like a baby bottle in a cartoon. The thing was, she didn't *have* to steal it. Anyone—her mother, grandfather, grandmother—would have bought a baby bottle for her. But she wanted *this* baby bottle—she couldn't *wait* for another one. Perhaps there would never *be* another one. It was from this incident that she knew how irresistible a compulsion could be. The need to have that bottle was not a choice. Many things in her life were like that.

Her grandmother painted, her mother had written books and now ran a famous gallery, and for the longest time she did not know what she could possibly do to distinguish herself. She knew she had a musical gift—her piano teacher raved about her, but it was not until she was given a guitar when she was twelve that she truly found her calling. Becoming one with that guitar, she felt entirely safe for the first time, as if the instrument and the music it made were an all-powerful shield against all the dangers of the world. Nobody could call her a thief when she had that guitar in front of her. Nobody could take her to task for patrolling the house at night or for the wicked thoughts she had had about Lorenzo when he was a baby. She picked out the chords and sang "Greensleeves" over and over to herself, imagining a beautiful lover to whom she was plaintively singing:

Alas, my love, you do me wrong
to cast me off discourteously,
For I have lovèd you so long,
Delighting in your company. . . .
Greensleeves were all my joy . . .
Greensleeves were my delight . . .
Greensleeves were my heart of gold
and who but my lady
Greensleeves. . . .

Sally commuted from PLaza 7 to RIverside 9 to study with a black-listed folksinger of the thirties called Mason Herbst, who lived way uptown in a dusty apartment filled with stacks of crumbling sheet music. His upright piano was out of tune. His teeth were yellow, his stomach made basso noises, and he smelled funny.

Once, she made the mistake of mentioning her grandfather Levitsky to him, and his expression became so black she was afraid he would refuse to teach her.

"Not your fault," he muttered almost to himself, "that your grandfather's a stool pigeon."

"You know my grandfather?" she asked.

"I'd know him in *hell*," said Herbst. He went on demonstrating technique.

At the time, Sally didn't really comprehend what had happened, but later she understood. Things had occurred before her birth that people were still furious about.

Mason Herbst knew about Child ballads, blues, "progressive jazz." He was friends with Woody Guthrie, Alan Lomax. He subscribed to *Sing Out* magazine. Mason Herbst liked to stroke her long red hair with his trembling fingers. She hated his touching her hair. She hated especially the pathetic way he looked at her, smiling crookedly with yellow teeth. But she made no move to stop him. She didn't want to offend. She let him touch her hair and blow his foul breath in her mouth. But one day, after he had taught her "Barbara Allen" and "Black is the color of my true love's hair," she left his apartment and never came back. He was just too spooky. She would teach herself to play, she decided, by being a sponge, absorbing music everywhere. It was true that later she would miss that link with the radical past— "We want bread and roses too" was another song he taught her—but by then she knew how to find it elsewhere. She never even dreamed then that her darling grandfather knew all there was to know about those forgotten days. He had stopped talking about them in the fifties—and besides, he was old and somewhat forgetful now.

By the time Sally was a junior in high school, she discovered the coffeehouses in the Village, where, as a lark, she called herself Sally Sky. (Sally Wallinsky seemed much too cumbersome a name for a singer, and she liked the spaciousness of Sky.) "This land is your land, this land is my land," she sang. "This land was made for you and me."

She also delighted in driving her grandfather crazy by singing the "International":

> *Arise, ye prisoners of starvation!*
> *Arise, ye wretched of the earth!*
> *For justice thunders condemnation!*
> *A better world's in birth!*

"Vat better world?" her grandfather would ask. "The Communists all became capitalists—that's all! We *forgot* the wretched of the earth to mine opinion. The wretched of the earth were damned ungrateful—and they smelled bad too!"

"What happened to your idealism, Papa?" For Sally knew that much from her mother.

"A long story. America has no room for idealists and dreamers. Making a living is the American religion." (Only, he pronounced it "making a *leeving*.")

"I hope I never get as cynical as you, Papa."

"Just live long enough." He sighed. "For a long time I asked why the old had to die. It's not because your heart attacks you or because of cancer-schmancer—but because we lose our illusions. Without illusions we die. Without illusions there's no energy, no enthusiasm for life. So we have to be replaced—by the young who have fresh illusions. God planned it that way."

"Then you believe in God?" Sally asked.

"I have decided that God believes in me."

Papa went to his bookcase, extracted a yellowed anthology of poems, and opened it with a loud crack and a cloud of dust. He read a poem to Sally in his gravelly voice with its Russian accent:

> The clock in the workshop, it rests not a moment;
> It points on and ticks on; eternity—time;
> Once, someone told me the clock had a meaning,
> In pointing and ticking had reason and rhyme. . . .
> At times, when I listen, I hear the clock plainly:
> The reason of old—the old meaning is gone!
> The maddening pendulum urges me forward
> To labor and still labor on.
> The tick of the clock is the boss in his anger.
> The face of the clock has the eyes of the foe.
> The clock—I shudder—dost hear how it calls me?
> It calls me "Machine" and it cries to me, "Sew!"

When he had finished reading, Papa rocked back in his chair and said: "To mine opinion, it's better in Yiddish." But he tried to remember it in Yiddish and just couldn't.

"Dat's my memory—a sieve—but I won't forget the *schreiber*—a great man, Morris Rosenfeld, who wrote poetry and worked in a sweatshop. Your grandmama did too. . . ."

"My grandmama wrote poetry and worked in a *sweatshop*?" Sally asked incredulously. Sally knew her grandmama as an elegant lady in gold half-moon glasses and perfectly tailored suits from Balenciaga and Dior.

"A sweatshop?" Sally was agog.

Levitsky said: "There's plenty you don't know, *mayne kind, mayne shayner kind.* . . ."

With a guitar you could go anywhere in New York in those days. Sally wore her frantic, frizzy strawberry hair down to her waist, and on her feet she wore rough-hewn sandals she had bought on Eighth Street in the Village. She dressed all in black. She sang as if her life depended on it. In a way, it did.

Boys started turning up when she was fourteen, first in the person of Gaiter Rowland—"Gaiter Gaiter Masturbator," as his friends called him—the six-foot string bean of Washington Square. He had soulful black eyes and dangled a smoldering Gauloise from his lower lip. Gaiter was a banjo player, Scruggs picker, pot smoker, finger fucker, and all-purpose rebel. He hung out with Izzy Young at the Folklore Center. In its back room, Gaiter initiated Sally into orgasm with his banjo-picking fingers, and for a long time she thought she was the only girl in the world to have experienced this gasping release. She began to starve herself in penance. No food, no water, long, tortured telephone conversations with Gaiter, in which she tried to break up with him and he begged her not to. He wrote songs for her. She wrote songs for him. He would win her back by singing under the town house window with two musician pals and strewing the stoop with rose petals.

The guilt Sally felt about what she did with Gaiter was all mixed up with stealing the bizarre toy baby bottle and not being the best dancer but going on TV anyway. The pain and anxiety were so great she had to ease them somehow. Music shut them out for a while, and so did pot. The problem was, you needed more and more and more to exit the panic and pass into the smooth concentric waves of feeling. Sally always *felt* too much. Some people do drugs to feel *more,* but she did them to feel *less*. When she was straight, people were hideous. They looked like gargoyles by Goya. When she got a little high, their features smoothed out. They were prettier. They stopped being grotesques.

And sex was also a way of exiting the panic. Sex was a way of smoothing everything out. But then you became dependent on it. And that was dangerous, because sometimes the one you depended on would go away. It was unpredictable. It put you at the mercy of men.

If only there were some way to get that smooth, soothing feeling without being at anyone's mercy. That was what Sally wanted. She didn't know how to get it. She would have done anything to learn the secret.

Later in her life, whenever she got sober, she would remember all too clearly why she had drunk and done drugs. To make the ugly world less ugly. To take the sharp edges off everything. To pretend that people were nicer than they were. People in the Program talked about "being present for your life." But what was so great about being present for your life? She never got to that point. She would dry out, sober up, the world would get these ugly edges, and there was nothing to soften anything. Conversations were endless and dull. People at parties were grotesque, stupid, disappointing. Life lacked all sweetness. For we must admit that the sweetness of intermittent oblivion is as necessary to human life as sleep is to waking. Without illusions, we are lost. There is vinegar, not honey, in the rock.

Then, just when things were bleakest, Sally would fall catastrophically in love, hoping for the chemical endorphin high of loving but forgetting how much love put you at the mercy of the one who could give that release. Love led inexorably to drugs. The looseness of love required the looseness of drugs. And then she was back on the roller coaster again.

There was nothing Sally liked better than the beginning of a love affair. Long lunches spent gazing into each other's eyes. Imagining all the qualities you longed for in the other person. Imagining the perfect sexual union, all needs fulfilled, all contact points meeting so the juice of love could flow right through your bones. Sally could fall in love so easily. And out of love so easily. Sally lived to fall in love. And she always fell in love with the wrong person. Her music was inspired by it. And so was her madness. Were the music, the madness, and the love all somehow the same?

The pulse of the music went through her body like an orgasm, making her feel that *she* was an instrument and the whole cosmos was playing her song. "Dear God," Sally would say, "make me an instrument for your music. Play through me what the universe needs to hear. Make me a conduit for your message." She promised to sacrifice everything for that. She had made her pact with the devil. (But a pact you make with the devil at twenty may not be one you want to keep at thirty.)

Sally was capable of doing anything onstage. She didn't feel her separateness from the audience. She became their spirit, screaming, singing, moving to their rhythm. She was in a trance, entranced. It was only offstage that she had a problem.

She thought that everyone else knew how to live but she did not. Secretly she thought she was broken inside. Or missing some part. "The balance wheel is missing," was how she put it to one of her many therapists. And she felt that literally: broken inside. "Teach me to live, teach me to love," was how she put it in one song. "Teach me to balance on my heart."

If Sally always fell in love with the wrong person, it was because she wanted transformation from love. Between her mother's dogged bohemianism and her father's suicidal madness, she was often left to be mothered and fathered by her grandparents. And they were ancient. They had grown up in a different century. Naturally they wanted her to make them young. They wanted immortality, as all progenitors do. They had left their parents and struck out into the world when they were just teenagers—though that word did not exist then. But they were horrified to see the same impulse in her. They coddled her. They tried to hold her too close.

Predictably, she bolted. But what she ran *to* proved worse than what she ran *from*. The music business was a harsher family than the family of her birth. She discovered she hated the road. It smacked of abandonment, and abandonment was what she feared most. The hotel rooms smelled of someone else's cigarettes. Nicotine on the phone receivers, nicotine in the ashtrays, burns on the tabletops. In the diners, the eggs always had a thin film of grease floating on top. And the grits all over the South were either runny or lumpy. And the "home fries" all over the West had brown bits that looked like fried cockroaches. Cups of watery coffee were served with supper in the Midwest. And there were huge bloody steaks that looked like minia-ture abattoirs. Sally hated the food you got outside New York and California. It was a barbaric diet, a diet for cannibals. She became a vegetarian early (for the sake of the animals, she said), would carry dried fruits and nuts with her and buy bananas on the road. For a long time, she lived on banana-and-peanut-butter sandwiches washed down with screwdrivers or cranberry juice and vodka. She lived on vitamin pills and fruits and nuts and vodka. Lots of vodka. "My Russian roots," she used to say.

Later, much later, when she formed her second group—Nobodaddy's Daughter and the Suns, she bought a bus. A big silver bullet that resembled a dirigible on steroids and was outfitted with everything a traveling band might need—even a water bed in the back, which, of course, leaked. The silver blimp was painted with psy-chedelic designs in Day-Glo colors. Day-Glo daisies and Day-Glo sunflowers bloomed above Day-Glo dahlias and Day-Glo tulips. The bus always had an aroma of cannabis and an infestation of ants (no roaches, thank God). On its side was painted NOBODADDY'S DAUGH-TER AND THE SUNS, in livid pink. It was photographed a lot. But the smell. Nobody could photograph the smell.

It was the sixties, and jealousy was not cool, so everyone slept with everyone. Sally slept with her main man, the drummer, Peter Gootch, and with the keyboard man, Harrison Travis, and with whoever else she fancied on the road. She had expanded from her pure folk roots into a hybrid sound the diehards thought a sellout but the record-buying kids adored. The money rolled in and rolled right out. Money managers sprang up like weeds, talking tax shelters, four-for-one write-offs, oil and gas, cattle futures, the lot. Only by the good sense of her grandfather Levitsky was Sally saved from the brink of perpetual tax trauma, since he had had the *sechel* to set up the Sally Sky Trust to catch her song-writing royalties. Thank heaven for that—or she would have been at the mercy of the IRS, whose agents could no longer be bought off with "hats"—as was her grandfather's old habit.

The truth was that Sally remembered almost nothing about the touring years. She was that stoned. When people asked her: "Was it fun being famous?" she said: "I don't know." And she didn't. She wasn't conscious for most of it. What she remembered might as well have been a shadow-puppet show. Auditoriums full of screams and sweat, buses rocking in the night, and always sleeping off some high with low companions. That she was able to go on singing at all was a miracle. It was also a miracle her heart didn't stop. She certainly gave it every opportunity to.

She was twenty-two in that miraculous year 1969, and her voice was heard from Tin Pan Alley to Haight-Ashbury, from SoHo to the Casbah, a sweet soprano sound singing of peace, love, and the danger of trusting anyone over thirty. Sally Sky was more than a singer; she was a symbol of her generation—and you know what happens to symbols. They are likely to be trampled in the mud.

After her third album, *Listen to Your Voice,* went platinum and she was on the cover of *Newsweek,* looking beatific in sky blue—her signature color—she had all kinds of offers from Hollywood, but she chose instead to disappear. She had an accomplice in this disappearance—the first of many.

He was someone whose writing she had loved throughout high school. When she first saw the letter, she couldn't believe it. Max Danzig was her hero. His novel, *A Girl Called Ginger,* about a

bohemian Jewish girl growing up in the Village, was the novel she
identified with most, of any book she had ever read. She had kissed
the misty author picture on the dust cover over and over again. She
believed Max Danzig was the only man who could understand her.
He was known to be a recluse. He never gave interviews. And here
he was, inviting her to come and visit. And signing his name "Max." It
had never occurred to her that anyone called him Max.

> *Dear Sally Sky,*
>
> *I listen to your music and think you are the saddest and most
> beautiful girl in the world. You remind me of my heroine,
> Ginger. Like her, you deserve happiness. Will you let me help
> you give it to yourself? If you ever find the world is too much
> with you, you have a friend and fan in the Northeast Kingdom.*

The invitation came at just the right time. Sally hated the road and
she hated the way she was being preyed upon in the wake of her platinum record, and Danzig miraculously seemed to know this.

She drove to St. Johnsbury, Vermont, and asked the owner of an
antique teddy bear shop where Danzig lived. The owner pointed to a
ridge where a red barn peeped out of the birch trees, surrounded by
wilderness. She gave Sally directions. To her amazement, Sally found
Danzig's barn.

What she later remembered was how *old* he'd looked when she first
saw him outside his house. Slight, small, long white hair. (He hardly
looked that old on the dust jacket.) Tufts of white hair curling out of
his ears. It must be the hired man, she thought, her entire knowledge
of Vermont being Robert Frost's poems. For a moment, she thought
he was her grandfather's age, and she had the impulse to get back in
her car. Then she imagined how wretched her mother would be if she
vanished, leaving no trace, and she made up her mind to stay.

"I knew you'd come," said the writer, looking at her in the most penetrating way. "Am I much older than you expected? I must be. The book picture was taken long ago."

Sally was astonished that he knew what she was thinking. She wanted above all to be known, and he knew her. And there was another moment of panic when she saw those white hairs curling out of his ears, but after a while, she didn't see him or his white hairs at all.

His barn was filled with books and heated by a woodstove. Cats patrolled the rafters. A husky named Nanook guarded the door. Danzig made her a marvelous vegetarian nut loaf for supper that first night. She stayed two years.

Danzig got letters from all over the world. His books were published in languages Sally had never even *heard* of—like Serbo-Croatian and Macedonian. He had foreign editions of his books lining the walls of the barn. The letters Danzig received were heartbreaking. "Dear Mr. Danzig, I am a boy in India who is just like your Ginger. What shall I do with the rest of my life?" Or: "Dear Mr. Danzig, I would like to come and study with you. I have enclosed my first novel in the hopes that you will be able to persuade a publisher to take it on." Or: "Dear Mr. Danzig, You are my sister's favorite writer. She is dying of leukemia. Would you be kind enough to visit her in hospital in Leeds. It would mean the world to her. If you cannot, I understand, but would you please sign these first-day covers?" And then there would be envelopes featuring other writers—Mark Twain or Carl Sandburg, for example. Danzig never signed anything.

It was Sally's job to read them and devise answers—answers that were kind but not too encouraging. Danzig had found over the years that too-encouraging letters promoted more demands, which, when unmet, provoked sheer rage and hatred. It was an impossible task. The misery and heartbreak of the world was in those letters, and no response seemed adequate. Danzig was the Mr. Lonelyhearts of the world's adolescents.

"The saddest thing I have learned is that the line between fan and assassin is perilously thin," Danzig told Sally. "The world is *full* of people who never got enough love, not ever, and all of them write to *me*. If I write back too enthusiastically, they want more and more and more, until eventually I disappoint them. Then they want to kill me. I can't fulfill their dreams. I wonder if God feels that way."

The event that had caused Danzig to stop publishing took place when a prisoner to whom he had written for many years was released from prison and came immediately to Vermont, wanting to move in with the writer. When, after a month, Danzig tried to explain to this fan that much as he empathized with him, he needed to be alone to work, the prisoner felt betrayed and tried to strangle him. In the scuffle that followed, Danzig accidentally shot the man.

"I decided fame was a fraud," Danzig told Sally. "You write to seduce the world, you make it your best friend, but then when the world comes, you have no time, because you are too busy *writing*. And writing requires shutting other people out. More honorable not to build up false expectations."

So instead, Danzig meditated. He wrote haiku, which he taught Sally to copy in calligraphy.

"Only what is not for sale can be uncontaminated," Danzig said. "Poetry is free because publishers do not want it. It remains a private, noncommercial, thus consecrated, act."

His was a philosophy that a twenty-two-year-old who had been traumatized by sudden fame in the music business could find solace in. And Sally did.

Max Danzig read Sally poetry—Dickinson, Roethke, Rukeyser. He encouraged her to write it—a habit that lasted the rest of her life. Sally sang him folk songs, taught him to play the guitar. For a long time they slept in the same bed and did not become lovers. This was a novelty to Sally after the compulsive drugged fornication that went on in the music business. Max understood that Sally trusted no one, and he wanted to win her trust.

"I promise never to fuck you," he said, "but only to make love to you." Sally thought that was the nicest thing a man had ever said to her. When at last they came to physical coupling, Max, who had studied tantra and many other meditative techniques, would remain inside her forever without moving. He would look at her with the softest expression as she reached climax again and again, but he would not lose his erection.

"Why don't you come?" she would ask.

"When you come, the feminine part of me comes," he'd say, "and the manna is released into my soul." They would lie entwined for hours and hours. Sally felt as happy then as she had as a little girl in bed.

Still, she tormented herself with questions. Was it because of her essential fatherlessness—her father had committed suicide when she was a little girl, but no one had told her until years later—that she was with a man forty years her senior? Was it healthy? Was it right? She shared these questions with Max.

"Was what you were doing *before* healthy?" he'd ask. "These questions are pointless, a form of self-torture. Self-torture is your greatest talent. If anyone else were as mean to you as you are to yourself, you'd shriek in pain. Sally—*let it be*. The point is, you aren't drinking, aren't smoking pot. You've never been this healthy, this serene. You say so *yourself*."

"But can I just stay here while the world passes me by?"

"What is the world anyway? The music business? The world is what you choose to make the world. This is your world, our world. We make it ourselves. Everything else is delusion."

Whenever the weather permitted, Sally and Danzig would snowshoe across his property over the deep snow. They would follow animal tracks, put out seed for the birds, salt for the deer. Even the raccoons, those little scavengers, they fed.

"This is real," Danzig would say. "Everything else is delusion."

The mountains were purple, and the smell of wood fires followed them as they crunched through the snow, talking about what was and wasn't real.

Nanook leaped on ahead. At times like this, Sally felt entirely blessed. She thought of neither past nor future. Only the crunch under her feet existed and the smell of burning wood in the air— applewood and oak. The stolen baby bottle was far away. Her questions about her lost father were far away. She refused to remember she had a mother.

There's plenty to do in the country. Danzig read her Blake—not only the "Songs of Innocence and Experience" but the "Prophetic Books," which she hardly understood.

"Don't worry—nobody understands them, not even Blake."

"And Mrs. Blake?"

"Not her either."

They'd walk awhile in the snow.

"Who is Nobodaddy?" Sally would ask.

"Blake's god—the disappointing father figure."

"Like my father!" Sally shrieked. It was an *aha!* moment.

"If you like. . . ."

"Nobodaddy, Nobodaddy . . . I must write a song to Nobodaddy!"

"You must," Danzig said.

And that was how Sally came to write "Nobodaddy's Daughter"—a song that captured a generation's hunger for an absent father.

> *Silent and invisible*
> *as a misplaced glove,*
> *my nobodaddy daddy*
> *sends me nobodaddy love.*
>
> *I seek him in the darkness,*
> *I seek him in your arms,*
> *my nobodaddy daddy*
> *cannot shelter me from harm. . . .*

Shall I bind him with my singing?
Shall I bind him with my joy?
My nobodaddy daddy
My winged life destroys.

I could fly
without him, I could fly—
I know why,
without him I could fly—

Danzig's reading Blake to Sally inspired that song—and his tales of Ireland, which he loved above all other countries, inspired many others. They talked endlessly about going there.

"I want to take you to Ireland, to the Black Valley, the Back of the Beyond, where the elves and sidhes play and glaciers have turned the rock layers upside down. There is a land inhabited only by ghosts and prophecies, a 'land of scholars and saints'—Ireland. A land where the rain wails and 'her name keeps ringing like a bell in an underground belfry. . . .' Or so said Louis MacNeice. I'd love to take you to the last unspoiled place in the world."

"I'd love to go."

"I want to share with you what I've learned about making things. When I used to write for publication, I was always tense. My back would go into spasm when I was finishing a book. But now that I write only for myself, everything is sheer play. Making the words dance together is now a way of being happy. I dance with them. I no longer fret. I would like to teach you how to do that."

"Teach me! Teach me!"

"What I learned in Ireland was that anxiety is the enemy of art. If you relax, treat it all as play, put one foot in front of the other and do the jig, and knock the critic off your shoulder with a nimble walking stick, there's *nothing* you can't do. We were *made* to make things, to play, to dance. We ruin it all with competition, with wanting always to be the best, to win a prize or make a dollar, when actually there is *no* best and the prize is the doing itself and the dollars are never enough and anyway we don't do it for the dollars. The cosmos is in a *constant* state of creation. We have only to tap into the flow. We are already part of it. We have only to say yes to the universe."

Sally would have stayed with Danzig forever, but forces were aligning themselves against her that would make this impossible. Danzig was old. His children were possessive. The second act was waiting in the wings.

She never came to kiss the Blarney Stone until much later. And by then it was too late. By the time she paced upon the battlements and stared, by the time she arose and went to the Lake Isle of Innisfree, peace could never drop slow for her again.

> All forms of mental flow depend on memory, either
> directly or indirectly. History suggests that the oldest
> way of organizing information involved recalling one's
> ancestors, the line of descent that gave each person his
> or her identity as a member of the tribe or family.
>
> —MIHALY CSIKSZENTMIHALYI

Lisette de Hirsch had invited Sara to a luncheon party at her house in Connecticut on a Sunday afternoon in May. It was not the sort of party you could bring a little kid to, so she had to get a sitter for Dove. She took the train to Darien, painfully aware that this was not the chic way to arrive. That would have been by vintage car or new ecological electric wagon, but Sara didn't have options. Still, she knew she looked good in her beige linen jumpsuit with beige linen three-inch platform clogs, her chic new pith helmet swathed in veils against the ravages of the sun.

Lisette's son, a dark-eyed, long-lashed, very tall young man named David, picked her up at the station in one of those new Chinese electric runabouts and took her out to the house, on a gated promontory overlooking Long Island Sound. There were waiters in white jackets lofting trays of champagne in flutes, but Sara didn't drink. She never drank. Her mother had drunk enough for both of them.

David, a lawyer who seemed a few years younger than Sara, led her across the green lawn to where Lisette was waiting, greeting her guests with double-cheeked air kisses.

Sara was introduced to various paunchy elderly tycoons, who fell under the rubric "board members." She had seen a few of them at the Council. It seemed the men all had the names of investment banks—Lazard, Morgan, Goldman, Rothschild—but surely this was a delusion.

Introductions were made, then David took her arm and led her on a stroll along the path that looked out on the Sound.

"How do you like working at the Council?" he asked.

"Is this a trick question?" said Sara.

"Not at all. My mother says you're absolutely brilliant. She has great hopes for you."

Sara watched the sailboats scudding along under puffy white clouds.

"That's good—because I have great hopes for myself," Sara said.

At lunch, Sara was seated at a table with a famous abstract expressionist painter of the sixties who had just married an investment banker, a famous black opera singer of the eighties who had just married an investment banker, and a famous feminist of the seventies who had just married an investment banker.

Once renowned for leading a liberated life, each of them now waxed poetical over engraved stationery, joint bank accounts, and renovating multimillion-dollar real estate. (A house on the Sound cost twelve million and up these days, and on the ocean, thirty million and up.)

The painter, Rebecca Lewin, a willowy brunette with a thrice-lifted face, said, looking uxoriously at her new husband, Laurence Morgan, "I used to feel the whole world was Noah's ark and I was the only one not going two by two."

"I know just what you mean," said the stately opera singer, Roberta Chase.

"I never thought I could be with anyone for *life*," said the tall, slender feminist, Lily Crosswell, "but when I met Philip, I knew. . . ." Toasts were made to love and matrimony and marrying your best friend. Sara felt sick. Suddenly she said, "But if all of you—my heroines—are subsiding into matrimony, then who's to set an example for women like me?"

Lily said: "Of course it's not *necessary* to be married to live a full life."

Rebecca said: "I was so productive during the twenty or so years I was alone."

And Roberta said: "I don't think any woman of ambition should even *think* of marrying until she's fifty! There's plenty of time after that, even for children. My best friend just had triplets at fifty-four!"

Sara felt even sicker. She thought of Dove—so inconvenient, yet so lovable.

David squeezed Sara's hand under the table and shot her a look that said: I understand. But did he?

Later that afternoon, when they were having coffee on the lawn, he asked:

"Has my mom given you the keys to the secret storeroom yet?"

"What secret storeroom?"

"I guess not," said David. "But I know where they are—and if you're nice to me . . ."

"Is this blackmail?" asked Sara.

"I guess so," David said. "Has anyone ever told you how beautiful you are?"

"Yes," said Sara. "Actually they have. . . . Now tell me about the secret storeroom. So far I've been immersed in the photographs, traveling through time as I catalog them for the database. The photographs are fabulous enough—a whole vanished world, the vanished world of our mothers . . . to coin a phrase."

"I don't know if I should tell you about the storeroom . . . yet."

"I have ways of making you talk," said Sara, kicking him gently in the shins.

"I need to know you better," said David.

"You seem to know me pretty well already," said Sara. "What a disgusting conversation at lunch!"

"It does make you wonder, doesn't it?"

"*I'm* trying to figure out how to get divorced, and all these women want to do is get married. Marriage is much overrated."

"Only if you're with the wrong person. If you're with someone who is right for you, it's the most wonderful thing in the world—two best friends venturing through time and space. The three graces back there are right about that. Marriage can mean joint real estate or it can mean freeing each other to do your work, loving each other in good times and bad."

"Have you ever been married?"

"No. That's why I'm such an expert."

"Now—the secret storeroom."

"Oh," said David. "What do you think is the real agenda of the Council on Jewish History?"

"Beats me," said Sara.

"Oh, come on—what do people want when they're rich enough to have everything else?"

"Ummm . . . Immortality? Eternal life? Their names in marble? In gilt? Their brains suspended in nutrient agar, their bodies frozen for the future?"

"You got it!"

"So they're preserving rich old Jews and keeping them on ice?" Sara asked. "Is that the secret storeroom?"

"Almost . . . ," said David. "But not nearly so gruesome. Actually they're collecting family archives, and my mother is charged with figuring out what to do with them. That's where *you* come in."

"I thought your mother was head of development."

"That and everything else," said David. "She endowed the place, and like a lot of people, she thinks money translates into *control*. Fortunately her board agrees with her. That's why they're her board. You see, she's looked at some of these family papers, and they don't necessarily prove what she *wants* them to prove."

"What's that?"

"What do *you* think?"

"That the Jews are the most perfect people on the planet. . . ."

David laughed. "Exactly."

Sara said: "People are people. What's interesting is how mixed up they are."

"So if you were asked to tell your family story through an archive, what would you do?"

"I'd let the materials dictate how the story should be told and what it should say."

"Right," said David. "I'm with you. But there are plenty of other people who would like to destroy any part of the record that says anything negative about the chosen people."

"But weren't we chosen to be *human*?" said Sara.

"*I* think so . . . *you* obviously think so. But my mother thinks we should suppress any details that might be bad for the Jews or give the anti-Semites ammunition. . . . Let's continue this later," said David. "Here comes the lady of the house."

Lisette de Hirsch sailed over to them in her white silk caftan.

"*Here* you are!" she said.

"Here we are," said Sara and David in unison.

By June, New York was steaming like the tropics. A grayish-yellow haze hung over the city, and the humidity became the major topic of conversation. But the underground vault of the Council on Jewish History, David's so-called secret storeroom, was frigid.

Sara had once read about a man who buried portions of his treasure all over his native city, then left his grandchildren nothing but crude, hand-drawn maps as their legacy. Whether they found the treasure or not was up to them.

That was the way Sara felt excavating ancestors in the crypt of the Council.

She had worked her way from photographs through oral history interviews to letters and journals in backward script, but what it all meant was baffling, and what she was meant to do with it was even more baffling. Lisette spoke of a great exhibition, a richly illustrated book, a documentary film. Perhaps all three. Money was no object. It never was an object with her. The point was to show the way the past informed the present, the sanctity of memory, the heroism of the people who embodied memory itself.

The previous night, Lloyd had come to see Dove, walking into Sara's apartment as if he had every right to be there. He had strolled into the kitchen, flung open the refrigerator, and helped himself to an apple. It was a symbolic apple. He bit into it with a loud crunch.

"Daddy! Daddy!" Dove had cried, throwing her arms around his long legs.

Sara was in the process of making dinner after a long day of trudging through archives at the Council. She was deep in thought about what she might do with these materials, and Lloyd's presence was an unwelcome distraction. Sensing that, he seemed to want to stick around.

Lloyd pulled up a kitchen chair and sat down. Dove climbed on his lap. What a cozy scene this was! The profligate papa returns. All is forgiven. Sara's anger at him was temporarily gone. He seemed to know it.

"How's your new job?" he asked.

"Fine," Sara said. She wasn't going to give him the satisfaction of saying anything else.

"Is it okay if I give Dove her bath and put her to bed?" Lloyd asked.

"Yes!" said Dove. How could Sara dent her enthusiasm?

While Lloyd bathed Dove and happy sounds emanated from the bathroom, Sara thought: If I could stop time here and now, we could be together again. And why not? We're a biological unit after all. She remembered the strong sense of fleshly connection she had felt when she first held Dove in her arms and looked at Lloyd through eyes that were blurry with tears. Who could have imagined such a miracle? Such an *everyday* miracle, so ordinary, yet so transcendent. The ubiquity of the miracle made you believe in God. In Goddess.

After Dove was safely tucked in bed, Lloyd came to talk to Sara in the kitchen.

"I still love you," he said.

"What good does that do *me*?" she asked.

"Maybe we can work it out," he said.

"Maybe I'm the queen of Romania," she said.

They went to bed anyway. The worst part of it was that bed still worked for them. It had never stopped working. His smell, his touch, his breath on Sara's neck, all felt perfectly right. No matter how enraged she was at him, he could cut her open and rub sugar in her wounds.

What would the indomitable Sarah Sophia Solomon Levitsky have done? Sara quickly consulted her. She had—she always had—the right answer.

"You can't ride two horses with one behind," Sara said to Lloyd.

"What?" he asked.

"It's the wisdom of the grandmothers of our tribe. Either stay or go, but don't ride two horses with one behind. Or dance at two weddings at the same time."

Was she telling him, or was she telling *herself*? She thought she was telling herself.

However great the sex was, she didn't really want him back *all* the time. She was taking on some of the fierceness of that other Sarah, and she was tempted, for the first time in her life, to bet on herself—something her own mother, Sally, had never really done.

Sara was already half grown when she met her mother. Fourteen, with breasts and periods and lots of questions she was afraid to ask. Her father and his friend Sandrine had taken her to Montana when she was two. At fourteen, she had run away to find her mother, after discovering a furious letter from her that her father had hidden in his sock drawer.

Running away was *exciting*. With money she had saved, she took a series of filthy buses to New York, deeply gratified by knowing that her father would be worried sick. Once in New York, she thought she would stay at a scuzzy Y and call her mother in London. Then she'd ask her to wire a ticket.

But wonder of wonders, Sally was *in* New York when Sara got there. The family gallery was having a show in honor of its late founders, Sarah and Lev. And Sally had come to New York for the opening.

Thrilled to see her long-lost daughter, Sally scooped her up and took her everywhere in New York—from tea at the Mayfair (where she plied her with scones and jam and clotted cream) to shopping on Fifth and Madison (where she bought Sara clothes she had never *seen* in Montana, let alone worn).

Sara would never forget the transition from the Port Authority Bus Terminal to the Mayfair! Nor would she forget what she always thought of as her Holden Caulfield day alone in New York, talking to pigeons and bus drivers and bums sitting on park benches. Even though it was not even a whole day but only a few hours, Sara had mythologized it as a turning point in her life.

Sally was the most glamorous creature Sara had ever seen, and their reunion was ardent. But after that burst of ecstasy, their relationship had never really worked. Sara had always called her mother Sally, not Mom. It was hard enough to call her *anything*, because for

much of her Montana childhood, her father had claimed her mother
was dead. She would never forgive him for that. It was one of many
things she would never forgive him for.

Of course, there had been a scandal and a custody suit—but Sara
learned the details only later, from Sally. She also learned later that
her mother was more than a singer, she was a sort of mascot for
everyone born in the postwar baby boom.

At twenty-two, Sally had been on the covers of *Newsweek* and
Time. By thirty-two, she was in rehab—and Sara had already been
taken away from her. Her fiery grandmother, Salome—still beautiful, still auburn-haired, in her late sixties—had wanted to jump into
the breach and raise Sara on stories of Paris in the crazy years, stories that would get more and more vivid, no doubt, as fewer and
fewer witnesses were alive to contradict them. But Sara's father,
Ham Wyndham, a poet who had once been jailed as a war resister,
had sued for custody, won, and spirited Sara away to Montana long
before it was the "next place." For much of her childhood, she had
helped with the herding of cattle under the jagged mountains,
thinking she had no mother and having no idea where she came
from.

Sara didn't meet her mother again until she took the mad initiative
of running away at fourteen. She was never sorry she had done that,
even if it didn't turn out quite the way she had expected.

After their passionate reunion, her mother of course sent her to
finishing school in Switzerland with the sons of Arabian oil sheiks and
the other neglected daughters of rock stars. Eventually Sara wound
up at university in England, reading history. By then Sally was living
on her ASCAP earnings in Europe, mostly sober but something of a
shadow of her former self. She hated fame and all its trappings, didn't
want a TV in the house, and made sure Sara had one of those
European educations that make you a misfit in America forever after.
Sara was determined to be a historian, not an artist of any sort.
Empirical truth was what she was after—science, not art.

Sally had tried to evoke for Sara what it was like growing up in the sixties: how Yoko Ono was a conceptual artist who did photographs of people's bottoms (before she became the most famous Beatle wife), how you could walk down the streets of New York and suddenly be hit by a dense, aromatic cloud of marijuana smoke, how people suddenly started dressing like maharajas, African chieftains, ragged gypsies. For all that, Sally said, "the sixties" were more a creation of yearning journalists (yearnalists) than anything else.

For a while Sally lived in London because her AA group was there. She took up AA like a religion. Sobriety was her revelation. Day and night, she made herself available for people with problems, people who were in danger of losing their sobriety. She gave service. Sara remembered being jealous of Sally's "pigeons" and wondering what *she* had to do to become one of them. They seemed to get more mothering than Sara did. She wanted Sally to be a mother so badly that she mothered *her* in propitiation. It didn't work.

What did Sally live on? ASCAP and art. But she lived far more modestly than she had to. Levitsky had left her enough paintings to take care of several old ages, and she received a steady flow of income from her songs—which were still being played around the world.

From time to time, someone would want to make a movie based on one of Sally's ballads, and there would be long pointless meetings, endless negotiations, until eventually Sally threw up her hands and scuttled the project over some detail. She really sought obscurity and hated the thought of losing it. But all her protestations were of no use, because Hollywood, being Hollywood, would take all the details of her story and rip it off anyway. At least half a dozen movies used versions of her hegira—from *A Star Is Born* to *The Rose*. Her life was in danger of becoming a cliché.

◆

"My generation," she used to say, "was told that fame was the greatest good. Stupidly we believed it—at least as credulous teenagers we did. In fact, fame is merely the fact of being misunderstood by millions of people."

As an example of this, Sara's mother always used to point out how people's attitudes toward her changed when they realized she was "Sally Sky."

"They become suddenly respectful, hesitant, looking for some benefit, some angle. But I am the same person—a stumbling human being. Why do they want me to be omnipotent?"

Sara wanted her mother to be omnipotent. All children wish for this. Sara did *not* want her mother to acknowledge being a stumbling human being. Sara needed a rock, an altar, a goddess. And what she got instead was "Easy does it," "Feelings are not facts," and "Ego equals Easing God Out."

Sara came to hate the Program. "A cheap synthetic religion for a godless generation," she called it privately. And as soon as she got the chance, she called it that publicly too. Sally was devastated. She didn't understand her only offspring. And that was why Sara was so ripe to fall in love with someone like Lloyd.

Sara fell in love with Lloyd the way an orphan falls in love. He was older, of course, and her teacher in all things.

They met at a Sunday lunch in Hampstead. A motley assortment of people: Sally's friends and pigeons, some poets, novelists, creative flotsam and jetsam. She spotted Lloyd immediately. He was handsome, for starters, and he had that cynical smile that said: I don't belong here and neither do you. He was dark-haired, green-eyed, clever, tall. He looked at Sara as if she were the only woman on earth.

They made excuses and went to walk on the Heath. It was late March. There were daffodils everywhere. Sara felt suddenly grown up, being with him. She wanted, more than anything, to be out of the grip of her feuding parents. She wanted not to be the hostage in some ancient war, begun before her time. Lloyd kissed her at the top of the Heath among the daffodils. Then he told her she was too young and they should go back.

"Too young for what?" she asked. She had that perfect self-possession and poise the children of alcoholics have. It made her seem much older than her age. If he was going to resist her, then she was going to have him. It was as simple as that. She knew most people are so indecisive that if you make up your mind to have something, *anything,* you can. She made up her mind to have Lloyd. He didn't know what hit him. Sara moved in on his life and facilitated everything, as she had learned to do for her mother.

"I believe there is no man you cannot have if you will do everything for him," she told her best friend in London, Cecily Hargrove.

Cecily said: "Dunno."

But then Cecily was a Sloane Ranger, with her own BMW, a family manse in St. John's Wood, a sixteenth-century castle in Kent, a restored farmhouse in Tuscany, and an amazing Art Deco villa in Beaulieu, used only two months a year: December and August. There was also an oceangoing yacht called *Cecily,* registered in Panama, where Cecily had never been.

Cecily's banker father raised money for the Tories. Her mother was a famous interior designer, who did up hotels all over the world. She even had a hotel named after her in London. The Augusta, it was called, and it was tiny, fully booked, and madly chic. Famous actors stayed there. And opera stars. And well-heeled young Chelsea matrons who booked rooms for midweek afternoons and paid only in cash.

Cecily's mother was a dame in her own right, and her father was a knight. *Arise, Sir Rafe* (spelled "Ralph"). Nobody remembered that his parents had been born in Hungary and fled in 1956. And certainly nobody had to know that her mother was a Russian-Jewish baby brought to London from Moscow via Berlin at the age of oneish— whenever that may have been. Dame Augusta was so plastically surgerized that she couldn't close her eyes. Naturally she never told her age or place of origin. As far as anyone knew outside of *Burke's Peerage*, her country seat in Kent had been the home of her ancestors.

Cecily had been born so privileged that she was languid. She loved Sara because Sara was definitely *not*. She adored get-up-and-go. She adored Sara's adamancy about not drinking or smoking dope. Cecily had a problem with dope. She had already been to three of the most expensive rehabs in the States. And she hung out with Sara, hoping that she would be the fourth.

Sara was right about Lloyd. She had his number. She troweled on the charm, and Lloyd got hooked on her in record time. She followed all the rules in a book that told women how to catch men. The book was written for people with room-temperature IQs, but it *worked*. It argued that men were hunters and women were gatherers and if you wanted to catch a man you had to understand that.

Sara understood. She'd understood it even *before* she read that book. She knew it instinctively.

Lloyd was astonished to find out that Sara was a virgin.

"Girls aren't virgins anymore," he said.

"If your mother has had the entire musicians' union," Sara said, "you have to do *something* to distinguish yourself."

"How can I sleep with you when it's such a heavy responsibility?" he asked.

"Stop thinking of it as a heavy responsibility."

"I can't," he said.

So she seduced Lloyd. Even though she was a virgin and he was "experienced," she had her way with him. And he felt honor-bound to marry her. She had counted on that all along.

Of course she seduced Lloyd in her mother's London flat. How could she *not*? She brought Lloyd home and had him in her own bed. In the morning, Sally made them breakfast.

Sally and Lloyd were faintly embarrassed. Sara was exultant. It was the very best moment of her life thus far when Sally came to wake her up and found Lloyd draped nakedly around her. Sara was oh so pleased with herself.

"I guess you'll just have to accept the things you cannot change," she told her mother.

"It's *your* life," her mother said, wanting a drink so badly she could taste it.

Sara consciously made an old-fashioned marriage with Lloyd. She took care of him. She took care of Dove. She collapsed her identity into his. Sara was convinced that all the unhappiness she sensed in her mother's life came from her desire to be the most flamboyant of a flamboyant clan. Sara would instead cling to *Kinder, Kirche, Küche*. She would travel back to the past.

"I suppose I am a typical member of the class of 2000," Sara wrote in her journal:

Since our parents were credulous enough to think that a drop of LSD in the water supply would bring world peace, we were cynical about everything. Since our parents were all divorced when we were young, we were never going to get divorced. We were as skeptical as they were naive, as tough as they were tender. We thought they were dopes— undisciplined hippies. We hated their narcissism, their self-indulgence. We thought their values sucked. We called ourselves slackers—with pride. A slacker was the opposite of a hippie. A slacker knew life was no rose garden. A slacker expected so little, she could *never* be disappointed. A slacker was disillusioned even before she—or he—could vote.

In prep school and college we all wrote memoirs—even though we had not yet much to remember. We were told the novel was dead and all that counted was personal experience—but we had had so little personal experience that it was hard to know *where* to begin. I decided it was better to study history. At Oxford I was taught by historians who believed that *all* subjective data was suspect, but now I am beginning to wonder whether there is anything *but* subjective data.

When Lloyd was writing his dissertation about the history of the Third Reich—his thesis, of course, was that the average German *delighted* in murdering Jews—he had found all sorts of proof: photos, home movies, diaries, journals. I helped him to assemble this material. We pay homage to the past first of all by documenting it. This is a great lesson for a historian to learn.

Like me, Lloyd was trained by Namierian historians, who believed that only impartial documents can tell the story of a given period. His research was always heavy with inventories of *things*: bank records, legal documents, birth and death records. He loved primary sources, mistrusted the secondary ones. This will probably turn out to be a terrific preparation for my work at the Council—whatever it turns out to be.

And then she scrawled at the bottom of the page: "*I am never sleeping with Lloyd again!*"

11

Sarah to Sara ✦ RUB OF LOVE

> *Little children don't let you sleep, big children don't let you live.*
>
> —YIDDISH PROVERB

Sarichka, my love, I left off my story when Mama and Tanya and Bella and Leonid arrived from the old country. You will remember that Levitsky had disappeared, that Sim was in jail, that Lucretia eventually laid claim to poor weak Sim, who had not the strength to resist. When Mama and the family arrived, I realized that no matter how much I had missed them, I was *never* going to be free again. Now I had to live in worriment about their welfare. Every decision I made had to be made as part of a family. And families may be all we know of heaven but they are also all we need of hell.

I am telling you this because I want you to appreciate the rare moment you find yourself in—lonely, yes, but also free. My mama used to say: "You can get married in an hour, but troubles last a life-time." The same is true with families. You miss them, you yearn for them, and then they come back—and troubles last a lifetime.

My brother, Leonid, for example, thought that Leonid Solomon was a good enough name for Russia, but in America he had to be Lee Swallow, the Sanitary Star. It was not enough he should make a fortune; he also had to have a wife to squander it. This is what America meant to him. Bella and Tanya turned into "sweaters"—they ran a sweatshop—and exploited new girls from Russia the way *I* had once been exploited. Then Bella and Tanya got married, and their husbands exploited both the girls *and* them. You wouldn't want to know how most of your family made their fortune—and that was *before* Salome introduced Levitsky to Robin the forger—who eventually put his mark on the Levitsky gallery and made another bundle. All I am going to say is that the world has a few more "Vermeers" than the master knew about.

When you look at the names of benefactors on buildings, notice that they don't engrave up there how their ancestors made the money in the first place. Behind every great fortune lies a great crime. I believe it was George Bernard Shaw who said that. He knew a thing or two, for a *goy*.

Nobody ever encourages you to tell how *Zaydeh* really made his money. Sweeping his competitors' goods from the shelves, a little harmless price fixing, *a bissel* collusion, a soupçon of antitrust . . . the family would be furious if you remembered any of *that*. Sweet little *Zaydeh* no longer had a bodyguard when *they* knew him. Or a driver who packed a rod, excuse the expression. Or a revenue agent he bought off when an audit loomed. ("Buy him a hat," Levitsky used to tell his son-in-law Robin when there was a problem with the taxman.) The audits were always mysteriously forgotten, or they came out "no change." How Levitsky *loved* that expression, "no change"! In those days revenue agents were just *nudnicks* who wanted a nice "hat" like anyone else—imagine! But when we remember sweet little *Zaydeh*, we don't think about this *chazerei*—we only remember his pockets lined with chopped liver.

I know you are feeling pretty rotten about jumping into bed with Lloyd—who I never liked, by the way. But as my mama used to say: "A slice off a cut loaf is never missed." (I may have quoted it once too often to my Salome, who took it more seriously than anything else I told her. You should only pray never to have a daughter like her.)

Nowadays, looking at my family, I am not so very thrilled and delighted about the way they all turned out—but you, my little namesake, I think you have a real chance to redeem your mother, of blessed memory. *You* could become like the woman I knew who danced all the way to America. Your grandmother Salome, if the truth be known, was something of a wild one—a *kurveh,* as we say in Yiddish. But Salome had a lot of good theories, I'll give her that. She was something of a philosopher. About anti-Semitism she was never wrong. She had a nose for it. Many Jews have this nose, but Salome had something more. She was brilliant. She wrote poetry, which she never published. She was prophetic, ahead of her time. You know that she wrote one of the first novels of what is now called the Holocaust—even though she wasn't there, Charlie. Of course her *meshuggeneh* Aaron, of blessed memory, *was.*

Now the Holocaust has become a miniseries. (There's no business like *shoah* business.) It *wasn't* then. In the forties, it was hell to even convince people that there *was* such a thing as a Holocaust. The newspapers in America didn't write about it. Even the newspapers owned by the Jews. They were afraid to be too sympathetic to foreigners. So the Holocaust was a secret. God forbid the allrightnik American Jews should get too cozy with refugees.

Oh, yes, we all had friends from Europe who came here talking about horrible things: mass murders in the East, relatives who disappeared, concentration camps, mail that returned "addressee unknown," businesses seized, houses, farms . . . But we didn't always know *what* to think. Refugees are always full of *bubbameisehs.* They're always *a bissel meshuggeh*—and who can blame them?

But Salome understood the Holocaust long *before* it was a miniseries. She heard stories from Aaron, of blessed memory. Of course she used some of his experiences in her novel—which, by the way, you should read. Men have been writing novels using their wives' stories for six thousand years, but a woman does it and suddenly it's a *shande*? I call it discrimination against women, that's what I call it. Salome was the closest thing I ever knew to a genius, the smartest person in a very smart family, but she was so *meshuggeh* she didn't always *use* her talents. She was too *meshuggeh* about men. Boy-crazy from the start. Let that be a lesson to you. She also had no *sitsfleish*.

Talent is talent, but it's not *enough*. You have to be able to sit in your chair and work. And work. And *work*. And WORK. When they reject your work or cheat you out of your payment, you just work some *more*. You *never* give up. Never. I *had* that tenacity. Salome did not. She was a regular princess of Israel. *My* fault. I showered her with goodies. I gave her all the love I lacked from Levitsky, all the kisses I could not give to you know who. And it spoiled her. And so did the money. By then we were making a living. We were comfortable. (In truth, we were rich, but I was too superstitious to admit it. *Kayne hore*—God might strike me dead.)

When Salome left for Paris, I missed her terribly, as only a mother could miss a daughter. I felt rejected, abandoned. I knew she had to seize her life—but why did it have to be at my expense? I wanted her home with me forever. And knowing that, she had no choice but to run away. She had to run away at first to come home at last. She had to lose herself in Paris and the Berkshires to find herself at last.

Mothers and daughters—it's a comedy, but also a tragedy. We fill our daughters with all the *chutzpah* we wish for ourselves. We want them to be free as we were not. And then we *resent* them for being so free. We resent them for being what we have made! With grand-daughters, it's so much easier. And great-granddaughters.

The truth is, Salome was more like me than I ever thought. That was the problem. Like me, she thought too much. About everything: life, art, anti-Semitism. Especially anti-Semitism. She always believed that as Jews we were resented mainly for our refusal to compromise. We believe our God is the most superior God of all, and we laugh when the *goyim* try to convert us. Later we cry.

Salome would brazenly say to *goyim*—any who would listen: "We worship a book, and you worship a bloody corpse on a cross—I fail to see why that's preferable." And people would look at her as if she'd taken leave of her senses. She would say *anything* to shock, but usually she restricted this comment to the bohemian circles in which she normally traveled. When she said it at a cocktail party at *my* gallery to the canon of the Cathedral of Saint John the Divine (Levitsky and I always liked to have a few Episcopalians around—it added class, we thought), he didn't quite know what to say, ecumenical though he was. I think he said, "Hmmm. I see." I believe this is the *goyishe* equivalent of *Gevalt*.

Why are Jews funny? Consider the alternative. We laugh so as not to drown in our own tears.

Leave Lloyd alone. You have a nice new suitor, in that young fellow whose mother is the queen of the Council on Jewish History. But the truth is, you don't *need* a man. Don't make the mistakes I made. Even in my day, marriage was not any longer a woman's only destiny. I took that traitor Levitsky back because my mother *blackmailed* me into it. Or maybe I blackmailed myself. I felt I had to be *coupled*. For Mama's sake. And the world seemed too dangerous for a woman alone. But the truth is I carried him more than he carried me.

I am trying to help you to be strong. "Why *should* I be strong?" you may ask. Because you owe your life to your ancestors' strength. Because we are all *counting* on you to be strong. Your strength is *our* strength now. We live through you. And by the way, we're *watching*! Not to make you feel guilty or anything. . . . But we are your guardian angels now.

I will never forget the day Mama and the rest of the family arrived at Ellis Island. It was the day after Yom Kippur in . . . it must have been 1912, but I'm never sure of dates. I waited in a gang of people at Battery Park under the elevated for my darling family, my very own *greeners,* to arrive from the island of tears.

American relatives, eager to show off their broken English, their bowler hats, their clean-shaven faces, their Yankee finery, waited in a throng held back with billy clubs by the high-helmeted Irish cops. What a contrast there was between the new arrivals and those who waited for them! The *greeners* wore kerchiefs, wigs, shawls, carried battered pots and pans, packs of bedclothing on their backs. Bedraggled from their wretched days at sea, blinking their eyes at the American sunlight, they actually *looked* green around the gills as they greeted their sleek American *landsleit*: another race—no, another species.

The Yankee cousins were unencumbered by baggage, wore three-piece suits, bow ties, elegant skirts and waists, hats brimming with feathers and flowers. They had gold teeth where the immigrants often had *missing* teeth. Gold teeth then were a sign of prosperity. (I should have a nickel for every one the Nazis later pulled out and melted down.) They wore their gaudiest Yankee finery to Battery Park. They wanted to impress. They wanted to blind the eyes of their relatives with their success.

The day before had been the holiest day of the year, and I wondered what Mama had done to worship on that sacred day. I wondered and worried. I was already six months pregnant and beginning to be unable to hide my condition.

Suddenly there they were! *Mamele* with her *sheitl* and kerchief, her shawl, her clumsy shoes—and cousin Bella with her huge bosom, her ruddy cheeks, her boisterous manner. My sister Tanya had grown up in the seven years since we parted. And Leonid was a man! He pushed forward to meet me, held his strong arms on my shoulders, and said:

"*Mayne schwester, meine shayner schwester . . .*"

And *Mamele* cried. She could hardly *talk* for crying. And then she patted my belly.

"*Nu*?" she said.

I nodded my head in its gorgeous hat. "This one is blessed," I said. (That's how well I could predict Salome's future!)

The first few days with them were delicious. They raved about my studio on Union Square, told endless tales of Russia, of the ship, the *Fatherland*, of Yom Kippur services on Ellis Island, where the fine ladies from HIAS—the Hebrew Immigrant Aid Society—had served a delicious dinner to break the fast: matzo-ball soup, fish, lamb, dried prunes and apricots, cakes and tea, all presented on paper plates so we wouldn't worry if the dishes were kosher. As the *greeners* left the dining hall, each was given dried prunes, fresh apples or oranges.

"In Russia, they beat us and burn us. In America, they feed us *pflommen*, oranges, apples!" Leonid said. "Even on the boat I made dozens of deals. . . . God bless America, kiddo! I bin learnin' English. In America, you got to speak English—right, *schwester*?"

I looked at Leonid with his greenhorn clodhopper shoes, his one good suit, made out of heavy Russian wool, far too thick for a warm New York September. He *looked* like a *greener*, but he already understood what there was to understand about America.

"Time *ist* money—*nu, schwester*?" he said, pinching my cheek. He made the universal money sign with his thumb and forefinger.

"*Gelt*," he said, "is the king of America, *nu*?"

Tanya meanwhile hugged me, and Bella assessed my elegant clothes.

"*Soora*," said Bella, "*du bist eine Yankee!*" And I laughed and hugged them all to the belly containing your grandmother Salome. Then we all went back to Union Square.

I was working for the picture fakers Filet and Cooney in those days, so I often traveled. I would take the overnight train to Palm Beach, and Mama would worry about "*das kind, das kind*. . . ."

"*Mamele*—in America pregnant women *work*, ride trains, walk in the streets. . . ."

And Mama would cluck her tongue, and produce amulets from the old country to protect my baby, and worry, worry, worry.

She was shocked at how irreligious the Jews were in America. Where was the *mikveh*? Why did the men shave their faces and work on Saturdays? Why did the married women wear their own hair? Why were the children so disrespectful to their elders? Where could you get fresh-laid eggs?

I installed Mama in the kitchen, where she felt most comfortable, and I found sewing jobs for Tanya and Bella, but Leonid needed no help from me. He was out like a shot, drumming up business, learning English, working first as a butcher's boy, then somehow getting the use of a borrowed wagon and making a deal with a Chinaman to wash and starch the butchers' gowns. From these humble beginnings, he became the "founder and president" (as he always used to say) of Sanitary Star, which, by the end of the Great War, was providing linens to all the swellest restaurants in New York. And so Leonid Solomon became Lee Swallow, with diamond cuff links and diamond studs and a string of mistresses—Ziegfeld girls mostly—not to mention his glittering wife, Sylvia, whom I *never* liked. It must have been 1912 when they came—I'm sure of it—because a few months later, right after Christmas, I took the whole family—the *ganse meshpocheh*—to see *Peg O' My Heart* at the Cort Theatre, starring a younger-than-springtime Laurette Taylor. I attribute many of my brother's tastes to this outing. He *never* forgot the first Yankee play he saw in America. Mama hated it, not understanding a word. To her it was all *goyishe mishegas*. But Leonid—or Lee, as he already called himself—fell in love with Laurette Taylor as Peg (as only a *yiddel gruber yung* can fall in love with a *shiksa* actress), and I believe he determined then and there to have an English Tudor house like the one in the stage set—not to mention a *goyishe*-looking wife. As for Bella, she always preferred *The Gold Diggers,* which we saw a few years later. And Tanya was a devotee of Second Avenue (which in those days meant the Yiddish theater and only the Yiddish theater).

And Mama? Well, Mama never liked *any* play but *Der Dybbuk* at the Yiddish Art Theatre.

"Dat's vat I call a *play*," she said in English. "Broadvay you can have. . . ." And Leonid and I applauded, because she rarely said a word in English—though she understood a lot more than she let on.

Ah, my little mama—*Mamele*—how I miss her! And the older I get, the more she is with me. She is always with me. She used to drive me absolutely *meshuggeh* with worriment, but she is part of me. She is also part of you.

It was your mother, Sally, who began the whole project of interviewing me. This was when you were very small and she was overcome with family feeling. She could hardly believe how strong her feelings were. She fell head over heels in love with you—the way we all fall in love with our babies. Then, when your father kidnapped you (she had all kinds of plans to kidnap you back) and did all that legal *hoo-ha*, she wanted me to narrate the family roots for you, to talk to you on tape for the future, so you would know where you came from and why.

The future is such an odd concept. What do we know of the future? What do we even know of the present or the past? Your mother was not really a bad sort. It was never easy for her, with her father threatening to commit suicide all the time—and finally succeeding. I blame that side of the family for the alcoholism too, by the way. Levitsky used to say: "To mine opinion, they were all *shickers*, those Wallinskys, and if Hitler hadn't got them, the bottle would have." "*Oy oy oy—shicker* is a *goy*" was one of his favorite lines—never mind whether or not it was relevant, the Wallinskys being, of course, as Jewish as we.

Sally's life was hard from the beginning. Salome batted her back and forth to California depending on her romantic life—Marco,

Robin, God knows who else. Levitsky and I adored her, but how could we make up for the father she did not have? We tried, God knows. I think even Robinowitz tried—but he was another *vantz*, it turned out. He tried to steal the gallery from all of us, and your mother eventually threw *him* out too. (Sally's long lost half-brother, Lorenzo, turned out to be a nogoodnik also. That's why I think he really is Robin's flesh and blood—though Salome was never one hundred percent sure *who* the father was.) After Salome threw Robin out, she invited her old friend Marco to live with her, but she never married him. She'd had enough of marriage. And now she decided that Lorenzo—your uncle who finally took over the Levitsky Gallery—was *Marco's* son. *Veys nicht,* as my mother used to say. "Little children you hold in your arms; big children stand on your head." Of course, it's better in Yiddish, like all these things. . . .

Sally finally seemed to find herself when she found that guitar, but then she got *too* famous—there *is* such a thing as too famous. When she vanished and nobody knew where she was all that terrible time, Salome nearly lost her mind.

"Mama—Sally is missing!" she screamed to me on the telephone. And she hired all sorts of detectives to find her. I tried to comfort her. "Daughters always come back," I said. "After all, even *you* came back."

"This is different—you don't understand," Salome yelled.

Sally had taken up with that old writer in Vermont, as I suppose you know by now. Who doesn't? It was in the *New York Times*. Then, after he died, his children descended and kicked her out. She ran away again and this time joined up with a commune of women who called themselves witches. She claimed that the Jewish religion was *patriarchal*—her word—and witchcraft was better. She was always looking for some sort of salvation. That was her problem. There is no easy salvation—patriarchal, matriarchal, schmatriarchal. Mama used to say: "God gave more wit to women than to men." But I'm afraid Sally was the exception that (as they say) proves the rule.

No, I don't really mean that. I loved Sally—*how* I loved her. She was a wonderful little girl, so smart, so clever, so *musical*. She wrote music before she could even put down the *notes*. She would sing to her piano teacher, Lillian Zemann, and Lillian would say: "Perfect pitch! The child has perfect pitch! And she composes like a Mozart! A Mozart she is! I never met a child like her! God help her. Sometimes I think she's too talented for a girl."

"Lilly," I would say, "bite your tongue! How can a girl be too talented?"

"I have to explain this to *you*—of all people?" Lilly would ask. "You *know* what means too talented. You, Salome, your granddaughter. It's a curse and you know it: smart, talented, headstrong, opinionated women get their own way everywhere but in bed! I should tell *you* this? *You should be telling me!*"

Lorenzo was also part of the problem. Salome couldn't help being in love with him, the only *boychik*, and Sally felt displaced. He was a little *vantz* too—spoiled by Levitsky, spoiled by both his daddies (they both claimed him), and treated like the Prince of Wales. He had riding lessons in Central Park, wore handmade boots from Hermès in Paris, was driven to school by the chauffeur. I told Salome not to do it, but she couldn't help herself. She made her only son into a monster. Of course he assumed the family business was his—and the truth was, Levitsky wouldn't ever have thought of training a girl to it, however smart she was. Later, when Sally discovered she hated fame and all its trappings, she figured she'd have a place with Renzo in the family business—but Renzo didn't want the competition. He figured he had the inheritance all sewed up. Then he married that tough cookie, and she didn't want her sister-in-law around either, wanted *her* children to inherit. It was not that Sally lacked for money. She needed a job, a cause, something to do—but Renzo and Babs kept her out. That was the beginning of the end.

Lorenzo really had delusions of grandeur. He was an expert at bossing the staff, having suits made in London, sending home cases of wine from France, collecting starlets and polo ponies. Levitsky used to say he was working on growing a foreskin. He would send his mother pictures of himself on horseback and she would *kvell*. *My* mama used to say: "If a poor man ate a chicken, one of them was sick." God knows what she would have said about polo ponies! Probably: "If a Jew rides a pony, one of them is an ass." Never tell that to your uncle Lorenzo. He doesn't have such a sense of humor about himself.

12

Falling Stars

If the rich could hire people to die for them, the poor would make a nice living.

—YIDDISH PROVERB

David de Hirsch kept phoning, and Sara kept saying she had no baby-sitter and couldn't go out to dinner. He offered to come up to her apartment and make her dinner, and eventually—it was the fifth call—she agreed.

David turned out to be an extraordinary cook. He brought fresh vegetables from his parents' Connecticut place, live lobsters from a fish market downtown, shallots, herbs, wine, newly baked bread. While Sara put Dove to bed, David happily made dinner.

"Do you do this all the time? Or is it special for me?" Sara asked.

"The latter."

"Why?"

"Because I want to. Because this was the only way I figured I'd see you again. You're pretty resistant."

"Like a strain of flu outevolving an antibiotic?"

"At least I'm the *cure* in your figure of speech, not the disease."

"Don't be so sure. I'm a bad bet for romance. I'm still married, for starters. And I'm through with love."

"Nobody who looks like you is through with love."

"You're wrong. Looks are deceiving."

"Have some lobster," said David.

"When in doubt, eat *trayfe*."

"I know the way to a woman's heart—feed 'em and fuck 'em."

"How delicately you put it," said Sara.

"I try," said David, "to cover my terror with bravado."

They talked about their lives. Sara told David about her childhood memories of Montana—now distant as the moon—how strange it was to suddenly realize she *did* have a mother, her finding Sally, her estrangement from her father, many other things she was surprised to find herself able to talk about.

"So where is your mother now?"

"Dead, unfortunately. I would like to ask her so many things. I'm hardly ready to be motherless. Though actually I was often motherless even when she was alive."

"What happened to your mother?"

"She started to drink again after I married Lloyd and left London with him. She was furious with her brother for some financial shenanigans he pulled. She felt abandoned by me and everyone. She fell apart. Supposedly it was a car crash that killed her. I know it was the booze in her blood. She was allergic to alcohol. When she picked up a drink, she was actually *saying* she wanted to die. She was an alcoholic, and I made fun of her support system because I was ignorant and stupid and angry—a snot-nosed kid—and I feel responsible. She was much more fragile than anyone knew. And all those meetings were holding her together. I should never have made fun of what was essential to her—her religion."

"It's not your fault."

"But I think it *is* my fault." Sara started to cry. "I blew it with my only mother. You don't get a second chance. Or a second mother."

"Maybe she blew it with you. A mother is supposed to be able to take guff from her own daughter without falling apart. It's the deal."

"It is?"

"Look," David said, "I found out only last year that I was adopted. I was furious with my mother for not telling me—then, gradually, I worked it through. I railed and screamed for several months, and then it hit me that I was not promised perfection. Who has an uncomplicated life? The truth is, we all have to make up our own lives, invent our own ancestors, sort out our own memories. In the end, we are all self-made."

"How do you know that at your young age?"

"I'm not so young," said David.

"How old are you?"

"I was born in 1980. I'm old enough to know I'm madly in love with you and plan never to let you out of my sight."

"You can't know that. You hardly know me."

"I can. I do."

"David, this is ridiculous," Sara said.

"Why? Because I'm so sure and people aren't supposed to be sure? Look, I'm not asking you for anything—just the right to make you dinner from time to time and talk to you. Why is that so scary?"

Sara looked at his sweet, earnest face and asked herself why she was so scared.

"I don't want to be dropped on my head again," she said. "Anyway, I don't need a man. . . . Why should I need a man?"

"For fun," said David. "Isn't that enough of a reason? And of course because I was the one who got you into the secret storeroom."

He did the dishes and went home without making a pass—the first of many nights he did that.

✦

When Lloyd discovered that Sara was busy nearly every night, that she seemed to have a regular dinner date—even though she was always home—he became very agitated.

"Why can't I come up and see Dove?" he asked. "Are you trying to keep my child from me?"

"You can take her on the weekend. I just can't have you wandering in here as if you still live here. It's too difficult for me."

"You have a boyfriend."

Sara said nothing. She didn't have a boyfriend. She had, merely, a friend. It was nice to have a friend. She didn't say: You have a friend, too. She didn't say: You had one first. She knew that Lloyd could be dangerous if aroused to ire. She was going to outsmart him. It was a matter of survival.

"I'll see you on Friday when you come to pick up Dove," she said. "Got to go."

"Good for you," said David when she hung up. "You don't owe him anything."

How could she explain that she felt she owed him everything even though there was no reason for it.

"Then why do I feel my life is tangled root and branch with him?"

"Because it *was.* But you've started to untangle it. Now I'm going to make you homemade *orechiette.*"

"Now that you know you have my guidance, Sarichka, what are you afraid of?" Sarah Sophia Solomon Levitsky seemed to whisper in her ear.

"Everything and nothing," said Sara.

"What did you say?" asked David.

"I think I was just talking to myself," Sara said.

The truth was that Sara was looking for flaws in David, signs that he was insincere, a bounder, the sort of man *Sally* would have become involved with, but she couldn't find any—not yet. Her mother had been a terrible judge of character, had constantly fallen in love with sycophants, interviewers, managers, R and D men, people who had hidden agendas. Sara had always been afraid that her mother's bad judgment would come to trip her up. She was very hard on herself, always looking for her own Achilles' heel.

"Does your mother know we're friends?" Sara asked David later when they sat down to eat his homemade pasta.

"Not from me, she doesn't. I think it would be too complicated if she knew. You haven't said anything, have you?"

"It's the *last* thing I'd talk about with her."

"Good," said David. "Stick to work. Talk to her about what you're finding in the archive."

"That's the problem," Sara said. "What I'm finding is not going to fulfill her theories about Jewish women. She's not going to *like* what I'm finding. My feeling is that she wants glorious heroines, and what I'm finding are women dancing with feet of clay."

"So maybe that's your story."

"It *can't* be my story."

"Let your story be whatever your story is," David said.

Sara remembered when she was summoned back to London to say goodbye to her mother's body. They had tried to put the pieces back together, but it was obvious they were held together by her clothes. Sara flung herself on the coffin, weeping, but even as she did that she wondered what she was weeping for. For the mother she never really had? For her own guilt? For her mother's wasted life?

The AA pigeons gathered around, clucking. They were kind, but they had no idea what Sara needed. Lorenzo made a brief appearance, weeping for his own mortality and he tried to enlist Sara in a scheme to sell her mother's remaining artifacts to some rock and roll museum. Sara was so offended that she fled from him.

He returned to the Connaught, where he had a girlfriend the age of his niece waiting. And the *crowds* that showed up! Hundreds of diehard fans arrived in the rain, holding aloft banners and pictures of Sally Sky. One scuzzy-looking man had an umbrella hung with pictures of Sally, circa 1969, hand-painted by someone with absolutely no talent. His raincoat was covered with buttons from Sally's concerts in the sixties and early seventies. One pathetic old hippie tunelessly sang Sally's most famous songs. "Listen to your voice," he croaked. "My nobodaddy daddy," he whined.

The fans even jostled forward in the chapel, wanting to touch Sally's corpse, tear off a piece of her shroud (a floaty Zandra Rhodes dress), or clip a lock of her hair. But the coffin was closed. So they turned to Sara instead. They tried to photograph her, to tear off bits of *her* clothes, at least to touch her. She recoiled. Her skin crawled. Why did they want *relics*? Should she have brought "pigges bones" to sell, like Chaucer's Pardoner? The best part of Sally was in her *music*. Why did they want pieces of her daughter's clothes? No wonder John Lennon never left the house! If Sally's fans loved her songs so much, why didn't they know that all that was left of her was in her music?

Sara found the funeral so upsetting that she wanted to flee, to see no one, but she was trapped in the chapel by all the surging fans. Pushed by the crowd, she *couldn't* escape. She wanted to scream, but no sounds came.

Sara suffered terribly from claustrophobia, which she could usually conquer when she was calm, but at times like this it hit her full blast. She was starting to panic. She thought she might hit people or wet her pants. And the worst thing was that nobody realized how close to hysteria she was. Except for one woman—an American who had grown up in the glory days of Hollywood with a film director father. She was at least twenty years older than Sally. And she seemed to have gotten her accent from Glinda, the Good Witch of the West. Tiny, she had a pretty doll-like face and curly hair, and she gave off an aroma of essence of roses. Sara imagined that a rainbow would be illuminated over her head if she ever sang "When you walk through a storm, keep your head up high . . ."

"I want you to know this about your mother," the woman said. "She loved you more than anyone in the whole wide world. She wanted the very best for you. She couldn't always show it. She was funny that way. But she wanted you to know how much she loved you."

Words do not make up for much, but sometimes the right words at the right time can open a door. The door opened as soon the door to the crematory fire would open. Sara's tears flooded out and would not stop.

The doll-like woman had a doll-like name: Shirlee Tuck. She took Sara by the hand and waited with her through all the rites at the hushed funeral parlor in Chelsea: the playing of Sally's recordings, the speeches by Judy Collins, Lucy and Carly Simon, Joni Mitchell, Joan Baez, Patti Smith, and a very rambling Dylan, who allowed as how much he had *loved* Sally, how he *wished* he could have saved her, how she was *always* his muse. Then came the nondenominational cremation, with the coffin rushing into the flames as if in a ride in Disneyland. At least, Sara thought, I don't have to put a shovelful of earth on her coffin and leave her alone in the graveyard. She always hated that moment. She always thought the dead would be cold and lonely. But Sally would be dispersed in the moist English air. Eventually the molecules that once were her mother would drift toward the Pale, and her ancestors would reclaim her.

At last she would meet the angel Dovie, the *malech ha-movis,* who is also the Messiah. Does everyone have her own angel? Sara wondered.

When the endless day was over, Shirlee took Sara back to her place in the West End and stayed with her, soothing her.

Shirlee lived in a narrow house in a little mews off Berkeley Square, where the nightingale sang no more. Inside were white walls, red roses, a warm fire, a narrow staircase. Tea was brought by a gentle Filipina wearing white pajamas and white flip-flops.

"This is Sally's daughter, Sara," said Shirlee.

"Sorry for your loss," said the Filipina, whose name was Dolores. She had a sad face to match her name. Which came first—the name or the sadness?

Shirlee let Sara cry as long as she needed to. Then she produced a letter from Sally, written just days before her death.

> *Dear Sara,*
>
> *I suspect that when I am gone and you try to add up the bits and pieces of my life, you will not be able to make sense of much. It's in the nature of things for daughters to dismiss mothers rather than vice versa. You will know you have done well with your daughter when she storms out of the house without your permission.*
>
> *Lives are not given; they are seized. If you do well as a parent, you give your child that fierceness—the fierceness of a baby eagle who snatches nourishment out of the mother's mouth, then flies away. We have to learn to compliment ourselves as parents. It's vain to expect compliments from our children. I have not done all I wanted with you. You must do the rest yourself. I must learn now to detach. The hardest thing in the world is to love a child fiercely, then to detach—but they are the two halves of love. This is the only way I can detach, so that you may seize your life someday. I know you will forgive me—if not now, then perhaps later.*
>
> *Your loving Mother,*
> *Sally Sky*
>
> *P.S. I was fascinated to read once that mothers and daughters (and the grandmothers and great-grandmothers before them) carry identical DNA in their cells. Thus the feeling that they are alike has a biological basis. It is not merely conjecture. But just*

because the DNA is the same does not mean the destinies are. We do have choice about our lives, and our destinies are not wholly out of our control. I do not mean that we can be God-like or make our wills override God's, but intention counts for a great deal. What I have discovered in my life is that whenever I have wanted something deeply and badly enough, I have achieved it, and whenever I have been lazy and careless, it slipped through my fingers.

I wanted you. I was never happier than at your birth. But somewhere along the line I lost my fight and surrendered to other forces. Perhaps I was afraid to fight for fear of losing. The truth is, we have to concentrate intently, keep attention focused every day of our lives. Without that we slip and fall, slip and fail. Be the part of me that did not slip. Do not fail. Fear passes if you keep on fighting. Just try to remember that. Some old rabbi once said: "The whole world is like a very narrow bridge, and the main thing is not to be afraid." I have become quite interested in Judaism lately. There is great wisdom in our traditions—great and very diverse wisdom. I am sorry now I never had you study to be bat mitzvah, but other things distracted me. Like your father, who kept kidnapping you, suing for custody, and all that shit. Besides, when you were thirteen you were in Montana, thinking you were a goddamned Wasp! Never mind. You come from a line of women who were fighters. And the hearts of mothers and daughters beat in eternal unison.

The best part of me flowered in you.

All my love,
Sally

Sara read the letter and asked Shirlee how she came to have it.

"She gave it to me for safekeeping, with a few other things. When you are ready, I'm supposed to give them to you."

"How will you know when I'm ready?"

She laughed musically. "Oh," she said, "*you'll* know and you'll tell me."

"I'm not ready to be an orphan."

"Nobody is ready to be an orphan, yet we all are orphaned. And still we have an obligation to those who orphaned us. The past lives only in us. The dead live only in the living."

"But didn't *she* have an obligation to *me*?"

"She fulfilled it as best she could. She couldn't do what she couldn't do. Your job is to love her and forgive her. It could take a lifetime, but your freedom depends on it. Stay angry—and you are tied to her forever. Only forgiveness sets you free. She also wanted you to have this. . . ." And Shirlee handed Sara a sheaf of papers, which she didn't read until she was back on the plane, flying home.

Transcript of Twentieth-Anniversary *Rolling Stone* Interview with Sally Sky

LONDON, 1989

Q: Let's just see if this is working. Testing, one, two, three . . . Okay. Let me just say how grateful I am to finally get to interview you—what with the twenty-year anniversary of Woodstock upcoming in August and—

A: How old were you at the first Woodstock? Five? Six?

Q: Well, ninish actually. But I have *read* everything about it.

A: And you want to know how an old-timer remembers it?

Q: A *legend* actually.

A: A legend is rarely young. (Laughs)

Q: Ms. Sky, if I didn't admire your music so much, I'd never have signed on for this.

A: That's what they all say. Then they stab you in the back. Luckily I have quote-approval.

Q: Let's go back to the beginning—how you fell in love with music, your first teacher, all that.

A: You didn't even read the *clips*!

Q: I want to hear it in your words.

A: Well, I studied piano first with some old *yenta* called Lillian Zemann, or was it Lehmann—who can remember?—and then guitar with Mason Herbst, a legend in *my* time. He was the guy who collected all the Child ballads, started the folk revival, but never got credit for it since he was bloody *blacklisted*. Since my grandmother was a painter and my mother a writer, it seemed that folksinging was the only thing that really *belonged* to me. My mother gave me a guitar when I was twelve, and I found myself in it. Took it absolutely *everywhere,* didn't feel safe unless it was hanging around my neck.

You could go *anywhere* in New York with a guitar in those days—Washington Square, the West Village, Central Park. All the stuff you call "the sixties" was well under way even the decade before—Beat poetry, drugs, the Merry Pranksters, Jack Kerouac, Ken Kesey, Allen Ginsberg, Gregory Corso, Peter Orlovsky—the lot. I wore my strawberry hair down to my ass, of course, and dressed all in black. The sackcloth-and-ashes look was very popular at the time. Had these rough-hewn Neanderthal sandals from Eighth Street. I was a regular non-conformist conformist—as my grandfather Levitsky loved to point out.

I started singing in the Village when I was—God knows—fourteen. It was a way of getting out of the house. And my house was *some* house: Papa, Mama—I mean my grandparents, of course—Salome, Robin, Marco—my parents (I had three of 'em)—not to mention 'Renzo, my brother, the bad seed. That was a joke. (Laughs)

Q: Tell me more about your brother.
A: I wish there were more to tell. He followed me into show business, but he didn't have the grit for it. He thought he was the Prince of Wales, and he got very good at choosing engraved stationery, playing polo, seducing starlets, squandering money, playing producer, but he never really produced very much. When his life proved to be a zero, he went into the family business and tried to destroy it. I was too busy destroying myself to stop him. Men were my drug of choice, and whatever drugs they were taking, *I* took. If I have any guilt about my life, it's for having been unconscious for so much of it.

Q: I find this astonishing. You? Guilty? What about the sexual revolution?
A: I hardly remember it.

Q: Ms. Sky, I find all this very hard to believe.
A: Of course you do. You were raised thinking Sally Sky was a *symbol of freedom,* not a person. Look, we were just kids who, like all kids, wanted to distinguish ourselves from our parents. In my case, that was hard since my parents were *already* weirdos. My mother had been in Paris in the thirties, with Henry Miller. And my grandfather was a big shot in the art world who knew *everybody*—Picasso to Pollock. *I* came to the music business because it was the only territory *left* for me. And I loved the music but hated the business part—the thievery, the mafiosi, the R and D men, the suits stealing money from the artists and manipulating their insecurities to facilitate this. The truth is, I never loved

anything as much as the warmth coming across the footlights from the roaring crowd. I *always* knew what to do up there— how to move, which songs to sing, how to sashay with my guitar. I could *feel* what the audience wanted and give it to them. In any room, any club, any coffeehouse, any bar, I could get up there and suddenly know in my gut what songs they wanted to hear. For a shy person it was extraordinary, a communion. It was only *offstage* that I had a problem.

Q: Did you have any idea how significant Woodstock was going to be?

A: Are you kidding? A mud slide in Bethel, New York, with hundreds of thousands of kids and no toilets! We all thought it was a nightmare till *Time* magazine told us it was the dawning of the Age of Aquarius.

Q: You mean you had *no idea*?

A: None whatsoever. Listen, when *Listen to Your Voice* went off the charts, I had no idea what hit me. If you sell a million records in America, suddenly everyone wants to touch you for luck—as if you're God. That's very disconcerting. Stressful, you might say.

Q: Why?

A: Because there's *no way* you can live up to it, that's why. People want stuff from you that not even God can deliver. Salvation, for example. Or else they want to *become* you, suck up your talent by osmosis—which is impossible. So you have a very narrow window in which to be golden. Then you're dross. I always knew this. I knew a hit record or two or three wasn't a *life*. I knew I had to figure out what I wanted to be when I grew up. You may have noticed that many of my contemporaries didn't. Many of my contemporaries—you may have noticed—are dead. Which is actually preferable, in my opinion—or, as my grandfather used to say, "to mine opinion"—to living too long. I have no wish to be a centenarian, singing "Nobodaddy's Daughter" on my walker, getting a telegram from the White House at a hundred and three.

Q: What was the difference between you and all those who died too young?

A: Grace.

Q: I mean *really*. Our readers want to know.

A: Look. There's no way to talk about this stuff in *words*. Your readers can't learn from words. They have to want the answer so badly that they're banging their heads against a brick wall. Then maybe they'll listen. I reached a point where literally I couldn't get out of bed in the morning. I was living with the man I thought was my great love—living in a five-million-dollar beach house in Malibu. I had a hit record. The phone was ringing off the hook. People came by, offering me any drug I wanted. There were tabloid photographers with telephoto lenses hiding in the bougainvillea. It's *supposed* to be the American dream, but I would lie in bed in the morning trying to think of ways not to get up ever *again*. I was terrified every time the phone rang. I really don't know how to talk about this stuff. By now it's *banal*—what with people confessing to recovery in public all the time. But it was no less real for that.

Q: There is a rumor about your disappearance.

A: It's not a rumor. I went away for a long time.

Q: What brought you back?

A: Am I back? (Laughs) I am not going to fall into the trap of talking about spirituality and recovery. When I say it can't be put into words, I mean it. It has to be *experienced*. Next . . .

Q: Tell me how you got the idea for your first big breakthrough album, *Listen to Your Voice*.

A: I think for women born in the forties, the idea of listening to your own voice was a new and radical thing, something that had to be *discovered*. We learned our craft singing traditional songs (that is, songs made by men, in which women were objectified as virgins, whores, dead virgins, dead whores), and we had to learn now how to sing in our own voices. We had to discover we had something to say.

Of course, the blues singers got there first. In the teens and twenties, African-American women discovered everything it took us a half century to discover—us white girls, I mean. They were *way ahead* of us—Ida Cox with her "Wild Women Don't Get the Blues," Bessie Smith with her "Empty Bed Blues," and "Ain't Nobody's Business If I Do." *They* were our role models, and we didn't even know it. White women had to go black to find their own voices. That's why Janis Joplin sang black and Mama Cass and countless others. Black women wrote about the tragedy of gutsy, feisty, independent women who still wanted to get laid. *They* were the avant garde. We're just catching up *now*. Not even . . . And most of them died broke, lost their copyrights to small-time operators, couldn't get into hospitals when they were sick, because of Jim Crow laws, got hooked on drugs by their so-called lovers. . . . Their stories are hideous. Nothing I went through even comes *close*.

But we couldn't even *hear* our own voices at first. Our struggle was just to *listen* to our own voices. Maybe that will be our legacy. I just happened to write the song that tuned into that struggle. But where my songs really came from I can't say. In that period I was able to take just about *anything* in my life and make a song of it with no self-consciousness at all.

"My Old Man" came straight out of a visit to my dad at the funny farm when I was four. "My Mother's Men" came out of the fact that my mother always had three or four guys she was rotating, including her husband Robin and her main man Marco. "Nobodaddy's Daughter" came out of reading William Blake with Max Danzig, my mentor. "Thorazine Dreams" was another song that came out of trying to identify with my crazy father—who was dead by the time I was five or six, but nobody told me. I had to find out for myself! Another story . . .

You write what you know, what you have at home. You don't even *think* about it. Only later, when it has become a phenomenon—read: "has made a lot of people rich"—do you analyze and answer questions about it. Then your innocence is gone. You analyze *after* the fact, but where the inspiration comes from is *mysterious*. It *has* to be. It is made underground. "We work in the dark, we do what we can—our work is our passion and our passion is our art. The rest is the madness of art." I think Henry James said that. I've probably misquoted it, but then I come from a family of aphorists. They always quoted everything, and they quoted everything askew.

Q: Some feminist critics have written that you gave your power away to men. They refer, of course, to your many marriages. Do you want to comment on that?

A: No. But I will. In a way, my generation was destined to find out who we were through the men in our lives. We tried on men as a way of trying on lives. In the beginning we didn't know that we could *have* those lives without using the men as the excuse. What we found out in the end was that we were actually much *stronger* than the men in our lives and that what weakened us was precisely our not *knowing* we were strong, looking for mentors, advisers, strong men, to father us. In my case, especially, since my father was certifiably insane and then certifiably dead by his own hand, I was always attracted to father figures, healers, doctors, shrinks. I married a few of them and lived to regret it.

Q: What about your daughter, Sara?

A: The best thing I ever did, my finest creation, my arrow into eternity.

Q: What are your hopes for her?

A: That she will be as *unlike* me as possible.

Q: Can you elaborate?

A: She hates it when I talk about her in interviews. I dare not say a word.

Q: Can you talk about your relationship with Max Danzig?

A: Since it's part of my legend, I guess I *have* to.

Q: How did you meet him?

A: He sent me a fan letter. I still have it. You can imagine that I was flabbergasted. Max Danzig was a famous recluse. After his novel *A Girl Called Ginger*, he stopped publishing entirely and retreated to Vermont. He never gave interviews. He was much smarter about that than me. (Laughs)

Q: I'll let that pass. Ms. Sky, tell our younger readers why Danzig was so important to your generation.

A: Shall I translate for your lip-readers? For all your nonreaders who nevertheless want to *hear* about books? Why not? He was the writer who got adolescent angst just right. He read our hearts. He showed the interior of an adolescent's brain. I thought he was the only man on earth who could understand me.

Q: So what did you do?

A: I disappeared from my California life and drove to St. Johnsbury, Vermont. I had no idea where Danzig lived, but I figured that *someone* would know. And they did. I asked the fat, blowsy blond proprietor of an antique teddy bear shop. She wandered out to the covered bridge with me, pointed up to a ridge above the town, featuring a red barn surrounded by birches and wilderness. She gave me directions. To my amazement, I found my idol.

What I remember was how *old* he looked when I first saw him outside the barn. His book picture had been taken a long time ago. He was slight, small, with long white hair. He even had puffs of white hair curling out of his ears. That told me he was *really* old.

"I knew you'd come," he said.

"How could I not?" I said.

His barn was filled with books—stacks and cartons of books everywhere—and heated by an old-fashioned pot-bellied stove. Various cats patrolled the rafters. A husky named Nanook was top dog. Danzig made me a vegetarian nut loaf for supper. I stayed for two years. During most of that time nobody knew where I was. My mother and grandmother went crazy. *And* my stepfather and grandfather. I showed *them*!

Danzig was the closest thing I ever met to an enlightened being. He knew that life was a divine comedy, not a revenge tragedy. He had the gift for passing this news along. That was why so many people worshiped him—even though he had stopped writing for publication.

Danzig felt overwhelmed by his fans. How can a mere writer heal the ills of the world? He *can't*—any more than a mere singer can. But people see you on your spiritual path, and they are so hungry for spirit that they want a piece of you. If you give away all those pieces on their terms, nothing will be left of *you*! *Your* own journey will end. But how to refuse the sincere seekers?

Instead of building up false expectations, Danzig meditated.

He wrote haiku, which he taught me to copy in calligraphy.

"Only what is given as a gift can be uncontaminated," Danzig used to say.

I sang him folk songs—Appalachian ballads, Irish songs, English songs, Spanish, Portuguese, and Greek. I sang him Woody Guthrie, Pete Seeger, and Aunt Molly Jackson songs. I sang him "Union Maid" and "Bread and Roses" and "This Land Is Your Land." I sang him "Bourgeois Blues," and "Midnight Blues," and "Nobody in Town Can Bake a Sweet Jelly Roll Like Mine." I sang about boll weevils, unemployment compensation, and Banks of Marble. I sang "We Shall Overcome," "Follow the Drinking Gourd," and "No Irish Need Apply." And then I sang him *my* songs—*all* my songs. I even wrote him a few—like "Nobodaddy's Daughter." (Don't look so eager. I ain't gonna sing them for *you*.)

I taught him to play the guitar. For a long time we slept in the same bed and didn't become lovers. This was definitely a novelty to me after the drugged fucking that went on in the music business. He understood that by then I trusted *no one*. He wanted to win my trust. And he did. It was a long time since I had trusted anyone.

We used to talk about what was and wasn't real. He would recite Yeats to me. And Blake:

He who binds to himself a joy
Does the winged life destroy.
But he who kisses the joy as it flies
Lives in Eternity's sunrise.

Q: So why did you ever leave? It sounds like heaven.
A: The world was too much with us even there. Danzig was always afraid that his kids would publish his cache of manuscripts if he died. He'd given me strict instructions to burn everything if

anything happened to him. But when he had that stroke, I was so traumatized that I was just *unable* to burn his notebooks and manuscripts. I *knew* where they were. I *knew* what to do. But I just *couldn't*. He lay there for almost a year, immobilized, unable to speak, while the vultures came and carried away his treasures, his manuscripts, his letters, his notebooks. The rest is, as they say, history.

Q: You were a major character in Danzig's last novel?
A: Are you asking me or telling me?

Q: Well, are you the folksinger in that book?
A: I never answer questions that can only be answered yes or no.

Q: All right, then, shall we discuss your marriages?
A: I never discuss my marriages. Except, of course, in the most *theoretical* terms.

Q: What do you think gave you the confidence to become a star in the first place?
A: I *always* felt special. From the time I was a little girl, I believed I was fated for great things. This was probably because my grandfather Levitsky made it clear I *was* special. He walked me to school every single day. He dropped everything when I came home in the afternoon. Most successful women are daddy's— or granddaddy's—girls. My daddy was dead, my daddy was nobodaddy, but Levitsky was like a double daddy—he was *that* powerful. I also knew I was special because there were portraits of me (painted by my grandmother) at every stage of my life. But most of all I knew I was special because my mother wanted me and my grandmother wanted me and my grandfather wanted me.

There was a black smudge on this rainbow, and that was my

father, who lived far away in a sort of hospital place and was
whispered about. Then he killed himself, and he was *still* whispered about. I never knew if he was alive or dead. I invented a
fictional father in my head. I sing about him in "The Ghost in
My Life," in "Nobodaddy's Daughter." But if I didn't think of
him and thought instead of my grandparents and my mother,
everything seemed secure. Until, of course, my brother was
born. Even Robin, my mother's husband, loved me. And Marco,
her main man. Not to mention all her other lovers.

   Bed, it turned out, was her favorite place to be.

Q: Many of your commentators say the same of you.
A: Fuck my commentators.

Q: There are also rumors about that. Would you like to correct
   them?
A: No.

Q: It seems you've lived in all the places most important to your
   generation: Malibu, Vermont, Venice, London, New York, but
   not the Hamptons. How is it you've never landed in the
   Hamptons?
A: How is it the Hamptons always make me feel *poor*? Even if you
   fly out there in your own plane, drop into misty, damp East
   Hampton airport like a grasshopper on a leaf (green as money),
   suddenly there you are surrounded by Lear jets, Queer jets,
   Fear jets, all the flotsam and jetsam of real wealth. And suddenly the farm in Vermont, the apartment in Venice, the co-op
   on the Upper East Side, all feel like *trayfe*. And the parties—
   from Hollywood to Broadway to Finance and back again.
   Washington pundits (*The Pundit Did It*—good title for a mystery, huh?) diddling 28-year-old over-the-hill supermodels,
   Broadway babies with their toy boys, middle-aged lady walkers

and underaged boyfriends ... Everyone with a multi-million-dollar house on the ocean, filled with Anglo-Indian antiques, everyone with a huge pool, a golf course, two tennis courts—of two different surfaces—everyone with Italian fountains, man-made mountains and rivers, and a Range Rover just for the nanny. How did you ever get so far *behind*? Whatever you have, wear, do, is *less, less, less*. Whichever party you go to is not quite the right party. Whichever friends you stay with are not the ones who are hottest this year. Heat is everything. And the Hamptons always make you feel like you are returning to room tempera-ture.

Movie moguls with helicopters just for their flacks, retired investment analysts with eighty-foot sloops, novelists who pub-lish *two* number-one best-sellers a year and *kvetch* that their publishers think *they write too much*. Hamptonitis. I have Hamptonitis. It's a lot like pericarditis—an inflammation around the heart. Not that it isn't the same in Cap Ferrat or Venice, in Martha's Vineyard or Aspen—but the rituals are slightly foreign and therefore not so galling. In Europe, the people seem *less* like us, so we are somehow less aggravated, and in Aspen, they're all so bonhomously *Western*. At the Vineyard, they're more genteel and pseudo-Wasp modest—though they're just as rich. The Hamptons are Manhattan brought to a boil and going sockless. The Hamptons are everything I hate about my generation: greed, money hunger, cynicism, display. Their parents sum-mered in the Catskills, so they discovered the Hamptons. From Poland to polo. From Grossinger's to the Hampton Classic. It makes me puke.

Q: Wow ... Tell me how you *really* feel—but seriously now—tell me about your big comeback, the new CD you're issuing next month. It's called—

A: *Sally in the Sky with Diamonds*.

Q: A tribute to the Beatles? The sixties? What?

A: A tribute to my own amazing powers of survival.

Q: Tell us about it.

A: It's better listened to, of course. But let me just say that it is really my autobiography in music. Everything important in my life is in those songs.

Q: I'm looking forward to it. . . . Tell us about your mother, would you—she seems quite some woman.

A: When I was little, I thought she was the most amazing mother who ever lived. She seemed younger than the other mothers, and she liked to skip in the streets and ice-skate in Central Park, and she always had a vast array of admirers. But I made her crazy once I became an adolescent. And when I disappeared with Danzig and never told her where I was, I think I took *years* off her life. She didn't deserve that.

Q: "Lullaby for My Mother" is one of the most touching songs on the new album. She should be very proud of it.

A: It's the *least* I could do for her.

Q: How old is she?

A: She's seventy-seven and still going strong, God bless her.

Q: Do you get along?

A: Finally, we do.

Q: And your father?

A: Don't you listen? My father is bloody *dead*!

Q: Oh, please forgive me, Ms. Sky.

A: I've never forgiven *him*—why should I forgive you? (Laughs)

Q: There has also been the persistent rumor that you were working on a musical about your grandmother—a sort of female *Fiddler on the Roof*. True?

A: Truish. I spent a lot of time interviewing my ancient grandmother Sarah on tape about a decade ago—inspired in part by wanting to make a family chronicle for my daughter, Sara, who was then just a baby. Now she's eleven and lives in Montana with her father. Her father has sweetly told her I am dead, so of course she doesn't know her own mother and grandmother— my mother visits her secretly and observes her from a distance, or even from up close, aided and abetted by Sandrine, who lives with my ex and is not a bad sort. Not really. I have been separated from my daughter for so long—I'm still fighting for visitation—that I wanted her to know her great-grandmother—in case she died before I got little Sara back. You see I named my Sara for *my* grandmother whom I adored.

Q: I thought Jews didn't do that.

A: Only certain Orthodox Ashkenazim don't. The point of it is to confuse the angel of death—as in so many Jewish rituals. The Sephardic Jews don't have this taboo, and most American Jews are *not* Orthodox. Odd how increasingly proud I am to be Jewish—despite my lack of Jewish education. My grandmother Sarah Solomon Levitsky was amazing. Lots of women were amazing then. Sarah was sort of *Yentl* meets *The Age of Innocence*. What a musical she would make! *Hello, Dolly!* ain't nothin' compared to my grandmama Sarah.

Q: Where is that project now?

A: In development hell. It has so far been through development at three regional theaters—the Old Globe in La Jolla, the Yale Rep, and I forget which other. Right now the director and producer don't talk to each other. I hear that's *normal* for musicals.

Now there's talk that HBO wants to develop it as a movie musical starring Bette Midler—whom I adore. "*Alivai!*" as my grandmother would say. If I'm lucky, my granddaughter will eventually do it.

Q: Is there any question I haven't asked that you'd like to answer?
A: Yes. What are you doing for dinner?

[It must be assumed that the interviewer was just the sort of young flatterer Sally liked. Soulful, hairy, adoring. What happened next is anyone's guess. The Rolling Stone *interview never ran, of course, because Sally changed her mind and had her lawyers write to the magazine threatening dire consequences if it did. She also pulled her new CD.* Sally in the Sky with Diamonds *became a collectors' item after she had most of the copies destroyed. Ed.]*

13

Inventing Memory
1995, 1992

> *God invents us, but we invent our own ancestors.*
>
> —VENETIAN PROVERB

Sara remembered when she first realized that her mother might not make it. It was the summer she was seventeen and she had joined Sally in Venice, where she had rented a sixteenth-century house on a canal, a house with a long back garden, rumored to have once been a cemetery. The garden was wild—huge Rousseauesque palm fronds, enormous crimson roses that looked as if they had been fed on human blood, two tortoises who made love all the time, grunting noisily—and a blue mirrored ball reflected this Edenic scene.

Sally was drinking again—tentatively at first, then enthusiastically. She was keeping company with a descendant of doges whose name identified *palazzi* and *campi* in Venice as well as many country estates in the Veneto. He was called Prince Alvise Grandini-Piccolini, and his high-bridged aristocratic nose was red from the wines of his region. White-haired, paunchy, courtly, he escorted Sally about in a custom-made motorboat, a re-creation of a wooden *motoscafo* of the 1920s—though in fact it was new.

Sara understood there might be a problem when her mother said on the first night they had dinner together: "I am starting to think I might not be an alcoholic after all. I appear to be able to take it or leave it."

That night at Montin's, they drank only bubbly water, and Sally seemed proud of this—as if she had *not* been drinking only water with Alvise. They ate grilled fish, smothered in fried zucchini, and salad made of carrots, radicchio, and tender baby lettuce.

Later they were met by Alvise and his gorgeous green-eyed son, Gianluca, and were taken on an evening tour of the self-consciously romantic city, winding up at a small, red-lacquered *osteria* near the Rialto, where platters of baby octopus and bowls of steaming bright-yellow polenta were put before them, together with an icy bottle of prosecco. Sara watched in trepidation as Sally dipped first her nose into the prosecco, then her mouth.

"Whatever you do, don't let her pick up the first drink," her father had cautioned. "She can't stop."

But the process was not so obvious to Sara. What she saw was a gradual loosening of inhibitions, accompanied by a giddy laugh, rather too much preening and flirting, and tiny sips of prosecco alternating with large gulps of water.

Sara didn't know what to do. Stop her? Let her go on drinking? Empty all the bottles into the canals? The results were not dramatic at first. But after a week, Sally was finishing bottles of wine with Alvise and ordering more and sleeping all day in the dark and depressing front room of the little house, with the shutters closed against the morning sun.

Another intriguing feature of the house was that the people who rented it to Sally—a flea-bitten Venetian contessa named Fiammetta Malfatti and her beautiful young gigolo, or possibly son, Sante—

never really seemed to vacate the premises. They lived, supposedly, in a *mansarda* (or attic) at a friend's house, but in truth they were always around; they appeared to scuttle into the house like rats whenever Sally, Sara, and Alvise went out for meals.

Sara hated Venice, hated the decrepit house with its rotten shutters, its ghostly owners, its too lush garden, its cobwebs in corners, its ants making a procession across the fruit that sat on the breakfast table. Venice was death and decay to her. People who loved it, she thought, were in love with death, drawn there by an unhealthy desire to be out of the mainstream, in a backwater where life was placid and mild because nothing, in fact, had mattered there for five hundred years. The trade routes had shifted to the Atlantic and Pacific, and the people who continued pottering about the Adriatic were, to Sara, the world's losers. No wonder they gave themselves such airs.

What did Sally do there? What was she saving herself from by fleeing her work? She slept most of the day and drank with Alvise most of the night. Americans would come and be impressed by the dark little house with its moth-eaten antiques and luxuriant garden—and then they would go away raving about what they had seen. But what *had* they seen? Entropy and decay in exotic surroundings—that was all. Life was supposed to be a battle against decay and death, and Sara saw her mother willingly succumbing. She hated what she saw. She hated her mother for her passivity, for her bad Italian (Sally imagined she could speak it, but her phrases seemed to come out of nineteenth-century operas or twentieth-century cookbooks), for her embracing death with outstretched arms.

"I need you to set an example for me," she told Sally. "I need you to be strong for me."

"*I* also needed plenty of things I never got," Sally said. "What makes you immune to the human condition of death and disappointment?"

"It is *not* the human condition," Sara said. "It's *your* condition.

Despair and disappointment are not all there is to life—but you make it seem that way! It's your choice!"

"Stop lecturing me," Sally said. "I'm supposed to lecture you. *I'm* the mother."

"Then *act* like one," Sara said.

Sally took another drink.

Sara went for a long walk alone. Then she jogged along the Fondamenta where the *Dogana*, the old customhouse, stood. She sat and drank a coffee and looked at the glittering waters below the church of the *Redentore*. She did not understand her mother's pessimism, but she felt its tentacles reaching out to engulf her like an octopus. If she stayed here with her mother, despair would win. She did not have to understand this black thing with suckers to reject it. All her life, it seemed, Sara had fought her parents' despair. But in Venice, the despair was winning. Sally had put herself in a kind of exile here. Surely the music business and the stress of New York could not be worse than this living death under a sky painted by Turner or Tiepolo.

Later Sally got sober again in London and resumed her addiction to AA. But what Sara had seen in Venice left an indelible mark. It was in Venice that summer that she decided she had a total aversion to alcohol. She still had not taken a drink—to this day.

Something else she saw in Venice left a mark too. The crumbling old house on the canal had an extraordinary library, full of books on philosophy and mysticism and religion—many of them in English. One passage in one of these books left such an impression that she had copied it into her notebook, even though there were a great many things in it she did not fully understand:

> *When the Baal Shem had a difficult task before him, he*
> *would go to a certain place in the woods, light a fire, and*

meditate in prayer—and what he set out to perform was done. When a generation later the Maggid of Meseritz was faced with the same task, he would go to the same place in the woods and say: We can no longer light the fire, but we can still speak the prayers—and what he wanted done became a reality. Again, a generation later, Rabbi Moishe Lieb of Sassov had to perform this task, and he too went in the woods and said: We can no longer light a fire, nor do we know the secret meditations belonging to the prayer, but we do know the place in the wood to which it all belongs—and that must be sufficient. And sufficient it was. But when another generation had passed and Rabbi Israel of Rishin was called upon to perform the task, he sat down on his golden chair in the castle and said: We cannot light the fire, we cannot speak the prayers, we do not know the place, but we can tell the story of how it was done. And the story which he told had the same effect as the actions of the other three.

The passage was by a man called Gershom Scholem, whom she had never heard of. But it intrigued her; could writing chronicles be a magic act? So she also dated her interest in history to that summer. And her interest in things Jewish. If telling a story could make magic happen, she needed to know more about this religion.

"I feel like a castaway," she wrote in her notebook during that summer. "My mother is less than a mother and my father is less than a father. Actually they are a lot alike. My mother likes Europe because she imagines herself out of the competition there. And my father likes Montana for the same reason. If I ever have a child, I will try to set a better example."

◆

From Venice, Sara jumped back in time to Montana. When Sara thought of Montana she saw in her mind's eye the weathered log cabin with the tin roof where she spent most of her childhood, the house she'd fled when she was just fourteen. Jagged peaks frosted with snow, dark-green forests on the flanks, wide valleys where you might see baby moose loping on splayed legs in the long-awaited spring. The western larch is yellow, the conifers are dark green, and the rivers are wide and serpentine and crammed with fingerling trout. The rivers in this last Eden have names like Belly, Big Blackfoot, Bighorn, Milk, Powder, Yellowstone, and Wisdom, and the mountains are called things like Bitterroot, Swan, Tobacco Root, and Yakt.

Sara lived on Bear Creek. When she was older she was shocked to learn there are many Bear Creeks in Montana; in her childhood it was, of course, the only one. Her father and the gypsy artist woman he lived with, Sandrine Kaplan—she was French, but her parents had blue numbers on thin arms—had torn down an old log cabin with crowbars, labeled the beams, and floated them down the river to their property, bought in 1968 for the equivalent of twenty-six dollars and a bottle of booze.

Sandrine was big, busty, exuberant, and her love for Sara was never a mother's unconditional love, but since Sara didn't have any other mother for a long time, she bonded to Sandrine and learned a lot from her—how to manage her father in particular. Sandrine also made her want to be Jewish even before she knew for sure she was.

"Flexibility is Jewish survival," Sandrine used to say. "It's important to be able to pack up and move, learn new languages and customs. The rabbis may inveigh against assimilation, but it's why we've survived for six thousand years. We assimilate, but we still keep our pride of identity. And we keep our holy books. Never forget that, Sara."

Sandrine was the first woman who had made her feel that being

Jewish was a heroic destiny. Sandrine's parents had passed along to her the conviction that life was a gift carved out of a universe of death. Sandrine desperately wanted children, but she and Sara's father never were able to conceive. So she adopted Sara as her spiritual daughter.

Sandrine had been there the day Sara got her first period. Sara was thirteen and a half. She had been weeping for weeks. Weeping over a baby grouse with an injured leg, weeping whenever her father said: "Shhh. I'm writing." Weeping whenever she was asked to do a household chore. Finally Sandrine was so exasperated with her that she dumped a bucket of well water on her head. This sobered Sara up immediately, and she threw her arms around Sandrine, saying, "I love you, Sandrine, I really do."

Later she found blood on her white underpants, a blackish cherry-colored stain that looked as though it would never wash out. She closeted herself in the single bathroom, wondering if she was ill or if this was "it." Sandrine began banging on the locked door.

"Wait a *second*!" Sara yelled.

"Let me in!" Sandrine countered.

Sara reluctantly turned the lock. She looked up sheepishly from the toilet seat.

"Is this *it*?" she asked Sandrine.

"Oh my God—my baby!" Sandrine yelled. Then she slapped Sara on the cheek and hugged her right after.

"Why did you slap me?"

"Good luck," said Sandrine. "An old ritual."

"*Why* is it good luck?" Sara asked.

"Damned if *I* can remember!" said Sandrine. "But I had to do it. My mother did it to me."

"I think that's a stupid reason," said Sara.

"You may think so now, but you won't if you ever have a daughter."

"Do you think of me as your daughter?" Sara asked.

"Why do you ask such silly questions?" Sandrine said, tears running down her cheeks. And she rummaged under the bathroom sink for a box of pads, went out and got Sara a clean pair of underpants, and showed her how to stick the pad on the crotch of the underpants. Then she dumped her bloody pants in the sink and ran cold water over the crotch.

"Cold water only," said Sandrine. "Otherwise the blood sets." To Sara's astonishment, she rubbed her bloody pants between her hands under the cold water.

"Nothing wrong with blood," she said matter-of-factly. "Basis of life, in fact."

"What's going on in there?" Sara's father shouted from his desk.

"Nothing!" Sandrine yelled. "Mind your own damn business!"

But Sara thought she might have told him later, because he was very tender with her that day and the day after.

Her father. How to describe him? He was a man who used his political consciousness to cover human deficits—a sort of male Mrs. Jellyby. He was a lot more emotionally dense than Sandrine—but he wrote poetry that made women think him sensitive. That and his handlebar mustache and sad, puffy eyes. (Sara knew it was just the booze.) He and Sandrine had come to Montana with a copy of *The Whole Earth Catalog* and a chain saw. They were utterly unprepared for the Montana winters. Stronger types than they had broken their teeth, noses, and backs on this landscape.

But they persevered. Once they had rebuilt the log house, given it a new glittery tin roof, the house owned them as much as they owned the house. In the winter the snow could be waist high. When it melted, blue lupine, Indian paintbrush, asters, alpine poppies, and columbines all bloomed at once. But even this blossoming could not assuage Sara's primal loneliness. Only Dove's birth would later assuage it. Dove's birth had filled the bottomless hole in Sara's heart. She remembered the wholly unexpected thrill she had when she saw that soft skull, those inky eyes, for the first time. She was at once madly happy and terrified. Suddenly all the holocausts of history seemed to threaten that little skull.

One night in Venice, Sara went out drinking with Gianluca, the son of Grandini-Piccolini. She supposed he was a princeling, since his father was a prince. She "fooled around" with him—meaning they tongue-kissed ("sucked face," as Sara's smart-ass friends liked to say) in a narrow alley and he felt her breasts and pressed his erection against her. AIDS and her mother's reputation had made Sara cling to her virginity, but she figured "fooling around" was okay. Nevertheless she felt like a fool when Gianluca said, "I will call you," in his careful English and then did not.

"They always say that," her mother said. "It means nothing."

His failure to call had been the first stab in the vitals, but her mother's commentary was the second. Whenever she felt bad, her mother knew exactly how to make her feel worse.

"Don't you think *I'd* like to start all over again?" her mother yelled. "Be young again? But I can't, goddamn it—I'm too fuckin' old!" Sally was only in her forties. She was still foxy, and sometimes she walked like she knew it. Men still propositioned her in all languages. What the hell was the matter with her? Whatever it was, it was all in her head.

"You're beautiful, Mom, and men are crazy about you!" Sara was making a special effort to call Sally "Mom," even though it felt weird to her.

"Men are crazy—that's true. I'm such a dope!" Sally started to cry. "When I was young and beautiful I didn't know it, and now that *you're* young and beautiful, I *do!*"

Then, prompted somehow by Sally's outburst, and wanting to make herself feel better, Sara did something that made her feel even worse: she called Gianluca. To her horror, a girl answered, giggling. "*Una straniera,*" she said derisively in that Italian way which implies that to be a foreigner is the worst sin of all. Sara quickly hung up the phone. She was devastated.

Remembering all this from what seemed like a century ago—both the disappointment and her mother's disappointing reaction to it—Sara thought she should not have been so surprised by Lloyd's recent fickleness. Somehow she knew that men were led around by their cocks, that they tended to fall in love, fleetingly, with whoever made these fickle organs rise. It didn't even *mean* much. They were as confused by their emotions and erections as the women they betrayed and disappointed. They were at the mercy of a length of muscle, blood vessels, and skin that never seemed long enough, durable enough. At least women had solider values. Sara was starting to know that what mattered was her work and Dove. Sara's work right now was inventing her own ancestors, inventing memory itself.

In Sara's dream, there is a sooty-winged angel with a tall black silk hat, a cloak lined with sable the same color as his long beard, and the inky blue eyes of a baby. Looking at him, she understands that he is *her* angel as much as he is Sarah Sophia's. This is, in fact, the angel who has brought them all to America, who has choreographed their hundred-year dance. This angel will protect Dove from the vicissitudes of her life. He will perch on her shoulder as Sarah perches on her great-granddaughter's shoulder. He may, in fact, be Dove's alter ego, Dovie. Do souls transmigrate across generations? "Why rule out the possibility?" the dreaming Sara mutters to herself, starting to awaken.

Then, in that unpredictable way of dreams, the angel turns into David de Hirsch.

With the dream still holding sway over her reality, Sara takes a sleepy morning shower. When she emerges and looks in her bathroom mirror—still fogged with shower mist—she suddenly sees Sarah Sophia as she appeared in that first defiant photograph. The same ropes of hair, the same determined mouth, the same soft, deep eyes. At that moment, Sara knows for certain that Sarah Sophia is her great-grandmother and that she is growing into her great-grand-mother's bravery as surely as a geranium cutting soon fills up its pot of soil.

Sara hasn't written poetry for a long time, not since she married Lloyd, but now she sits down at her desk and scrawls this poem into her notebook:

> *I plant my heart in the earth.*
> *I water it with light.*
> *The sweet green tentacles*
> *of spring urge toward the light.*
> *They nudge the earth like fat worms wriggling,*
> *loosening light in the darkness.*
>
> *They open the channels and passages*
> *that allow the flow of life.*
>
> *Sweetness follows them.*
> *The sweetness of the new pea pod,*
> *the ginkgo leaf in May,*
> *the sticky buds of the weeping cherry*
> *not yet burst,*
> *the fuzz of the pussy willow*
> *in the pink hour*
> *before dawn,*
> *the small green arrows of the crocus*
> *pushing through a glaze*
> *of bluish snow.*
>
> *O light that nourishes life—*
> *let us be mirrors*
> *of your splendor.*

Let us reflect your pure energy,
not dampen it.
Let us be givers of the light.

The dull earth turns
on its rusty axis.
The dolorous echoes of the dying
fill the ears of God—

who responds by planting
hearts with light,
hearts in the moving earth.

Let us learn to imitate
this infinite making of new hearts.

Air, water, earth are all we need.
And the miracle of the heart
alive with light.

Sara writes almost as fast as her thoughts, which tumble over each other like pebbles in a rushing river. And then Dove wanders in, rubbing her eyes with sleep.

"I had a scary dream, Mommy, but I don't remember it. There were monsters. . . ."

"The light sends the monsters away, darling. Even at night, they aren't as powerful as they look. It's all a bluff on the part of the monsters, because, really, they're afraid of *you.*"

"Really?" asks Dove. Her expression is one of those can-I-really-trust-you expressions six-year-olds specialize in.

"Really," says Sara. "Monsters are the most scared animals of all."

Sara can see that Dove has decided to trust her. She feels suddenly jubilant. Dove's faith in her makes up for any number of betrayals.

Later that day, working in the Council's book stacks, Sara is moved to write a letter to the real David de Hirsch:

> *Dear David,*
>
> *I'm going to ask you not to make me dinner for a while. You don't know me, and the truth is I don't really know myself. I can't give away what I don't own, namely myself. Maybe there will come a time when I know myself better and can be your friend. You have already been a sort of guardian angel to me in ways you don't even know.*
>
> *Sara*

And to Lloyd, she writes:

> *Dear Lloyd,*
>
> *I realize now that I married far too young, didn't really know my own mind, but was looking for refuge. I think you should decide to stay where you are for both our sakes. But I expect you to share the raising of our child fairly with me and I hope I won't have to take you to court to make that happen. Someday I hope we can be allies for Dove's sake.*
>
> *Sara*

Sara knows that she will have to cut herself off from these two men to take the journey with the angel she is destined to make. Except for Dove, she will have to dwell among shades for a while. Hadn't Sally hoped she would be as unlike her as possible? Sara knows she is only starting that process of separation now.

"I had to find my ancestors," Sara writes in her notebook, "to

separate from them." And then she scrawls the following notes to
herself:

> *Sarah's oral history tapes are priceless—even in their raw form.*
> *Of course I will have to cut a lot of her ering and uming about*
> *how much she hates tape recorders and all her puzzlement*
> *about whether she is doing it right. I will also have to organize*
> *her recollections in roughly chronological order. I wish I could*
> *give a taste of her accent. She sounds like an ancient Yiddish*
> *comedian—but she believed that people thought she had a*
> *French accent and that was why they sometimes found her*
> *hard to understand!*

> *Salome's files consist mostly of letters and journals—but I*
> *am still convinced that* Dancing to America *(or pieces of*
> *it) must be somewhere buried in the Council's crypt. To*
> *be lost in a library has been the fate of many great works.*

> *But the documents of Sally's life are nothing like Sarah's*
> *narrative or Salome's letters and journals. Her files consist*
> *of masses of visual materials, glossies of concerts, folded*
> *posters, album covers, press kits, fragments of interviews.*
> *The only complete one is the* Rolling Stone *that never ran.*
> *As I pick my way through the boxes, I see Sally age from a*
> *pure-faced teenager to a strong-jawed woman of middle*
> *years. In her youth, she could play the audience—the*
> *great anonymous audience—instinctively. She was a shy*
> *person who could be embarrassed by a conversation in a*
> *living room, but with an audience of thousands she felt*
> *loved, secure, adored—especially if no one she knew was*
> *in that room.*

◆

*It was not surprising that there was no afterlife to that
life. Performing on huge stages, becoming the voice of the
voiceless crowd, their sweat, their smell, uses a person up
totally. What could you become afterward? How could
you reinvent yourself? She went up in flames in the usual
way of her generation: alcohol, drugs, men. Looking for
spirit, she found spirits. Looking for ecstasy, she found
self-destruction. The cure was recovery. But how can you
"recover" from being an artist? If your essential job is to
give birth to yourself over and over, how do you do it
without becoming God?*

Back in Venice that awful summer, Sara remembered how much
she wanted to leave and how trapped she was there.

"Don't go—wait for *Redentore*," her mother said. *Redentore* was a
feast day to commemorate the ending of a fifteenth-century plague.
The Venetians built bridges of boats from San Marco to Salute to
Giudecca, festooned their boats with flowers, and lay outstretched in
them, getting drunker and drunker and staring at dazzlingly ostentatious fireworks that exploded in the night sky to the sound of Vivaldi's
music.

Redentore was a popular holiday, one of those bones thrown to the
common people since the time of the Roman Empire to make them
tolerate their wretched lot. Sara wanted to leave Venice after her
humiliation with Gianluca, but everyone was waiting for *Redentore*,
waiting for the Redeemer—weren't we all? So she stayed. Stayed in
that filthy, disorderly house with her mother drinking, stayed in the
heat and smell of that sewer city, stayed amid the deceiving Venetians,
who saw her only as a *straniera*, and finally escaped the day after the
Feast of the Redeemer, with thousands of day-trippers who had slept
in boats or in the streets and doorways of the city.

She was never as glad to leave any place in her life. On the train, she promised herself never to take a vacation with her mother again. She doesn't wish me well, she said to herself, and even if she *is* my mother, I have no reason to be around people who do not wish me well.

✦

The other late memory she had of Sally was much sweeter than the Venetian one.

She always thought of it as her "Holden Caulfield Day in New York."

In Montana, at her father's house when she was fourteen, Sara had found a letter from her mother—so she had a mother after all!—folded around a yellowing birth announcement (her own!), hidden in a cigar box in the bottom drawer of her father's desk. It started with this mysterious fragment:

JAZZ AGE POEM

Jass, jazz, jazzbos
and flappers in their beaded dresses
doing the black bottom
on the Great Black Way
slumming in Harlem
the twenties
the original Broadway babies
drinking bathtub gin

my mother what a world you grew up in
my world now

Then it went on:

> *Sara must be fourteen by now. Your cruelty in depriving*
> *me of contact with her is not to be believed. My meditations*

*on my own mother remain an important part of my identity.
(See poem above.) I know Sara needs me, and I need her. She
will only* hate *you for keeping us apart. Don't you realize
that? I will never stop cursing you until you tell her I am
alive and love her! My curses are powerful. Look what
they've done to me.*

   Sally

And the birth announcement, from a 1978 *People* magazine, read:

*Sally Sky's latest hit: Baby Sara Sky-Wyndham born in
New York City on August 1st to singing legend Sally Sky
and war-resister poet husband Ham Wyndham. Baby
Sara sings her first lullaby to Mama Sally Sky.*

And then there was a grainy, faded color photo of a beautiful smiling strawberry-haired woman crooning to a little lump of a newborn
baby whose mouth was open in a howl.

The blood rushed to Sara's face as she read the hidden letter and
the astonishing birth announcement. She knew now that she had a
real mother, and the return address proved it. And how amazing
that her mother was someone whose *songs* she knew! "Listen to
Your Voice" had been her favorite song ever since she could
remember.

Sara had a bit of money saved from birthdays and baby-sitting. She
had a New York address—some gallery on Fifty-sixth Street. She left
a scrawled note that read: *Gone to find my mother!* and took the bus
to Bozeman that stopped in front of the hardware store in Bear Creek.

In Bozeman, Sara transferred to a bus to Chicago. In Chicago, she
transferred to a bus to Cleveland, and in Cleveland she transferred to
a Pittsburgh bus. From there New York City was only a hop, skip, and
a jump.

The Greyhound tickets set her back $149. One way. "It's a dog of a way to get around . . . ," as the Harry Chapin song goes. But she had a mission—a real live mother in New York City. And she was going to *find* her.

Let the blue chemical toilet in the back of the bus slosh; let the passengers fart; let the guy with the two-day growth and lazy eye stare at her breasts—she was going to find her birthright.

New York was a revelation—starting with the filth and menace of the Port Authority Bus Terminal. Sara had never seen bums sprawled out on the street, festering men rattling filthy paper cups full of change or women sitting on ragged blankets, holding smeary babies aloft, along with signs that read HELP ME BUY PAMPERS or HOMLESS N' HUNGREY. The ride had been purgatory; the bus terminal was hell.

Sara didn't know New York—except from TV shows. She was a country girl. New York assaulted her with its frenzy, its sad, wandering homeless people, its busier-than-busy rich people (who walked fast and looked straight ahead so as not to *see* the homeless people), its side streets crammed with belching trucks, its traffic jams, its gridlock, its greasy soot that settled in your eyes and on the sides of your nose.

She walked east from the Port Authority, not really knowing where she was going. She had an old knapsack on her back, Doc Martens on her feet; she wore Levi's, a purple turtleneck, and a green nylon parka to protect her from the cold. It was January, and the day was freezing but glaringly sunny.

Discarded Christmas trees threaded with tinsel stuck out of trash baskets or lay askew between the curbs and the streets. New York had more garbage than she'd ever seen in one place! She hadn't slept all night, but the sheer energy of New York woke her up with a rush. The city was like a dynamo, making its own power, turning all day and night to produce heat, light, and fire. What drove the dynamo? Ambition. The yearnings of millions upon millions of people, coming from everywhere in search of everything: excitement, money, sex, fame, a better life.

Did they find it? Most of them didn't. Some ran shrieking through the streets, having gone mad in New York. Some got hooked on crack and wound up in seedy hotels in Forty-second Street's vomit district. Some made it to the other side of town, where they would avert their eyes from anyone who reminded them of their origins.

But the pulse of the city was unlike anything Sara had ever felt. It was a great heart beating, and the arteries that fed it pulsed with bright-red arterial blood. Sara walked east to Times Square, then made the mistake of taking Broadway downtown for a block or two, thinking it was Fifth Avenue. She became slightly disoriented. On Thirty-ninth Street she walked east again, hoping she wasn't lost. A dazed-looking man with dreadlocks lurched up to her, blowing pungent smoke in her face. "Smoke, baby?" he asked. She started to run. When at last she got to Fifth, she turned left and started uptown.

It was only when she saw the great Beaux Arts hulk of the New York Public Library—with its white lions, its shallow marble steps, its carved names of antique benefactors—that she knew for sure she was going the right way. She sat down on the library steps and took out a tattered map of New York that was at least twenty years old (she had taken it from her father's shelf of travel books, actually torn it out of a book—a crime in her family). Then she continued north up Fifth Avenue. When she came to Rockefeller Center, she had to detour to see the skating rink, great, golden Prometheus capturing fire (apparently without consequences to his liver), and the channel garden—that little alley with the angels of wire and light, still trumpeting the holiday season. She walked past Atlas holding up the empty world, gawked at Saint Patrick's across the avenue, and then she crossed to the other side to admire the clothes and shoes and jewels in store windows. In Montana, you'd have no place to wear such things, but here . . . the very thought made her heady and dazed.

On Fifty-sixth Street, she turned east by mistake, and then she corrected herself and turned west. The house she was seeking was between Fifth and Sixth, and at first she panicked, thinking it wasn't there at all. She traversed Fifty-sixth Street twice before she caught sight of the discreet sign, LEVITSKY GALLERY, in stainless steel on a white marble facade.

As she rang the bell, she thought of how she must look—a hick from Montana ringing the bell of a chic marble town house in New York.

The door opened. A staggeringly pretty blonde, in a short, flared black wool dress that skimmed her thighs (which were almost visible under shiny semitransparent black tights), opened the door. She looked at the country bumpkin figure Sara made and said: "We don't want any."

"You don't what?" asked Sara, taken aback.

The blonde started to turn away, her hand on the door. (Within, Sara saw a white room, hung with paintings, creamy Japanese screens as dividers, and beyond, a long rectangular back garden, with a Japanese teahouse and a Japanese raked sand garden and boulders frosted with snow.)

While the blonde tried to close the door, Sara took off her backpack and fumbled in it. She extracted a piece of paper that had been folded so many times it looked like an ancient treasure map.

"Ms. Levitsky?" Sara asked nervously, and "Ms. Sky?"

The blonde hesitated. She wanted to get rid of this kid, but clearly she was more than just an intruder.

"I am Ms. Robinowitz," said the blonde, "one of the owners of the gallery. Ms. Levitsky is upstairs. Ms. Sky is with her. Who are you?"

"Sara Wyndham, ma'am, Ms. Sky's my mother," said Sara, feeling

like a fool—like Huck Finn being "sivilized" or Holden Caulfield
sneaking into his parents' apartment while they were out. Or maybe
Sara was more like Pip from *Great Expectations*, her absolutely
favorite book in the world when she was fourteen. Other kids
watched the tube, but Sara liked nothing better than to lose herself in
a book. Sitcoms seemed moronic to her.

Sara was freezing out there on the marble steps. The tiredness and
fear had just hit her.

The blonde eyed her warily, seemed to calculate the potential
gains and losses.

"Come in," she said reluctantly.

The gallery looked like a gallery in a movie, starring Meg Ryan or
Goldie Hawn as the blonde. There was a show in progress. Sara rec-
ognized works by Picasso, Braque, and other important artists.

"We're doing a memorial show," the blonde said, without
explaining. She walked in her clunky black platform boots to the
telephone, pressed some buttons (it had more buttons than Sara
had ever seen, except in a bank!), and whispered into the mouth-
piece. Suddenly there was a commotion in the stairwell, and a middle-aged woman with long red hair, a Wedgwood-blue cashmere
sweater, black cashmere tights, and soft cobalt-blue leather boots
ran down the stairs.

"Sara! My baby!" she shouted as she ran toward her ragtag daughter.

And shortly after, an elevator door opened at the back of the
gallery and out stepped a silver-haired lady in elegant black slacks
and a gray silk blouse and masses of silver-blue pearls.

"Can it be true? Is it Sara?" the older woman asked. "Let me look
at that *punim*. . . ." And walking toward Sara, Salome Levitsky
Wallinsky Robinowitz began to cry. "I never thought I'd see *mayne
shayner kind* again!"

By now Sally had her arms around the stunned teenager.

"Darling," she wept. "Darling."

And time seemed to stop as the three elegant New York women contemplated Sara from Montana, with her backpack, her scuffed Doc Martens, baggy jeans, and dirty parka.

"Sally? Sally Sky?" Sara asked. And Sally couldn't say a word—that was how hard she was crying. Sara was crying too.

Later Salome kissed her and kissed her, and Sally was delirious. Sally wasn't drinking then. She was religiously going to AA meetings at Saint Thomas Church and the Citicorp Center. She was serene, centered, accepting of life's complications.

"We have so much catching up to do," she told Sara, "so much catching up. Where to begin?"

By then Sally lived in London. She had come back to New York only for the memorial show dedicated to her grandparents—Sarah and Lev Levitsky. They had died within weeks of each other, Sarah at just a hundred, Levitsky at possibly a hundred and something—but who could find his birth certificate? Their passing was as strange as their marriage had been. First he was hospitalized for pneumonia; then she was. She died, muttering about how her great-granddaughter should never have been given her name, for fear of confusing the angel of death. But Sara was in Montana, and perhaps the all-seeing *malech ha-movis* couldn't see that far. The family was afraid to tell Levitsky she was gone—he might die of a broken heart—and they buried her. But the night of the funeral, while Salome stood beside Levitsky's hospital bed, with silent tears running down her cheeks, he said: "I hear Mama calling to me from heaven. She keeps saying: *Nu—what's taking so long?*" He died early the next morning.

Sally was staying with Salome, and they for once were getting along—mostly because they had a common enemy, the estranged wife of Sally's half-brother, Lorenzo, who had come to claim her husband's (and children's) share of the gallery and wasn't leaving until she got it. (Renzo had left other children scattered here and there in Europe, and they might eventually claim their patrimony too.) The very blond, very bossy Babs Hart Robinowitz was an art historian, who had worked at the gallery before marrying Renzo. She was after the keys to the fabled safe-deposit box in Lugano, and she wanted to force the sale of the gallery and divide the spoils. Sara had walked in on this ugly struggle.

Renzo, meanwhile, having gone through all the money he could beg, borrow, or manipulate out of Lev, Sarah, and Salome, claimed to be broke again. He was a *luftmensch* who fancied himself a producer, and he always had crazy schemes: the gay musical *Hamlet* that bombed, the musical based on the Book of Genesis that bombed (Raquel Welch was signed to play Eve), the newly discovered Shakespeare comedy that turned out *not* to be by Shakespeare or even the Earl of Oxford. All his producing projects hemorrhaged money for as long as possible, then went belly-up. Babs was sick of him too, but they had never bothered to get divorced.

Renzo was living in Lugano with an aging German supermodel named Ursula, who thought he could make her a star as the Dark Lady in a London musical based on the Sonnets.

The Levitsky wills and trusts were so complicated that in the few short years since Sarah and Lev passed on to their reward, no one else except the lawyers had been rewarded—which perhaps explained why Renzo was secretly negotiating with the Council on Jewish History to sell the Levitsky family archive.

Sara barely understood any of this till much later, but she could feel a strong undercurrent of hostility between Babs and Salome, Babs and Sally.

◆

Sara kept studying Sally and Salome to see how she resembled them—if at all—but it was all too overwhelming.

Sally said: "Well, let's take the darling girl to dinner—but first let's clean her up. I think she'll clean up well."

Then ensued a movie montage of days of shopping. Shopping at Bergdorf's, Bendel's, Saks, so that Sara-from-Montana could become Sara-from-Manhattan.

"I should write a song about this," Sally said. "A shopping ballad. Maybe I should write it to the tune of 'Turkey in the Straw.'"

Sally was the perfect mother during those days in New York, and Salome the perfect grandmother. Sara felt like the princess she had always dreamed of being.

During those January days in New York, Sara explored the city— the Metropolitan Museum, the Cloisters, the Frick, the Empire State Building, even the Statue of Liberty and Ellis Island.

Salome went with her on some of these trips. She was eighty then and slightly breathless in the cold wind that blew off New York Harbor, but she was certainly game. Still a beautiful woman, she dressed in the softest silk knits, cashmere and mohair, all in shades of gray, mauve, amethyst. And she wore beautiful antique jewelry from Italy, England, Japan, China, India.

Sara was too shy and inexperienced at fourteen to ask Salome all the things she would know to ask later. She could not even formulate the questions. Trapped in her own adolescent angst, she knew that her grandmother was remarkable but didn't know how to *begin* with her.

Sally, for her part, adored her daughter, but she didn't really know *how* to be a mother. She could not substitute *we* for *I*. Imprisoned in her own skin, she was always smarting over some real or imagined hurt. Sara was surprised to find her a bit of a disappointment compared to her songs. The best part of her was in her music.

But Sara did learn one very important thing from her mother:

"Discover what you love and do it." Even after Sally started to drink again, even when Sara was in boarding school in Switzerland with all those rich nerds, she asked herself, "What do I love?" And she decided that when she could answer that question she would be launched on her own life.

Sally was glad that Ham and Sandrine were worried sick.

"Fuck 'em!" she said. "Let them worry. I worried so much it took years off my life." She was right about that, but not for the reasons she thought.

14

Dancing to America

2006

*What are the Jews after all? A people that can't sleep
and let nobody else sleep.*

—ISAAC BASHEVIS SINGER

Freud believed that the impulse to destroy was greater
than the impulse to create. Her mother's self-destructiveness made
Sara agree with him about that. And the archive bore him out. For all
the beautiful dead women in "waists" who died of nothing more violent than childbirth, there were hundreds, even thousands, of children who had died in *pogroms*, at the hands of Nazis and related
thugs. The last century had been an Armageddon for a people with
no shortage of Armageddons. Whenever it seemed that things could
not possibly get worse for the Jews, they *did*. In this context, what
was a heroine? One who raised the most children? One who killed
her own children? One who took it upon herself to *chronicle* all these
horrors while at the same time raising children?

And what comfort was history? None. On the last day of Passover,

1389, a bloody *pogrom* was visited upon the Prague ghetto. (The old familiar accusation was that Jews had desecrated the Host.) At least three thousand people were killed, and their blood was left on the walls as a memorial.

The famous Rabbi Avigdor Kar composed an elegy to commemorate the massacre and called it "All the Hardships That Befell Us":

More than one father killed his own son, and more than one mother slew the very child she carried in her womb. . . . Too many fell to be named: young men and women, old men and babes in arms. . . . So much torment has engulfed us, yet we have not forgotten the name of God. . . . The days of hope must come! Injustice and desolation must be driven out! Let us return together from Exile and let the prophecy of Isaiah, our constant comfort, come to pass: For my salvation is near to come and my favor to be revealed.

Sara had read enough of this sort of thing to know that she—and even her daughter, Dove—was born in a peaceful parenthesis in Jewish history, an unaccustomed time of bloodlessness when her people seemed safe in America. But were they *really* safe—any more than they were safe in Prague in 1389 or safe in Spain in 1492 or safe in Germany in the 1930s? Storm clouds and storm troopers might be gathering everywhere. In Christian America, you could never tell when it might be un-American to be Jewish. The conversion mania might well start again. Fringe hate groups were plentiful enough. The Aryan Nation and the Christian Coalition were joining forces with the Southern Baptists to *convert* the Jews. Portents were ubiquitous if you cared to look. Militia groups and Christian fundamentalists might very well ally themselves with Farrakhan's forces to kill the Jews. Such madness had happened before. *Many* times before.

If the Council on Jewish History had a significant exhibition, should it be called "All the Hardships That Befell Us" or "Dancing to America"? Pessimism or optimism? Give the people what they wanted, or tell them the truth? Sara knew that Lisette was going to ask for her ideas about this, and the fact was that Sara was still debating with herself. Who wasn't *sick* of Jewish pessimism? She was sick of it herself! The days of hope must come! And just when you decided to live by that optimistic faith, someone showed you a picture of a mountain of eyeglasses or wedding rings or human hair—and hope was proved illusory again. The Holocaust had put a curse on Jewish history, obscuring all the joy, all the creativity, all the laughter of this ancient people with images of victimization and death. If the Jews were to be seen hereafter only as victims, then hadn't Hitler really *won*? Was *his* to be the final definition of this six-thousand-year-old people? Sara hoped not.

What kind of God had the Jews chosen to be chosen by? A God with the conscience of a jackal, the obduracy of granite, and the sense of humor of a Nazi? The God of Job was hardly a God who refused to play dice with the universe. How could you possibly fault people who turned away from all that pain? Who became Jewnitarians or Ethical Culturists or even Bill W.–cultists like her mother? Other tribes worshiped gods who gave rain or coconuts or manna. Other tribes had soft praline gods who forgave everything with honey tongues. But the Jews delighted secretly in the harshness of their God the way the English used to think they were more virtuous for having no central heating. The God of the Jews was a sadist who required his people to be masochists. Or so it sometimes seemed.

Who was it who said pain leaves deeper traces than pleasure? The God of the Jews was indelible and eternal because of all that pain. Soft gods had come and gone. Forgiving gods had come and gone. And the God of the Old Testament remained—with his thundering voice, his impossible tests put to Job, Abraham, Isaac, even Jesus himself, until there were holes in their hands and dust in their hearts. This God was no wuss. This was a macho God. No wonder the Jews were so proud to have been chosen to suffer by such a butch God, Yahweh of the *cojones*.

"Heresy!" she could just hear old Sarah Sophia saying. The whole point of the story of Job is that God does not want to be worshiped only in the *good* times. *This* is the wisdom of Yahweh. We cannot fathom the will of God any more than we can create what God creates. Any weak, pusillanimous people can worship a God who gives goodies. It takes an iron-willed tribe to cleave to God even when God sends boils, death, destruction. *This* is the true surrender to God's power. And surrender is the *only* wisdom. "How do you think *I* survived," Sarah Sophia seems to say, "but through surrender?" This is the paradox: surrender is the greatest strength.

So went the ancient argument in Sara's head as she prepared her notes for the meeting Lisette de Hirsch had called. Lisette wanted to discuss the future of the Council, the best way to raise membership and donations, the major exhibition she had in mind.

The meeting took place in the room sunken into the bedrock of the city. Sara remembered the first time she had come here with Lisette, and she felt like a different person now. The room no longer scared her, nor did the big-cheese donors with their names like banks, who sat at the round conference table with their pristine legal pads and their twinkly expensive pens. Guys like this all looked alike to Sara. She was sure that was unfair to them, but they all seemed homogeneous.

Lisette began by saying that the Council needed to celebrate itself, show the world its work, its value.

"We have been doing all this excellent work in private, and now it's time to let the world see what we're up to. I'm looking for a theme for our exhibition, which will also become the theme for the illustrated book that goes with the exhibition. . . . I have some ideas myself."

Now came the moment everybody dreaded: the moment when one's idea would be ridiculed or it would be seen that one *had* no ideas. The three board members—three kings, as it were—were brilliant at nondisclosure. They had arrived where they needed to be by saying as little as possible. Silence is always brilliant—surely old Sarah's mother would have had a proverb for it.

"I would defer to Mrs. de Hirsch," said the first board member, a hunched-up man who had made billions in Wall Street.

"I would love to hear what you both have in mind," said the second, a silver-haired lawyer who protected himself and his wealth by contributing equal amounts to both major political parties.

"My expertise is elsewhere," said the third, a banker who advised popes and presidents and loved calling his clients from the Lincoln Bedroom—whoever was president.

"Sara, what do you think?" asked Lisette.

"I've been reading and thinking to prepare for this, and I keep coming back to the same thought: Can we let Hitler define Jewish history for us, or should we define it ourselves?"

Lisette looked alarmed. "Explain what you mean," she said testily.

"It's not easy to explain," Sara went on, "but let me try. We have this glorious history, which has now been eclipsed by the Holocaust. There are Holocaust museums, Holocaust studies . . . It's as if we spend all our time arguing with Hitler. It's a trap, I think. It's letting the anti-Semites say what Jews are and aren't."

"But you wouldn't *deny* the Holocaust?" Lisette asked.

"Of course not," said Sara, "but I don't believe that the greatness of our people is demonstrated only by the hands raised against us. I would rather stress the days of hope than the days of despair. Maybe we've been chosen because of our abundant life force, our refusal to surrender—and maybe we should celebrate *that*. The more I think of the history of the Jews in America, the more struck I am by the fact that we are all descendants of survivors, not victims. Rather than defeat ourselves with pessimism, why don't we show our ancestors dancing to America?"

"What a clever title for an exhibition!" said Lisette.

"*What* title?" asked Sara. "I wasn't aware I had proposed a title. . . ."

"'Dancing to America,'" said Lisette. "That's the title of our exhibition. So optimistic and upbeat, so positive. People are tired of negativity, I think. . . ."

"And then we take the story of a family and show its odyssey over a hundred years. . . ."

"I love it!" said Lisette.

Suddenly the board members began vying with each other to regale Sara with heartwarming family stories about impoverished ancestors. One started with a pushcart, one with a tailor's shears, one with nothing but a shovel. The pushcart peddler became a department store king, the tailor became a garmento whose sons built a Hollywood studio, and the man with the shovel founded a real estate empire.

"But if it's to be *real,* it can't only glorify the family. It has to show them—warts and all," said Sara.

"Of course," said Lisette. "No whitewashing."

"You say that now," Sara said, "but what if you learned that there were black sheep in the family . . . ?"

"*All* families have black sheep—even mine," said Lisette with a laugh. "My great-great-great-grandfather was a horse thief. . . ."

"And mine," said Mr. Goldman—or was it Mr. Lazard?

"We think it's a great idea," said Lisette. "We're a thousand percent for it."

And that was how Sara talked herself into taking on the most difficult project of her life, *Dancing to America.*

The research was compelling. Sara found herself increasingly seeing the world through the eyes of her ancestors. Sarah Sophia seemed to take over her thoughts, her way of looking at the world. And as she entered into the consciousness of this woman who had to be so much braver than she, Sara became more and more courageous herself, almost as though she were clothing herself in another soul, as if some transmigration had occurred.

Every biographer knows that any soul may be yours if you follow its contours and learn them by heart. This is what Sara did. She felt that she was being led through a deep fog and that as the fog cleared, she was beginning to suspect who she was.

Of course, Lisette de Hirsch vetoed most of the texts and exhibits she proposed. Did old Sarah *have* to have an affair with a *goy*? Why couldn't she marry nice Levitsky right off the bat? And did Levitsky *have* to be impotent? And a forger's fence to boot? Surely there were Jewish art dealers who *weren't* crooks? And what about Salome's affair with Henry Miller? Couldn't she have an affair with Chagall or Pascin, for example, or some other *Jewish* artist? Even Modigliani. Wasn't Miller an anti-Semite? And wasn't Salome a bit too wild, never knowing whether her only son, Lorenzo, belonged to Robin or Marco? And why was Lorenzo such a failure, such a no-good? And would he sue if the Council included him—or a character based on him—in the exhibition? And Sally's alcoholism? Was addiction really such a problem for Jewish girls? Lisette didn't want to censor—far from it—but was that *realistic*? Realism was the key here.

Lisette was already writing fund-raising letters and drafting press releases trumpeting the exhibition: "Exhibition to Chronicle One Hundred Years of Jewish Immigration."

Let Lisette sanitize the exhibition in any way she wanted, but in the family story Sara was now writing (in lieu of her dissertation), not a line, not a comma, would be changed. Nor would Lloyd or David distract her. Once the family chronicle took over her life, she had little desire to be interrupted by either of them. David was too good to be true—how could anyone persist in loving someone who offered so little in return?—and Lloyd might just be a charming psychopath. There would always be men—but unless she captured the story of Sarah Sophia, Salome, and Sally, it was likely to be lost forever. Now was the time for her to get their stories down on paper. She had to complete their tales to begin her own.

Each one of these women had left some unfinished business.

Sarah Sophia at first stopped painting under her own name and became a ghost painter. Even when she achieved fame in her own right as a Hollywood portraitist, she put her husband's gallery ahead of her work. She became rich, but she let her own work come behind the gallery. Salome had also allowed herself to be derailed. She kept endless notebooks when she was young, but she really gave up writing seriously after the disappointment of *Dancing to America*. At that time, nobody wanted to publish a book that honestly showed a woman's point of view. (Even Anaïs Nin's unexpurgated journals appeared only in the eighties and nineties. The first versions—in the seventies—were totally sanitized by Nin herself! No wonder they seemed so nebulous in places. All the real stuff was cut out! The affair with Henry Miller, the truth about her marriage, her incestuous father—everything!) And Sally deliberately destroyed her talent—with men, with drink, with bitterness, with lethargy. She even pulled her greatest album. How self-destructive can you get?

Sara had come to understand that she was fated to be the author of their stories as she was to be the author of her own life. The women in her family had always written letters to their daughters, and the chronicle she was writing would eventually be her own letter to Dove.

At first Sara found herself wrenching the material this way and that, trying to make a story with a moral. She started with the *pogrom* in the Pale and the death of little Dovie (as if she were making a movie), and then she followed Sarah to America on the creaky old ship. She liked the transition from the sweatshop to the grand "cottage" in the Berkshires, and she liked the love triangle with Levitsky and Sim Coppley. She liked Salome in Paris during *les années folles* and Salome's Berkshire odyssey. But no matter what she did, she could not find a conventional moral in the story. It astonished her that she should have been seeing a man named David (also called Dovie when he was little) during the research for her family history. Synchronicity . . . but what did all these more-than-coincidences mean?

Again and again, Sara came back to the question of whether women were better off now than they had been a hundred years earlier. It just was not *clear.* She wondered about old Sarah. "If I let her speak, what would she say?" Sara asked herself; and then answered herself by letting old Sarah narrate the beginning of her tale.

She remembered that early notebook in which she had written down the quote about making magic by telling a story. *We cannot light the fire, we cannot speak the prayers, we do not know the place, but we can tell the story of how it was done.* . . . Wasn't *that* what she was doing?

And sometimes she caught herself dreaming Sarah's dreams or Salome's or even Sally's. For in truth she was all these women. Each of them had a part in making her who she was. But she was also herself. Their blood ran in her veins. Their DNA spiraled in her cells. Their memories teemed in her brain. She was telling a story—*their* story—the story of how one generation gave way to the next, the story of how the strengths of one generation rescued the next generation even in its darkest moments.

When we dream, we invent our own memories, and this is also true when we write. The holy teachers were right: telling a story *is* a kind of prayer, a kind of meditation, a sacred act. It makes magic happen.

Or is the story *itself* the magic?

The exhibition was only a way of beginning. Sara used the exhibition as a means of getting into the story. But at the same time as she was being a good little girl with Lisette and the board members, she was telling the true, the secret history in her own way—whether or not the Council approved its contents. And as she wrote, she began to see that only by telling *this* particular story, by inventing memory itself, would she be free to go on with her life.

But who would be the heroine? Sarah Sophia, Salome, Sally—or Sara herself? Did it really matter? After all, wasn't *she* the portrait painter with the robber baron bleeding on her stoop, and the flapper in Paris who goes home to find her country sunk in Depression, and the singer of the sixties who throws away her talent and her life? She had to try on the souls of all these women in order to become herself.

And so she began with what she knew had to be the first line of her story. *Sometimes, in dreams, my firstborn son comes back to me. . . .*

Glossary of Yiddish Terms

alivai	I hope, I wish, if only I had
alter cocker	old fart
bar mitzvah/bat mitzvah	boy's/girl's coming-of-age ceremony at age thirteen
beshert	destined
bissel	little
boychick	a kid
broykis	angry, resentful
brucha	a blessing
bubbameisehs	old wives' tales
challah	Sabbath bread
chazerei	junk, worthless things (literally, pork)
cheder	Hebrew elementary school
chuppah	wedding canopy
chutzpah	nerve, brass
das kind	the baby
der fremde	the foreign world (America)
doven	pray
dreyer	operator
du bist eine Yankee	you are a Yankee
dybbuk	spirit
emis	truth

eppis	thus
feh!	pooh!
fersteh?	understand?
feygele	male homosexual (literally, little bird)
fussgeyers	those who go on foot (especially across Europe)
ganaiven	thieves
ganse meshpocheh	the whole family
gay vais	go know (who could have known?)
gelt	money
gevalt	expression of astonishment
gonif	thief or chiseler
goy, goyim; goyishe	gentile, gentiles; gentile (adj.)
goykopf	gentile mind
greeneh, greener	newly arrived immigrant— a greenhorn
gruber yung	upstart
kaddish	mourner's prayer
kayne hore	may the evil eye be avoided
kiddush cup	ritual wine goblet
kishkes	guts
klezmer	musicians
kopeck	Russian currency
kreplach	dumpling
kum mit mir	come with me

kurveh	loose woman
kvell	swell with pride
kvetch	nag
landsman, landsleit	countryman, countrymen, particularly from the same town
luftmensch	a person with his feet firmly planted in air
malech ha-movis	angel of death
mamichka, mamanyu, mamele	darling little mother
matzo	unleavened flat bread for Passover
mayne kind, mayne shayner kind	my child, my beautiful child
mayne leben, mayne neshoma, mayne libe	my life, my soul, my love
mayne schwester, mayne shayner schwester	my sister, my beautiful sister
menorah	candelabra for Chanukkah
meshuggeh, meshuggeneh	crazy
mikveh	ritual bath
minyan	quorum of ten men needed for a religious service
mishegas	madness
mit geschmecht	with pleasure
naches	pride
narishkeit	nonsense

nebbish	weak, helpless person
nu	so?
nudnick	fool
oleha ha-sholom	rest in peace
pflommen	plums
pisher	jerk, squirt
pogrom	anti-Semitic raid
punim	face
pushke	collection box for charity
schlepper	one who drags, goes slow
schmearer	someone who bribes people/or a bad painter
schmegegge	fool
schnorrer	leech, sponge, moocher (literally, beggar)
schreiber	writer
schtupping	fucking
sechel	smarts, wisdom, common sense
shabbas goy	the gentile who lights candles on the Sabbath when Jews are forbidden to work
shande	scandal, shame
shaygetz	gentile boy
sheitl	wig worn by Orthodox wives
shicker	drunk
shifskarte	ship's ticket
shiksa	gentile woman

shoah	holocaust
shreiing	screaming
shtetl	village
shul	synagogue
sitsfleish	tenacity
starke	strong man, tough guy
street speilers	kids who dance in the street
takeh	so, thus
trayfe	unkosher food
tsuris	troubles
tush	behind, bottom
vantz	prick
veys nicht	I don't know
yenta	busybody (female)
zaydeh	grandfather